D0093637

THE SHADOW OF KYOSHI

降击神通

AVATAR
THE LAST AIRBENDER.

THE SHADOW OF
KYOSHI

F.C. YEE with AVATAR CO-CREATOR MICHAEL DANTE DIMARTINO

AMULET BOOKS · NEW YORK

Cataloging-in-Publication Data has been applied for and may be obtained from the Library of Congress.

ISBN 978-1-4197-3505-9

Jacket illustrations © 2020 Jung Shan Chang
Book design by Brenda E. Angelilli

Printed and bound in U.S.A.
10 9

Amulet Books are available at special discounts when purchased in quantity for premiums and promotions as well as fundraising or educational use. Special editions can also be created to specification. For details, contact specialsales@abramsbooks.com or the address below.

Amulet Books® is a registered trademark of Harry N. Abrams, Inc.

ABRAMS The Art of Books
195 Broadway, New York, NY 10007
abramsbooks.com

So I tell this story a lot at panels and interviews, but I want to preserve it for posterity here. During a time when I didn't know what I wanted to do with my life, and before I had ever written a novel, I thought about becoming a TV writer. To become a TV writer, you have to demonstrate your skills by writing a spec script, an episode of a currently running show—essentially, fanfiction. I had just watched Book Two: Earth of the original *ATLA*, so I wrote a spec script where Sokka feels bad about not being a bender, and finds a cool master to train him. In my spec script, he was going to learn to fight with Wing Chun and gadgetry (in retrospect, the result would have been a lot like Asami).

From these creative beginnings, I would never have dreamed that in the future, I'd be establishing canon for the Avatar world. In the truest sense, I have you, the fans, to thank for this opportunity. You've kept your love for this universe burning brightly for more than a decade, and the most I could ever hope for as a fellow fan and author is to add to your enjoyment. These books are dedicated to you. Thank you all so much.

Sincerely,

F. C. Yee

PROLOGUE

˙BOY!˙

Yun clawed at his own neck until he drew blood. The feeling of slime and teeth lingered on his skin.

"Boy! Stop your sniveling!"

He remembered Jianzhu lighting the incense. He remembered the sticky-sweet smell and the deadness it created in his limbs. Stingjelly venom, his training told him. He'd only just started his doses with Sifu Amak.

Yun blinked and tried to make sense of his surroundings. His hands clawed into wet, porous moss when it should have been the dust of the mining town under his fingernails. He was in a mangrove forest. The sky was the color of acid.

He crawled around, the juices of a swamp sucking at his knees. The trunks of the leafless trees twisted and gnarled as high as hills, barely lighter in color than silhouettes. Screened by the loose weave of branches, a great glowing eye stared at him.

It was the eye that had spoken. The eye that told him he wasn't the—

A pain, terrible and familiar, wracked his stomach and folded him in two. His forearms splashed into the swamp water. The landscape around him began to shake, not from earthbending but from something rawer and more uncontrollable.

He wasn't. End of sentence. He was nothing.

The shallow water danced, raindrops on a drum, spiking into geysers. The shoreline swayed, rattling the trees, bucking and clashing them together like the antlers of beasts locked in combat. Yun dashed his head against the ground in a frenzied corruption of a student bowing to their master.

Jianzhu. His entire mind was a screamed name, a single screeching tone on a broken flute. His skull thudded against the brackish mud. *Jianzhu*.

"Stop it, you miserable little brat!" the eye roared. Despite its anger it shrank back from him, afraid of his throes of agony. The ground squeezed and fluttered, the heartbeat of a man falling to his death, pounding louder and louder before the final impact.

Yun *wanted* it to stop. He wanted the anguish to end. It hurt so much, to see everything he'd worked for shredded to sparks and dust. It was destroying him from the inside.

So let it out.

The whisper came to him in his own voice. Not the eye's. Not Jianzhu's.

Put the pain outside. Put it somewhere else.

On someone else.

The rip started at his feet, a pinprick in overstretched silk. The tear birthed itself in the water and raced into the banks of the earth like lightning cracking the sky. The ground split apart, releasing all its quaking tension in one swift cataclysmic burst.

And then . . . stillness.

Yun could breathe again. He could see. The trembling had worn itself out, spent its energy in the creation of a long lesion in the ground, an unnatural wound upon the landscape. Swamp water poured into the injury, masking a depth he knew he shouldn't explore.

Things were so much clearer when there was relief. Yun used this moment of respite to look around. The musty grove resembled no forest he'd ever seen. The dim light in the sky came from no discernible sun. This place was a hazy reflection of a real landscape, painted with ink that had been thinned too much.

I'm in the Spirit World.

He backed away from the ravine that lay before him, not wanting to be dragged in by the force of the water's flow. Turning around, he pulled himself to drier footing using the exposed roots of a leathery tree. The air smelled like sulfur and rot.

Master Kelsang had told him about the Spirit World. It was supposed to be a beautiful, wild place, full of creatures beyond imagining. The realm of the spirits was a mirror held up to its visitors, a reflection of your emotions, a reality that shaped around your own spirit's intangible projection.

Yun flexed his fingers, finding them as solid as they could be. He wondered if the gentle monk had ever explored a nightmarish bog like this one. They'd never talked about what happened if you entered the Spirit World while you were still in your body.

The rustle of branches gave him a start and reminded him he wasn't alone. The eye. It watched carefully from the darkness of the forest, circling him on translucent appendages studded with what he knew to be human teeth. He'd felt its bite back in the mountains when it had sampled his blood.

A pulsing panic rushed through the chambers of his heart. Yun knew he was on borrowed time. He tried to remember what Jianzhu had called the spirit. "Father . . . Glowworm?"

The eye suddenly rushed closer, socketing itself in the gap between two nearby trees. Yun shrieked and fell backward on his elbows. He'd made a mistake. A crucial, invisible barrier had been broken by saying the name aloud, and now he was more connected and vulnerable to it than ever.

"I call myself that," the spirit said. Father Glowworm's pupil darted around unnervingly, the iris squeezing narrower. Its gaze had the heft of a probing tongue. "Now, child, I believe you owe me your name."

Like a fool, Yun had fallen into the role of the bumpkin from cautionary Earth Kingdom folktales, the poor field hand or woodcutter who fell under a curse or was simply eaten. He could only think of how he'd be consumed. Rasped into pulp, maybe, and absorbed into the slime.

"My name is Yun." His palms were slick with fear. In some of those tales, the stupid boy survived through sheer pluck. Yun was already prey; his only chance was to become interesting prey. "I—I—"

His poise was failing him. His slickness under pressure that had impressed the Fire Lord and the Earth King, the chieftains of the Water Tribes and Head Abbots of the Air Temples alike, was nowhere to be found. Maybe Avatar Yun had the confidence to talk his way out of this, but no such person existed anymore.

Father Glowworm shifted in the trees, and Yun knew he was going to die if he didn't say something quick. His mind leaped back to the moments in his past when his fate was cradled in someone else's hands.

"I wish to submit myself for consideration as your student!" he yelped.

Was there a way for a single eye to look surprised? The forest was silent except for the rush of falling water. "I . . . kneel before you as a humble spiritual traveler seeking answers," Yun said. He shifted around so his posture matched his words. "Please teach me the ways of the Spirit World. I beseech you."

Father Glowworm burst into laughter. It had no lids to narrow, but its sphere tilted upward in the universal direction of amusement. "Boy, do you think this is a game?"

Everything is a game, Yun thought, trying to still his shaking. *I will draw this one out as far as I can. I will survive a turn longer.*

There was no more Avatar Yun. He would have to be Yun the swindler again. "I can hardly be faulted for wanting to ask questions of a spirit wiser than the best of humanity." *When in doubt, flatter the mark.* "The Earth Kingdom's finest sages couldn't identify the Avatar for sixteen years. And yet you did it in a matter of seconds."

"Hmph. You don't fight the kind of battle Kuruk and I did and not be able to recognize your opponent's spirit. I could already feel Jianzhu bringing his reincarnation closer to one of my tunnels. It had to be one of you children."

Yun's ears perked at the word *tunnels*. "You have routes to the human world? More than one?"

Father Glowworm laughed again. "I know what you're doing," it sneered. "And it doesn't impress me. Yes, I can create passages to the human realm. No, you will not trick or convince me into sending you back. You're not the bridge between spirits and humans, boy. You're the stone that needed to be pitched away by the sculptor. The impurity in the ore. I've tasted your blood, and you're nothing. You're not even worth this conversation."

The eye crept closer. "I can tell how upset you are by the truth," it said in a soothing sweet tone. "Don't be. Who needs Avatarhood? You will find your own use, and your own immortality. Once I strengthen myself on your blood, part of your essence will exist within me, forever."

The problem with any game was that eventually, the opponent decided to stop playing. Father Glowworm suddenly rushed Yun, spiraling through the forest, tendrils of slime grasping and parting the trees like the beads of a curtain.

"Now, be grateful!" the spirit roared. "For we are about to become one!"

UNFINISHED BUSINESS

BROTHER PO once told Kuji the nickname for the *dao* sword was "all men's courage." Hold the sturdy chopping blade that let you hack away at a foe with abandon, and you'd feel braver immediately.

Kuji did not feel braver as he gripped the haft of his *dao* with clammy palms and watched the door. And his blade did not feel very sturdy. It was a rusted, chipped specimen that seemed like it would shatter if he waved it in the air too vigorously. As the most junior member of the Triad of the Golden Wing, he'd had to wait at the back of the line as weapons were passed out in turn. This sword had come from the bottom of the crate.

"Now you're a real soldier, eh?" someone had joked at the time. "Not like the rest of us hatchet men."

Brother Po stood by the doorway holding his small axe, the favored weapon of most of the Triad's seasoned fighters. He looked calm on the outside, but Kuji could see his throat bobbing up and down repeatedly as he swallowed, the same way it did when he was going for a big money play in Pai Sho.

If Kuji had confidence in anything for protection, it was in his gang's turf—Loongkau City Block was practically a fortress. On the surface, Loongkau looked no different than its neighboring districts of Ba Sing Se's Lower Ring. The visible portion on the block rose a haphazard couple of stories into the air like a budding mushroom, in defiance of gravity and sound architecture.

But it was an open secret that the complex extended illegally into the ground layer by layer, far below the surface. Each level had been dug out below the previous one without a solid plan or understanding of safety, shored up by using only improvised supports of wood scrap, mud brick, bits of rusty scavenged metal. And yet Loongkau held solid without caving in, possibly with the aid of the spirits.

The inside of the block was a knot of twists and turns, staircases and empty shafts. Hives of squalid apartments squeezed the available pathways into narrow choke points. Loongkau was littered with natural traps like the room where Kuji and Po waited, which was one of the reasons why lawmen never went inside the City Block.

Until now. The boss had gotten a tip that the Golden Wing's stronghold was going to be hit this very day. Every brother was to take up positions until the threat was gone. Kuji didn't know what kind of enemy could get his elders so riled up. By his guess it would have taken more lawmen than the Lower Ring possessed in order to lay siege to Loongkau.

Regardless, the plan was sound. Anyone trying to make it to the lower floors would have to file through a narrow bottleneck that ran by this room. Kuji and Ning could get the drop on an intruder, two-on-one.

And it was unlikely they'd see action, Kuji reminded himself. The level above was being prowled by Throatcutter Gong, the boss's best assassin. Gong could stalk and kill a mongoose lizard in its own jungle lair. The number of heads he'd taken could have filled a haybarn—

A crash came from one floor up. There was no sound of a voice accompanying it. The little apartment began to feel less their turf to hold and more a box confining them like animals in a crate.

Po gestured with his hatchet. "We'll hear them coming down the stairs," he whispered. "That's when we strike."

Kuji tilted his ear in that direction. He was so desperate to hear any approaching signal that he lost his balance and stumbled. Po rolled his eyes. "Too loud," he hissed.

As if to prove his point, someone flew through the doorway, snapping the hinges, and collided with Kuji. He shrieked and flailed with his *dao* but at best managed to smack the person in the head with his pommel. Po grabbed the attacker and raised his hatchet to strike, but checked his swing at the last second.

It was Throatcutter Gong, unconscious and bleeding. His wrists bent the wrong way and his ankles were bound with his own garrote wire. "Brother Gong!" Po shouted, forgetting his own lesson in stealth. "What happened?"

From the wall opposite the hallway they were supposed to be focusing on, a pair of gauntleted arms burst through the brick.

They wrapped around Po's neck from behind in a chokehold, cutting off his words. Kuji saw his elder's eyes go white with terror before Po was pulled out of the room straight through the wall.

Kuji stared at the emptiness in stupefied disbelief. Po was a big man, and in a blink, he'd been taken like a raven eagle's prey. The hole he disappeared through revealed only darkness.

Outside, the floorboards creaked from the weight of a person walking, as if complete silence were a cloak the enemy could wear and discard at will. The treading of heavy boots came closer and closer.

The doorway filled, blacking out the faint light from the hall, and a tall, incredibly tall, figure stepped inside. A thin line of blood trickled from its throat, as if it had been beheaded and glued back together. A dress of green silk billowed underneath the wound. Its face was a white mask, and its eyes were monstrous streaks of red.

Trembling, Kuji raised his blade. He moved so slowly it felt like he was swimming through mud. The creature watched him swing his sword, its eyes on the metal, and somehow, he knew it was fully capable of putting a stop to the action. If it cared to.

The edge of the *dao* bit into his opponent's shoulder. There was a snapping noise, and a sudden pain lashed his cheek. The sword had broken, the top half bouncing back in Kuji's face.

It was a spirit. It had to be. It was a spirit that could pass through walls, a ghost that could float over floors, a beast impervious to blades. Kuji dropped the handle of the useless sword. His mother had told him once that invoking the Avatar could safeguard him from evil. He'd known as a child she was making up stories. But that didn't mean he couldn't decide to believe them right now. Right now, he believed harder than he believed anything in his life.

"The Avatar protect me," he whispered while he could still speak. He fell on his behind and scrambled to the corner of the room, blanketed completely by the spirit's long shadow. "Yangchen protect me!"

The spirit woman followed him and lowered her red-and-white face to his. A human would have passed some kind of judgment on Kuji as he cowered like this. The cold disregard in her eyes was worse than any pity or sadistic amusement.

"Yangchen isn't here right now," she said in a rich, commanding voice that would have been beautiful had she not held such clear indifference for his life. "I am."

Kuji sobbed as a large, powerful hand gripped him by the chin with thumb and forefinger. It was gentle but gave the assurance that she could rip his jaw clean off his head if she so desired. The woman tilted his face upward. "Now tell me where I can find your boss."

Kyoshi's neck itched terribly. The garrote had been coated in ground glass, and though she'd managed to avoid getting cut too deeply, sharp little fragments still vexed her skin. It served her right for being so sloppy. The gang's wire man had been stealthy, but not at the level of the company she used to keep in her *daofei* days.

Speaking of which, she'd taken a risk by not incapacitating the boy like she'd done his elders. But he'd reminded her of Lek. The way his stupid babyface tried to arrange itself in a mask of hardness, his obvious need for the approval of his sworn elder brothers. His sheer, idiotic bravery. He was too young to be running with a gang in the slums of Ba Sing Se.

No more exceptions for today, she told herself as she stepped over rusting junk and debris. She was still in the habit of labeling anyone roughly her age as boys and girls, and the language made her inclined toward softness, which was dangerous. Certainly no one would show Kyoshi grace because she was only nearing eighteen. The Avatar did not have the luxury of being a child.

She pushed through a hallway barely wider than she was. Only the slightest cracks of illumination came through the walls. Glowing crystals were expensive, and candles were a fire risk, making light a premium in Loongkau. Networks of pipes dripped above her, pattering on the gilded headdress she wore despite the cramped environment. She'd learned to account for the height it added, and having to stoop had been a fact of her life since childhood.

The smell of human density wafted through the corridors, a concoction of sweat and drying paint. She could only imagine what the lower levels offered the nose. The City Block packed more people into its limits than any other in the Lower Ring, and not all of its residents were criminals.

Loongkau was a haven for the very poor. People with nowhere else to go squatted here and applied their industries, eking out livings as garbage pickers, "fell-off-the-wagon" marketeers, unlicensed doctors, dodgy snack vendors, and the like. They were ordinary Earth Kingdom citizens trying to get by on the margins of the law. Her folk, essentially.

The shadowed confines of the City Block were also home to a more violent sort, evolving gangs of the Lower Ring whose memberships were swelling from the influx of *daofei*. Bandits who could no longer hold territory in the countryside were fleeing for the cover of Ba Sing Se and other large cities, blending in with the populace, hiding among the same refuge-seeking citizens they'd brutalized in years past.

Those were not Kyoshi's folk. In fact, many of them were running from *her*. But given it was just as likely for an apartment to be holding scared residents who had nothing to do with her quarry, Kyoshi was keeping her movements in check. Garden-variety earthbending that ripped up huge chunks of the surroundings would cause a dangerous collapse and harm innocents.

The interior opened into a small market area. She passed a room full of barrels leaking bright ink over the floor—a home dying operation—and an empty butcher stall clouded with buzzing ant flies. Jianzhu's study had contained his notes on the political and economic situation of Ba Sing Se, and the small reference to the City Block noted how enterprising its residents were. Curiously, it also mentioned that the land it was built on held some value due to its prominent location in the Lower Ring. Merchants in the Middle Ring had tried to purchase the block in the past and evict the residents, but the dangers of the gangs had always made such projects fail.

Kyoshi paused near a vat of spoiled mango pomace. This was her spot. She bent an assortment of rock debris into a small circle and stood on it. She crossed her arms over her chest to make the smallest cross section possible.

Before she went, though, she noticed a tiny object in the corner. It was a toy, a doll made of rags scavenged from a fine lady's dress. Someone in the block had gone through great effort to sew a doll made of fabric from the Upper Ring for their child.

Kyoshi stared at it until she blinked, remembering why she was here. She stamped down with her foot.

Her little platform of earth, held together by her bending, turned as hard as the point of an auger. It burst through the clay tiles and rotting struts of wood, dropping her fast enough to make her guts lurch. She plunged through the floor and into the next level down, before doing it again, and again.

Jianzhu's tactical manuals noted that in enclosed fights most casualties happened at doorways and stairs. Kyoshi had decided to skip over those parts of the building and bore her own passage. She counted fourteen stories—more than she'd estimated—until she came crashing through the ceiling of a room that was solid earth underneath. The bottom of Loongkau.

Kyoshi stepped off her platform, dust and crumbs of masonry cascading off her arms, and looked around. There were no walls in here, only supporting columns that propped up the great weight of the levels above. *So the City Block has a ballroom*, she thought wryly. The empty expanse was similar to the entertaining halls of wealthy nobles like Lu Beifong. There was a space like this in the Avatar's mansion in Yokoya.

She could see all the way to the far end since the walls held lumps of glowing crystal, as if the light for the entire building had been hoarded for this room. There was a desk, a wooden island in the emptiness. And behind the desk was a man who hadn't given up his pretensions since Kyoshi had last seen him.

"Hello, Uncle Mok," Kyoshi said. "It's been a while, hasn't it?"

Mok, the former second-in-command of the Yellow Neck *daofei*, goggled his eyes in surprise. Kyoshi was like a curse he couldn't shake. "You!" he fumed, shrinking slightly behind the furniture as if it could protect him. "What are you doing here!?"

"I heard rumors about a new boss settling into Loongkau and thought he sounded very familiar. So I came to investigate. I heard this group is calling itself a Triangle now? Do I have that right? Something with three sides." Kyoshi found it hard to keep track. The *daofei* who were funneling into the cities brought their grandiose customs of secrecy and tradition into the realm of urban petty crimes.

"The Triad of the Golden Wing!" he yelled, infuriated by her disinterest in his rituals. But Kyoshi was long past caring about the feelings of men like Mok. He could throw whatever tantrum he desired.

The drumming of feet grew louder. The men Kyoshi had bypassed on the middle floors came filing into the room, surrounding her. They brandished axes and cleavers and daggers. Mok's men had preferred outlandish weapons when they still roamed the countryside, but here in the city they'd abandoned the nine-ring swords and meteor hammers for simpler arms that could be hidden in a crowd.

Bolstered by more than two dozen men, Mok turned calmer. "Well, girl, what is it you want? Besides checking in on your elders?"

"I want you all to surrender your weapons, vacate the premises, and march yourselves to a magistrate's courthouse for judgment. The nearest one is seven blocks from here."

Several of the hatchet men burst out laughing. The corner of Mok's mouth turned upward. Kyoshi might be the Avatar, but she was vastly outnumbered and trapped in an enclosed space. "We refuse," he said with an exaggerated roll of his hand.

"All right then. In that case, I only have one question." Kyoshi cast her gaze around the room. "Are you sure this is all of you?"

The Triad members glanced at each other. Mok's face swelled with rage, reddening like a berry in the sun.

It wasn't insolence so much as pragmatism, her instinct for tidiness and efficiency rising to the surface. "If not, I can wait until everyone arrives," Kyoshi said. "I don't want to have to go back and check each floor."

"Tear her apart!" Mok screamed.

The hatchet men charged from all directions. Kyoshi drew one of her fans. Two would have been a bit much.

Kyoshi stepped over the groaning bodies. When one of the Triad members was too still, she nudged him with her boot until she saw signs of breathing.

Mok's robe had blown off in the scuffle. He managed to budge the chair he was sitting on a few inches in flight before Kyoshi put her hand on his shoulder, pressing him back into his seat.

"No need to get up yet, Uncle," she said. Past enmity or not, he was still older than her.

Mok roiled with an anger and fear that Kyoshi could feel through her grip. "So, you're going to murder me in cold blood like you did Xu. May you be ripped apart by thunderbolts and many knives for slaying your sworn brothers."

Kyoshi found herself bothered, more than she should have been, by Mok calling her a murderer. She and Xu Ping An had agreed to a duel, and the man immediately tried to kill her. Once she'd gained the upper hand, she'd given him a chance to yield. The former leader of the Yellow Necks had amply demonstrated he was beyond saving.

And yet, during sleepless nights, she thought about Xu. The vile man infected her thoughts when she could have been dreaming of those she loved. She thought about Xu a great deal, his weight in her hands, and how, at the end of their fight, she'd *decided*.

Kyoshi cleared her head. "Anything goes on the *lei tai*," she said. Justifying the act out loud was bitter, ineffective medicine that she forced herself to swallow anyway. "I'm not going to kill you. You and your men got a foothold inside the walls rather quickly for a gang of countryside bandits who spent most of their history bullying farmers. You have a contact in Ba Sing Se helping you, and I want to know who it is."

Mok stiffened with purpose. True *daofei* never surrendered information to the authorities, even if it would benefit them. "The day I squeal to you, girl, is the day I—*aieee!*"

Kyoshi reminded him that times had changed since they first met with a crushing squeeze of her fingers. She dented the nerves of his arm until the terms of their new relationship sunk in.

"It was someone from the Middle Ring!" Mok said, once he stopped squealing in pain. "We used go-betweens; I don't know their name!"

Kyoshi let go and took a step back. She'd been expecting him to name a Lower Ring criminal, a local who'd maybe sworn brotherhood to him in the past. The Middle Ring was the domain of merchants and academics. Something didn't add up here.

Mok clutched his shoulder and scrambled away from the desk. "Wai!" he shouted at a door behind him. "Now!"

In her distraction, Kyoshi had forgotten the third leading brother of the former Yellow Necks. The door burst open in an ambush before Kyoshi could react.

Brother Wai sprung out, knife raised, a snarl on his lips. He wasn't wearing the leather strap that covered his severed nose, and without it his gaunt face had a skull-like appearance. Wai had been a fast, vicious man back in his Yellow Neck days, and he still was.

But when he saw the intruder was Kyoshi, dressed in her full makeup and regalia, he gasped and nearly halted in midair. Wai was one of the few witnesses who'd seen her in the Avatar State, and the experience had overawed the spiritual man. He stepped back to give her space, nearly knocking his brother over in his haste, and dropped to his knees. The knife that had been aimed at Kyoshi a second before, he placed at her feet like an offering.

"Oh come on!" Mok screamed as Wai bowed his head to the ground and prostrated himself before the Avatar.

Kyoshi stepped out of the City Block into the street. The day had gotten brighter and hotter. A squad of peace officers, uniformed guardsmen of Ba Sing Se, waited for her, lining in wings to the left and right of the exit. The junior men who'd never seen the Avatar before stared at Kyoshi as she emerged from the darkness. One of them dropped his truncheon and fumbled to pick it up.

Kyoshi walked past the rank-and-file guardsmen, ignoring the whispers and barely acknowledging the bows, until she reached Captain Li by the door. He was a sallow-faced man who'd been on the job too long, his retirement delayed by gambling debts. "The cordon is set," he said to Kyoshi in a pipe-smoker's wheeze. "No trouble out here so far."

Most of the Lower Ring citizens went about their business, ignoring the presence of the law, but Kyoshi noticed a few people watching with fake disinterest, probably spotters for other unsavory organizations. Working with Captain Li meant flirting with a violation of Kyoshi's *daofei* oaths. She'd sworn to her elder sister Kirima under a blade held by her elder brother Wong never to become a lackey of the law.

But Li had been her tool, her informant, not the other way around. He'd provided her the intelligence she needed to close her unfinished business with Mok, and numbers for cleanup once she was done. "Is the building safe?" Li asked, tilting his cap to dab at his forehead with his cuff.

"The Triad members are down and ready to be extricated," Kyoshi said. "You should summon a doctor."

"I'll get right on that," Li replied in a dull tone that let Kyoshi know how seriously he took the suggestion. He put his fingers to his lips and whistled. "All right, boys! Get the vermin out of there!"

The guardsmen hustled into the City Block, free to move fast after Kyoshi had swept the twists and nooks of danger. She waited patiently to see the results of her work. The Triad of the Golden Wing needed to be counted and catalogued in the light of day. Being hauled away like dry goods would cause their mystique to blow away in the wind. Hopefully.

She heard loud voices and the sound of a struggle emerging from the darkness of Loongkau. Two officers dragged out a man who hadn't been among the Triads who'd attacked her. He was dressed poorly, but a pair of glasses fell from his head. He had to have been a jeweler or a tailor to have invested in such an expensive device.

A boot crushed the glasses into the dust before she could say anything. With mounting horror, Kyoshi watched another set of officers come out, hustling a woman by the back of her neck. She held a wailing child in her arms. The man with bad vision heard the cries and began thrashing harder in the guards' grasp.

These weren't Triad members. They were one of the poor families who lived in the City Block. "What are your men doing?" Kyoshi shouted at Li.

He looked confused at her question. "Getting rid of the bad element. Certain folks have been waiting to demolish this eyesore for a long time." He turned hesitant, a haggler afraid to part with too much of his money. "Do . . . you want a cut? If you do, you have to talk to my man in the Middle Ring."

The Middle Ring. In a flash, she understood.

Someone with big, lucrative plans for Loongkau wanted the residents scrubbed from the city block but needed an excuse to do it. They'd let the Triads in first, to get the law and the Avatar involved, and then bribed Captain Li to clear out innocent and criminal folk alike.

"Stop this!" Kyoshi said. "Stop this right now!"

"*Aiyaaa,*" Li lamented without a speck of sincerity. "I'm sorry, Avatar, but I'm acting within the confines of my duty. Rightfully, I can vacate these premises of criminals as necessary."

"Mama!" It was the little girl's sobbing that set Kyoshi over the edge. *"Papa!"*

Kyoshi drew her fans and snapped them open. She raised clumps of earth from below the dusty top layer, where the clay was still moist and malleable. Fist-sized clods shot forth, slamming over the mouths and noses of Li and his officers, clamping over their skin like muzzles.

The guards let go of the family and clawed at their faces, but Kyoshi's earthbending was too strong to be resisted. Li sank to his knees, his eyes goggling out.

They had time before they would suffocate to death. Kyoshi put back her fans and slowly went to each guard in turn, yanking off their headbands one by one, checking the square metal seals of the Earth King fastened to the cloth.

The badges of every official in Ba Sing Se had identification numbers engraved on them, a testament to the city's massive bureaucracy. These men, despite the shrinking supply of air to their brains, could understand the gesture of her taking their headbands and tucking them into her robes for safekeeping. One visit to an administration hall, and she could learn their identities. She could find them later. Most residents of Ba Sing Se had heard the rumors. They'd heard stories of what Avatar Kyoshi was, and what she did to people.

Kyoshi saved Li for last. He'd turned purple in the time she'd taken to make the rounds. After snatching his headband from under his cap, she let the clay fall from his mouth, and the others' at the same time. Li's squad dropped to the ground, gasping for breath. The captain landed on his side and his inhalation rattled like dice in a cup.

She leaned over, but before she could say anything, Li threw a name at her, hoping to buy clemency. He really had no backbone. "His name is Wo! The man paying me is Minister Wo!"

Kyoshi needed to shut her eyes so her frustration wouldn't leak out. There were probably a dozen Minister Wo's in Ba Sing Se. The name alone was meaningless to her. The city was too big. The Earth Kingdom was too big. She couldn't keep up with the corruption leaking from its holes.

She gathered her breath. "Here is what's going to happen, Captain," she said as calmly as she could. "You are going to clear the block of the Triads and no one else. Then you are going to find paper and brush. You will write me a full confession, detailing this Wo person and every bribe you took from him. Every stroke of it the truth. Do you hear me, Captain Li? I will check. I want you to pour your very spirit into this confession."

He nodded. Kyoshi straightened up to see the woman and her daughter looking at her with wide, frightened eyes. She started to approach them, wanting to ask if they were hurt.

"Don't touch them!" The man who'd lost his glasses threw himself between Kyoshi and his family. With his near blindness, he wouldn't have seen her trying to help. Or maybe he had, and decided she was a danger to his wife and child anyway.

Farther away, around the edges of the cordon, more bystanders had gathered. They whispered to each other, the seeds of fresh rumors taking root in the soil. The Avatar had not only ripped apart the occupants of Loongkau, but she'd turned her insatiable wrath upon the officers of the Earth King's justice as well.

The stares of the ordinary citizens and the terrified family made Kyoshi's skin prickle with a feeling that corrupt men like

Li or Mok could never force on her. Shame. Shame for what she'd done, shame for what she was.

Her makeup covered the flush in her cheeks and camouflaged the furrow in her brow. She gave Li one last meaningful tap and then walked away from Loongkau as slowly as she'd arrived, an impassive statue heading back to the altar that gave it life. But really, underneath her paint, she was fleeing the scene of her crime, her heart threatening to pound her chest into dust.

THE INVITATION

PEOPLE WHO complained about how long it took to travel across Ba Sing Se were usually factoring in the congestion. That wasn't a problem for Kyoshi. Crowds tended to part out of her way like grass before the breeze.

She had another shortcut to exploit as well. It was possible to waterbend a makeshift raft upstream along the drainage canals running from the Upper Ring all the way out to the Agrarian Zone for irrigation. It was extremely fast, if you could stand the smell.

She reached the Middle Ring by the evening. Despite the orderly layout and numbered addresses, she struggled to find her direction in the uniformity of the white-painted houses and green-tiled roofs. She took paths leading her over peaceful bridges that spanned gently flowing canals, and along tea shops redolent with jasmine blossoms and trees shedding their pale pink petals over the sidewalks. As a child living in the gutters of Yokoya, Kyoshi used to imagine a paradise much like the Middle Ring. Clean, quiet, and food at hand anywhere you looked.

Store owners sweeping their floors would look up in surprise at her, but soon returned to their business. She passed a gaggle of dark-robed students that stared and elbowed each other to get a glimpse but didn't flee her gaze. People who were comfortable with their station in life tended to have less fear. They couldn't imagine danger in any form visiting their doorstep.

Kyoshi slipped out of sight into a darkened side street. She opened an unmarked door with a key she kept in her sash. The hallway she entered was as full of twists and stairs as Loongkau, but much cleaner. It ended with a passageway into a plain second-story apartment, furnished only with a bed and a desk. This room was one of several properties around the Four Nations that Jianzhu had bequeathed her, and it served as a saferoom where she could sleep overnight when she didn't want to announce her official presence with the Earth King's staff. She unbuckled her bracers and peeled them off, tossing them on the bed as she crossed the floor.

She sank into the chair and dumped the pilfered headbands on the desk, the badges clattering over the surface like gambling winnings. She was more careful removing her headdress. A breeze rustled her freed hair, coming from the window that gave her an expansive sunset view of the Lower Ring in all its vastness and poverty, the brown shacks and shanties stretching over the land like leather drying in the sun.

It was an unusual layout for the apartment. Many Middle Ring houses did not have views that faced the Lower Ring. The merchants and financiers who lived in this district paid so they didn't have to look at unpleasantness.

Her fingers moved on their own, organizing the badges into neat stacks. A dull ache of exhaustion settled into her head. Today had added another complication to the pile. She would need to plan another visit to Loongkau to make sure the residents were safe within their homes. And she'd have to follow up on Li's information, or else the captain and his backers would know they could simply wait until the Avatar had passed like a cloud overhead for them to resume their corrupt activities.

She knew it was a losing battle. In the grand scheme of things, singling out one dirty lawman in Ba Sing Se would have as much effect as pulling a raindrop out of the ocean. Unless . . .

Unless she made an example of Li and whoever bribed him. She could hurt them so badly that word would spread about what happens when the Avatar catches you exploiting the defenseless for your own gain.

It would be quick. It would be efficient. It would be brutal.

Jianzhu would have approved.

Kyoshi slammed her hands against the desk, toppling the badges. She'd slipped yet again into the mindset of her deceased "benefactor." She'd heard his words in her own voice, the two of them speaking with as much unity as the Avatars were supposed to be able to do with their past lives.

She opened a drawer and pulled out a hand towel that had been resting in a small bowl of special liniment. Kyoshi dragged the moistened cloth hard down the side of her face, trying to wipe away the deeper stains along with her makeup.

A shudder of revulsion ran up Kyoshi's back when she thought of how she'd smothered Li with the exact same technique

Jianzhu had once used on her. She should have abhorred it, knowing exactly what it felt like to die slowly as your lungs caved in on themselves. In dealing with Li, she'd slipped as easily into Jianzhu's skin as she had her clothes.

The ones that had *also* been a gift from him.

She slammed her fist on the desk again and heard part of the joinery crack. It felt like every step she took as the Avatar was in the wrong direction. Kelsang would never have entertained violence as policy. He would have worked to improve the fortunes of the Loongkau and Lower Ring residents so they could push back against Triad domination and Middle Ring exploitation. He would have acted as their voice.

That was what Kyoshi had to do. In essence, it was what Kelsang had done for her, the abandoned child he found in Yokoya. It was the right course of action and would be the most effective in the long run.

It would just take time. A very . . . very long time.

A knock came from outside. "Come in," she said.

A young man wearing the billowing orange and yellow robes of an Air Nomad opened the door. "Are you all right, Avatar Kyoshi?" Monk Jinpa said. "I heard a loud noise and—*aagh!*"

The stack of letters he was holding went flying into the air. Kyoshi whipped her hand around and around in a circle of airbending, corralling the papers with a miniature tornado. Jinpa recovered from his surprise and caught the pile of letters from the bottom of the vortex up, re-creating the stack, but with the corners sticking out at all angles.

"Apologies, Avatar," he said when he'd secured her correspondence once more. "I was surprised by your, uh . . . " He gestured at his own face in lieu of pointing rudely at hers.

She hadn't finished wiping off the rest of her makeup. She probably looked like a doctor's illustration of a skull with the skin halfway stripped. Kyoshi grabbed the towel to finish the job. "Don't worry about it," she said as she worked the cloth along the corner of her eye, taking care not to get the compound that would dissolve the paint into it.

In defiance of her order, Jinpa still looked worried. "You're also bleeding from your neck."

Yes. Right. With her free hand she opened a fan and aimed the leaf at the garrote wound around her throat. The shards of glass in her skin plucked themselves out under the force of her earthbending and balled into a floating clump that dropped to the floor when she switched her focus to a nearby pitcher.

A tiny wriggle of water snaked out of the vessel and wrapped itself around Kyoshi's neck. It was cool and soothing against the itch of the wound, and she could feel her skin knitting together. Jinpa watched her heal herself, both worried and horrified by the crudeness of her self-administered first aid.

"Isn't healing water supposed to glow?" he asked.

"I've never managed it." The mansion's libraries in Yokoya were full of extensive tomes about the medical uses of water-bending, but Kyoshi lacked time and a proper teacher. She'd read through as many of the texts as she could anyway, and the wounds she'd been accumulating as the Avatar gave her plenty of opportunities to practice on herself.

She'd made a vow. No matter how limited her knowledge was, or how flawed her technique, she would never again watch someone she cared about slip away in front of her while she did nothing.

She tossed the water back in the pitcher and ran a finger over the marks left behind on her neck. *At this rate I'm going to look like Auntie Mui's latest patchwork quilt.* She could hide the scar with more makeup or a higher collar. But the mottled, healed burns on her hands, courtesy of Xu Ping An, reminded her she was running out of body parts to injure and cover up. "What are the updates?"

Jinpa took a seat and pulled out one of the many letters addressed to the Avatar that he'd already broken the seals on. He was allowed the privilege. During her first visit to the Southern Air Temple as the Avatar, he had helped her constantly with planning and communication, to the point where his elders shrugged and officially assigned him to Kyoshi as her secretary. Without his assistance, she would have been overwhelmed to the point of shutting down.

"Governor Te humbly submits a report that Zigan Village has surpassed its former peak population and can now boast of a new school *and* herbal clinic, both of which are free of charge to the poorest townsfolk," Jinpa read aloud. "Huh. The Te family's not known for generosity. I wonder what's gotten into young Sihung recently."

What indeed. Te Sihung had been the first official of the Earth Kingdom to learn Kyoshi was the Avatar, right after she'd decided not to assassinate him during a *daofei* raid on his house. After her public revealing, she'd made it clear to Te that the life debt he owed her still applied and she'd continue to watch him. Knowing his power didn't make him immune to consequences seemed to have bolstered both his compassion and skill as governor.

Good news was hard to come by these days. "What's next?" she asked Jinpa, hoping for more.

His lips pulled to the side. "The rest of the letters are audience requests from nobles you've already rejected or ignored."

"All of them?" She eyed the tall stack of papers and frowned.

Jinpa shrugged. "You reject and ignore a lot of nobles. Earth Kingdom folk are nothing if not persistent."

Kyoshi fought the urge to set the whole pile of correspondence ablaze. She didn't have to read every message to know each one was a demand for the Avatar's favorable judgment on matters of business, politics, and money.

She'd learned after the first few times. Kyoshi would accept an innocuous invitation to attend a banquet, preside over a spiritual ceremony, bless a new canal or a bridge. Inevitably, her host, the governor or the largest landowner—oftentimes the same person—would corner her into a side conversation and beg for assistance in material affairs they would never have bothered Kuruk or Great Yangchen with. But Kyoshi was one of their own, wasn't she? She understood how business was done in the Earth Kingdom.

She did. It didn't mean she liked it. Sages who'd vehemently denied her Avatarhood despite Jianzhu's last will and testament, nobles who claimed trickery after watching her twirl water and earth above her head with their own eyes, suddenly became true believers when they thought she could aid them in biting off greater mouthfuls of wealth and power in the endless hierarchies of the Earth Kingdom. The Avatar could settle where a provincial border lay, and which governor got to claim taxes from a rich cropland. The Avatar could speed a trade fleet along its route safely, protecting the lives of the sailors, but ultimately ensuring a massive profit for its merchant backers. Couldn't she?

Kyoshi soon learned to ignore such requests and focus on what she could wreak with her own hands. "Those messages can wait," she said. She secretly hoped the stack of correspondence would blow away into dust if she sounded cold and authoritative enough.

Jinpa gave her a gentle but chiding look. "Avatar . . . if I may be permitted, you have to participate in high society to *some* extent. You can't keep putting off the leadership of the Earth Kingdom forever."

The Earth Kingdom doesn't have leadership, Kyoshi thought. *I helped kill the closest thing to a leader it had.*

"The duties of your role extend beyond being a powerful bender," he went on. "You've scrubbed the countryside of the largest bandit groups, and it's impressive you were able to track down this Mok person and keep him from hurting more innocent people. But at this point you're running yourself ragged simply so you can beat up the same bad men you've already beaten up in the past. Is scraping the bottom of the criminal barrel truly the most good you could do for the Four Nations? Not to mention the risks it poses to your personal safety."

"It's what I know." *And it's the only way I can be sure what I'm doing is right.*

They'd had this conversation before, many times, but Jinpa never grew tired of reminding her. Unlike the other Air Nomads she'd met, who prized detachment from the world, he was constantly pushing her to engage in a higher level of discourse with the very people who sought to exploit her. He wasn't much older than Kyoshi, slightly on the other side of twenty years, so it was strange when he spoke like a political tutor trying to guide a wayward pupil.

"At some point, you will have to stand upon a greater stage," Jinpa said. "The Avatar creates ripples in the world, whether they mean to or not."

"Is that a saying among your mysterious friends whom you won't tell me about?" she retorted.

He merely shrugged at her clumsy attempt to change the subject. That was the other frustrating thing about Jinpa. He wouldn't trade jabs with her like Kirima or Wong. He showed her too much respect, a problem her old companions never had, even after learning she was the Avatar.

She wondered what would happen if the monk ever met the remaining members of the Flying Opera Company. She could imagine Jinpa offering them assistance in escaping the *daofei* lifestyle. They probably would have tried to steal his bison.

There was only one thing that could get her to talk to the sages. "None of the letters mentioned—"

"Master Yun? No, unfortunately. He has yet to turn up."

Kyoshi exhaled, a long hiss through her teeth. During the period where the world thought Yun was the Avatar, he had focused a great deal of effort on treating with the Earth Kingdom's elite. Which meant they were the only people who knew his face. Without a lead from someone who recognized him, finding one man in the entirety of the Earth Kingdom was like looking for a single pebble in a gravel pit. "Let's try bumping up the reward again."

"I don't know if that'll help," Jinpa said. "The prominent figures of the Earth Kingdom lost a lot of face as a result of Master

Yun's misidentification. If I were them, I wouldn't want him to resurface. I would want to pretend the whole episode never happened. I hear Lu Beifong forbids anyone in his household, guests included, to speak of Jianzhu or his disciple."

Jinpa had a strange amount of access to political gossip for a simple Air Nomad, but his observations were usually correct. *That blasted pricklethorn Lu.* As Jianzhu's backer, the Beifong patriarch was just as guilty in Kyoshi's eyes for the mistake in identifying the Avatar, and he continued to cast off any further responsibility in the matter.

She'd begged Lu Beifong in person to help her find Yun, expecting the old man to have some semblance of grandfatherly attachment to him. Instead Lu coldly revealed that the letter Jianzhu had sent to sages across the Earth Kingdom proclaiming Kyoshi to be the Avatar also said Yun was dead. Between Jianzhu's final words and Kyoshi's confused testimony of the incident in Qinchao, Lu chose to believe what was most convenient for him. As far as he was concerned, the scandal had resolved itself. A victory for neutral *jing*.

Jinpa gave her a smile out of sympathy. "No one's asking you to give up your search for the false Avatar, but maybe—"

"Don't call him that!"

Her rebuke echoed through the room. Thinking about how easily Yun had been abandoned, first by Jianzhu, then by Lu and the rest of the Earth Kingdom, had set her back on edge. Jinpa avoided her gaze, lowering his head. In the awkward silence he wiggled his foot nervously. She didn't need bending to feel the tremors through the floor.

"I'll send word of Master Yun's description to every major passport-checking waystation I can," he said. "It's the job of such officials to match names and appearances. They'll be paying closer attention than your average bystander."

It was a good idea. Better than any she'd had so far. She felt doubly bad for losing her temper. She needed to apologize for her outburst, needed to stop having such outbursts if she and Jinpa were to ever shorten the distance between them.

But she was fearful of what lay at the end of friendships. She had been a danger to every companion she ever had. And she still couldn't shake the memories of an Air Nomad who gave her jokes and warmth and easy smiles.

"Make it happen," Kyoshi said curtly.

Jinpa nodded. Then he paused, as if wondering how to frame his next statement. "I didn't open all of today's letters. One of them came by special courier."

"Half the letters we get are by 'special courier,'" Kyoshi scoffed. Grandiose deliveries with envelopes stamped with *Urgent* and *For the Avatar's Eyes Only* in loud green ink were common tricks the Earth Sages tried, in order to grab her attention.

"This one is genuinely special." Jinpa reached into his robe and pulled out a message tube he'd been safekeeping.

It was red.

The sturdy metal tube was end-capped with gilded flames. In the surroundings of the staid but clearly Earth Kingdom furnishings of the apartment, the scroll case looked like an ember in a forest, threatening to catch. An army of wax seals guarded the seams.

Jinpa passed it to her with both hands like an object of reverence. "I believe this is from Fire Lord Zoryu himself."

Her first direct correspondence from a head of state. Kyoshi had never met the Fire Lord, nor had he ever written her before. The only contact she'd had with the Fire Nation government was the envoy who'd visited her in Yokoya soon after the news broke of her Avatarhood. The sharply dressed minister had watched her raise a modicum of all four elements, nodding to himself as each one was checked off in turn. He'd saluted Kyoshi, politely stayed for dinner, and then left for his homeland the next morning to report the new state of affairs. She remembered appreciating the lack of grief the foreign delegate gave her in comparison to her own countrymen.

Breaking the seals and opening the case felt like damaging a historical artifact. Kyoshi kept as much of the wax's original shape as she could and unfurled the scroll inside.

The writing was direct and to the point, devoid of the flourishes Earth Kingdom officials thought were necessary to curry favor with her. Lord Zoryu needed the Avatar's assistance on a matter of national importance. If she would come visit the royal palace as his honored guest to celebrate the upcoming Festival of Szeto, a significant holiday in the Fire Islands, he could explain further in person.

"What does it say?" Jinpa asked.

"It's an invitation to visit the Fire Nation." A debut on the world stage. She swallowed the nervousness that had suddenly clumped in her throat.

Jinpa saw her hesitation and clasped his hands together, beseeching. "This is exactly what I'm talking about, Avatar. The Four Nations aren't going to let you remain out of the public eye forever. Please don't tell me you'd snub the Fire Lord, of all people."

Kyoshi mulled it over. She doubted the ruler of the Fire

Nation would waste her time with a frivolous request for help. And her frustrations with her own country were threatening to push her past her breaking point. A change of scenery might be called for.

"And it's a holiday festival," Jinpa added. "You might even have fun. You *are* allowed to enjoy yourself from time to time, you know."

Leave it to an Air Nomad to fall back on fun as the last argument. "You can write back and tell the Fire Lord I am honored to accept his invitation," she said. "We'll start planning the trip tomorrow. I don't think I can handle any more business for today."

Jinpa bowed solemnly, hiding his satisfaction that finally the Avatar was stepping up to her responsibilities. "No one needs their rest more than the Avatar." He left the room for the office they'd set up down the hall.

Alone, Kyoshi stared at the cream-colored paper in silence. She hadn't mentioned to Jinpa the portion of the letter that tipped the scales in favor of the visit.

It was a very specific piece of news at the end of the Fire Lord's message. The former Headmistress of the Royal Academy had returned home after a long convalescence in Agna Qel'a, the capital of the Northern Water Tribe. So had her daughter. Perhaps the Avatar would like to see them, given the three had been acquaintances in Yokoya? They certainly wished to see her.

Acquaintances. Kyoshi didn't know it was possible to feel such relief and distress at once. She wasn't in the Fire Nation yet and already she could picture who was waiting for her, the walking blaze of pure heat and confrontation. In the darkness of her exhaustion, a point of shining light beckoned.

Rangi.

Kyoshi carefully folded the paper and tucked it into her robes, close to her thumping heart. Despite her secretary's wishes, she was not going to be getting much sleep tonight.

PAST LIVES

JINPA'S BISON Yingyong had only five feet instead of the usual six. As a calf he'd been attacked by a predator and lost his left forelimb. As an adult, the injury caused him to list slightly to the side when he was flying, which required Jinpa to give a gentle tug with the reins in the opposite direction every so often to maintain a straight course through the air.

Kyoshi had gotten used to traveling in Yingyong's arcs. Kelsang's bison Pengpeng was busy raising calves of her own at the Southern Temple in a well-deserved retirement, and Kyoshi had never expected their relationship to be permanent. Pengpeng might have been willing to put up with her, may have even liked her, but only a single Air Nomad could truly partner with one of the great beasts for life.

She and Jinpa flew a little lower than usual on their way to the Fire Nation, close to the green waters of the Mo Ce Sea, where the air was warm and easy to breathe. The beautiful weather allowed it. Scoops of clouds drifted overhead in the blue sky, providing little pockets of shade for them to dip between.

If Kyoshi missed anything from those days after she fled Yokoya on Pengpeng's back, it was these little in-between moments of travel. Most people would have assumed that floating on a bison with the breeze against her face was calming, but for Kyoshi, the upside was very different. Taking to the air gave her the assurance that for once, by default, she was doing the best she could. There weren't any faster ways to get from one point to another than a sky bison. She had no other options to fret over.

An unsecured bag began to slide from one edge of the saddle to the other. Jinpa gave the reins another little yank, and Yingyong righted himself. Kyoshi caught the sack and tucked it under a lashing. "Is he okay?" she asked. "Does he need to rest?"

"Nah, he's fine," Jinpa said. "Lazy boy got distracted by a school of winged eels. Didn't you, boy? Who's a lazy, distracted boy with a poor attention span?" He gave Yingyong an affectionate scratch behind the ear. "But if you do want to stop, there's an opportunity up ahead with an interesting piece of history. A small island where it's said that Avatar Yangchen performed her first act of waterbending. Want to see it?"

She did, honestly. Kyoshi held an intense curiosity about one of the greatest Avatars in history, her predecessor from two generations ago. Yangchen was the woman who'd done everything right. She was the Avatar whom, to this day, was still invoked by people for protection and luck. Kyoshi often wished she understood Yangchen's leadership like a real scholar. She'd been making do with her commoner's knowledge of the blessed Air Avatar who'd successfully kept the world in balance and harmony.

She would study Yangchen's work more the next time she returned to Yokoya. There had to be useful materials in the mansion's great libraries. Right now, though, she was in a hurry. "We don't need to land. I'll take a look from above."

"Of course, Avatar. I'll let you know when it comes up."

Kyoshi settled back into her seat. The letter under her jacket made a slight rasp against the fabric and a loud scrape against her nerves.

She hadn't communicated with Rangi in a long time. Messenger hawks had trouble withstanding the extreme cold of the north, where her mother Hei-Ran had been recovering. As a new Avatar, Kyoshi was always on the move. The mansion was as far away from the Northern Water Tribe as a point in the Earth Kingdom could be. It seemed like the world had conspired to keep them apart and mute their voices.

She wanted to think about something else. Or talk to someone else. She still found it hard to make casual conversation with Jinpa, and a bison saddle was a large, empty seat for one person. She was more accustomed to fighting for space with at least four other people, jostling shoulders, complaining about whose breath stank from eating too much pungent food.

After a while she felt Yingyong turning into another roll, sharper this time. "So . . . where's this island?" she asked Jinpa as she balanced herself against the rail. The sea was a flat sheet with nowhere to hide for a landmass.

Jinpa leaned into the circle and examined the water. "Hmm.

Everything I've read said it should be around here. I don't see anything but that dark patch under the surface."

"Look, if we can't find it, we can just go. It's not important—"

KYOSHI.

She screamed as a bolt of pain drove into her skull from temple to temple. It seized her by the neck and scoured her vision into a blur. Her hands went limp and lost their grip on the saddle. Kyoshi keeled over the edge and fell off the bison, her ears filled with the sound of her own name.

She hurt the entire way down. A sharpness like daggers bounced from one side of her head to the other. It found an outlet down her spine where it could ransack her body. She was barely aware of how fast and far she was plummeting.

KYOSHI.

A man with a deep voice called to her, his words shredded by the wind speeding past her ears. It wasn't Jinpa.

KYOSHI.

The shock of cold salt water as she hit the ocean was a relief from the heated agony. She lost her sense of up and down. Her limbs drifted weightlessly. When she opened her eyes, there was no sting.

Out of the endless blue, a figure drifted in front of her, mirroring her slackness in the water, as much of a prisoner as she. The shape of it was hazy, an ink painting dipped in a river, but she knew who the apparition clad in Water Tribe furs was.

Avatar Kuruk.

—KYOSHI—NEED YOUR HELP TO—

The voice of Kyoshi's immediate predecessor in the Avatar cycle was much louder in the water, his native-born element. It thundered between her ears.

—KYOSHI—YOU MUST—I CAN'T—IT CAN PASS—

A hand plunged through Kuruk's body, dissolving it into the surrounding liquid like thin syrup. It grabbed Kyoshi's lapels and tugged her toward the surface. The salt water, which hadn't bothered her until now, dug into her eyes with a vengeance. Forgetting she was still below the surface, she gasped for air and got her throat splashed for her troubles. If Kuruk's spell could have kept her from drowning indefinitely, it was broken now.

Jinpa kicked toward the rippling sunlight, holding tightly to her with one hand. At first Kyoshi tried to help him by swimming upward herself. It took her an embarrassingly long time floundering like that to remember she was a Waterbender surrounded by water. A quick raise of her arms and a rolling bubble carried her and Jinpa to the surface.

They burst into the air and emptied the contents of their lungs. Kyoshi hacked and coughed until she could breathe once more. Yingyong floated in the water nearby, growling in worry.

"Are you all right!?" Jinpa sputtered. "Are you hurt?"

"I'm fine," Kyoshi said. The headache had mostly dissipated into the ocean. "I just lost my balance and fell."

"Just fell?" Jinpa was as visibly upset with her as an Airbender could be. He was raising his voice. He was *frowning* at her.

"It was Kuruk." Kyoshi squeezed the sides of her head to dull the lingering throb. Her bending spared them the need to tread. "He was trying to tell me something."

"Avatar Kuruk!? You . . . you communed with Avatar Kuruk? You looked like you were having a fit!"

"It's usually not this bad. It wasn't so painful the last couple of times."

Jinpa's jaw threatened to unhinge and fall into the ocean. "These episodes have happened before and you haven't told me? Kyoshi, an Avatar communing with their past selves is supposed to be a hallowed experience, not a life-threatening seizure!"

Kyoshi grimaced. She knew. She knew exactly how lacking her spiritual connections were. She'd found out through trial and error.

The Water Tribe Avatar had manifested before her in his complete form exactly once in the Southern Air Temple, where he had the gall to ask *her* for help before dissipating just as quickly. She'd been left in a lurch, not knowing what to do with such a useless vision.

But the experience did remind her she had access to a trove of worldly advice in the form of her past lives. A vast wealth of experience and wisdom lay at her fingertips, if she could only master her own spirit.

Kyoshi had tried reaching out to previous generations of the cycle by meditating in the sacred places of the Southern Air Temple, wayside shrines of the Earth Kingdom dedicated to the great Avatars like Yangchen and Salai, spots of natural beauty atop mountains and next to flowing rivers. She wasn't expecting it to be easy. She'd read that spiritualists had taken lifetimes to gain the skills of meditation, trance, and enlightenment. Kyoshi had fully prepared herself to be greeted by the silence of failure when she tried to commune with her past selves.

What she wasn't ready for, though, was getting jagged fragments of Kuruk.

And *only* of Kuruk.

Every . . . single . . . *time.*

The results of her meditations were always the same. She would reach inwardly, attempt to harmonize with her past, and be met by the blotchy form of the Water Avatar spitting garbled nonsense. It was as reliable as a dropped stone hitting the bottom of a well. She tried deciphering his mysterious request, but whatever connection they shared wasn't strong enough for her to figure it out.

And the sessions often hurt in a teeth-rattling, convulsive way. That was why she'd never asked a sage who'd been to the Spirit World to guide her in meditation. She feared the same reaction as Jinpa's if anyone saw her fail so loudly and painfully. An Avatar who struggled to reach her past lives was one thing, but an Avatar who was violently rejected and roughed up by the process like a thief caught sneaking into the wrong house was another. Kyoshi didn't need her legitimacy doubted more than it already was.

Eventually she'd stopped trying to commune. She hadn't been the greatest admirer of Kuruk anyway, and if he was the only past life out of a thousand generations willing to make contact with her, then she could do without. But sometimes her predecessor forced the issue and appeared unbidden.

"It's not a big deal," she said to Jinpa. "Occasionally, I'll have a vision of Kuruk, or hear his voice. I can never tell what he's trying to say."

Jinpa couldn't believe she was talking about it like a bad knee aching before it rained. "Kyoshi," he said, summoning the tranquility of his ancestors to keep from breaking down and weeping at her ineptness. "If an Avatar of the past has a message for you, it's usually of the utmost importance."

"Fine!" she yelled. "The first chance we get, we'll find a great enlightened master and I'll learn how to talk to Kuruk! Now can we please get back to our *other* top-priority mission? Or are you somehow going to fix everything that's wrong with me all at once?"

The look of hurt and disappointment on the monk's face confirmed it. Kyoshi might have been a bad Avatar, but she was also a bad master to her secretary, one who not only yelled, but insulted. Not even Jianzhu put his staff down to their faces. She would have thought her experience on the other end of the relationship would have made her better at this.

And Jinpa had saved her from drowning. Had she been wearing her heavy robes and bracers instead of a light traveling outfit, she might have sunk too fast for him to reach.

"I'm sorry," she said. "Jinpa, I'm really sorry. I've no right to speak to you like that." He would have gotten along better with Yun. The two of them would have become fast friends and played Pai Sho from sunup to sundown. "I . . . I wish you were serving a worthier Avatar."

Her apology didn't seem to be quite what he was looking for, but he acquiesced with his usual gentle smile. Jinpa clambered onto Yingyong's withers and began wringing out his wet robes. Kyoshi sighed and plunged her face back below the surface, hoping the shame would rinse away.

She saw something under the water that hardened her spirit again.

The dark patch Jinpa had spotted from above was a wrecked

and sunken atoll, an island blown apart and scarred by what could only be bending of the highest power. The reef structure was split and pitted, giant chunks of earth scattered like marbles, and swathes of coral had been ground smooth by unimaginably intense waterbending.

Kyoshi recognized the telltale marks of destruction well. This was Yangchen's island. It was the same place where Kuruk and his companions had gone so he could practice going into the Avatar State for the first time. Maybe they didn't know. Or maybe they'd chosen a location associated with Yangchen to receive spiritual assistance from the great Air Avatar. But Kuruk, in his lapse of control, had destroyed the atoll and sunk it below the waves.

A spot holy to Yangchen and the Air Nomads was gone because of his carelessness. As she pulled herself back onto the saddle, Kyoshi tried to model herself after Jinpa's calm. Some very unkind opinions were running through her head, and right now, the less she thought about Kuruk, the better.

THE REUNION

IT WAS strange to think that getting closer to a string of active volcanoes would make them feel better, but here they were, approaching the Fire Nation.

Jinpa wisely avoided the plumes of noxious smoke emanating from the active peaks but wove Yingyong over the thermals in between, riding bumps of heated air in a playful, winding course. It was enough to make Kyoshi forget herself and smile.

Clumps of settlements could be seen on the smaller islands, usually by the coasts but sometimes higher up in the mountains, where level pastures and shade-grown tea farms dotted the slopes. The landmasses formed a thickening tail that led them to the body of Capital Island, where the earth doubled over on itself to form First Lord's Harbor.

They swooped lower to see the city that had formed around the Fire Nation's largest port already preparing for the upcoming celebration. Strings of red paper lanterns crisscrossed the streets, in some places thick enough to completely obscure the carts and sidewalks below. The sharp clack of vendors hammering their wooden stalls together filled the air. Kyoshi spotted one alley overtaken by a half-finished parade float. A team of dancers practiced their moves in rigorous unison atop the platform.

"This seems like a serious party," Kyoshi said. She secretly wished she could be down there, among her fellow commoners for the celebrations, instead of attending a state function. There'd certainly be less pressure on her.

"You know how Fire Nationals are," Jinpa said as he waved at a bunch of gawking children on a rooftop who were thrilled to see a bison fly overhead. "Buttoned up until the moment they let loose."

They left Harbor City behind and continued flying up the slope of the caldera that dominated the big island. Trees and vines clung tenaciously to the steep, rocky surfaces, and the humidity grew heavy like a blanket.

"Should we stop here and announce ourselves?" Jinpa said. He pointed to the stone watchtowers and bunkers built into the lip of the dead volcano.

Kyoshi shook her head. Impatience was rising in her chest, tidewater threatening to spill over its levees. "The letter said we should head straight to the palace."

Sure enough, the pointy-armored guards watched them fly by with hardly a reaction on their unmoving faces. Yingyong crested the edge, and the capital of the Fire Nation revealed itself like the burst of a firework.

Royal Caldera City. The home of the Fire Lord and the highest ranks of nobility in the country. Where Ba Sing Se equated power with expansiveness, Caldera City concentrated its status like the point of a spear. Towers rose into the air, brushing shoulders with their red-shingled neighbors. They reminded Kyoshi of plants competing for sunlight, stretching ever higher lest they fall behind and perish.

Several glossy, shining lakes lay in the bowl of the caldera, one much larger than the others. She'd forgotten their official names, but outside the Fire Nation they were often referred to as the Queen and Her Daughters, renowned for their crystalline beauty. It was said that no boat disturbed them on pain of death, but Kyoshi now knew that to be a silly rumor. Lantern barges were already paddling across the mirror surfaces to set up for the festival.

In the center of the depression was the royal palace, stern and barren. It was surrounded by a wide ring of naked beige stone that would force anyone who approached on foot to be unsettlingly exposed to the ramparts and watchtowers. Only within the inner walls did a garden dare to take root, and it was as sparse as a young man's beard. Kyoshi knew that was likely a security measure to prevent thieves and assassins from moving from tree to tree undetected.

With defensive concerns taken care of, the palace complex itself focused on grandeur over any other priority. A central spire pointed to the sky, flanked by two golden pagodas with an excess of upturned eaves, making it appear as if the roofs were adorned with animal claws. It looked more like a great shrine than a residence. The steep angles of the structure would have made it difficult to sneak in from above.

Kyoshi mentally slapped herself once she realized she was casing the home of the Fire Lord. The old habits of the Flying Opera Company were sprouting from her head like dormant seeds after a fresh rain.

"Do you know where we're supposed to touch down?" Jinpa said, interrupting her reverie. "I'm a little wary of flying over the wall. I'm guessing that families who own mounted crossbows tend not to like that sort of thing."

"The main gate, but not too close." As a former servant Kyoshi knew that the higher classes liked their visitors to enter their residences in just the right manner, to be awed and cowed by a well-designed display of culture and power. And the ruling family of the Fire Nation was the highest class it got.

Yingyong settled on the avenue that bisected the stone ring. They dismounted to walk the rest of the way to the gatehouse. On the ground, the bison had a bouncing gait from his single foreleg that made it hard for riders to stay in the saddle. Luggage would get thrown off his shoulders if it wasn't securely tied down.

They came to the heavily barred, unbendable iron gate. There were no slats, viewholes, or other means to show themselves. Kyoshi wondered if she was supposed to knock before a grinding metal noise broke the awkward silence. Somewhere inside, the gears of heavy machinery bit into each other, groaning with friction. The gate moved, not outward or inward, but straight up.

A girl stood on the other side, revealed by inches, as if she were too much person, too much force for any one mortal to handle all at once. Sometimes Kyoshi believed that. In her mind, the grand scape of Caldera City and the royal palace was nothing compared to the splendor being unveiled right now.

The gate finished its agonizing journey with a heavy metallic slam. The archway inside was lit with torches, none of which shone as bright as the pair of bronze eyes that flickered over Kyoshi from head to toe. Other than wearing the armor of a higher-ranking officer that had fewer spikes and overhanging flaps and more gold trim, Rangi looked the same. Her ink-black hair had grown back to its usual length. Her posture was as stiff and unyielding as Kyoshi remembered.

And she still wrapped herself in the same air of unquestionable superiority. To be in Rangi's presence was to not meet her standards. A mere few seconds of silence were enough to make Kyoshi tremble.

Her worst fears pushed their way to the forefront. Enough time had passed that Rangi might have changed into Kyoshi's *former*. Former teacher, former bodyguard, former . . . everything.

The stillness of the moment was broken by a strange noise that Kyoshi had heard only once before. Rangi laughing and choking at the same time.

The Firebender slumped over, leaning her hand against the nearest wall, and gasped for breath like she'd been holding it since the gate cracked open. "I had to sprint over here . . . all the way across the grounds . . . so I could look impressive greeting you," she wheezed. "I must be out of shape."

The bands snapped from around Kyoshi's heart, giving it room to beat once more. "Is that how you've been doing it?" The whole time they'd known each other, Rangi would often be waiting for her, ridiculously early, or she'd suddenly and dramatically appear out of nowhere at the last minute. Knowing she'd simply been running at top speed from place to place hurt the mystique a little.

Rangi grinned and nodded as she caught her breath. "At least I don't have to worry about other Fire Nationals seeing me right now. The only blind spot in the defenses is right here, directly under the gate itself. Which means I can do this."

She reached up and yanked Kyoshi inside the wall, right into a searing kiss.

CULTURAL DIPLOMACY

KYOSHI FORGOT what she was supposed to be doing. Where she was. Which way was up. Memories faded before the warmth of Rangi's lips. The two of them melded into each other, alloyed.

And then, in a supreme display of cruelty as far as Kyoshi was concerned, Rangi broke it off and took a step back. "Welcome to the Fire Nation, Avatar," she said, professional once more. She smoothed a strand of hair that had fallen out of place but otherwise acted like she hadn't just robbed Kyoshi of her wits using nothing but her mouth.

The Avatar was still reeling, too dazed to respond. "Mistress Rangi," Jinpa said, stepping deftly around her to greet their host. He bowed, palms pressed together in the Air Nomad way. "It's good to finally meet you in person."

Kyoshi flushed in spite of herself. Jinpa knew who Rangi was, but she didn't necessarily want her secretary witnessing her private moments. *Day one of Kyoshi's first visit to the Fire Nation*, she could imagine him documenting for posterity. *The Avatar inappropriately kisses the love of her life while standing in the threshold of the most fortified place in the world.*

"Brother Jinpa," Rangi said with a friendliness she rarely showed anyone. "I am honored by your presence. You can leave your bison by the gate while the two of you follow me. Our stable masters are trained in the care of mounts from every nation." She leaned in and gave him a wink. "I let them know that I'd make them suffer immensely if they mishandled your companion."

Jinpa laughed until a look from Kyoshi told him that Rangi wasn't kidding. His chuckle died in his throat. He went back and loosened Yingyong's reins. *"Be a good boy and stay here,"* Kyoshi heard him whisper in the bison's ear, to which the animal made a plaintive rumble. *"Yes, I know she's scary. I'll be fine."*

Once Yingyong was settled, Kyoshi, Rangi, and Jinpa walked down the tunnel. It had been designed to kill people. Small holes pricked through the iron plates that coated the passageway, apertures designed to let arrows or fire blasts through. The floor was solid but hollow, implying a sudden drop if the defenders pulled a lever.

A single cough echoed through the hall before being forcibly swallowed. It hadn't come from them. If each firing hole had a soldier behind it, then a whole troop was watching them go by.

Kyoshi glanced nervously around the iron gullet until they emerged on the other side of the wall into a paved plaza that ran through the garden. The stark nature of the greenery stripped it of any calming effect. A single minister waited for them, wearing the red-and-black silks of a civilian authority and the unhappy expression of a tightly wound fussbudget.

"Avatar Kyoshi," he said. His deep bow made his lengthy gray mustache droop off his face. "I am Chancellor Dairin, Head Palace Historian. On behalf of Fire Lord Zoryu, I extend our country's greetings."

"The honor is mine, Chancellor," Kyoshi said. "Where is the Fire Lord? His message indicated that we have important matters to discuss."

Dairin's face pickled further. "He is . . . indisposed at the moment. You will see Fire Lord Zoryu tonight."

This was a brusquer greeting than Kyoshi was expecting. Though to be fair, she had no business criticizing anyone for their lack of diplomacy.

Rangi stepped in to ease the awkwardness. "I believe the first item on the agenda is the palace tour, Chancellor," she said. "Kyoshi has been telling me nonstop how she's been looking forward to learning more from one of the world's foremost Avatar scholars."

The flattery was like sticking candy in the mouth of an angry child. Dairin couldn't show how pleased he was for fear of looking silly. "Of course," he said, frowning harder with all his might. "I assure you it is *very* long and comprehensive. This way inside, please."

Kyoshi and the others padded solemnly down the corridors of power as her predecessors had done since the unification of the Fire Islands. The great halls of the palace were empty in a way that could only be achieved by the household staff watching them, moving out of their path, guards and servants shuffling behind corners so as not to offend the Avatar's sight with their presence. Kyoshi knew *this* trick very well. It gave the illusion of calm and solitude when maintenance of such a great manor required the chaos and numbers of an army.

As they walked, pretending they were alone, Dairin pointed out works of Fire Avatar poetry and policy on scrolls preserved in boxes of clear crystal. Kyoshi nodded appropriately at jewels and gilded hairpins worn in her past lives, tucked into alcoves for display.

No toys, she noted. But plenty of *jians*, *daos*, engraved daggers. The relics of each nation had their own personalities, and Fire and Air couldn't be more different.

Jinpa asked Dairin questions and begged for elaborations on the answers like an eager student, the two of them slightly outpacing Kyoshi and Rangi. The furtive wink he gave Kyoshi over his shoulder let her know he was purposely creating an opportunity for the laggards to talk to each other.

Kyoshi really needed to give him a raise. She didn't pay him anything, the monk serving her out of some self-imposed duty to the Avatar, but he deserved a raise nonetheless. "How is your mother?" Kyoshi whispered to Rangi. The last time she'd seen Hei-Ran, the woman was barely clinging to life.

"Well enough that she wants to speak with you tonight, at your reception," Rangi said.

As if this visit wasn't nerve-wracking enough. Still, Hei-Ran being healthy was a blessing. It explained Rangi's ease, her ability to pick up right where they left off. "So who's this Dairin person then?" Kyoshi asked. "I thought there was a special Fire Nation minister in charge of handling Avatar relations."

"There's supposed to be. I don't know why Dairin was the only official sent to greet you either. Maybe Lord Zoryu's having some problems with his staff, but I don't dare ask. I have some privileges from my connection with you, but really, I'm only a First Lieutenant here in the palace."

Kyoshi nearly laughed. "Only" a lieutenant, a rank many adults in the Fire Nation strove for and failed to reach. Rangi's casually overachieving nature was one of the many little things Kyoshi missed about her.

"Tell me about your secretary." Rangi tilted her head at Jinpa's back.

What was there to tell? "He's part of some kind of secret Pai Sho club and he acts the complete opposite of an Air Nomad sometimes. I haven't figured him out. But he's been a good—"

"And here we are at the Royal Portrait Gallery," Dairin said loudly, stopping short.

Kyoshi nearly collided with him and Jinpa. She was steadied by Rangi grabbing the back of her tunic. She could imagine news of the disaster spreading over the Fire Nation, the Avatar bowling over her entire entourage.

The chancellor hadn't noticed how close he'd come to being trampled. He gazed upward at the walls with sheer pride bursting from his expression. "I could spend days here and never get tired of it," he said.

His reverence was well-deserved. The portrait hall was one of the most overawing works of man-made craft that Kyoshi had ever seen. Paintings of the Fire Lords adorned one side, reaching from floor to ceiling, triple the size of their real-life subjects. Cloaked in red and black with halos of gold behind them, the rulers of the Fire Nation looked down at their audience like a race of giants.

Even a first-time visitor like Kyoshi could tell that these were works of art that took years, careers, to finish. The late Fire Lord Chaeryu's portrait, the most recent entry into the gallery, wasn't complete. Stencils where gold inlay and orange hues had yet to be filled in spread across the background near his feet.

Rangi nudged her to look at the other side of the gallery. Opposite the Fire Lords stood the Fire Avatars, painted in matching size and grandeur, equally breathtaking in artistic glory. These portraits were spaced farther apart. Judging by the way there was roughly one Avatar per four Fire Lords, and how the gaps were not perfectly even, Kyoshi guessed that the likenesses of her predecessors formed a timeline that stretched down the hall.

The viewing party stopped at Avatar Szeto, depicted in his trademark tall minister's hat. Where most of the other figures held a ball of fire in one hand, Avatars and Fire Lords alike, Szeto hefted an abacus, rendered with as much loving detail as any of the illustrated flames or weapons wielded by his compatriots. Each bead of the counting instrument was set with real pearl, and they were racked to a calculation that ended in an auspicious number.

In his other hand he wielded a stamp made gigantic for artistic license. It was unlikely that the real item would have been so large or carved from solid cinnabar like it was shown in the painting. Szeto would have blanked out whatever was written on the paper he was trying to approve.

"Here we have the namesake of our festival," Dairin said. "The Fire Nation owes a great debt to this man."

"Can you tell me more about Avatar Szeto?" Kyoshi asked. "I'm afraid I don't know as much about him as I should."

The chancellor cleared his throat for a long lecture.

"During Szeto's childhood years, the Fire Nation teetered on the verge of collapse, struck by plague and natural disasters," he said. "The wrath of the spirits was terrible, and Fire Lord Yosor was in little position to halt the fracturing of the country along the old fault lines of the clans."

"The clans?" Kyoshi said.

Dairin sighed, realizing he'd have to cover some remedial history as well. "Each noble house of the Fire Nation is descended from one of the old warlords from the period before the country was united. That is why the noble clans retain certain rights such as governance of their home islands and the retention of household troops. During Lord Yosor's reign, the clans set their warriors against each other, ravaging the countryside in futile bids for power and resources. Many historians, myself included, opine that without Szeto's intervention, the Fire Islands would have splintered apart, reverting to the dark days of Toz the Cruel and the other preunification warlords who caused so much suffering for our people."

Kyoshi was surprised at how much this story sounded like the Yellow Neck uprising. From what she always heard as a commoner, the Fire Nation was a model of harmony and effectiveness, the counterpoint to the bickering Earth Kingdom polities. Szeto's era was not that far away in the distance of history.

She didn't have to fake her interest or rely on Jinpa for this part of the tour. "What did he do to fix the situation?" she asked.

"He applied for a job," Dairin said. "Though as the Avatar his material needs would have been met and his decrees heeded,

Szeto took a government post as a minister of the royal court, technically subject to the same rules and regulations as any other official. He showed up to work at the Capitol and sat at a desk. Furthermore, he insisted that his career advance at the pace of his achievements rather than leapfrogging his seniors just because he was the Avatar."

"And that helped?" Kyoshi said incredulously.

"It turned out to be a brilliant strategy," Rangi said. "Rather than chase emergencies all over the nation, he concentrated his efforts on a central location and spread his influence from there. Szeto was an extremely capable bureaucrat, accountant, and diplomat. And since he was working for the royal family, there was no split in legal and spiritual authority in the country. His victories were the Fire Lord's victories."

Dairin nodded, satisfied that the youth of today were being educated suitably about their nation's past. "Once he was promoted to Grand Advisor, Avatar Szeto was able to end the open hostilities between rival noble houses. A lasting peace followed, in which he continued to serve his country with dignity and excellence."

"He put an end to the debasement of coins," Rangi said. "It rescued the economy from the brink of disaster."

"One of the scrolls we passed on the way here said he set up the first official programs to give relief to the peasantry in times of famine," Jinpa said.

"And most important, he kept proper records of it all," Dairin said. He wiped the corner of his eye out of habit, as if he'd been moved to tears in the past when thinking about Szeto and was just making sure right now. "Truly, Avatar Szeto was an ideal for us officials to live up to, and a shining example of Fire Nation values in general. Efficiency, precision, loyalty."

Kyoshi gazed with new admiration at the dour, long-faced man whose festival they were here to celebrate. She liked this Szeto fellow. Or this version of herself, as it were. A strong work ethic and an eye for organization were traits she respected. Perhaps she should have tried communing with him instead of focusing on Yangchen so often.

Dairin graciously allowed their party to drift toward the art pieces that interested them. Kyoshi wandered over to the portrait of Lord Chaeryu again. Knowing more about him could help ingratiate her with his son, the current Fire Lord Zoryu.

Kyoshi tried to interpret some of the imagery. Chaeryu's theme seemed to be vegetation. She could see bundled rice stalks, a harvest bounty. There was a penciled outline yet to be painted, a detailed flower arrangement with two blossoms sprouting from the same vase. In the vessel, a large stone camellia greatly overshadowed a smaller winged peony.

That was odd. Kyoshi knew the basics of flower arranging in the Fire Nation style, and that kind of off-balance spacing was normally frowned upon. In real life, the bigger plant would have blocked off the sunlight from the lesser one and caused it to wither.

"Chancellor," she said. "I have a question about these flowers."

Dairin tensed up unnaturally at the word *flowers*. He hurried to her side with a sense of dread, not waiting for her to ask anything, and peered frantically at the stencils like he expected some sort of unpleasant revelation.

It took him a little longer than Kyoshi to see the outlines, but when he did, his reaction was unmistakable. The chancellor turned white and trembling, and beads of sweat gathered on his nose.

"*Do not speak of this to anyone but the Fire Lord,*" Dairin muttered under his breath.

"Wait, what?" Kyoshi had heard him clearly, but she didn't understand the life-or-death conviction in his voice.

The chancellor clapped his hands, the sharp noise startling Rangi and Jinpa, who were still looking at other paintings. "The tour is over!" he declared. His eyes darted to the entrance of the gallery, fearful of the empty space. "Avatar, my apologies for prattling on when you must be tired from your journey. I will show you to your accommodations. Immediately."

The floors and walls of the Avatar's quarters in the Fire Palace were so laden with antiques and artwork it could have passed for a small museum in itself. For the remainder of her stay Kyoshi could look forward to enjoying landscapes painted in cinnabar, vermillion sculptures of preening birds, tapestries woven with carmine threads. The overwhelming redness of the space made it hard to tell distances inside. The room where she was going to sleep might have been as big as the bottom level of Loongkau.

"I feel like I'm staring directly into the sun," Jinpa said. He pressed his palms against his eyes and blinked.

"It took me a while to get used to so much red again myself,"

Rangi said. She sat down on the corner of what Kyoshi had thought was a large raised platform and bounced softly, which meant that the scarlet-quilted square wide enough to hold a *lei tai* on top of it was the bed. "Agna Qel'a is the same thing, only with ice. You need special goggles to move around the brightest parts or else you'll go snowblind."

The mention of the north made Kyoshi's innards clench. It was a reminder of how far Rangi had journeyed to seek treatment from Water Tribe healers for her mother's poisoning, and a warning of how demands on the Avatar could steal away time in the blink of an eye. Kyoshi hadn't been to the North Pole yet. She was lucky that Rangi wasn't angry at her for not visiting.

She thought about bringing up Dairin's cryptic actions in the gallery but didn't, less out of concern for his wishes and more because she and Rangi had more important things to talk about. Kyoshi turned to Jinpa. "Can you give us some time alone?" she asked him, motioning at the door.

"Not so fast," Rangi said. "Report please, Brother Jinpa."

The monk stepped forward like a first-day recruit and addressed her directly, completely bypassing Kyoshi. "She hasn't been eating properly despite my repeated admonitions."

"Hmm." Rangi pressed her lips together in disapproval. "She can be stubborn like that."

"Hey!" Kyoshi said. "Don't talk about me like I'm not here!"

Jinpa continued to count out various offenses on his thumb and fingers, bending them back one by one. "She barely gets any sleep. I'll find her passed out late at night, on top of a book or a map or a manual. She doesn't give herself enough time to recover from her injuries. And she insists on reacting to random reports of violence throughout the Earth Kingdom in person! Do you know how hard it is to manage her schedule when she does that?"

Out of all her fears for this visit, Kyoshi hadn't been prepared for this scenario, her secretary and her bodyguard ganging up on her. "Have you two been writing each other behind my back!?"

"Only the one time," Rangi said. "I sent Jinpa a letter at the same time as I sent your invitation. It was the only way I would get a truthful update on whether you've been taking care of yourself. Apparently, you haven't."

"She hasn't," Jinpa confirmed. "Quite the opposite, in fact. If I didn't know any better, I would say she's intentionally seeking out the most dangerous situations and hurling herself into them without any regard for her own safety!"

"That's not true!"

"Oh, so then I suppose you fell neck-first into a sharp object by accident?" Rangi said. A deep scowl crossed her features. "Don't think I haven't noticed your new scars. It's like you're ruining my favorite parts on purpose."

Jinpa wiped his eyes, the release making him emotional. "She is *so* taxing," he said into his fist, sniffling a little.

Rangi got up from the bed and patted him on the back. "I know. I know she is. She's the worst. You've done a heroic job taking care of her, and I'm here to help you now."

"*I* am the *Avatar*!" Kyoshi said in a desperate last resort to shield herself from further judgment. "Not some helpless child!"

The way she stamped her foot undercut her message. Rangi and Jinpa gave each other a squint. *Are we sure about that? I'm not so sure.*

Kyoshi's head hurt. She had spent long months building fortifications around herself, establishing a reputation and self-image in the Earth Kingdom as someone not to be trifled with. It'd taken Rangi less than an hour in the Fire Nation to tear those walls down and invite Jinpa inside.

Jinpa's growing grin told her this was revenge, glorious revenge aged like fine wine until the perfect moment. This was payback for all the times she'd ordered him to drop the conversation about her injuries or ignored his reminders to put the books away and get some rest. She finally figured out how she felt about the young man who'd been there quietly in the background, providing her care with grace and compassion.

He was a dirty snitch. "You can't talk about me like this!" Kyoshi fumed, pointing her finger at Jinpa. In the *daofei* code, snitches were punished by thunderbolts *and* knives. "I am your boss!"

"That may be, but *she's* clearly the one in charge." He tipped his bald head at Rangi, positively gleeful with the new method of Avatar management he'd been gifted. "If squealing is what it takes to keep you healthy, then slap me with a feather and call me a pig chicken."

"Get out," Kyoshi snapped.

Jinpa shared another knowing smile with Rangi as he backed out the door. *Look at her, trying to be tough. How adorable.*

And then, suddenly, for the first time in a long time, Kyoshi and Rangi were alone together.

It was like being granted a wish from a spirit before she was ready. Kyoshi felt the need to choose her words carefully or else her boon would vanish.

Rangi helped her with the selection. "How are things back at the mansion?" she asked quietly. She'd lived there alongside Kyoshi. Yokoya had been her home too, until that night they fled together into the storm.

"Less busy." The mansion was no longer the vibrant, bustling place it was during Kyoshi's servant days. Much of the staff had quit immediately after the Earth King's investigators closed the poisoning case. As the new master of the estate, Kyoshi didn't replace them, not wanting to manage a large household anyway, which left most of the halls empty and the gardens untended. The villagers avoided the hollowed-out manor and called it an unlucky place. "Auntie Mui is still there, doing what she can. I don't know why she hasn't left yet."

"*You're* why." Rangi looked pained and frustrated, as if an old injury that should have long since healed had been prodded too hard. "She's trying to support you, Kyoshi."

She was going to say more on the matter but decided to hold it for another day. Their next topic needed every possible inch of space cleared around it before they could approach. For a while, the two of them stared at the same patch of red threads woven into the rug.

Again, Rangi got there first. "Yun?"

One of the promises that Kyoshi had made to Rangi before she boarded the ship bound for the frigid reaches of the north was that she would find their friend, no matter what it took. The declaration had been slipped in among tears and embraces so tight Kyoshi's shoulders ached for days afterward. The witnesses were the dockworkers and sailors weaving around them on the pier, grumbling at their obliviousness to anything but each other.

But in the expanse of the Earth Kingdom the force of her vow had dissipated. She'd quickly learned that without some kind of edge, it *was* functionally impossible to find a single person in the depths of the largest continent, even one as famous as Yun had been. She hadn't a shirshu to track his scent, nor spiritual trigrams to read for his location. Asking commoners in the villages she visited in the course of her Avatar duties if they'd seen a particular Earthbender was a laughable exercise. *Gray hand? Sure, my cousin's got a skin problem like that.*

Looking back on it now, her grand ambitions had been reduced to pathetic letter writing campaigns to sages who had no inclination to help. And why would they? Lu Beifong wasn't the only one who preferred to believe he was dead.

"I thought if I could figure out how he survived, it might give me a lead," Kyoshi said. "But every story I found of people taken bodily by spirits was a folktale, and none of them live. I don't have an explanation for how he came back." *Or why he changed.*

She rubbed her eyes. The sting of reliving her failures made it hard to see straight. "The closest piece of information I could find was an account of a spirit possessing the son of a provincial governor during the Hao dynasty. It said a dragon bird flew through his body, altered his physical appearance, and gave him unusual abilities."

"Is that the answer?" Rangi said. "Maybe people touched by spirits can pass through the boundaries between the Spirit World and the human realm easier than others."

"It's hard to say. The text didn't mention crossing between worlds. It just said the boy sprouted feathers and a beak when the dragon bird flew into him. Yun didn't look any different on the outside when I saw him in Qinchao. But he's not the same as before. I just know it."

Kyoshi felt like screaming in the red chamber. This was the best she had done for their friend. An old story and a wild guess. She couldn't pretend in front of Rangi. The full weight of her futile, wasted efforts crushed down on her shoulders.

"Kyoshi . . . have you ever considered that he's moved on?"

She looked up at Rangi's question, confused. "From what?"

"From us." Rangi swallowed, the words hurting her as she spoke them. "Based on what you've told me, I don't believe he wants to be found."

She held up a hand to cut off Kyoshi's protest. "Think about it. There are numerous ways he could have gotten in contact with the Avatar. He knows the sages of the Earth Kingdom. He could have left a message with them. The fact you *haven't* heard from him yet is telling."

Kyoshi could believe the nobles of the Earth Kingdom wanted to stick their heads in the sand when it came to Yun. But Rangi? How could she?

"You're talking about forgetting him," Kyoshi said, her breath already shortening in her chest. "Erasing him, like Lu Beifong and the rest of the sages want to do." *Like Jianzhu wanted to do*.

"No, Kyoshi, I'm not. I'm talking about letting our friend come back to us when he wants to, not when we demand it. I want the people I care about to have a moment's peace, instead obsessing over the other.

"You said he was healthy when you saw him," Rangi said. "I don't think we need to worry about his survival. Someone as talented as Yun can flourish anywhere in the Earth Kingdom. I'd stake my honor on him showing up when he's ready, and when he does, we'll take him to task for everything that's happened.

"And then afterward," she declared with the force of a fresh oath, "you, me, and him will go back to Yokoya and eat the biggest dinner Auntie Mui's ever cooked. *That* should be our plan."

Kyoshi forced a smile. Jianzhu. The teahouse in Qinchao. How Yun had escaped that infernal spirit's clutches to emerge once more into the daylight. It might have been possible to unravel the knot—provided they were still dealing with their old friend.

The three of them together, like it was before Avatarhood severed a corner of the triangle off. She wanted the old days back, more than anything else in the world. But deep down, she was afraid of a truth the world kept pushing on her. Kyoshi rarely got what she wanted, if ever.

Rangi saw she wasn't getting through. She decided on a different tack, coming closer with a hint of sway in her hips. "You know, the party's not for a few hours." Her voice grew heated and breathy. She reached out and ran her thumb and forefinger lightly over the lapel of Kyoshi's tunic. "I have an idea how to get your mind off your troubles until then."

A dumb grin spread across Kyoshi's face. She leaned down so Rangi could brush her lips against her ear.

"*Stance training,*" Rangi whispered. Her grip on Kyoshi's clothes suddenly turned into a grapple. In one swift motion she kicked Kyoshi's feet wider and forcibly bent her knees into a deep hinge.

"Do you know how easy it was for me to pull you off-balance at the gate!?" Rangi yelled. "You haven't been practicing! I thought I could trust you not to go soft in my absence, but I was wrong!"

Kyoshi stuttered in dismay. "But . . . I thought we were . . ."

"What we do without guidance defines who we are!" Rangi seemed determined to flay those months of missed exercises out of Kyoshi's hide, one way or another. "Twenty minutes without a break, or I bust you back to square one of your training! You'll be doing hot squats with ten-year-old Academy washouts! You want that? Huh?"

As the burning began to spread through her legs and lower back, Kyoshi grasped her mistake in coming here. Reuniting with Rangi meant having to deal with the cruelest and harshest person she knew—the Avatar's firebending *sifu*.

"Lower!" Rangi bellowed.

THE PERFORMANCE

KYOSHI STEPPED out of the dressing chamber feeling readier for the trials ahead. She'd grown more skilled at wielding the many layers of her outfit and could pull them on without assistance now. As she entered the bedroom, she cinched her sash as if buckling down a shield.

Rangi waited for her in an overstuffed, throne-like chair. "You've made alterations," she said, eyeing the sections where the colors were slightly different from her memory.

"I kept mending the original fabric, but eventually it took too much damage. I picked out new patterns I liked and had some pieces replaced." Despite Kyoshi's ill repute, the best tailors in Ba Sing Se had tripped over their own feet for a chance to dress the Avatar. Free advertising was still free advertising.

As she took Kyoshi in, Rangi landed on a detail that made her frown. "You kept the chainmail liner though. Made it heavier."

The comment was loaded. Kyoshi could see the thoughts running through Rangi's head. *What kind of dangers have you been putting yourself through without me?* She tried to say something that might relieve her friend's worry. "Safety first?"

Rangi sighed. "Kyoshi, it's more than that. You're the guest of honor tonight. You could have worn the finest robes in the world and instead you picked the same clothes you fight in. This is a small, informal reception with a handful of guests on the personal invitation of Fire Lord Zoryu. You're not going into battle. You don't have to be constantly at war."

Kyoshi remembered the last time she'd let herself fully relax without a care. She could relive every detail, all too easily.

It had been a sunny afternoon in Zigan Village, made brighter for having survived and scattered the Yellow Neck menace. Her healed hands smelling faintly of herbal tincture. Kyoshi walking down the street side by side with Rangi.

And Lek.

She often wondered how Rangi felt about those days, whether their time spent with the Flying Opera Company was real or just a mantle to be cast off on the way to proper Avatarhood. Would Rangi mention the rest of Kyoshi's bending masters during the party? Would their exploits in the *daofei* town of Hujiang, their illicit raid on Governor Te's manor, make for an amusing story? Or would Rangi pretend their gang never existed? That journey certainly hadn't lasted long in the grand scheme of things.

Kyoshi cleared her throat of a welling, thrashing bitterness. "I suppose you're not going to let me wear my bracers then."

"Of course not. We'll get you some gloves if you want, but

in this country your hands are nothing to be overly surprised about. Half the attendees tonight have dueling scars hidden here and there underneath their clothes."

"You don't." Rangi's skin was unmarred everywhere Kyoshi had been lucky enough to see it.

Rangi snorted. "That's because I don't lose duels."

She pushed herself out of the chair and twirled, swishing her dress so she could inspect her own hem from all sides. Rangi wore a formal silk gown that gave her the swept, elegant appearance of a stamen emerging from a flower of blood-red petals. She looked lovelier than a garden after a brisk rain.

"I know it sounds frivolous and wasteful, but appearances matter here in the palace," Rangi said. "Fire Nation nobles dress and act to represent their clan affiliation and rank. Our peers notice our smallest choices and assign meaning and intentions to them."

She smoothed a crease in Kyoshi's skirt. "Deep in the bowels of the Earth Kingdom, no one was watching us. That's how we got away with half the antics we did. Here in the Fire Nation, *everyone* is watching you. I want you to remember that. Everyone. Is. Watching."

Kyoshi's stomach gurgled from the mounting stress. "So, it's not going into battle," she said. "It's worse."

Rangi didn't disagree. "Your clothes will pass for now, but as the festivities progress, you should choose different looks. And it goes without saying, but no face paint during the length of the holiday."

Kyoshi was going to protest, but Rangi poked her in the chest. "The paint is for pulling jobs with our sworn brothers and sisters," she whispered, her eyes glistening with memories. "Not for mingling among abiders and square folk who don't understand the Code."

Kyoshi stared at her. Then slowly, deliberately, she enveloped the smaller girl in her embrace and kissed her on the forehead. Rangi squeezed back tightly.

There should have been no doubt in Kyoshi's mind. The Firebender hadn't officially taken the oaths, but the Flying Opera Company were her friends too. And Rangi's friends were as sacred as honor to her. Kyoshi had gone so long without her center she almost forgot what it felt like. Rangi made her human again, balanced and whole.

"You better get your fill of this now," Rangi murmured as Kyoshi brushed her lips against her. "When we're in public, you *cannot* touch my head or my face or my hair."

But those were Kyoshi's favorite parts. "Really? You've always let me."

Rangi unraveled herself from Kyoshi and fixed the arrangement of her hairpins. "That's because back in the Earth Kingdom it didn't matter, but here, touching someone's head outside of your closest family is one of the most disrespectful gestures imaginable. It's best if you avoid touching anyone in general, including me. I hate it as much as you do, but now that we're actually inside the gates of the palace, we have to follow decorum."

She eyed Kyoshi with suspicion, having been on the receiving end of many kisses to the scalp due to their height difference. "I mean it. Hands off from the neck up."

"I get it, I get it!"

A knock came from outside the room. "Avatar, Mistress Rangi, it's time to go," Jinpa called. From his carefully measured pitch, it was obvious he was trying to give them as much clearance as possible. They joined him in the hallway.

The monk had chosen the version of Air Nomad traditional robes that pinned up at one shoulder and left the other uncovered. His arm and the side of his torso were exposed in a bare sweep down to his waist, revealing a surprising set of muscles on the lanky young man.

"What?" Jinpa said at their silence. "Too pastoral?"

Rangi shrugged. "Usually people don't go shirtless in the royal palace, but there's bound to be exceptions for national dress. It's fine."

Kyoshi was glad her fans had escaped commentary. They rested in her sash, passable as court fashion unless she thumped someone with their heavy weight. It was ironic that she first thought them less useful than a blade. She'd need the comfort they provided, given the daunting task ahead.

She exhaled through gritted teeth. "All right. Let's go meet the Fire Lord."

"You two are worthless," Kyoshi whispered, doing her best to direct her ire equally between Rangi and Jinpa, who kneeled on either side of her. "You're both fired."

"Lord Zoryu promised me it would be twenty to thirty people, at maximum!" Rangi said through a tightened smile. "A small gathering!"

"Does this look like a small gathering to you?!"

Over five hundred pairs of golden eyes stared at the Avatar and her companions as they perched on a raised dais that had been erected with unbelievable speed in the same formerly empty gardens they'd observed from above on Yingyong. It seemed like the entire assembled nobility of the Fire Nation was present, standing at attention, watching Kyoshi their one and only objective.

In a banked row off to the side, percussionists bellowed over their mallets thundering against drums the size of wine tuns. *Erhu* players sawed at their instruments with such ferocity that a pile of destroyed bows lay behind them. They tossed the casualties of their performance over their shoulders and drew fresh ones from nearby quivers without missing a beat. The speed and martial intensity of the music was at odds with the calm, almost meditative stillness of the listeners. Kyoshi wouldn't have known if they were enjoying it if not for the slight approving nods she caught here and there from the members of the court nearest her.

She should have known something was wrong from the start. Chancellor Dairin had ambushed them outside their quarters and whisked them through a series of baffling passages, explaining there had been a last-minute change to the program. Now here they were, being deafened and honored in equal measure.

Having supported a few grand events as a servant, Kyoshi knew that hosts only pulled out the stops like this if they had something to prove. But there was nothing for the Fire Lord to be insecure about, unless he thought she was evaluating him on how lavishly he feted her. She would assure Lord Zoryu this kind of reception was unnecessary, if she ever made it to his side.

Right now the Fire Lord was very far away, on the other side of the sea of nobles, nested on a platform that mirrored Kyoshi's. In the distance she could only make out the gold-on-black edging of the royal armor shoulder pieces he wore over his robes and a couple of his most prominent features. She could tell the Fire Lord was a young man with a pointy chin and a tall forehead, and that was about it for now. Squinting for more details would have been rude, and detectable by the entire gathering.

To make matters more uncomfortable, Lu Beifong was here, of all people. The old man sat near the edge of the crowd on a folding stool. He was surrounded by a small group of Earth Kingdom sages. Based on the faces she recognized, they appeared to be handpicked solely on the criteria of who disliked Kyoshi the most.

"I'm sorry, Avatar," Jinpa said. He shifted on his knees, not used to the position, compared to the way Air Nomads sat cross-legged to meditate. "None of my sources indicated there would be an Earth Kingdom delegation. I'll try to keep them from troubling you with petty requests."

The performance ended in a crashing halt, the musicians shouting at the top of their lungs one last time in unison. The ones who were sitting to play leaped to their feet, their arms spread wide, and the drummers held their sticks over their heads like victory flags. They posed for a moment, breathing heavily.

The crowd responded with polite applause that ended equally abruptly. If the performers were disappointed by the muted response, they didn't show it. They began packing up their instruments without a word while the assembled nobles turned to each other. Earsplitting music was replaced by the murmurs of delicate conversation.

"That's it?" Kyoshi asked, her words suddenly too loud. She looked behind her to see Dairin motioning the three of them to get off the platform. They joined the chancellor on the ground level. "What happens now?" she asked him.

"According to palace garden-party etiquette, now you . . . *mingle* in the general direction of the Fire Lord," Dairin said, as tense as Auntie Mui before a banquet. His mustache wiggled from the strain. "He will do the same to you. This allows for the two of you to encounter each other as equals, as perfectly as two leaves drifting together on the surface of a pond. This method of reception is one of the highest honors the ruling family can grant a guest. It is beyond my station to linger at your side."

"Okay," Kyoshi said. The objective was straightforward. "Go talk to the Fire Lord. Got it."

"No!" Rangi said, already knowing what Kyoshi was thinking. "You can't go right to Lord Zoryu, or else that would be rude to the other guests." Behind the cover of the platform she hastily adjusted Kyoshi's lapels and sash, brushing lint and garden pollen off the fabric.

"So I have to chat with everyone I bump into?"

"*No!* Only certain individuals here have enough status to speak in your presence!"

Kyoshi was getting desperate. "How will I know who they are?"

"Those with the right to approach the Avatar by themselves will introduce those who do not," Rangi said. "Remember, between Fire Nationals, higher rank always introduces lower rank. The introduction is the pivotal juncture that sets the tone for the rest of the conversation."

She saw the anxiousness in Kyoshi's face. *"You* may directly address whomever you want without preface, up to and including the Fire Lord. To be greeted by the Avatar herself is a great blessing. But I *strongly* recommend you reserve that honor for Lord Zoryu. Jinpa and I will be by your side, but we won't necessarily be able to speak unless the situation allows it."

There was so much to remember. "I'm going to die here, aren't I?" Kyoshi said with a groan.

"Don't worry, Avatar," Jinpa said. He stepped forward and rolled his shoulders. "I've failed you once tonight as your chamberlain. It won't happen again."

Despite his bravery, Jinpa was the first to fall. As they entered the crowd, a little circle of courtiers interested in meeting an Air Nomad for the first time quickly isolated him from the group. Apparently, speaking to an Airbender was fair game for most of the attendees.

They had to leave him behind, trying to answer questions about the Western Air Temple and its unusual upside-down architecture. Kyoshi assumed he was improvising many of the inner details, given that the Western Temple housed nuns only.

Her exalted status as the Avatar kept people from approaching her, but not from scrutinizing her. The court made sure to provide a respectful amount of physical space, creating a little bubble that moved with Kyoshi and Rangi at its center, which only made the glances over the tops of their glasses, the sideways stares, the lulls in conversation as they passed more obvious.

It was deeply unsettling. Kyoshi found her pulse rising, a mindset of neutral *jing* failing to calm her. She had to distract herself by observing them back, taking mental notes the same way she did on her patrols through dangerous territory.

This was the first time she'd seen so many high-ranking Fire Nationals in one place. The nobility of this country favored more understated fashions than their counterparts in the Earth Kingdom, choosing red-on-red patterns for their robes and gowns. The broad expanse of their shoulder pieces seemed like the most common way they expressed their associations. She could see subtle geometric sigils imprinted on the swathes of fabric, or simple renditions of native flowers and animals.

One particular image she noticed again and again was the stone camellia, in small bunches or large asymmetrical designs or used as delicate edging. A good quarter of the attendees were wearing some form of it, by far the largest group. Noticing she was outnumbered by a particular faction set the hairs on Kyoshi's neck prickling before she tamped down the worry. She was among Fire Nation nobility, not in a back alley about to get jumped by Triad hatchet men. The flower must have had a link to the departed Chaeryu as she'd seen in the gallery, and the partygoers wore it out of respect.

Servants passed by them as smoothly as clouds, offering morsels of food so spiced that the drifting aromas nearly made Kyoshi sneeze. There were skewers of hippo-ox tail, rolls of ocean kumquat, and slivers of fish of all sorts, from waters near the islands and from rivers so far away they would have had to make the journey here packed in ice.

Kyoshi declined to eat out of nerves. This was how much she'd changed since becoming the Avatar. Refusing food. Younger Kyoshi would have punched her in the nose for that.

Rangi watched a few of the platters go by. "That's odd."

That's odd was now their official motto for the trip. "What is it?" Kyoshi asked.

"There's no stalknose mushrooms. They're a traditional Festival of Szeto food. The mushrooms grow on overcrowded ears of grain, so they're symbolic of a good harvest. I don't see them anywhere."

"So?"

Rangi turned to her with the utmost gravity. "Kyoshi, this is the royal palace. If we don't have them, no one in the country has them. This is not an auspicious sign for the holiday."

The slight pout on her lips that she was doing her best to fight was adorable. Rangi always tried so hard to hide her foibles, as if "liking certain things" was unprofessional. Knowing that she had a weakness for a particular snack made Kyoshi want to squeeze her tight. The next time the two of them visited Yokoya, she'd ask the remaining kitchen staff to find some stalknoses and cook them however they did in the Fire Nation.

"Avatar," came a squawk from somewhere around Kyoshi's belly.

She looked down to see Lu Beifong delivering a curt bow. Despite age confining him to a seat on the other side of the crowd during the concert, he'd appeared in front of her like he'd stolen the secrets of dust-stepping from the Flying Opera

Company. The old man must have wanted a transaction. Only business could make him so positively spry.

"Master Beifong," Kyoshi said. She nodded slightly. Lu was as high up in the Earth Kingdom hierarchy as a person could get without being a king, so this encounter was probably within the rules of decorum. "It's . . . good to see you. How are your grandchildren?"

A large flying boar symbol had been embroidered onto Lu's robe in an attempt to conform to Fire Nation clan customs, but it fell short in tastefulness. With his bony fingers, Lu picked a loose silk thread off the sewn animal and scowled. Somewhere, a tailor was going to lose their job.

"Numerous and unpromising," he said, flicking the thread to the ground. "What I wouldn't give for a talented leader to be born into my family, or a child with a good head for numbers. I would take a halfway-decent Earthbender at this point. With the way things are going, the Beifong name threatens to slide into obscurity."

"Would that children were fit to their parents' needs," Kyoshi said, the words coming out like ground glass through her teeth. Lu and the other sages only knew that she was an orphan and were content to leave it there. The tap of Rangi's toe against the back of her foot let Kyoshi know that she was likely turning red and betraying her anger. *This is why I need the makeup*, she thought.

"Yes, well put," Lu said. He gestured to another Earth Kingdom man by his side. This person was younger, in his forties, and had obviously tried to coordinate his green-and-yellow outfit to complement Lu's. "This is Governor Shing of Gintong Province."

Lu's hanger-on from the Earth Kingdom didn't bother with niceties. He pushed closer impatiently, nearly jostling a waiter trying to serve small vials of plum wine. "Avatar, I have a grievance. The misinformation you sowed among my people during your last visit to my lands has damaged the workings of law and order."

Kyoshi picked up the way Lu's eyes flashed at her. *Good leaders do not stir the pot. They do not cause disruptions.* The old sage valued stability above all else, and several of Kyoshi's recent escapades in the Earth Kingdom did not fit his definition of conduct becoming of an Avatar.

Kyoshi sorted through her mental notes. Gintong Province was close to Si Wong, a dusty scrubland that was relatively unproductive and difficult to grow crops on. But that didn't mean someone couldn't try to exploit it.

"Ah," she said. "Governor Shing. Now I remember. You were buying land at distressed prices from peasants who couldn't till their fields because of *daofei* raids, forcing them to later work for you as indentured laborers on the farms that used to be theirs."

The exactness of her terms surprised the older men. She wasn't supposed to *say* such unpleasant facts out loud in polite company. She was supposed to allude to them, dance around the matter, peck at it like a small feeding bird.

"Hmph," Lu muttered. "That's a tad different from the way you phrased it to me, Shing. You told me you were paying good money to keep your lands free of bandits."

"*I* took care of the *daofei* in the area," Kyoshi said. "And once I finished, I told the farmers that I considered ownership of the land reverted back to the state it was in before the Emerald

Claws first set foot in Gintong. I undid the problem and its aftershocks both."

"I had binding contracts on those lands!" Shing said. "I purchased them legally! I have the documentation!"

Kyoshi thought for a moment. Here was where an Avatar of old, skilled in diplomacy like Szeto and Yangchen, might offer him something in return to soothe tempers and save face. But she couldn't bring herself to try to imagine fitting compensation. Why exactly did Shing, a powerful man, deserve to exploit a catastrophe and become richer at the expense of his citizens?

She found the words marching forth from her lips with ease. "Well, Governor, if you value business terms so much, I can send you a bill for pacifying your province. Given the results, my cost would be the equivalent of supplies and wages for a medium-sized army. I'd need the payment immediately, in a lump sum."

Behind her, Kyoshi heard the nose snort of Rangi trying desperately not to laugh. Shing looked like he needed to suck on a wood frog. "These are the tactics of an urban racketeer!" he shrieked. "When they said you were a criminal, I didn't believe the rumors at first, but clearly—"

"*Shing!*" Lu snapped. "Mind how you speak to the Avatar. We are not in our homeland."

The Governor of Gintong wilted at Lu's rebuke. There was an uncomfortable pause. The nearby crowd watched with barely hidden glee as the noisy Earth Kingdom folk had it out with each other.

Lu sighed and shook his head. His hunch seemed to have taken on a steeper angle. "I'm afraid I must retire early from the festivities," he said. "Old bones and whatnot. It was a delight, everyone."

He shuffled back toward the garden entrance of the palace. Shing followed a few steps behind, somehow looking much worse for wear than the elderly man. Kyoshi could easily see Lu cutting Shing loose from the Beifong circle of influence after tonight, not out of any moral obligation, but for being a bad investment who'd gotten on the Avatar's wrong side and embarrassed the Earth Kingdom outside its borders. She might have just ended the man's entire career.

Once they were alone again, Rangi cleared her throat and leaned in. "As much as I love watching you verbally set people on fire, be a little more careful. That same conversation between two Fire Nationals could have ended with an Agni Kai."

Kyoshi knew she wasn't kidding. The Flying Opera Company used to tease Rangi mercilessly about honor and other Fire Nation values back in the isolated depths of the Earth Kingdom, but that was when she was the only Firebender for hundreds of miles around. Here, Kyoshi and Shing were the odd ones out. The stifling atmosphere made it easy to believe that no interaction was too small to have meaning.

"This isn't a game," Rangi reminded her. "This is a garden party. There are stakes."

"I'll do better next time," Kyoshi said.

"Good." Rangi mustered herself. "Because here comes my mother."

THE HEADMISTRESS

HEI-RAN'S ARRIVAL was preceded by a hush through the nearby crowd. Lower-ranked nobles parted to let the woman who'd taught their daughters pass through. Some of them gave her crisp salutes, a reminder Rangi's mother had also been a high-ranking military commander at one point. She returned the gestures with glances and nods.

Kyoshi swallowed hard. Even without the complications of her early Avatarhood, this was a reunion with someone designed from the ground up to pass judgment and cull the unworthy from her presence.

Hei-Ran approached slowly, using a cane to assist her steps. She hadn't bothered with dressing in finery. The stark parade uniform she wore enhanced the deliberateness of her movements. Her once solid-black hair was mingled with strands that had turned gray and wiry.

She looked older. That meant finally looking like Rangi's

mother, without a doubt, instead of her twin. The blaze in her eyes was still there, as clear and piercing as ever.

Kyoshi bowed, if only to escape the woman's gaze for a moment. "I am grateful to see you in better health, Headmistress," she said.

"And a little surprised, it seems?" Hei-Ran said.

Kyoshi tensed up. She'd made the wrong face. Again, this was why she needed her makeup, to hide the nuances of expressions she couldn't control.

Hei-Ran brushed her own comment away. "You don't have to pretend. I can't believe I'm up and about either. They're miracle workers, Water Tribe healers." She sighed unhappily. "I can barely firebend right now though. It's like being a child again, having to learn the basics and build my strength back up. A fitting punishment, given what I put Yun and you through."

Kyoshi winced. A firebending teacher of Hei-Ran's caliber losing her abilities felt like a tragic loss for the whole world.

"I still haven't discovered who was responsible for this crime," Kyoshi said. In her opinion the official inspectors had dropped the case prematurely. They'd found no records or messages as to why so many influential members of the Earth Kingdom had gathered in Yokoya that day, but that was suspicious in itself. "But I swear, I won't let it drop."

Pain coursed through Hei-Ran's face. "Kyoshi, it was him. It was Jianzhu."

It took a while for the dam to give way. Kyoshi's old hatred, long stilled, came rushing over the banks once more. She turned to Rangi, who gave her a grim nod.

"The victims in Yokoya were his enemies come to oust him as the Avatar's master," Hei-Ran said. Her voice was strained and hoarse. "He caught me and himself in the attempt. Whether it was out of sloppiness, or to throw off suspicion, we'll never know."

Kyoshi closed her eyes and gripped the handle of one of her fans. It took so long for the threads of mistakes and monstrous deeds to stop weaving into the future, to just tie themselves off and *end*. Maybe they never ended.

A different pattern hung out of reach, one where Kelsang was alive, Hei-Ran had never been poisoned, and Lek was still sulking in a run-down teahouse in Chameleon Bay, longing for a bison. "I'm sorry," Kyoshi said. "If I had been able to create a flame when you tested me . . ."

Remembering her past failure in front of Hei-Ran hurt all the more considering how much Kyoshi enjoyed the act of firebending these days. The flames came easily now when she danced with Rangi's native element, and yet she had been so lacking back then. Kyoshi thought often about that little ball of tinder she had failed to set alight. Sometimes it drove her to tears, what could have been saved but for her weakness. "I'm sorry," she repeated.

Hei-Ran laughed, a short, harsh bark. "*You're* sorry. *You're* apologizing to *me*." The indomitable former commander began to shudder. She pressed her fingers to her eyes so hard that it looked like she was trying to gouge them out. Rangi was at her side in an instant, steadying her.

The bystanders were as surprised as Kyoshi at the show of emotions. But Hei-Ran collected herself before she shed any tears. Kyoshi had a feeling this was the furthest extent of the woman's vulnerability.

"Kyoshi, *I* am the one who needs to apologize," Hei-Ran declared with nary a crack in her voice. "I am so sorry for what I did to you. And for what I allowed Jianzhu to do to you and Yun. I could have put a stop to what was happening. I could have seen things clearly if I'd wanted to see them. I can never make this right."

Kyoshi looked at Rangi's hand on her mother's elbow. It was a small gesture, the slightest touch, but it made Kyoshi think of the way she had wrapped her arms around Kelsang once, as he wept on an iceberg over his mistakes. It was hard to tell, given their stern, unyielding expressions, but here was a woman wracked by guilt, being comforted and supported by her loving daughter.

"Your recovery is a good start," Kyoshi said.

Hei-Ran looked at her, puzzled.

"Toward paying your debt to me," Kyoshi clarified. "What I demand from you, Headmistress, is your continued good health. I'll accept no less than what I'm owed."

"Kyoshi, this isn't the time for jokes."

"She's not joking, Mother." Rangi's smile overflowed with love for them both. "She's simply like that. Now swallow your pride and accept the decree of the Avatar."

Hei-Ran laughed again, though there was no gladness in the sound. She patted her daughter's hand. "I'm all right. Go find Sifu Atuat. I need a moment alone with Kyoshi."

Rangi clipped her heels together and left to retrieve whoever this Atuat person was. Hei-Ran gathered herself and stared down Kyoshi. How she managed to do that from her lower height was a mystery.

"Kyoshi, I want you to know something," she said. Hei-Ran's voice lost what was left of its earlier emotion and turned into a cold, unflinching whisper, simply measuring and reporting the dimensions of the truth. "I would kill him. I would kill him for what he did to you, and Kelsang, and Yun, and my daughter. I want you to know that, Kyoshi. I want you to *believe* it. If he were here, right now, I would kill Jianzhu in front of this entire crowd."

The space between Kyoshi and Hei-Ran changed like steel being quenched, hardening into an ancient and well-understood design. Her true reconciliation with Rangi's mother lay here, not in tearful public apologies.

"So would I," Kyoshi said.

"Good girl." Hei-Ran glanced in the direction her daughter had gone. "Rangi . . . ultimately, she is kind. No amount of drilling or hardship will ever change that about her. Which means there are places she will never go, places that are barred to her. You may have to visit them on her behalf, to protect her and others."

Kyoshi still struggled with the actions she took as the Avatar in defense of the world's peace and balance. But protecting Rangi was a matter that turned her into a different being, small and ratlike and vicious enough to live inside a thin shadow. She chose her words carefully to Hei-Ran, filling in the limits she was sure of. "I know exactly what to do with anyone who would hurt your daughter."

Hei-Ran's lips flattened into a line. Kyoshi knew that this was as close to a grin of outright approval as the woman ever gave. They gazed at each other in mutual accord.

The silence was broken by someone accidentally jostling Kyoshi's elbow. "I couldn't remember if you liked plum wine or sorghum liquor," a short, plump woman in blue robes said to Hei-Ran in a loud, piercing voice. She wielded a glass in each hand, threatening to spill the different-colored contents. "So I got both."

Rangi caught up like she'd been chasing the Water Tribe woman through the crowd instead of retrieving her. "Kyoshi, this is Sifu Atuat," she said. "Sifu Atuat is the greatest of the Northern healers. She personally saw to my mother's recovery. We invited her as our honored guest in thanks. While she's here, she's part of our family."

Hei-Ran pushed the proffered glasses away from her face. "And I'm still your patient, Atuat. I shouldn't be drinking. The other doctors said it would set back my recovery."

"The other doctors are cowards," Atuat said. "If your innards start failing, I can simply bring you back to life like I did before."

She turned to Kyoshi, acknowledging the Avatar for the first time. "I'm that skilled," she said solemnly. It was a matter of grave importance that Kyoshi understand the facts. "When the headmistress here arrived at my hospital, she was basically a corpse wrapped in a red shroud. To save her I picked the pocket of Death itself."

Kyoshi had to check that the good doctor wasn't already drunk. She wasn't. She was just . . . that way. "You must be one of the finest benders in the world then, regardless of element."

Atuat held up a finger while draining one of the glasses she'd brought for Hei-Ran. "I am," she said once she'd finished it.

"You know how women in Agna Qel'a aren't allowed to learn the fighting forms of waterbending?"

Kyoshi did not know that about the Northern Water Tribe capital, but no matter; Atuat was going to elaborate anyway. "I say it's the men who aren't allowed to learn healing from *me*. Any idiot can punch someone with water. *I* punch dying people's energy pathways with water such that they live for another handful of decades."

Hei-Ran rolled her eyes. "Don't flatter her," she said to Kyoshi, with the candor that one could only have when talking about a friend. "Atuat is arrogant enough without praise from the Avatar."

This was astonishing. The former headmistress of the Royal Academy and the mother of Rangi calling someone else arrogant. Kyoshi looked closer at the woman who warranted such a description. Atuat was a little younger than Hei-Ran and resembled Auntie Mui from the neck down, but there was an edge to her face and light blue eyes that Kyoshi found familiar.

Rangi noticed her trying to place it. "Sifu Atuat is Master Amak's sister," she explained.

So that was it. Kyoshi's spirits sank. She hadn't been the slightest bit close to the mysterious, disreputable waterbending master, but she'd been there when he died, stabbed through the back by Tagaka the pirate queen's waterbending. With so much blood staining her past, maybe Kyoshi really was as cursed as parts of the Earth Kingdom claimed. "I'm very sorry about your brother," she said.

Atuat sighed. "Thank you. Amak was never going to have a peaceful end, to put it mildly. But he died protecting people. That's far more honorable than what he was doing before."

Hei-Ran looked like she wanted to change the subject of Master Amak. "Where's this Airbender friend of yours?" she asked Kyoshi and Rangi. "I should meet him."

Kyoshi craned her neck, trying to see where they'd left Jinpa. His crowd was even bigger now, making a circle around him. The monk concentrated as he spread his arms wide, performing an airbending feat passed down through the Southern Temple that levitated him a few inches off the ground without causing a storm in the vicinity. Kyoshi had once involuntarily lifted herself with a larger version while in the Avatar State, but she couldn't do it under normal circumstances.

Jinpa said the party trick had supposedly been invented by Kuruk. It took a lot of skill and had no practical use, so Kyoshi believed it. As he drifted back to the floor, his audience of nobles clapped for the feat in the exact same manner as they'd done for the riotous music performance.

Kyoshi realized that Jinpa was enjoying himself, showing off for others. He hadn't had a real break the entire time he'd been serving her. "Would anyone like to try?" he said, indicating he could lift a willing volunteer.

"Me!" Atuat roared across the party. She hiked up her skirt so she wouldn't trip and marched off with haste toward the Air Nomad.

Hei-Ran pinched the bridge of her nose, a gesture of frustration she shared with Rangi. "I swear, it's like having a sister with no impulse control," she muttered. She limped after her own doctor, forgetting to say goodbye to her daughter and the Avatar.

The shocking lapse of manners from the headmistress warmed Kyoshi's heart. She liked Sifu Atuat, and her effect on Hei-Ran.

Rangi appeared to share the sentiment. "Sometimes I think making a friend cured her more than anything else," she said.

"Does she know about us?"

"Of course. Wasn't that what the two of you were talking about by yourselves? Her giving you the whole *You better treat my daughter right or else* speech?"

Kyoshi supposed that had been a part of the conversation, in a roundabout way. She decided not to mention the particulars.

"Avatar Kyoshi," said a deep, confident voice behind her.

She turned around to see a young man swathed in regal gold and black. His hair was pulled back tight, making his large forehead more prominent, and his sharp chin was clean-shaven.

Finally. She arranged her features in a welcoming expression that hopefully conveyed the right amount of respect for a foreign head of state. This was the introduction she had to make herself, without help.

"Fire Lord," she said. "Thank you for your gracious hospitality." While she was getting ready, she'd practiced over and over what she would say. From the way the crowd hushed, she could tell many eyes were watching her. "I have not been in the Fire Nation long, but already I have been awestruck several times by the natural splendor of your country, and especially the skill of its craftsmen."

"Oh, so you've visited the gallery then?" he said, grinning. "It's our national pride."

There was a slight tug on the back of Kyoshi's dress. She ignored it. She was doing well right now and didn't want to lose her momentum. "I did. Might I say, you resemble your departed father Lord Chaeryu a great deal. May your reign over the Fire Nation be as glorious as his."

A sharp kick to the back of her calf nearly made her buckle.

"Kyoshi!" Rangi's voice was a strangled squeak of mortification. *"That's not Fire Lord Zoryu!"*

ANCIENT HISTORY

THE CROWD had frozen. The waiters had frozen. The sun in the sky halted its arc. The celestial bodies had never seen such a colossal blunder in their thousand lifetimes of watching the Avatar.

"I should introduce myself," said the man whom Kyoshi had mistaken for the Fire Lord. "My name is Chaejin. Fire Lord Zoryu is my younger half brother."

Kyoshi looked around frantically for the real Zoryu. She spotted him, hurriedly working his way through the crowd in her direction, outpacing his own guards. She confirmed it was him like she should have done the first time by checking his topknot from afar. There it was, the headpiece in the shape of a five-tongued flame. Decidedly *not* resting in the hair of the man standing before her.

Kyoshi grimaced. It was as if this double had selected his

appearance to cause confusion. His robes were cut to resemble the silhouette of royal armor, and the gold brocade that hung from his shoulders was a shade that she thought was reserved for the Fire Lord and his immediate family. "Apologies for the error," she muttered. She had never heard of Chaejin before and had no idea where he fell in the court hierarchy.

"It's understandable; royal lineages can be confusing. My father was Fire Lord Chaeryu, but he never married my mother. We try very hard to hide our indiscretions here in the Fire Nation. Especially to outsiders."

She was too far out on a limb. She didn't know what to say when presented with delicate information like this. She glanced at Rangi for help. But judging from her panicked expression, Rangi didn't have enough rank to speak here. She'd spent all her capital already to warn Kyoshi of her mistake.

Kyoshi tried to read how delicate the situation was by glancing at the faces of nearby partygoers. The normally reserved Fire Nationals looked completely aghast. The tension grew thicker and heavier until finally their little bubble was pierced by the arrival of Zoryu.

"Avatar Kyoshi," the Fire Lord said, leaning over slightly from exertion. The hem of his outrageously delicate robe was grass-stained, and his headpiece had tilted out of alignment in his haste to get here. Their meeting had been anything but a graceful drifting together like two leaves in a pond.

"Zoryu!" Chaejin said. He genially slapped his brother on the back. "I was wondering when you'd get here. I'd like you to meet the Avatar. She thought I was the Fire Lord. Can you imagine?"

Kyoshi heard Rangi suck in her breath sharply, and she understood why. Chaejin had stolen the right of introduction, neglected his brother's title, and improperly touched the Fire Lord, all under the guise of a friendly gesture between family members. If court etiquette was a secret language, then it was finally opening to her, arranging concepts and syllables into sentences she could comprehend.

"How amusing," Zoryu said. "I need to talk to my guest now, Chaejin." The statement could have been a warning if delivered right, but the slight crack in the Fire Lord's timbre turned it unsure and plaintive.

"Of course, of course!" Chaejin said. "You must have wanted to discuss the recent crop failures. Or the precipitous declines of the fisheries. If there's anyone who could reverse our country's recent fortunes, it's the Avatar."

The strain in Zoryu's neck reached all the way to his temples. This must have been the problem of national importance he wanted to discuss with the Avatar, but not in such a public venue.

"A malaise has settled over the land since the death of our father and the natural bounties we used to enjoy during his reign have vanished," Chaejin explained, even though no one had asked him to. "Some of the older Fire Sages believe the spirits of the islands themselves are unhappy and have turned their faces away from us." He smiled at Zoryu. "I, of course, have argued otherwise. The strength of my brother's rule is not to be questioned."

The way Zoryu clenched his teeth and looked away told Kyoshi there was an element of truth to Chaejin's claims. Likely not the part where he supported his sibling though.

She knew what she had to do. The favor of the Avatar was the prize here, was it not? Men like Shing traveled across seas for a taste of it. Chaejin's little game of insubordination and disguise was obvious in hindsight. He wanted Kyoshi to shower respect upon him and criticize the Fire Lord.

She didn't appreciate being manipulated, especially by someone she just met. She narrowed her eyes at Chaejin. "If there's an issue with the spirits, I will resolve it on behalf of the Fire Lord." Her ability to communicate beyond the physical realm was sorely lacking, but he didn't need to know that right now. "He has my full support as the Avatar. Now, if you don't mind, he and I will talk in private."

Chaejin's mouth fell open.

"I believe I asked you to leave," Kyoshi said. Normally she'd wait longer before letting the cutting remarks fly, but this was a special case. She was on to Chaejin's performance, and she wanted the bystanders to see his efforts fail to bear fruit.

But instead of suffering the rebuke like Shing, Chaejin glowed with happiness. "I believe you did." He bowed and shuffled away, hurrying like he had to go share the news of their conversation with a friend.

That wasn't the effect she'd wanted. Kyoshi turned back to Zoryu. He stared at her like a gutted fish, unable to speak.

"Kyoshi," Rangi whispered, nearly catatonic, forgetting that the ruler of her country stood within arm's reach of her. "Kyoshi . . . what did you . . . what did you just do?"

She didn't know. It took the laborious, hurried arrival of Hei-Ran to provide an answer.

"What she's done is follow disaster with catastrophe," the headmistress growled once she'd limped her way over. "Everyone shut up and follow me, before you embarrass yourselves further."

Kyoshi fell in behind Hei-Ran. To her surprise, so did the Fire Lord. There was apparently no limit to the people Hei-Ran could boss around.

She detected pitying smirks on the faces of the nobles as they passed, but they weren't aimed at her, the ignorant foreigner who'd made a mess of things. They were directed at Zoryu, the man everyone here was supposed to owe absolute respect and fealty to. Whatever fluency she thought she had in court dynamics was being upended.

She took one last glance at Chaejin, who was already whispering enthusiastically to another guest. Emblazoned on the back of the Fire Lord's brother's robe was a large stone camellia, wrought in gold thread, meant to be seen like a beacon. The rendition was identical to the one she'd seen in the portrait gallery, only without its smaller peony rival. A single blossom growing strong, with no competition to worry about.

"Kyoshi, move!" Rangi whispered.

They left the mass of the crowd behind them, circling around the palace grounds. As large as the party was, there was still more empty garden where they could have some true privacy instead of counting on people not to snoop.

The sparseness of the flowering orchard was more attractive from ground level. The regular spacing between the zankan cherry and silver wisteria gave the impression of pink and white trees compressing into lines and then expanding again as their viewing angle changed.

The Fire Lord moved slowly, at Hei-Ran's pace. The stoic, silent royal guards had been dismissed. But Atuat and Jinpa had been pulled away from the party. Kyoshi had ruined the privilege of remaining unchaperoned for everybody in her group.

"I . . . Wow," Rangi muttered at Kyoshi. She pressed her fingers to her temples. "Huh."

"If I insulted this Chaejin person, I'm sorry," Kyoshi said under her breath. "But he was doing much worse, and no one called him out on it."

"It wasn't Chaejin you insulted; it was the Fire Lord!" Rangi could see Kyoshi didn't get it. "You declared in front of a crowd that you would fix a national problem for him!"

"Isn't that my job?"

"Yes, but you're not supposed to express it like that! The smooth running of the Fire Nation stems from the strength of the Fire Lord, both real and perceived. When you help him, you have to frame it as a partnership among equals. Simply claiming you're going to wave your hand and make it all better implies the Fire Lord is too weak to manage the country on his own!"

Kyoshi had the sinking feeling this information was buried somewhere in the libraries at Yokoya. She might have even read about this very aspect of Fire Nation culture, and simply forgotten. She could try and absorb the rules of diplomacy through text, but it wasn't the same as practicing them until they were second nature.

One of her past lives could have helped her with the information too, had she not been so deficient at communing. She imagined Avatar Szeto watching her blunder and hurling his hat to the ground.

"And then to top it off, you dismissed someone in front of Lord Zoryu," Rangi said. "Right of dismissal is the only custom more important than right of introduction." She ran her hand down the line of her jaw. "This is Chameleon Bay all over again. You charge in face-first, wreck the place, and then have to flee with your tail between your legs. I told you *minutes* before to be careful, did I not?"

Getting chewed out by Rangi was always going to be part and parcel of their reunion. Kyoshi just thought it would have taken longer to get around to it. "I'm sorry," she muttered.

They weren't being as quiet as they thought. "It's not the Avatar's fault," Zoryu said. "It's mine."

He'd come to a halt by a turtle-duck pond. The animals were napping quietly on water so clear they looked like they were hovering in midair. Under a willow tree was a stone bench, where Zoryu sat down, contemplating the peaceful scene. "A smaller reception would have avoided this, but at the last moment I thought I needed a bigger spectacle to enhance my image."

In defense of Kyoshi's first blunder, Chaejin and Zoryu were nearly identical in the face, down to the same prominent brow and jut of their chin. At a distance, it would have been impossible to tell them apart. But up close, she could see the Fire Lord was thinner, still a gangly boy underneath his voluminous robes. It was as if someone had sewn two copies of the departed Lord Chaeryu, one with less stuffing.

Zoryu's attempt to still his features in a regal manner was only half successful. As he gazed into the water, he smiled graciously at his reflection like someone who would much rather be crying. "This whole disaster is entirely my mistake, not Kyoshi's."

"Permission to speak beyond my station, Lord Zoryu?" Hei-Ran said.

He waved halfheartedly. "Granted. To you and everyone here."

"It *is* partially her fault!" she shouted. The sudden noise woke up the ducks and caused them to scatter to the other side of the pond, quacking as they fled. "Or at least you have to declare so! What kind of Fire Lord preemptively blames himself for everything?"

Permission or not, that seemed overly familiar of Hei-Ran. Unless Zoryu was a former private student of hers. The master-student relationship was one of the few to cut across all boundaries.

"You can't be that mopey little boy I used to teach anymore!" Rangi's mother snapped, confirming Kyoshi's suspicion. "Act with the dignity of your position! You've let Chaejin walk over you for far too long without repercussions and now he thinks he can get away with anything!"

Kyoshi watched Zoryu wither under Hei-Ran's scolding and felt a painful stab of recognition. "Was I like that, early on?" she asked Rangi in a low voice.

"Are you kidding me?" Rangi said with a snort.

"And what's so funny to you, Lieutenant?" Hei-Ran turned upon her daughter. "You're telling me you couldn't think of a tactic to prevent the situation? Not even a basic diversion?"

Rangi suddenly blanched. She trembled with a fear that Kyoshi had never seen before, not when taking on a brutal *lei tai* champion without her firebending or fighting a monstrous shirshu.

"You are responsible for the Avatar in every regard, not just physical safety!" The daughter might have been good at scolding, but the mother was the founder of the entire school. "Her reputation reflects on yours, and tonight I overheard an Earth Kingdom man call her a *daofei* to her face!"

Kyoshi and Rangi glanced at each other with eyes as wide as plates. They'd kept more than a few details of their journey to themselves. That the rumors were technically true and Kyoshi really was a *daofei* by oath was one secret they'd have to work together to keep from the headmistress, for fear of Capital Island setting ablaze.

"I'm also to blame," Hei-Ran muttered. "I shouldn't have left your side, but I was distracted." She glared at Atuat, who had just finished a skewer of meat she'd taken along from the party.

"What?" the Water Tribe doctor said, picking her teeth with the sharp sliver of bamboo. "*I* haven't offended anyone tonight. Frankly I found everyone else's behavior imprudent and shocking."

Jinpa, ever the peacemaker, raised his hands. "I am extremely confused. I understand court manners are important, but why is everyone acting like the nearest volcano is about to erupt?"

"It's because the very problem I requested the Avatar's assistance with has now become much worse," Zoryu said. He turned to Kyoshi. "I was going to explain everything under more private circumstances."

"Now's as good a time as any," Kyoshi said. "I trust everyone here." She was willing to take a gamble on Atuat's discretion.

THE SHADOW OF KYOSHI

Zoryu rearranged his robes so they wouldn't wrinkle, conscious of them for the first time this evening. "My father, the late Lord Chaeryu, was renowned for his exceptional strength, and . . . prodigious appetites. Chaejin is probably not my only half sibling born out of wedlock. But he is the one my father couldn't ignore completely. His mother is Lady Huazo, of the Saowon house."

"The Saowon are a powerful clan that controls Ma'inka Island, in the eastern part of the country," Rangi explained. "It's both one of the most prosperous and heavily fortified territories in the nation outside of the capital. Lady Huazo wasn't here tonight but many of her relatives were. They were the ones wearing stone camellia patterns, the Saowon family crest."

Based on the insignias Kyoshi had seen, the Saowon outnumbered the next two largest factions combined. "What about your mother?" she asked Zoryu. "Where is she?"

"My mother was Lady Sulan of the Keohso clan," Zoryu said, his lips twisting into a sad smile. "And I never knew her. She died giving birth to me. I'm told she was a lovely and wonderful person by all accounts."

Kyoshi's throat tightened in sympathy. If royal blood couldn't shield a child from being orphaned, then what chances did the castoffs of the world ever have?

"To avoid dishonoring Lady Huazo and the Saowon clan, my father officially recognized Chaejin as his child," Zoryu went on. "But somehow also managed to exclude him from being an official member of the royal family. It placed my elder half brother in an unclear position when it came to the line of succession, so he was removed from the palace. Sending him away to the Fire Sages was a convenient method to get rid of an embarrassment to the Fire Lord, and my father forbade the matter to be talked about at court while he was alive."

He caught Kyoshi's scowl of disapproval before she could mask it. "Fire Lords and Earth Kings did worse to their siblings in ancient times. And I've attended performances of Water Tribe sagas with similar themes. In hindsight, I'd have gladly taken Chaejin's end of the deal and traded ruling for solitude and study."

"Stop saying things like that!" Hei-Ran snapped. "Weakness is practiced and learned as much as strength is! What if one of the Saowon were to hear you?"

Zoryu shrugged, a gesture that looked strange when performed by the leading figure of an entire country. His sturdy shoulder pads weren't designed for ambivalence and almost swallowed his head as they rose upward. "It's too late to be worried. I set the wrong tone with Chaejin long ago. After my father's death, when I first heard the Saowon clan were sending Chaejin back to court as a High Temple liaison, I was delighted. I thought the playmate of my youth was returning. My only living blood relative.

"But being sent away by our father embittered him." Zoryu tapped the side of his hair, causing his headpiece to wiggle. "He came at me wanting 'his' crown. Chaejin exploited my initial lenience to show the clans how much kinglier he is than me and has continued to do so ever since. Tonight was merely one example in a long list of petty jabs and undermining."

"The Saowon have always been skilled at subtly shaping public opinion," Rangi said. She spoke with the weariness of a veteran more befitting of someone her mother's age. Kyoshi had never seen her act this way. "Chaejin has plausible deniability.

He could say that he merely acted with the impertinence of family and wore the wrong clothes. Punishing him for it could look like an overreaction and the Fire Lord would fall even further in esteem."

"This is what Chaejin does," Zoryu said. "He is simply better at this game than I am. And day by day he comes ever closer to fully winning it."

"I don't understand," Kyoshi said. "So he wishes he was Fire Lord instead of you. Insults and opinions can't change the laws of succession."

"They can when they're backed by enough troops," Zoryu said wryly. "Chaejin was telling the truth—the Fire Nation struggles, Avatar. The harvests have been borderline failures for two years in a row. Fishermen pull up empty nets from the shores of First Lord's Harbor to Hanno'wu. We had to cull half of the pig chickens in the country due to sickness a few months ago. To most of the commonfolk, it appears as if my entire reign has been cursed by the spirits of the islands themselves."

He rubbed the back of his neck, another fidget made ridiculous by his outfit. "Now, the noble clans might not believe in curses, but they do need revenues from their fiefdoms to pay their household warriors. If they can't, then I have a bunch of very angry, unemployed, highly trained fighters on my hands, suddenly willing to entertain the concept of 'Fire Lord Chaejin.'"

"If I may," Jinpa said. "Respect for the will of the spirits is one thing, but the misfortunes you're describing seem beyond anyone's control. How can the people of the Fire Nation lay these troubles at your feet?"

Zoryu snorted. "With great ease. My father was an unintelligent boor, but during his rule the rains fell, the fields were green, and the fish were so plentiful you could pluck them from the seas by hand. In contrast, I've had to empty the royal treasury to keep some of the poorer islands from going hungry. The Saowon homeland of Ma'inka is faring relatively well these days, which gives my brother even more credibility and influence. He appears to be the son of Chaeryu better favored by the spirits."

Kyoshi was beginning to understand. "You invited me here to bolster your reputation within your own country."

"You are correct, Avatar. Granted, I don't expect you to snap your fingers and have spirits fill the barns with grain. But I thought if you stood by me in solidarity during the holiday, it might help settle some of the unrest in the palace."

He made a face of longing for something going right for once. "Chaejin hijacked my plan and outmaneuvered me yet again. You . . . pretty much blessed his future reign, Avatar. In front of the whole court, no less."

"I see," Atuat interjected, tapping her chin thoughtfully as if she were the intended audience of the explanation. "But you're talking about conflict like an inevitability."

"Welcome to the Fire Nation, everyone!" Zoryu said with a grin that was equal parts cheekiness and deep, regretful sorrow.

Hei-Ran shot him a look that could punch its way through a stack of shields. Zoryu coughed. "What I mean to say is the history of this crown tends to repeat itself. Fire Lord Yosor nearly lost the country to civil war and was only saved by Fire Avatar Szeto."

"After a certain point it becomes a matter of strategy over spirits," Hei-Ran said. She stared at the pond, rolling her cane between her fingers. "In times of upheaval, every lesser clan wants to ally themselves with the eventual winners. If the

Saowon continue to wax in power and reputation, then at some point they'll have enough supporters to openly rebel against the throne."

"Chaejin works the courts while his mother Huazo consolidates wealth and power throughout the islands," Zoryu said. "In the meantime, I lack the political and military resources to check them. The standing Fire Army is an elite force, but it is small. To win in pitched battle against a clan as large as the Saowon, I'd need the rest of the noble houses committed in lockstep behind me, and that wouldn't happen without an *extremely* just cause."

He puffed his cheeks in frustration. "This is what I get for not wanting to spill the blood of my countrymen. I have borne the insults of Chaejin as best I could so as not to accelerate us toward civil war. I've traded away my image in bits and pieces, trying to delay the inevitable. But in the eyes of my people, I don't know how much more honor I have left to lose."

Kyoshi pondered the trap the Fire Lord lay in. Jianzhu had once complained to her that the Earth Kingdom was too big to govern properly. But its size meant it could suffer grievous injuries in one quarter and not feel them in the other. The Earth Kingdom's nature was to persist, muddling through floods, famines, bandit uprisings, and incompetent governors.

The Fire Nation, on the other hand, was of the right size to be transformed and consumed by its disasters. Kyoshi might not have been an expert in court politics, but she was well-versed in the motions of violence and suffering. She could see the sky-bison's view of war spreading across the map of the islands, and she understood how vicious a close-quarters fight for power could get.

Zoryu seemed fairly shrewd to Kyoshi, and decent enough at heart. It was just . . . for being one of the most powerful people in the world, he was remarkably powerless. He'd been handed a title by virtue of his birth, and a map to his life where every route led clearly to a dark, terrible destination.

She could sympathize.

"We need to engineer a response," Hei-Ran said. "Chaejin went too far tonight. There's plenty of time left in the evening to show him and the rest of the guests where the line is."

She spun around to march back to the party, but the sudden motion left her wobbling. Atuat grabbed her before she fell. "*You* need to rest," the doctor said gently. "You're done for the night. I'll take you inside."

Hei-Ran shook her head and gripped her cane tighter. "The children can't be left alone. Look what happened already."

Atuat's presence seemed to explode in size. Gone was the unserious, diminutive woman, and in her stead rose an implacable spirit of the north itself. "That's funny," she declared. "I thought I heard one of *my* patients back-talking me on a health matter just now. It must have been the wind."

Hei-Ran glowered at her friend, but like a master Waterbender, Atuat calmly rode the storm until it petered out. Finally, Hei-Ran sighed in surrender. "Fine."

"Monk," Atuat said. "Help me help her back, will you?"

Jinpa, acclimated to taking orders from people he just met, gently grasped Hei-Ran by the arm. He and the doctor led her back to the palace.

"Forget trying to rebuke Chaejin for now then," Hei-Ran called over her shoulder. "Don't do anything until we can come up with a plan. Stick with neutral *jing*."

Kyoshi watched them leave, fascinated. Someone had managed to cow the headmistress, the woman whom both Rangi and Fire Lord Zoryu feared. By this logic, Sifu Atuat must have answered only to the Moon and Ocean spirits themselves.

"Looks like the 'children' are on their own," Zoryu said, rubbing his eyes.

Kyoshi looked around. The sudden departure of Hei-Ran and Atuat had put into stark contrast the relative youth of their remaining group. Most of the nobles attending the party tonight were the same age as Rangi's mother, or older.

"I suppose we have to go back," Zoryu said. "Though I'd personally rather spend the rest of the evening reading or playing Pai Sho. Do you play, Avatar?"

"I am asked that often." She couldn't keep the note of tetchiness out of her voice. Across the Four Nations, people equated skill at the game with wisdom. It made her feel like her lack of skill at it was a character flaw. "The answer is no."

Zoryu winced. "I didn't mean anything by it. I became acquainted with your predecessor over the game."

She had to take a moment to understand he was talking about Yun, not Kuruk. "You do realize Yun wasn't the Avatar before me, technically speaking?"

The corners of Zoryu's mouth turned in opposite directions. "The Fire Sages would censure me for saying this, but in a certain way, he was Avatar enough. Master Yun burnished my image at court and pulled more diplomatic strings for me than any of my ministers. And he made me forget my station, in a good way."

"He had a talent for that," Rangi said. Her eyes were lost somewhere among the reflections in the pond.

"His visits to the palace were the only time I didn't feel like I was so alone," Zoryu said. "But I understand he was your friend before he was mine. My condolences to you both. The world is poorer without him."

Such a basic sentiment, and yet so rare. Kyoshi could count on one hand the sages in the Earth Kingdom who grieved for Yun the person, instead of distancing themselves from Yun the mistake. "Thank you," she said, her throat drying out a little. "Maybe one day I can be as much of a help to you as he was."

"I mean, given how gravely you've insulted me tonight, there's nowhere to go but up," Zoryu said with a glare she realized was meant to be a wink. He and Yun even had similar senses of humor. Kyoshi relaxed for the first time tonight. By no one's standards but hers, she and the Fire Lord had gotten off to a good start.

The smile vanished from her face when she considered how to break the news to Zoryu that the Earth Kingdom's preferred version of events was a lie. She looked at Rangi, who bit her lip.

Yun being alive was too much to drop on Zoryu tonight, Kyoshi decided. Perhaps once they found more leads. There was no point in telling the Fire Lord that their friend had been swallowed up by the mainland, forgotten, until they could do something about it.

The three of them walked back to the party, Rangi occasionally tugging on the back of Kyoshi's robes to make sure she followed the requisite distance behind Zoryu. There was a completeness to their formation she appreciated.

She remembered Chancellor Dairin's warning about the flowers. "Lord Zoryu," she said. "Is the Keohso clan sigil the winged peony by any chance?"

"Yes, that's the symbol of my mother's family. Why do you ask?"

She told him about the stencils on the portrait of his father, the Saowon's flower ascendant over the Keohso's. Zoryu swore in a manner very unbecoming of a head of state and clawed the air like he wanted to strangle someone.

"Wonderful. Now the royal artists are disrespecting me," he said. "Chaejin must have struck a deal with them. I'll have to replace the painters and have the images covered before any Keohso hard-liners see it and go berserk. Chaejin's other goal is to provoke someone in the Keohso clan into committing an inexcusable act of violence against a Saowon. Then *he* has the just cause for starting a conflict. History would say he was defending his honor."

Zoryu sighed. "Clan rivalries have been major impediment to the progress of the Fire Nation since its inception. My mother's side of the family despises the Saowon and would rather burn the country down than accept Chaejin as their ruler. Sometimes I wish I could abdicate, if it weren't for the violence the Keohso would create in my wake."

Kyoshi continued to be surprised by Zoryu's frankness. He was less power hungry than some small-time mayors she'd met in the Earth Kingdom. "It's a very Air Nomad idea," she said. "Running away, following the path of negative *jing*. Maybe it's a wise course."

She heard the smack of Rangi's hand colliding with her own forehead. "Spirits of the Islands, Kyoshi, you can't just encourage the Fire Lord to abdicate!"

"Please don't tell your mother I said that, Lieutenant," Zoryu said, suddenly and genuinely worried. "She'd beat the idea out

of me. I still break out in cold sweats when I think of her training programs."

Kyoshi snickered. It had been a very long time since she'd
connected to anyone her age. It was strange to think she could
relax around a smuggling gang and the ruler of the Fire Nation,
but nothing in between.

"We're getting closer to the party," Rangi lilted under her
breath. "So, could I please ask the two most important people I
will ever serve in my life to *start acting appropriately*?"

The Avatar and the Fire Lord straightened up, neither wanting to incur her wrath. Evening had settled and torches had
been lit to cast a gentle glow over the festivities. The crowd was
still dense, forming a grove of red silks over the pavilion. The
only sound was the chirping of insects drifting over the warm
air. A peaceful scene.

"Stop," Kyoshi said. It was a *daofei*'s suspicion that made her
come to a halt, but the feeling was strong. "Something's off."

"What is it?" Zoryu said. "I don't hear anything."

Rangi had noticed it too. "Exactly. It's too quiet." She slid in
front of Kyoshi and Zoryu, the marching order of rank no longer
as important as protecting her charges.

The conversations that filled the air earlier had completely
died out. The nobles were standing still, silently watching them
arrive. Zoryu had talked about a tipping point where he lost
too many supporters and the clans turned against him. But
there was no way it could have happened while they were gone.
Could it?

"Do you know what's going on here?" she whispered to Zoryu.
He shook his head.

Kyoshi advanced on her own for a better look. The men and women of the court were angry and confused, but most of all, they were utterly terrified. They stood at fearful attention, rigid like their lives depended on it. A crying waiter moved to wipe a tear but quickly caught himself, snapping his arms back to his side.

A sickening familiarity bloomed in the pit of Kyoshi's stomach. She'd seen this kind of behavior once before, when the pirate queen of the Eastern Sea had plucked Earth Kingdom natives from their villages and forced them to do her bidding upon pain of death.

"What's wrong with them?" Zoryu called over Rangi's shoulder. "Why are they acting like that?"

"They're hostages," said a familiar voice. "How else are they supposed to act?"

Kyoshi felt her chest being squeezed by powerful, invisible jaws, sharp fangs threatening to pierce her through in every direction. He hadn't spoken at the teahouse in Qinchao. Hearing him now, after so long, was an incantation that slowed her senses.

Up high, Yun sat on the edge of the Avatar's dais, letting his feet dangle over the side. He was dressed for the occasion in fine robes of green and black, looking every bit like a secret prince out of Earth Kingdom fables, hidden until the moment of his glorious ascension. Except for his one hand. It was still stained a rotting gray, like a dead thing affixed to his body.

Yun beamed at her, the same easy smile she knew from her dreams and nightmares alike. "It's good to see you again, Kyoshi."

THE CRASH

FOR ALL her desperate wishing, Kyoshi had never considered what she would actually say to Yun once she found him. He had been like the peak of a mountain, visible when she closed her eyes, attainable so long as she ignored the impassable terrain in between them. Now that he was here, she was too afraid to speak. The wrong word could pierce the illusion and send him away.

"If you're wondering what I'm doing here, I have a standing invitation to attend any and all Festivals of Szeto from my good friend the Fire Lord," Yun said. He waved cheerfully at Zoryu, and then feigned disappointment at the bewildered silence he received in return. "Oh, come on, Zoryu. Don't tell me the offer was rescinded simply because you thought I was dead?"

"Yun," Rangi said. "Get down from there. Now." She was both calm and stern, as if she'd caught him picking fruit from a tree he didn't own. But at the same time, she also shifted more of her body in between him and the Fire Lord.

Yun noticed the motion and gave her an unreadable smile. "Hi to you too, Rangi."

"Let's go inside, Yun," she said. "We'll talk."

He scrunched his nose. "That would have been nice, but I'm afraid I've already committed to a different line of play." He pointed to a lady in a voluminous pink gown near the dais who shuddered at his attention. "Madam, give a curtsy to my friends, will you?"

The woman sniffled and lifted the hem of her skirts. Underneath, her feet had sunk into the ground, the earth swallowing her up to the ankles. Kyoshi whipped around, looking at the other guests. Their long formal robes hid their feet from sight, but there were inches of bunched-up cloth puddled around every single one of them. The entire party had stepped into quicksand under the control of her friend's earthbending.

"You have to hand it to Fire Nation folk," Yun said to Kyoshi. "I threatened them *once* and explained that if they moved or made any noise, I'd make them regret it. And you know what? They were smart enough to comply! I didn't have to make any examples out of them! Don't you just love the discipline of these people?"

His expression darkened. "Earth Kingdom citizens would have blustered and yelled, '*How dare you! Don't you know who I am?*' I swear, Kyoshi, our countrymen can be so annoying sometimes. I would have just . . ."

He squeezed his hands, making a snapping, twisting motion. It was a gesture of frustration similar to the one Zoryu had playacted earlier, only this time Yun had a whole garden full of people in his grasp. The woman in pink screamed as she sank farther into the ground, up to her waist.

How could he do this? Holding people hostage was a line Kyoshi thought she and Yun shared, a distinction between them and their foes. Tagaka's slaving raid had been what provoked Yun to confront her.

"*Kyoshi!*" Rangi shouted.

They'd been through enough together for Kyoshi to know exactly what Rangi was trying to communicate. *Do something. Unfreeze. Now is your chance.*

Take him down.

But her body wouldn't move with the same certainty as Rangi's. Kyoshi had to fight her paralysis simply to get her fans out. While she fumbled with her weapons, Yun leaped over her head to the ground and slipped into the frozen crowd.

Kyoshi ran after him, cursing herself for such a clumsy, terrible draw. Wong would have disowned her from his operatic lineage had he witnessed it. She moved through the forest of people and felt the weight of their stares on her, some pleading with her to save them, many furiously accusing her of bringing this misery and humiliation to their door.

"So, Kyoshi—"

She spun around, swinging her closed fan in a backhand strike. Yun evaded the blow by leaning back, using a nearby Fire Nation minister as cover the way a swordsman fighting a duel in a bamboo grove might use the plants as a check on his opponent's blade. Kyoshi barely halted her motion in time before she cracked the poor man across the mouth.

Yun glanced at her fan and then her, his eyes wide, his

posture still angled. "Well, this is a first for our friendship," he said. "You just tried to hurt me."

She ignored the burning sting in her cheeks and thrust her weapon at his chin, but he swayed effortlessly to avoid it. She knew he'd received unarmed combat training, from Rangi herself perhaps, and it showed in his decisive movements.

She aimed a series of alternating stabs at his head and body. "Really?" he said, dancing with her like he'd been born a non-bending fighter. "After I dealt with Jianzhu for you, this is the thanks I get?"

The tips of her fans wavered. Yun had earthbent a rock through Jianzhu's chest, but it was Kyoshi who'd held him in place.

"Remember the look on his face as he died?" Yun grinned as if he were reminiscing over fire lilies instead of the time the two of them killed a man together. "Oh, I'd bottle it if I could."

In Qinchao, Yun had fulfilled Kyoshi's intent. Watching him remember the deed, and savor it so, was like staring into a mirror that revealed her own ugliness. She couldn't escape the crinkles of Yun's eyes, the satisfied contours of his mouth. Had she looked the same, standing in front of Jianzhu's body?

She noticed a Fire Navy officer behind Yun inhale deeply through his nose, seeking to aid her with a precision shot of fire from his fingers or mouth. He was trying to offer her another opening.

Kyoshi made eye contact with the uniformed man and shook her head. It was too risky. She had to talk her friend down. "Why are you doing this?" she shouted. "Tell me what it is you want!"

The reversion to their old roles calmed him, the servant trying to meet the master's needs. "Kyoshi," he said gently. "I want the same gift you received."

Avatarhood? The house in Yokoya? One she couldn't give, the other she cared so little about she'd have volunteered to draw up a transfer deed right here and now. He saw her confusion and leaned in to clarify.

"Justice, Kyoshi," he whispered. "I want justice. Everyone who lied to me is going to suffer the consequences."

"But Jianzhu is already—"

He shook his head. "Jianzhu was only the biggest name on a long list. Your mistake, Kyoshi, was that you stopped at him. My mistake was that I didn't save him for last."

Yun knelt down and placed his palm on the grass. He tilted his head and hummed. "The guards have come out and surrounded the party. Finally. I expected faster reactions from the Fire Nation's best."

Kyoshi's eyes widened. She thought she'd been buying time, but he'd been wasting hers. The whole spectacle of trapping the court where they stood had been a distraction to empty the palace.

"I think it's time I paid respects to my old *sifu*," Yun said. He winked at Kyoshi and dove into the ground. The hard-packed soil swallowed him as easily as the surface of a lake. She threw herself after him, scrabbling at the hole he left behind. It was filled with loose and crumbly castings like a shirshu's tunnel.

Yun's disappearance was the signal for general chaos to erupt. The nobles burst into screams, flailing and yanking at their legs, trying to free themselves. Palace guards flooded in between the rows of trapped guests. Kyoshi squeezed her way toward the edge of the gathering, shaking off the forest of hands trying to clutch onto her like a life raft.

"Rangi!" In her panic she nearly elbowed an angry nobleman in the face before emerging into the clear once more. *"Rangi!"*

In the distance, she saw Rangi hustling Zoryu into the arms of an arriving squad. The dazed Fire Lord disappeared into a phalanx of spears and spikes. Only after Zoryu was safe inside the formation did she break away and run toward Kyoshi.

"Where is he?" Rangi scanned the roiling crowd for Yun. "Where did he go?"

A long list. Everyone who lied to him. During their time together in Yokoya, Jianzhu had filled Yun's head with untruths about who he was, and what he could do.

So had someone else. Someone who demanded that he firebend.

Hei-Ran.

"He went inside the palace!" Kyoshi yelled. "Rangi, he's going after your mother!"

Rangi was a blur. She nearly scorched several bystanders with the jets of flame that shot from her hands. She extended her arms behind her, using the force to boost the speed of her bounding steps.

Kyoshi followed as fast as she could. There was no use telling Rangi to wait. One of them had to reach Hei-Ran before Yun did.

They tore past startled and indignant nobles, many of whom wanted to accost the Avatar for the harrowing experience they'd been put through tonight. As they neared the palace entrance, she saw the exit of Yun's tunnel. He'd already made it through the doors.

They barreled into the hallway, scraping paint off the walls and leaving smoke trails on the floors. Rangi led her to a section of the guest wing near the portrait gallery that Kyoshi hadn't visited yet, plainer than the Avatar's quarters but still lavishly decorated with baubles of Fire Nation history. When they came to the room at the end, Rangi brought her hands around and blasted the door open, nearly taking it off its hinges.

The force of their entrance scattered a tea set across the floor and sent Jinpa's robes flying over his head. From the smell of roasted flour in the air, he had been in the middle of serving Atuat and Hei-Ran tea in the Air Nomad style, using borrowed ingredients from the palace kitchen.

Atuat was the first one to stop screaming in surprise. "What is wrong with you two?!" the doctor said. "You could have injured us!"

"Did you see him?" Rangi said. "Was he here?"

"See who?"

"*Yun!* Yun is here, in the palace!"

The name didn't fall into place for the doctor. Jinpa, once he yanked the upturned layers of orange and yellow cloth off his face, looked to Kyoshi, confused that the man she'd been writing so many letters about in the Earth Kingdom was in the Fire Nation. And Hei-Ran simply closed her eyes to wait.

Kyoshi and Rangi both spun around to face the doorway. It smoked from their entrance. The clamor of bells could be heard, bouncing through the hallways, signaling an intrusion.

The seconds passed by like cricket snails. It occurred to Kyoshi that if Yun didn't know the way to Hei-Ran's room, they'd certainly left markers for him, a scorched, smashed path leading right to his target. But the assault never arrived. They heard a prolonged screech that sounded like a bird being clumsily slaughtered. Rangi cocked her ear at the sound. "That came from the portrait gallery."

"Stay here," Kyoshi said. She ventured carefully into the ruined hallway and stepped as quietly as she could through the maze of corridors, using what she could remember of the displayed antiques as her landmarks.

She arrived at the gallery and was greeted by the sight of Yun standing in the middle of the vast room, holding the limp body of Lu Beifong by his robes. "The old man's got a set of lungs on him," Yun said, digging a finger of his free hand into his ear.

He dropped Lu to the floor with a thud, the sound of a head bouncing against a hard surface wrenching a shudder from Kyoshi. "I took a wrong turn," Yun said. "You beat me to Hei-Ran because I took a wrong turn. Can you believe it?"

Yun's face distorted with a fury Kyoshi had never seen on him, as if losing his way in the palace was a worse experience than any he'd suffered. "I've *been* here before. Way more times than you. That awful red room used to be mine. Funny how fate works, isn't it? But at least I got a consolation prize."

He kicked Lu's body, folding it across the floor. The leader of the Beifong family had been Jianzhu's *sifu*, which meant he was considered Yun's as well, by the rules of teaching lineage and deference.

"Did you know that without the old coot's backing, Jianzhu would never have been able to declare me the Avatar?" Yun said, calmed by the act of disrespect. "Lu was partly responsible for what happened to us, in his way. Ending him was good, but Hei-Ran will be even better."

This wasn't him. This couldn't be the same person. The cave he'd disappeared into had spit out a simulacrum, an inhuman spirit wrapped in Yun's skin. "She's Rangi's mother!" Kyoshi cried.

"And Rangi's our friend. There are costs to this, Kyoshi. I thought you knew that. After Jianzhu, I thought you understood the price of justice."

He spoke with such concern, like he was comforting a victim of inevitability, a person trapped before the flood, the earthquake. "You should take Rangi away, so she doesn't have to watch her mother die. I plan on finishing my business in the Fire Nation before the end of the festival. It's your choice if the two of you are here for it."

Kyoshi heard footsteps clattering from the other end of the gallery. Chancellor Dairin had rallied a contingent of guards, blocking off the far exit. From the way his eyes darted to the walls, his first priority was the safety of the paintings, not the well-being of anyone near them.

One of the soldiers stepped forward to launch a barrage of Fire Fists. "No!" Dairin screamed, hurling himself over the woman's arm. "No flames!"

Yun stood trapped between the Avatar and the palace guard. "Stand down!" the squad captain shouted at him. "You're surrounded and you have nothing to bend with!"

He glanced at Kyoshi one last time before his face layered itself back into the public figure, the charmer, the showman. He held his hands up for his new audience. "As a matter of fact, I do."

Yun beckoned with his fingers and on one side of the gallery, the Fire Avatars began to dissolve.

The crowns of their heads dripped down the walls, leaving clear wooden backings behind. The brilliant colors of the portraits bled away from their stencils like wax thrown onto a bonfire and pooled into indistinguishable clumps of reddish-brown that floated through the air into Yun's waiting hands.

"The pigment in the paint," Yun explained. "It's usually made of ground-up rocks."

"No!" Dairin screamed, his fears coming to light in a way he could never have imagined. *"No no no!"* The guards behind him froze, stricken with horror at what they were witnessing. This was an assault on something deeper than their own lives.

As if bolstered by his celebration, mighty Avatar Szeto resisted the longest. But he too fell, the paint of his hat running down his long face, merging with the dark colors of his shoulders, then his waist, then his knees. His great stone stamp flaked away into cinnabar dust, joining the growing mass of pigment hovering under Yun's control. One side of the gallery was now completely blank. Instead of the wise faces of their Avatars, the portraits of the Fire Lords stared at an empty wall.

Yun held the finest work of the Fire Nation in a defiled, roiling blob above his head. And then, like a gleeful child permitted to break a jar, he hurled it on the floor. The pigment exploded in a storm of hardened pellets and sharp fragments and blinding mist.

Kyoshi managed to shield her eyes before flying shards embedded themselves in her forearms. A chunk of paint hit her so hard in the midsection that it knocked her on her back and snapped a patch of links in her chainmail, metal pouring out of her like spilled guts. Her windless gasps did nothing but coat her mouth with red dust.

By the time the blurriness in her vision cleared and the vapors from the paint explosion subsided, Yun was gone.

AFTERMATH

THE VOICES around her merged into a whirlpool of indistinguishable noise.

Kyoshi crawled her way toward the moans of the wounded on the other side of the room, dragging trails through the dark powder coating the floor. The palace guards had been wearing armor, but mainly ceremonial pieces. She saw lacerated faces, the telltale clutching of broken ribs. And those were the lucky ones, like her. Some of them weren't moving at all.

Chancellor Dairin had been completely unprotected. She found his body peppered with tiny holes, each one welling with blood. She tried to staunch his wounds with her hands but couldn't cover them all. She had no water to even attempt healing him.

More guards poured in from every side, shouting in confusion. Yun must have already escaped their encirclement. Kyoshi heard more than a few wails of anguish from the hardened fighters at the damage to their culture and history.

"Out of the way!" she heard Atuat bellow. "Give me space!"

The Water Tribe doctor slid to her knees beside Kyoshi. Instead of pulling out water from the skin at her hip, she prodded the fallen guards around Kyoshi with her bare hands, examining each one in turn for only the briefest of moments before moving on to the next.

"Why aren't you helping them?" Kyoshi yelled, her hands still pressed to Dairin's torso.

"There's too many wounded. I have to triage who can be saved and who can't."

"The chancellor is dying!"

Atuat took one look at Dairin. "He's already gone," she said with such dismissive neutrality it made Kyoshi think she was staring at Tieguai the Assassin himself. "Don't waste your time on him."

Kyoshi had read the woman completely wrong. She'd assumed the great doctor would fight for every breath of every victim. Atuat's friendship with Hei-Ran had made it seem like feeling emotions for those you healed was the key to their health. But here, she was clinically prioritizing, deciding fates quicker than she'd chosen what to drink at the party.

Kyoshi took her hands off Dairin's motionless body, his robes sticking to her palms from the blood. She didn't know what blessings Fire Nationals gave to the dead. She hoped her whispered apology to the poor man would do.

Atuat unslung her water skin and tossed it at her. "If you know any healing, do what you can. For the living." The doctor placed her hands over the chest of the unconscious guard she was examining. The air around them went cold, cold enough that Kyoshi's flesh prickled. "What are you doing?" Kyoshi asked, fighting off a shiver.

"Lowering his temperature." Atuat's temples pulsed in concentration. "It slows every process of the body down, including death. But if I don't stop at the exact right time, his fluids will turn to ice and destroy his own organs from the inside out." After a few chilling sweeps of her hands, she shifted over to the next guard and began the process anew.

"I've never heard of such a technique," Kyoshi said. Freezing liquids into solids was a basic skill of waterbending. Even she could do it by now. But she'd never considered the subtleties that lay in between water and ice, nor the blurring lines between the elements inside and outside of a person's body.

"That's because it requires too much raw power for most benders. And not damaging anyone with such power takes too much control. Misuse the technique, apply force in the slightest excess, and it kills. So perhaps you should shut up and let me focus?"

Kyoshi took the water from the skin and worked on who she could. She mostly knew how to stop bleeding and pop joints back into their sockets, and there was call enough in the room for her simple skills. As she healed the superficial injuries and glanced at the ruined Fire Avatar wall, a single thought pounded through her head.

It wasn't Yun who did this. It couldn't be. If she wasn't sure before, the heartlessness toward Rangi and Hei-Ran, the wanton vandalism, the offhanded slaughter of Lu and Chancellor Dairin made her certain now.

This was the work of the spirit. The foul, glowing apparition who'd identified her as the Avatar and dragged Yun into the darkness of a mountain had seized his mind. No one could go through that kind of experience unchanged. The Yun she knew would never be so cruel and destructive.

Atuat finished chilling the last of the victims she deemed savable. She swatted the leg of a nearby guard. "Take them to the hospital ward, but be careful," she commanded. "They're not actually healed yet, but your surgeons can start working on them now. I'll be there to help soon."

Kyoshi only had one question for the woman. "Can you teach me this technique?" Saving lives, pulling people back from the brink of death—there was no worthier use of bending in her opinion. Just the ability to keep someone stable until a real doctor arrived could have made such a difference in her past.

Atuat snorted in derision. At first Kyoshi thought she might have accidentally belittled how much study it took, but it turned out Atuat viewed it from a different angle. "When it comes to healing, *I* can teach anyone anything, in a fraction the time it normally takes," she said. "Whether I have a student of the right qualities is a different matter."

They got to their feet, only to see the leader of Zoryu's personal security detail waiting for the Avatar. The armored man's face roiled with bottled, silent anger, as if he'd been handpicked to represent the outrage of an entire nation. Only his duty kept him from bursting at the seams.

"We can talk about it later," Atuat muttered to Kyoshi. "I think you have more pressing matters at the moment."

Kyoshi followed the guard captain through the palace. They passed a torrent of furious nobles heading in the opposite direction, a crowd that had been recently dismissed from an unsatisfactory meeting. The courtiers, who had taken so much care in their order of speech during the party, muttered and hissed to themselves about "never having been so humiliated" and "the child being a disgrace to the crown." Some of the most livid men and women wore the winged peony, which meant they were Keohso, the same clan as Zoryu's mother.

The captain stopped at a set of massive bronze doors and indicated he wasn't allowed to go any farther. "Where are my companions?" Kyoshi asked. "The lieutenant and the head-mistress?" She had a feeling she'd need the guidance of Fire Nationals for what came next.

"Coordinating the palace lockdown," came the gruff reply. *Being useful, unlike you,* was the additional silent commentary.

Kyoshi pushed the doors open herself, revealing the throne room, the same place where the Fire Lord received his war council. The ceiling of the great hall was supported by four towering red pillars with dragons of painted gold spiraling around them to the heavens. In the back, up a series of steps, lay the throne of the Fire Nation, a flat, blocky platform that would have given the sitter little comfort. A giant sculpted dragon weaving through the coils of its own body hung over it, threatening to burst from the wall. She guessed that if she peeked under the red silk carpet that covered the entire middle third of the floor, she might find yet more dragons staring back.

A straggling minister sidestepped his way past her, the last remnant of an audience she'd missed. It was the man she'd nearly struck with her fan. He glared at Kyoshi and stormed out, leaving her in the throne room with only two other people. The Fire Lord and his brother.

It was not a good moment for a stranger to walk in on. Zoryu was ashen and stooped, his eyes half shut as if the light were causing him pain. Chaejin stood tall by his side, regal and calm. An artist capturing the scene could easily have gotten their subjects mixed.

She waited for Zoryu to dismiss Chaejin, but the order never came. "He's alive?" the Fire Lord said once the doors closed. "Yun was alive, and not a single member of your country thought to tell me? Did everyone in the Earth Kingdom decide to ignore this fact together?"

He didn't know how right he was. And Kyoshi was to blame more than any Earth Sage. She couldn't bring herself to answer.

"Why would he do this?!" Zoryu's cry was directed at the skybound spirits as much as Kyoshi. *"Why?!"*

"He was attacking the people who wronged him," she whispered. "Lu Beifong, Hei-Ran, the people who told him he was the Avatar." Vengeance sounded so alien a reason, coming from her lips, even though she knew exactly the depth and shape it could take.

"I was briefed on what happened in the gallery," Zoryu said. "How many are dead?"

Kyoshi forced herself to remember how many bodies Atuat pointedly ignored on the floor. "Lu. Chancellor Dairin. Two guards. Possibly more, depending if they make it through the night."

Zoryu slumped in the corner of his throne. The act made him look like a child trying to hide from getting called on in a classroom. The mantle of being the Fire Lord was too heavy for him right now. "The chancellor didn't deserve this," he muttered. "None of them did."

Chaejin reacted to the list of casualties much differently. "This is terrible," he said, rubbing his chin with exaggerated strokes. "A high-ranking official of the Fire Nation killed in the palace? A foreign dignitary under the Fire Lord's hospitality, murdered? Not to mention the destruction of our cultural heritage and the humiliation of the entire court in the garden. The disgraces to our country keep mounting. I can't imagine what would happen if the intruder had successfully assassinated the headmistress of the Royal Academy."

Kyoshi noticed he didn't count the fallen guards. She'd had enough of trying to play by decorum. "What exactly are you doing here?" she snapped at Chaejin.

"Representing the voice of the Fire Sages in response to this heinous assault upon our nation," he replied. "And if I can get a word in for the Saowon clan as well, then so be it."

Chaejin stepped down from the stairs leading to the throne. He probably shouldn't have been standing on them in the first place. "I'd be lying to my Fire Lord if I claimed to see a way out of this disaster. We've been gravely dishonored as a people. There are calls for retaliation against the Earth Kingdom."

"The Earth Kingdom—" She was going to say the Earth Kingdom wasn't responsible, but couldn't finish the sentence. "The Earth Kingdom didn't send Yun to harm your country."

"I know." Kindness oozed from Chaejin's every word. "I spent the last twenty minutes assuring the court our friends across the sea are not to blame. It took some doing, but I've convinced them."

He had no need to lie. If everything she heard tonight was true, it benefitted Chaejin to direct the court's anger at the Fire Lord, not at a foreign power.

And it should have been Zoryu doing the diplomatic work. Kyoshi looked to the Fire Lord, but Chaejin's presence had compressed him into a younger sibling and nothing but, unable to speak over his elder. The enraged Keohso were likely angry about Chaejin taking charge of the situation.

"Fire Lord, may I speak to your brother alone?" she asked. She'd only just arrived, but it was clear she wasn't going to get anything useful from Zoryu right now. His head bobbed in an indiscernible direction.

"Zoooryuuu," Chaejin crooned, like he was singing his younger brother to sleep. "May we be dismissed?"

A feeble wave. Good enough. Kyoshi slipped through the heavy doors and Chaejin joined her outside.

"I'm sorry you had to see that," Chaejin said. He looked down the long hallway to confirm it was empty. "My little brother's not the best under pressure."

Kyoshi examined his face. "I still can't get over how much the two of you look alike for not being from the same mother."

"I've been told I could serve as his political decoy. We still have those here in the Fire Nation, you know. The Fire Army keeps tabs on random villagers who resemble important figures. I don't think any of them have been pulled into service in the last century though."

"Zoryu has not impressed me so far," Kyoshi said. "Maybe he should be your decoy instead of you his."

Chaejin's brow lifted at the implication. "In truth, I fear for him," he said carefully. "If he can't bring the perpetrator to justice swiftly, the clans will no longer consider him fit to be Fire Lord."

"What would happen then?"

"He'd be replaced." Chaejin paused to gauge her reaction before continuing. "I have no idea with whom, mind you. But no Fire Lord in history has ever left the throne and lived very long afterward."

Kyoshi nodded slowly. "Who's to say that wouldn't be for the best? No one wants loose ends lying around. A single, unopposed, popular ruler would be much better for the Fire Nation." She leaned in and whispered into his ear. "I know what I said at the party, but really, the Avatar works with whoever wears the crown. It doesn't have to be a weakling like Zoryu."

Chaejin grinned. "It sounds like I can count on your backing should the worst come to pass."

It did sound like that. "Answer me this," Kyoshi said. "Once you're Fire Lord, what will you do about your country's fortunes?"

His smile faltered. "I'm sorry?"

"What will you *do*? You told me yourself how much trouble the Fire Nation is in. What actions will you take to help your people?"

Chaejin shrugged. "I'll think of something. I'm sure once a real ruler sits upon the throne, our people's problems will resolve themselves."

"I see. So, you'll be better than your brother, and the natural order of things will be restored on their own."

"Yes, exactly!" He delighted in her understanding. "Avatar, I am correcting a mistake. This country is mine by rights, no matter what my father twisted the law into declaring. I will get what is owed to me, and if a little blood must flow, then so be . . . it . . . . "

The remnants of Chaejin's grin melted away. His eyes narrowed. "Avatar, are you playing me right now?"

"Playing? No. I was forming an opinion." The court intrigue of the Fire Nation might have been too complex for her to navigate perfectly, but judging character was simpler. In Chaejin she saw a man who wanted power for its own sake and was willing to burn his own country to get it. How utterly familiar.

You know what to do with such men, cackled Lao Ge. It upset her to no end that she could imagine his whispers better than she could hear the voices of her previous lives.

She wasn't going to weed out a dignitary of a foreign nation like her former *sifu* might have wanted. But she was going to do everything in her power to prevent an entitled, shortsighted man from instigating a civil war for his own benefit. It was her duty as the Avatar.

Chaejin sensed her resolve hardening, which side she was coming down on. "Nothing I've said to you will hold up at court, or in court. Report me and it would be your word against mine. You're the Avatar, but you're an outsider."

"I know. I'll get more on you eventually."

He frowned at her directness. "Mark my words, the attack upon the palace will lead to Zoryu's downfall if it goes unanswered. Support my brother if you must. It will only delay the inevitable. Not even the Avatar can fight history."

Kyoshi turned and walked down the hall. "We have a saying in the Fire Nation," Chaejin called after her. *"Dishonor is like a bird in flight. It has to land somewhere."*

It was as she expected then. Peace in the Fire Nation, protecting Hei-Ran, all of it pivoted around a single axis.

Yun.

THE RITUAL

KYOSHI DRIFTED on her great raft of a bed in the red ocean of the Avatar's quarters. She couldn't tell how many times she'd been woken up throughout the night by her dreams. Each time her eyes opened, she would stare up at the painted ceiling, her mind racing until her vision blurred into the patterns of swirling crimson.

She was wide-awake and already dressed when a servant came to rouse her. Nor was she surprised to hear that Rangi and Hei-Ran were also up and waiting to speak with her.

The servant guided her to a balcony on an upper floor, set with a small table for breakfast. The sunrise view was marred by the gray wall that ringed the palace, but they were high up enough to see light peeking over the edges of the caldera. The Fire Nation capital residing in a dormant volcano was common knowledge, but Kyoshi had never considered what the view would be like from inside the sunken depression. She could have been sitting on the palm of a giant, its stone fingers threatening to close around her.

Rangi and Hei-Ran were already wolfing down their breakfast of bland gruel and salted vegetables. The blazing spices and oils that had slathered the party food now lay to the side of the table in small pots, to be added to taste. Even Fire Nationals took a break from hot flavors first thing in the morning.

Kyoshi was always amused by how swiftly Rangi plowed through her meals, her delicate features at odds with her voracious consumption. Her mother was no different. They'd probably developed a habit in the barracks of eating as fast as possible to avoid wasting time.

"Sit and eat first," Hei-Ran said to Kyoshi, pointing at the food with her chopsticks. "We're going to need our energy and I hear you're in the habit of skipping meals."

Rangi watched Kyoshi's every bite, a fresh humiliation brought on by Jinpa's tattling. The Avatar was no longer trusted to feed herself properly. *I am going to get you back for this, monk,* Kyoshi thought as she chewed and swallowed under Rangi's scrutiny. *Somehow, someday.*

Once they finished, Hei-Ran leaned back in her chair and let silence fall over the table. She watched the light extend its reach across the grounds.

"So," she said. "Yun wants to kill me."

The sound of Rangi's knuckles tightening could be heard in the morning stillness. But Hei-Ran stated it dryly, like she was noting the color of their napkins. A detail in an official report.

"He escaped not only the palace, but a full lockdown of the caldera," she went on. "All ports in the capital have been closed.

The festivities in Harbor City are on hold while the search continues house to house. No luck yet though."

Kyoshi was both impressed and disturbed by how efficiently the Fire Nation could conduct a manhunt. "Maybe there's another angle that could help us find him." She told them her conclusion that had germinated in the gallery and taken full root overnight.

She'd discussed the possibility with Rangi, but Hei-Ran was hearing it for the first time. "You think the spirit that identified you as the Avatar has possessed Yun," Hei-Ran said.

Kyoshi nodded. "Jianzhu called it 'Father Glowworm.' He said it fought with Kuruk in the past. This spirit could be controlling him, or maybe it altered his mind." She noticed Rangi frown deeply but put it aside for now.

"I've never heard the name," Hei-Ran said. "During the time our group spent together, spiritual excursions were never Kuruk's focus, to say the least."

Kyoshi sorely wished people would stop dancing around Kuruk's tenure as the Avatar with euphemisms. She didn't see what her predecessor had done to earn the favor. "Back in Yokoya I pulled apart Jianzhu's libraries, searching for mentions of a spirit fitting the description, but found nothing. I was hoping you would have some recollection."

"Better to ask Kuruk himself." Kyoshi thought Hei-Ran was brushing her off until she remembered she was supposed to be able to commune with her past lives. The statement was meant literally.

It would have been foolish to hide her spiritual troubles any further, so she gritted her teeth and confessed. "I can't," she said. "I can't fully reach Kuruk or any other Avatar."

To her surprise, they weren't upset. "Communing with their past lives is one of the most difficult and complex feats an Avatar can perform," Hei-Ran said. "Successful methods and experiences have been known to vary between generations. I wouldn't advertise your problem, but I wouldn't beat yourself up about it either."

Kyoshi was relieved down to the bone. In one matter regarding her broken, rocky Avatarhood, at least one matter, she wasn't at fault. What a difference it made having someone older *and* wiser to give her advice.

Hei-Ran stared over the edge of the balcony and drummed her fingers against the table.

"I have an idea," she said. "I know a friend of Kuruk's who spent more time with him after our original group went its separate ways. He used to be a Fire Sage stationed in the capital, but these days he maintains a small shrine in North Chung-Ling. He's an expert in spiritual matters. If anyone could give us answers, it's him."

"North Chung-Ling?" The town name held some meaning that Rangi disapproved of. "We couldn't go to the real Fire Sages?"

"They're in the pocket of the Saowon clan," Hei-Ran said. "The High Sage is Chaejin's maternal great-uncle. But my contact might know more about this Father Glowworm creature, especially if it has a link to Kuruk. If the Avatar successfully fought it in the past, perhaps it can be defeated again now."

The idea of her predecessor being useful to Kyoshi was a new one, but it filled her with hope. Kuruk's friend could teach her how to break the spell Yun was under. She could save him. This was her edge, the one she'd been missing in the Earth Kingdom. "We have to go to North Chung-Ling," she said.

Rangi slammed her fists on the table, clattering the empty dishes. The frustration building inside her since the beginning of the discussion had finally boiled over. "Are the two of you listening to yourselves?" she shouted. "The palace was attacked, and you want to go on a wild spirit chase?"

Kyoshi's optimism was too fragile to withstand any debate. She needed Rangi completely behind her, not throwing up resistance. "How else are we going to get the old Yun back?" she snapped.

"Kyoshi, he killed four people and defiled the palace. After what he did, there is no more 'old Yun.'"

She couldn't believe this. "I'm telling you he is *possessed*!"

Rangi's chair screeched as she rose to her feet. "And a day ago, you weren't even sure of that!"

"Lieutenant," Hei-Ran said. "Control yourself."

"No, *Mother*, I won't." Her choice of words was a retort to Hei-Ran's use of rank. "I'm not going to sit here calmly and listen to you entertain Kyoshi's wild guesses about spirits instead of coming up with a defensive plan for your own safety. I know you both feel terrible for what happened to Yun. I do too. But after what we all saw, it would be utterly foolish to treat him like anything but the danger he is."

There was only a limited amount of room on the balcony for Rangi to pace back and forth, but she made do. "I mean, he shouldn't have been capable of half the things he did last night. He infiltrated the capital, murdered Lu, and single-handedly foiled the entire security force of the royal palace. It doesn't make sense. Yun is a diplomat and a talented Earthbender, not some kind of trained killer."

"He is," Hei-Ran said. "He is a trained killer."

Rangi was caught in the middle of launching the next volley of her tirade, her finger crooked to the sky. "What?"

As methodically as if she were donning armor before a battle, Hei-Ran readied herself. She took several deep, controlled breaths. And then she told Kyoshi and Rangi a story about Yun they had never heard before.

Immediately after finding Yun in Makapu, Jianzhu started to fret. *Daofei* and corrupt politicians alike had profited greatly from the absence of the Avatar. Kuruk's early death showed how disastrous it could be for the world if the cycle were "renewed" at the wrong time. Yun needed to be able to defend himself from attempts on his life.

His physical safety wasn't Jianzhu's only concern. The new Avatar's legitimacy would be attacked with every underhanded trick in the book. Yun and his allies would inevitably suffer from slander, extortion, theft of secrets. He would have to maintain constant vigilance against attempts to destabilize his era of Avatarhood.

Yun's enemies would come after him as spies, sowers of chaos, and assassins. And in Jianzhu's eyes, there was no better protection than to make sure Yun possessed those same skills himself.

That had been Master Amak's role in Yokoya, Hei-Ran explained. The mysterious Waterbender had perfected his craft in the dark corridors of Ba Sing Se, where smiling princes attended feasts together by day and waged hidden wars of secrets and daggers against each other by night. Master Amak had not only trained Yun to resist poison, but also taught him how to use it. Atuat's brother had instructed him how to eliminate enemies with knife and bare hand. The lessons had been limited to theory. But like in every subject save firebending, Yun had shown to be a talented student.

Kyoshi tried to reconcile what she was hearing with the boy she knew. Yun had abhorred Jianzhu's butchering of the Yellow Necks, but he'd also mentioned how much he enjoyed learning from Master Amak. Jianzhu must have been slowly working on moving Yun from the abstract to the practical. He wanted another Gravedigger and was willing to be patient to get it.

"I turned a blind eye because I thought it would be best for the Avatar's protection in the long run," Hei-Ran said. *I am so sorry for what I allowed him to do to Yun*, she'd told Kyoshi. She hadn't been referring to bending training.

Rangi was quiet. And she was cold. No heat emanated from her body. Her face was like ice covering a river, frozen to a thickness that masked what flowed underneath.

She despised assassins. When pushed to the brink, Rangi had allowed the Avatar to work with outlaws, but there was no world where she compromised her morals and her honor like her mother had.

"A spirit didn't turn Yun into a monster," she whispered to Hei-Ran. "You did."

"I'm sorry—"

Rangi grabbed the table by its corners. She rose to her feet, her back muscles flexing as she lifted the heavy piece of furniture, dishes and cups sliding over the lacquered surface, and hurled the entire setting over the edge of the balcony.

The morning air was heavy before the crash. By the time the table hit the ground below, and the sounds of wood groaning and porcelain splashing like raindrops reached them, Rangi was already leaving. Hei-Ran made no move to stop her daughter. She sat across from Kyoshi as if this were a normal occurrence, a standard outburst.

With nothing between their chairs to occupy the space, Kyoshi felt overexposed. "Is anyone hurt?" Hei-Ran asked calmly. Kyoshi glanced over the railing and shook her head.

Hei-Ran pointed her chin at the door Rangi had vanished through. "You should go talk to her. You might be the only person who can right now."

"I need you to confirm something first."

Hei-Ran read the tightness in the Avatar's frown. "Kelsang didn't know. We took great pains to conceal such matters from him. He would have confronted the rest of us earlier had he found out."

Kyoshi was grateful to hear it. But in no mood to forgive. "And then maybe the rest of you would have killed him sooner too."

She didn't bother looking for a reaction in the older woman's eyes, to see if she'd successfully wounded the last living member of Avatar Kuruk's companions. She got up to go look for Rangi.

Kyoshi ran into Jinpa first. He already knew a delicate situation was afoot.

"Mistress Rangi is in the stables," he said. "I was grooming Yingyong when she came in and offered to assist. She, uh, seemed like she needed solitude, so I let her take over."

"She told you to get lost, didn't she?"

Jinpa shrugged. "I negative *jing*ed it out of there before my robes started smoking. Just make sure she doesn't yank my bison's fur out by brushing too hard."

Kyoshi followed his directions down the halls of the palace until she came to another garden-facing exit. It revealed a freestanding longhouse that smelled of fresh-cut hay. A gaggle of stablehands idled at a distance from the building, looking confused about what to do with their hands. Kyoshi knew they'd been ordered away. Where they stood marked the edge of Rangi's blast radius.

She went to the largest pen and saw Yingyong, his fluffy bulk taking up most of the room inside. His saddle hung off his back at an angle and only one side of his fur lay smooth and flat. He grunted at Kyoshi as if to ask, *Is someone going to finish the job?*

The sound of sniffling gave away Rangi's location. She found her by Yingyong's second and third right legs, sitting on the hay-strewn floor, tucked into a ball. Kyoshi's instincts were to lean down and wrap the smaller girl in her arms.

"Why didn't you stop him?" The kind of sharpness in Rangi's tone was rarely ever aimed at Kyoshi, but now it was out in full force.

"Who? Jianzhu?"

"Yun!" Rangi looked up, her eyes red. "I saw how close you got to him at the party and you did nothing!"

Kyoshi knew she was only lashing out from anger, but it still wasn't a fair hit. "Nothing!? He was standing in the middle of a crowd of hostages!"

"So you waved your fans at him; good try! You're the Avatar, Kyoshi! Did it ever occur to you to try *bending*? You had so many chances to drop him by force and you didn't take them!"

"I—" She had no response for why she didn't try fighting Yun with water or air. Hurting him with the elements, like she'd reflexively done to so many *daofei* and hatchet men, hadn't occurred to her. Looking back on it, even her strokes with her fans had been slow and hesitant.

The shame inside Kyoshi twisted into something hurtful. "What should I have done then? Kill him in cold blood like I did Xu Ping An? Put him down like a rabid animal? He's our friend!"

"Well, I'm glad you still have room to debate!" Rangi shouted. "I no longer get to decide how I feel about Yun! He took that choice away from me! What if he hurts *you*, Kyoshi? What if he attacks us again and you hesitate and he hurts *you*?"

Kyoshi punched the wall over Rangi's head. *"He wouldn't!"*

Dust trickled from the ceiling, catching the rays of the sun peeking into the stable. From where she sat, Rangi's voice turned smaller and younger. "You have a hole in your robes that says otherwise. If I had convinced you not to wear your armor, we'd be in a very different place right now. You'd be seriously injured or worse, and it would have been my fault." She lowered her eyes and curled her knees closer. "I couldn't live with that, any more than I could live with losing my mother again. I just got the two of you back."

Kyoshi slumped to the ground beside her. "Rangi, I swear to you, I will do what it takes with Yun. I won't let him harm anyone else, especially not your mother."

Rangi examined every inch of Kyoshi's face, looking for sincerity. She wiped the growing wetness from her own eyes before it became tears.

"When she opened her eyes in Atuat's hospital, I started to hope the past was done with us," Rangi said. "I thought we could begin moving forward, like how the traditional Avatar calendar counts the days. Did you know it's technically the six thousand four hundred fifty-fourth day of the Era of Kyoshi?"

Counting the days by where they fell in an Avatar's life was a formal and archaic method of timekeeping. It was mostly used by historians or trotted out during certain spiritual ceremonies.

"It doesn't feel like it," Kyoshi muttered. It didn't seem like her Avatarhood had ever legitimately begun. They sat there for a long time, saying nothing. Wishing things were different.

Kyoshi broke the silence. "You threw a table off the balcony."

Rangi laughed, a strangled noise of release. "I am in so much trouble. I could have killed someone. In the royal palace no less. What if the Fire Lord had been walking underneath us?"

"I no longer hold the title for worst breach of manners in the Four Nations," Kyoshi said. "And I am never, ever going to let you forget it."

Rangi reached over and took her hand. Red scars traveled down Kyoshi's wrist in wavy, branching patterns like the veins of a palm frond, a token from when she'd fought the lightning.

"For as long as you live?" Rangi asked solemnly.

Kyoshi smiled and nodded. "For as long as I live."

Rangi pressed her lips to the healed skin on Kyoshi's knuckles. The kiss sealed a promise to always give each other a hard time for the rest of their days. If Kyoshi held any longing for the past, it was for those simpler moments when she was Rangi's greatest and only headache.

"Avatar, Lieutenant, are you in there?" Zoryu called from outside. "I request your presence regarding a certain matter."

Rangi's head shot up from Kyoshi's shoulder. They looked at each other with growing panic. Maybe it had been a historically important table.

They sidled past Yingyong out of the pen. The attendants had been dismissed. The Fire Lord waited for them, wearing a lighter, morning-dress version of his robes. Kyoshi wondered if it took as long for him to put on his clothes as it did for her to don her chainmail.

"I didn't acquit myself well last night, immediately after the incident," Zoryu said to her. He fought the urge to look at the curling, pointed toes of his shoes instead of maintaining eye contact. "I should have taken command of the situation. I should have been the one talking to you instead of Chaejin. I swear, when it comes to my brother, I feel like my wits leave me. Certain people . . . they turn you into who you were before."

Zoryu had his flaws, but he was a ruler who cared about his nation. With Kyoshi's help he could grow into his crown. "You don't need to apologize," she said.

"Good, because apparently strong Fire Lords aren't allowed to." He sighed. "I've been speaking with my advisors and the situation remains dire. The only chance I have of keeping the court from turning on me is apprehending Yun."

"Then we want the same thing," Kyoshi said. "I will find him for the both of us."

"Thank you, Avatar." He bit his lip. "That's not the only reason I'm here, though."

He stepped aside to reveal Hei-Ran standing behind him, with Atuat by her side. The two women were stiff-backed, as if ceremony had suddenly intruded its ugly head again.

"What's the meaning of this?" Rangi said. She recognized something she didn't like in her mother's posture.

"Atuat is my second, and the Fire Lord is my witness," Hei-Ran said. Without her cane, she slowly, carefully, sank to her knees on the grass. She reached behind her and unsheathed a wickedly sharp knife.

"No!" Rangi started forward. "Mother, no!"

Hei-Ran pinned her daughter in place with a glare. "After what I've done, you would protest? Consistency, Lieutenant. No one gets to escape the consequences of their deeds. This was a long time in coming."

She grasped her topknot with one hand and placed the edge of the knife on it carefully. "For failing to recognize the true Avatar," she said, holding Kyoshi's gaze. "For not protecting my friend Kelsang."

Hei-Ran looked to the Fire Lord. "For letting my former pupil dishonor our nation."

And finally, Rangi. "For not being worthy of my daughter's esteem." With one swift stroke Hei-Ran lopped off the bundle of hair and tossed it on the ground before her. Her dark silken locks, salted with gray strands, billowed down her face and neck.

Rangi shuddered as Atuat carefully picked up the severed topknot and folded a clean silk kerchief around it. She'd lost her own hair, once, but that was due to the underhanded tactics of an enemy, far away in the Earth Kingdom. Regrettable and traumatic, but more akin to a war injury. Hei-Ran had acknowledged her personal dishonor right in the beating heart of their own country, in front of the Fire Lord.

"It's done," she said to Rangi with a sad smile. "You hold this family's honor in your hands now. You'll take far better care of it than I have." With a few more flicks of the knife, Hei-Ran cropped the remainder of her hair to match the severed ends, making it shockingly short, yet somehow still neatly fetching around her beautiful face. For this family, doing things cleanly and properly applied to everything, including rituals of ultimate humility.

Atuat took the knife from Hei-Ran and helped her up. In a way, the doctor made the ideal second. She would do as her friend requested, without the hesitance a noble of the Fire Nation might have at seeing one of its most illustrious figures fall from grace.

Rangi, on the other hand, was apoplectic. She'd been robbed of her righteous momentum, had her pockets picked. There was nothing she could say anymore to her mother in anger.

Hei-Ran let her daughter flap and fume another minute before deciding they'd wasted enough time. Letting witnesses have their say, even family members, did not appear to be part of the topknot-severing ritual. "All right then. North Chung-Ling." She peered inside the stable at Yingyong. "I see you haven't saddled the bison correctly. Five people will cause the floor to shift."

"What do you mean five people?" Rangi managed to spit out. "What do you mean North Chung-Ling? We didn't agree to go there."

"You were upset we weren't discussing a plan for my safety earlier," Hei-Ran said. "Well, standard operating procedure after a target comes under attack is to move their location. You should know this well; it's how you protected the Avatar from Jianzhu."

Hei-Ran turned to everyone. "We are going to hide out in North Chung-Ling," she declared. "While we're there, Kyoshi can make contact with Kuruk's friend to follow up on any spiritual leads to find Yun. It'll kill two spidersnakes with one stone. Brother Jinpa! Have you finished gathering the supplies?"

Jinpa teetered around the corner, crates and burlap bags stacked high in his arms. "I have, Headmistress. We can be in the air in fifteen minutes."

Hei-Ran had commandeered Kyoshi's secretary the same way Rangi had. Rangi stared at Jinpa, furious at his betrayal. He simply shrugged as if to say *Scariest Firebender wins* before sidling into the pen next to his bison.

"We haven't discussed our options!" Rangi said. "We have to take into account your condition!"

"She'll be fine," Atuat said with an uncomfortably cavalier wave of her hand. "Fresh air and movement will be better for her health than cooping her up in the palace. She survived the trip home, didn't she?"

"But—but—" Rangi looked to Kyoshi for backup. It seemed like she wanted to avoid a flight with her mother at all costs.

"But nothing!" Hei-Ran said before the Avatar could weigh in. "I may have no rank now, young lady, but you are still my daughter! I am telling you that we are going on this trip, and I don't want to hear any further complaints spewing out of your mouth! Now hush!"

Young lady? Kyoshi had seen the headmistress give the lieutenant orders before, but this was some kind of new and frightening relationship that had been unshackled. Rangi's mouth bent into a shape Kyoshi didn't know it could achieve.

"I'm officially an Avatar's companion!" Atuat whooped, throwing her fists in the air. The sudden noise startled Yingyong into squashing Jinpa against the side of the pen. "I'm going to get one of those fancy ink paintings of us commissioned for posterity!"

Hei-Ran was already inspecting the sections of Yingyong's coat Rangi had worked on. "You call this grooming?" she said, aiming her disapproval at her daughter. "It looks like you used a body brush instead of a dandy brush. It'll have to be redone. All of it."

"Somebody help me?" Jinpa pleaded from the other side, his voice muffled by his own bison's fur.

Zoryu watched the proceedings, gripped by horror and dismay. "I was going to give a great big speech about how the fate of my nation rests on the shoulders of this group," he said to Kyoshi.

A bag tore open, scattering grain everywhere. Yingyong roared in delight and began lapping it up, nearly knocking Atuat down with his tongue.

"We'll, uh, be careful," Kyoshi said.

Rangi and the others had to go back to the palace for a few more things. Hei-Ran cornered Kyoshi while she was straightening Yingyong's saddle blanket. The two of them were alone in the pen.

"It's not enough, and you know it," the older woman said quietly.

Kyoshi kept her eyes on her work. "What isn't?"

"My hair, my honor, they're not enough to balance the scale." Hei-Ran busied her hands along the saddle so it would look like they were talking about something else, something trivial. "There is no escaping the past. Yun is the sins of my generation, come back to haunt us. One way or another, he will catch up to me."

She cinched one of the buckles tighter. "Rangi may view this trip as traveling for my protection. You see it as a search for clues. But from my perspective, we're luring Yun away from the palace, out in the open. I am coming with you to act as bait."

Kyoshi started to protest, but Hei-Ran would brook no argument. "You will use me to draw Yun in. You will let him kill me if you have to. I don't think you have a good chance of capturing him without a sacrifice."

"Rangi would never allow—"

"Which is why I am talking to you right now, and not her. The stability of the Fire Nation is more important than my life." She gestured at her shortened hair. "The other reason I cut my topknot is so that there will be no further disgrace to the country if he kills me. An honorless person does not need to be avenged. I can bear any insult, because there's no more person to insult."

Hei-Ran was as even and steady as the earth they stood on. "As far as I'm concerned, I don't deserve to escape Yun's wrath any more than Jianzhu deserved to escape yours. My death might actually close the books on this nightmare. An upside I'd accept without hesitation."

The fake work reached its limits, and they turned to face each other. "My daughter would never listen to me on such matters," Hei-Ran said. "But I can trust you to do what needs to be done. Right, Kyoshi?"

Caught between two family members, Kyoshi didn't know what to say. For the sake of Rangi she should have refused Hei-Ran immediately. But the headmistress's chilling logic was brutal and elegant at the same time. It boggled Kyoshi how easily Hei-Ran came up with the trade.

Hei-Ran took her silence for an answer and patted her on the shoulder. "Good girl."

THE FIRE SAGE

TRAVELING OVER the Earth Kingdom meant crossing vast mountain ranges, lakes the size of oceans, deserts that threatened to swallow their surrounding features. Kyoshi was used to idling large swathes of time away on a bison's back, watching the landscape grow and shrink as she flew from one city to another.

Traveling through the Fire Nation was a quick jaunt in comparison. Reaching their destination on Shuhon Island, the next landmass over from the capital, felt like flipping a piece of double-sided embroidery around to see what was on the back. North Chung-Ling lay nestled inside enveloping arms of volcanic rock, a small gap in the formation granting it access to the sea.

They found an outcropping on the forested slope where Yingyong could stay, rather than be forced into pens that weren't built to fit him. Despite the short journey, Rangi spilled out of the saddle, a ragged mess.

"Your landing zone selection needs work," Hei-Ran said, pursuing her mercilessly.

"It doesn't need work," Rangi muttered.

"Young lady, I have been traveling with the Avatar on bison-back since before you were born! I count two approaches from the downwind side and insufficient forage. Do you want poor Yingyong to get surprised by rustlers? Or starve to death?"

"We're not going to be here that long!"

"You don't know that! Does preparedness not carry the day anymore? Do we need to take down the door sign at the academy?"

It had been like this the whole flight. Kyoshi took Rangi by the hand before she burst into flames. "Why don't we, uh, scout ahead?" She dragged her away from the group, down the trail leading to the settlement. Jinpa and Atuat stayed behind, walking at Hei-Ran's pace. They'd been mostly quiet throughout the trip, not daring to get between any family arguments.

"Traveling with my mother is the worst," Rangi fumed once they had some distance. "It's like being twelve all over again."

"How did you manage going to the North Pole together?"

"She was *comatose*!" Rangi said, startling Kyoshi with her flippancy. "Having her constantly in my ear, on a mission with the Avatar no less, is a completely different story!"

It wasn't the reaction Rangi was looking for, but Kyoshi swelled with a sudden happiness. She couldn't help it. Rangi acting so completely, utterly normal tugged on a rope connected directly to her heart. It always would.

On a whim, she picked Rangi up by the waist and whirled her around. No one was there to scold them for inappropriate touching. Rangi laughed despite herself and tried to swat at her but couldn't reach as far. "Stop it! You're embarrassing me!"

"That's the point!"

Most Earth Kingdom cities of good repair and repute were square, created to be plain and rigidly four-sided in the unimaginative but sufficient Earth Kingdom way. When settlements were forced into circular plots of land though, Kyoshi was accustomed to seeing towns arranging themselves in rings, mimicking Ba Sing Se. The layout deliberately made it easy to see who was rich and who wasn't.

But inside their caldera, the residents of North Chung-Ling had opted to build in wedges. Houses and market stalls angled their way toward the center, separated by streets that resembled the spokes of a wheel. Without Earthbenders to raise walls and roofs, the buildings had been hewn from logs dragged down from the slopes of the mountain. The relentless humidity warped much of the wood construction, making the town slightly tilted and confusing to look at.

And no one was rich. Not in the way of the Fire Nation and Earth Kingdom capitals, or self-sufficient cities like Omashu and Gaoling. As they walked through the outskirts, passing haggard stallkeepers, peddlers selling rusted tools, staring mothers holding children at their hips, Kyoshi recognized the same symptoms in North Chung-Ling as in Yokoya. Trying to scrabble against unyielding soil wore down on a person in a particular way.

Kyoshi realized the vaunted Fire Nation prosperity that other countries sometimes envied was a bit of a stage trick. Whether it was intentional or not, the capital took up most of what outsiders imagined as "the Fire Nation," due to its smaller size compared to the Earth Kingdom. And the capital would always look fine as a point of pride, hiding weaknesses, never lacking for anything.

"Let's do some reconnaissance and explore the fairgrounds," Hei-Ran said. "The man we're looking for is named Nyahitha. He's of the Bhanti tribe, though he prefers not to make that known. Out of respect we should feign ignorance of his background."

"Who are the Bhanti tribe?" Kyoshi asked.

"Exactly," Hei-Ran said, giving her a pointed stare.

They walked farther into town, in the direction of the sea. Rangi's irritation grew with every step. A stranger might have assumed that the haughty-looking girl was turning her nose up at the hardships of the commonfolk on display, but Kyoshi knew her better than that.

"What's your issue with this place?" she whispered. "You've been against coming here from the start."

"It's a carnival town," Rangi muttered. "A glorified gambling den. North Chung-Ling used to be known as a place where spiritual experiences were common and anyone could see a vision of the other world, not just the enlightened. But instead of maintaining its hallowed ground, the village cashed in on its reputation. People come here to pay for a 'spiritual encounter,' and once they're bored of that, cheap entertainment."

Kyoshi hadn't known such options existed. If she could pay to talk to Yangchen, she would. She'd empty any one of the numerous accounts Jianzhu had bequeathed her.

"It's not real," Rangi said, knowing exactly what Kyoshi was thinking. "The success stories are from tourists unwilling to admit they wasted their money. And it sullies the very nature of the spirits. If I were the Avatar and the only way I could make a profound leap was to grease the palm of a stage medium, I'd bury my head in shame."

They'd have to agree to disagree on that front. Rangi trudged on a few paces, before her expression softened. "Still, the town shouldn't be this run-down," she said. "There must have been as much trouble with the harvests as Lord Zoryu said. It's as bad as—"

"As the Earth Kingdom?" Kyoshi said, raising an eyebrow.

"Yes, Kyoshi," Rangi said, as unflinching as always. "As bad as some places we've been to in the Earth Kingdom." She kicked at the dust. "I don't know what's happening in my own country anymore. Maybe I've been away for too long. I feel like an outsider."

Kyoshi looked up at the second floors of the buildings and read the weathered signage hanging from the windows. There were a disproportionate number of inns for a town this size, which made sense if lots of visitors came and went. But there were also fresh banners draped from poles and awnings, displaying winged peonies, the sigil of the clan Zoryu's late mother belonged to. Their pristine state made Kyoshi think of quilts that spent most of the year in the closet, used only during special occasions.

"Is this Keohso clan territory?" she asked Rangi.

"The Keohso traditionally have the strongest influence on Shuhon Island, yes," Rangi said. "Though a lot of those flags are locals trying to win business. I'd bet they have a banner for every major clan stashed somewhere, waiting to be used."

"You know, I've never asked what clan you're from." Throughout the entire time they'd known each other, Kyoshi had failed to learn such a basic fact about her friend.

Rangi laughed. There was a roughness to the sound. "Sei'naka. Our symbol is a stylized whetstone. We come from a teeny-tiny little island to the south of the capital. Sometimes it doesn't get included on maps made in the Earth Kingdom."

She purposely let a coarse up-and-down rhythm into her accent to let Kyoshi know how great the social distance was from the royal palace, if not physical. "It has no resources to speak of, so my clan exports the talent and skills of its members. We're teachers, bodyguards, and soldiers because we have little else to fall back on. If we're not the best at what we do, then we're nothing."

Nothing. The word echoed with bitterness and dread in Rangi's throat, and through it Kyoshi saw deeper into the fires of her glowing girl than she ever had before.

It was the fear of being nothing that put the steel in Rangi's words and actions. It made her unwilling to compromise— except, apparently, on the way she talked, even though Kyoshi would fistfight anyone who thought there was *any* part of Rangi that warranted hiding. It explained the tension between her and her mother, two perfectionists under the same pressure, locked in the same cage.

"I'd like to see your home," Kyoshi said. "Your own little island. It sounds lovely."

Rangi smiled sadly. "I was going to take you there during the festival, but then this happened."

Kyoshi brushed the backs of their hands together. "Someday," she said.

They slowed down so the rest of the group could catch up, walking as five the rest of the way. The town parted to let the view of the sea in. Between the caldera and the shore, the fairgrounds of North Chung-Ling spread over the hard-packed sand. There was no ordered arrangement to the brightly colored tents and stalls. They made a forest of amusements to get lost in. Judging from the signs for games and betting and overpriced food and liquor, a heavy trail of money would be needed to navigate the maze.

It was still morning, and this town lacked the penchant for earliness associated with the rest of the Fire Nation, so the barkers and dice-dealers were still setting up. Once the fairground workers noticed the party arriving, a great hurrah rose into the air. The loud welcome was not for the Avatar or two Fire Nation nobles, but for Jinpa. The workers shouted, trying to get his attention.

"Master! Give me a blessing!"

"Master Airbender! Master Baldy! Over here!"

"I lost a koala sheep in the mountains! Give me the luck I need to find it!"

Kyoshi wasn't surprised by the reception. Outside of Yokoya, whose tightfisted residents tended to view Kelsang as a nuisance, Air Nomads were often seen by Earth Kingdom commonfolk as bearers of good fortune. Since monks and nuns would have to stop at villages across the world along their journeys from temple to temple, most peasants gladly provided Airbenders hospitality in exchange for help with chores, news and entertaining stories from other parts of the world, or a promise to relay messages to distant relatives.

Having an Air Nomad say a few words of spiritual blessing

over a new barn or baby was considered great luck among those who rarely encountered members of the wandering nation. She was glad to see the same attitude prevailed here across the sea.

Jinpa stepped forward and raised his glider-staff. "May those whom this wind touches be successful in business and health!" he shouted.

He whirled his staff with its tail fins open, creating a wide, gentle breeze that swept broadly over the fairground. It was a speedy and equitable distribution of luck, more efficient than trying to bless everyone in turn. The workers sighed and held their arms wide, trying to catch as much of the invisible wealth as possible.

Jinpa closed his staff to the enthusiastic cheers of the crowd, a more boisterous response than the muted applause the Fire nobles had given him. "I have no idea if any of that stuff works," he whispered to his group. "But it makes people happy."

"Folk here seem less uptight than in the capital," Atuat said. The stall vendors had noticed her polar origins and reasoned that if Atuat had traveled very far to be here, she must have had a lot of money. They shifted their attention away from Jinpa, who might have had the spirits on his side, but not cold hard cash.

"Water princess!" they cried at Atuat. "Queen of the snow, this way! This way for the best games, the best drinks! Only the best for a queen!"

"I really *should* be treated like royalty more," Atuat said. She smiled and waved at the workers like a dignitary stationed atop a slowly moving carriage.

"Can we trust you two to keep attention off the rest of our backs?" Hei-Ran said.

"Of course," Jinpa said. "Sifu Atuat and I will see to it that the three of you can conduct your business with discretion. She and I will— Oh dear, that's all of our money, isn't it?"

Atuat was busy dumping a large purse of coins onto a table in exchange for gambling tokens. Jinpa nodded at Hei-Ran as reassuringly as he could before joining the doctor.

Hei-Ran tried to tamp down the veins in her head with her fingers. "This is my punishment," she said. Once she'd recovered from her friend-induced headache, she led them in a meandering path through the tents, choosing lefts and rights with certainty. Occasionally she would stop and sniff at the air, her nostrils flaring.

"Yes, it smells bad here," Rangi said. "What were you expecting? We're near a rotting seaweed bed."

"What I'm looking for has no odor," Hei-Ran said. "I'm trying to see if I'm getting any dizzier."

Instead of explaining her cryptic statement, she picked her way through two stalls that weren't meant to have a path between them. Their owners didn't appreciate her crossing the lines of business, but a sharp glare from the headmistress convinced them to withhold their objections. Kyoshi felt compelled to mumble apologies as she wedged herself into the gap to keep up.

They came to a large tent all on its lonesome. It was made of cloth greased with flax oil, in the manner of ship sails designed to let as little air through them as possible. The structure looked so stained and flammable that an errant cough from a Firebender would send the whole thing up in smoke.

A sign posted outside said *Spirit Visions of the Future*. Either the characters were painted in wavy lines in a blurred approximation of a dreamlike state, or the painter simply didn't care enough to keep his strokes neat. Hei-Ran lifted the entrance flap with the tip of her cane. The three of them ducked inside.

"Welcome!" the sole occupant bellowed, throwing his arms in the air to hail his potential customers. "Are you interested in divining the secrets of the Spirit World? Do you hunger for a glimpse of the great tapestry of the future? Unlike what fraudulent soothsayers and mystics might claim, dear visitor, the power for such visions lies within *you*! For a small price, let me merely be . . . your humble GUIDE!"

"Nyahitha," Hei-Ran said. "It's me."

The man blinked, adjusting to the light they'd let in. "Oh," he said, dropping his arms. "It's you."

He was about Hei-Ran's age. His pockmarked face bore the markers of a rougher life, more days in the open sun. He was wearing costume pieces intended to mimic a Fire Sage's ceremonial outfit, a pointed hat and wide shoulder pieces over bare arms. The effect was less convincing than Chaejin's mock–Fire Lord robes.

The tent was empty except for some throw rugs and cushions. In the center, a metal device that resembled a charcoal brazier was jammed straight into the ground. There was no fuel in it though, only a small knob on the side of the pot.

Kyoshi hoped the man would offer them a seat so she could stop cricking her neck to fit inside the tent. But he and Hei-Ran opted to stare at each other in cold silence, drawing upon what were obviously old memories and intense dislikes.

"Why are you here?" Nyahitha said. He'd stopped shouting and was speaking to them in a quiet, clipped tone.

"Kuruk's reincarnation needs your help," Hei-Ran said, gesturing to Kyoshi.

That was Kyoshi's least favorite way for people to refer to her Avatarhood. But if it got her what she wanted, then fine. She bowed to Nyahitha.

The sage pretender eyed her up and down. Kyoshi had the same uncomfortable feeling of being bored into that Tagaka and Lao Ge had given her. Older folk who would find her dark depths before she could herself.

"Sit," he said. He turned his back on them and left through the rear of the tent.

They arranged themselves as best they could around the metal device. "It would be great if Kyoshi and I didn't have to waste time guessing what problems you have with this man," Rangi said. "Especially since you're the one who said we should meet him."

"It's simple," Nyahitha said, returning much quicker than Kyoshi expected. "The headmistress thinks I ruined Kuruk."

"And Sage Nyahitha believes I and the rest of Kuruk's companions did," Hei-Ran said.

Neither of them was fazed by the other's open hostility. Nyahitha laid down a tray and filled teacups for each of them. Rangi picked hers up and frowned. "Pardon me, but this is cold."

"No fires allowed," Nyahitha said. "Do not create any heat in here."

Kyoshi had never heard of a holy man of the Fire Nation eschewing flame. In fact, she was surprised he wasn't burning candles everywhere in the tent. "Why?" she asked. "What is this place?"

Nyahitha sipped his ambient-temperature tea. From his grimace, it was a concession rather than a preference. "North Chung-Ling is built over a deposit of flammable vapors. Instead of gold or silver, we have gas below our feet. If too much of it gets out in a concentrated place, a single spark will cause an explosion."

"But control the flow, and it becomes useful," Hei-Ran said.

Nyahitha shrugged. "*Useful* is a strong word. The first visitors to North Chung-Ling who reported spiritual visions likely stayed too long over cracks in the earth that let the gas rise naturally. Breathing the vapors will make you woozy and prone to hallucinating."

He flicked the bronze pot on the ground. "This gadget, however, lets me moderate how much vapor comes out of a natural spout, once I've located one."

"You're a fraud," Rangi growled, forgetting they were here to seek his assistance. "You charge people for a spiritual vision and then crank up the vapors until their eyes deceive them."

"Yes, I'm guilty of that." Nyahitha clapped his hands together. "Now, what can this old fraud do for the Avatar?"

"Mother, we are not letting this scam artist anywhere near Kyoshi." Rangi made to get to her feet.

Hei-Ran grabbed her daughter by the side-buckle of her armor and forced her back down. "Despite my personal issues with him, Nyahitha was also a true Fire Sage, next in line for High Sage before the Saowon clan played dirty with the selection process."

Kyoshi thought of Kelsang, who would have been Abbot of the Southern Air Temple before he fell from grace. "I'd like to stay," she said. Rangi huffed but made no further protest.

Nyahitha listened to Kyoshi's story from the beginning. He waited quietly and patiently, saying nothing while she told him how the blood-drinking spirit named Father Glowworm had picked her out as Kuruk's reincarnation and claimed Yun as his price for the task. Once she was done, the former sage leaned back and crossed his arms. "The curse strikes again," he muttered.

"What are you talking about?" Kyoshi said. "What curse?"

"That name you bring across my door is some very bad luck," Nyahitha said. "Kuruk tangled with many hostile spirits during his Avatarhood, and Father Glowworm was one of the worst. He never fully defeated it, and after their battle it doomed him to suffer catastrophic fortune in the physical world. Anyone he told about Father Glowworm would be cursed in the same way, anyone who even learned of its existence. I believe the intent was to isolate the Avatar from any allies he might call on to help him defeat the spirit for good."

There was an uncomfortable silence in the tent, the moment after opening a tomb.

"With all due respect, a curse?" Rangi said incredulously. "Bad luck? Are we falling to superstitions now?"

"Misfortune from the spirits is what people across the Four Nations pray to ward off every day," Nyahitha said. "Too little rain, too much rain, sickness, where the fish school—these are matters of life and death. If you don't believe in curses, look at me. I used to be a leader at the High Temple back in those days and where am I now? Kuruk didn't meet a happy end and neither did Jianzhu the Architect, if what you told me is true."

Zoryu was supposedly cursed, Kyoshi thought. Many people in the Earth Kingdom thought ill of her in a similar manner.

Fortune was an invisible, unconquerable creature that ruled commonfolk and noble alike.

"You fell due to your own vices," Hei-Ran said to Nyahitha, forgetting in anger that she was the one who had pushed for his help. "Vices that you infected Kuruk with."

"I tried to make sure at least *some* of the emptiness inside him was filled with purpose," he snapped. "You, who spent so many years with him, what did *you* produce? A good Pai Sho player? Some companions of the Avatar your lot were."

Excuses upon excuses for Kuruk. Kyoshi was sick of it. She slapped her hand on the earth beside her.

"Kuruk was responsible for himself!" she shouted. "Now, are we going to weep over what could have been for the past Avatar? Or are we going to help the current one?"

There was a hiss in reply. She'd dislodged the brazier planted in the middle of the tent. Nyahitha hastily re-centered it and tightened the valve.

"Did your boy have any strange features when you last saw him?" he asked. "Animal-like parts of his body?"

Kyoshi shook her head. "Not that I could see. But when he came back for the first time in Qinchao, there was something wrong with him. I mean palpably wrong. It was like he was making everyone around him sick and afraid."

"I've never diagnosed a case of possession in the flesh, but I suppose he could have a spirit's essence inside him. It's difficult to say."

"Please," Kyoshi said. She needed more than a cautious verdict from him. "There has to be something else you can give me. Father Glowworm has to have some kind of weakness. A way to break its hold on my friend."

She wasn't afraid of learning it would take a great battle for her to save Yun, or a quest through the worst places in the world. She was at home with such things. "I can fight it," Kyoshi said. "Just tell me how."

"I don't have that knowledge," Nyahitha said, deflating her hope. "Kuruk was the one who confronted wrathful spirits. I was just his handler on those missions."

Kyoshi wanted to scream inside the tent, took the breath to do it, until she remembered they had one last option. "Then teach me how to ask him myself."

Since he had no sleeves, Nyahitha wiped his nose on the cloth of his shoulder piece, crooking his neck. He stared at her as he did so, and Kyoshi could tell he was judging her worthiness, as if she were making the request for selfish reasons. She knew what it looked like when old folks decided a young person's fate was a light, weightless thing.

"Come back to me an hour before twilight," he said. "I can help you commune with Kuruk. Not through this noxious garbage though. Don't inhale it; it'll rot you from the inside."

"Haven't you been breathing it with every single one of your customers?" Rangi asked.

He smiled narrowly at her in response.

A commotion came from outside. It was an angry noise, the brewing of trouble to come. Nyahitha got up and peeked out the tent flap. Whatever he saw made him swear through his teeth. "What is it?" Kyoshi asked.

"Saowon," he said. "They don't normally come to North Chung-Ling."

Rangi's tongue-lashing about running into situations head-long was still fresh in Kyoshi's mind. "Can we watch from here?"

Nyahitha ran his hand through a sticky seam between the roof and the wall of the tent, letting the four of them peer through the crack. It felt a bit childish, lining up in a row to peep, but it worked. Kyoshi could see the scrubby open area that surrounded Nyahitha's stall.

Heading straight for them was a large procession of nobility. The column traveled by foot, bearing a giant palanquin swathed in red and gold silks. Surrounding it was a contingent of armored warriors.

These men and women looked ready for a battle, not a day at the beach. They held their jaws with an arrogance designed to provoke. And they were personally adorned with so many stone camellia designs that the great flapping banner of the Saowon clan they carried at the head of the procession was wholly unnecessary.

The stall vendors, who had been eager for customers earlier, were not happy to see them. Many of them left their booths and formed up a mob to meet the arriving Saowon. One middle-aged man with bushy sideburns stood at the front of the pack. He was very well-dressed compared to the rest of the fairground workers, but they seemed to rally around him rather than resent him for it.

"That's Sanshur Keohso," Nyahitha said. "He's the town's cotton merchant and the fair's main sponsor."

The palanquin came to a stop, its bearers carefully lowering the box to the ground. The occupant stepped out. She was a pretty woman with a thin, puckered face, wearing outrageously expensive robes. Kyoshi was certain she had not been at the royal palace reception. Such grandiose taste would have stood out.

"Lady Huazo," Rangi said. "Chaejin's mother. I'm not sure why she's slumming it in North Chung-Ling." Nyahitha gave her comment an angry squint but went back to watching.

Huazo and Sanshur Keohso approached each other like the principals in a duel. Speaking for the benefit of their respective contingents like stage players meant they were loud enough for Kyoshi's group to hear from inside the tent. "Master Sanshur!" Huazo said. "How good to see you. I've written you so many letters with no response, I began to worry for your health."

"My health is fine, Huazo," the fairground leader said. "And I could have saved you the visit. The answer to your inquiries, as it remains since the first time I gave it, is no. The fair is not for sale, nor the croplands. My cousins have agreed. Not a single square inch of Shuhon Island will ever fall into the hands of the Saowon."

Huazo licked her lips and grinned. "That's funny," she said. "Given how I recently purchased Master Linsu's entire salt-making operation down the shore. *And* his vacation house right here in town. I suppose he's not as loyal to his home as you are. He couldn't wait to pack up and leave this place."

Sanshur's eyes turned muddy with rage. The crowd behind him grew heated. Huazo drank in their reactions like water in a desert. "After I signed the papers, it occurred to me I should celebrate the Festival of Szeto in the newest outpost of my clan," she said. "And thus, here I am."

"With so many of your household guards," Sanshur said, staring at the Saowon force.

"For my own safety. Haven't you heard? Last night an assassin, a madman, *an Earthbender*, of all people, infiltrated the royal palace." Huazo had to cover her own mouth to keep her shock and distress from spilling out. "Members of the court were nearly killed. And it happened right under our dear Fire Lord Zoryu's nose. I'm told it was humiliating. Absolutely humiliating!"

Hei-Ran grimaced inside the tent. "Chaejin must have gotten messenger hawks out to his clan immediately after the attack. The Saowon are like shark squids when they smell blood."

"That doesn't explain why Huazo's tromping around in the middle of Keohso territory instead of seeing to her new business," Rangi said.

Kyoshi watched the news of Yun's attack ripple through the Keohso side. The fairground workers understood the implications for Zoryu's honor as well as nobles would. She became keenly aware that many of Sanshur's men were holding large hammers used to drive tent stakes into the ground, ice saws as big as swords, pieces of driftwood that served no purpose other than being heavy clubs.

"I know what she's doing," Kyoshi said. "She's picking a fight." Sometimes when a *daofei* gang wanted to go to war but cared about appearing in the right, they made themselves vulnerable by strolling through enemy streets, noses held high, hoping to provoke a small amount of violence upon themselves that could be answered with overwhelming force. Zoryu had told her this was part of the Saowon strategy. They preferred a Keohso to strike at them first.

"Watch what you say about our rightful Fire Lord," Sanshur growled.

"I'm simply stating facts," Huazo said. "Check with anyone you care to back in the capital. The Inta or the Lahaisin. I heard Lady Mizgen nearly had to have her foot amputated from her injuries. Anyway, I'm not here to debate the strength and capabilities of young Zoryu. I simply came to your lovely little village to enjoy myself and take the waters." She looked toward the sea and peered at the rancid algae foaming up on the shore. "Well . . . you know what I mean. I hope to run into you again, Master Sanshur."

She walked leisurely back to her palanquin. It looked like the crisis might have been averted, but a member of her vanguard, out of sight of his lady, made eye contact with Sanshur. Then, as a farewell, he spat on the ground.

"Please tell me that's less of an insult here than in the Earth Kingdom!" Kyoshi whispered.

Rangi and Hei-Ran gave her an answer by bursting out of the tent, making for the space between the battle lines as fast as they could. Kyoshi glanced at Nyahitha. "Go after them!" the old man yelled.

She joined the charge not a moment too soon. Several large stones flew from the Keohso side, aimed at Huazo's turned back.

With a series of punches she altered the trajectory of the rocks with immense force, sending them so far out into the ocean she couldn't hear the splashes of them land.

"Lady Huazo, is that you?" Hei-Ran cried out with exaggerated joy, making she drew more attention than the attack.

Huazo turned around with a frown. It lingered for a moment as she took in the surprise, but she quickly adjusted it into a wide smile. "Hei-Ran! As I live and breathe!"

The sudden presence of the headmistress was enough to make

Huazo's side stand down. Hands left the hilts of their swords and the soldiers stepped back to give their lady space to greet her old acquaintance. Kyoshi focused on keeping her fellow rabble in line by standing in front of the Keohso mob. They might not have known who she was, but she didn't need recognition to be intimidating. She gestured at Sanshur and his men with her eyes. *Did you see what I did to those rocks? Hmm?*

"What a wonderful surprise!" Hei-Ran said, as if she hadn't been listening in for the past few minutes. "Are you here to celebrate the holiday as well?"

"Yes, I was just telling—" Huazo stopped mid-sentence. Her eyes drifted to Hei-Ran's head. She pressed her fingers to her lips again, her shock genuine this time.

Hei-Ran stared back until it struck her. She'd forgotten her hair had been cut in dishonor. Her hands tightened around her cane. She backed away from Huazo, her eyes downcast.

Kyoshi had thought she understood the significance of the ceremony before, but she'd been wrong. Huazo was the first Fire National of notable rank they'd met since Hei-Ran lost her topknot, and the proud, invincible headmistress was acting like she no longer had the right to speak.

Huazo's stance shifted. She went from being caught off-guard by a formidable presence to having the bearing of an almsgiver in front of a wandering mendicant.

"Oh, my dear," she said softly. "Did this have anything to do with the attack on the palace?"

"It did," Hei-Ran said. She'd found her strength and calmness again. There was no shame in answering her newfound better. "Among other failures."

"How fate and fortune rule us all," Huazo said. She thought for a moment. "Hei-Ran, honor is honor, but friendship is friendship. I will never disavow you, no matter the circumstances." She reached out for an embrace, and Kyoshi was nearly ready to change her opinion of the woman.

But then Huazo used her extended hand to pat Hei-Ran on the head like she would a child. Or a pet.

Kyoshi tried to gauge Rangi's reaction, but Rangi was blank, zeroed out, a null in the ledger. Her gaze bored through Huazo and into the stars beyond. If she wasn't moving, if she wasn't immediately challenging Huazo to an Agni Kai, then it was acceptable for Huazo to treat Hei-Ran like this. According to the rules of etiquette, it was acceptable.

Hei-Ran didn't look perturbed at all. She endured Huazo's ruffle of her shortened locks with nary a frown. She was less upset than the Keohso commoners, who murmured and scowled at the ungraciousness on display.

After what felt like an eternity, Huazo let go. She turned to examine the rest of Hei-Ran's group. "That would make you the Avatar," she said to Kyoshi. After what she'd done, the rules of introduction were an afterthought.

"I am," Kyoshi said, finding it difficult to speak with Rangi in turmoil a few feet away. "I suppose your son wrote to you about me."

"He did! Our family is twice-blessed for both of us to meet you in such a short time."

"When you write him back, give him a message for me." Kyoshi hardened her gaze. "Tell him he makes a good Fire Sage. And nothing more."

Huazo's lips parted as she figured out what Kyoshi was saying. It was interesting to watch her mind work and her face try to hide it, deducing what the Avatar knew and what her son might have revealed. The conclusion that she would have to go through Kyoshi to get to Zoryu didn't worry her in the slightest.

A happy noise came from Rangi, so out of place that Kyoshi nearly drew her weapons in surprise. "Koulin!" Rangi's feet dug into the sand as she ran to meet one of Huazo's guards on the far edge of the formation. She was a girl their age who was equally delighted to see her. She had a round, pleasant face and wore her hair almost identical to Rangi's.

"Rangi!" The two girls nearly collided. They clutched each other's hands and grinned, oblivious to their surroundings. The sudden turnaround in Rangi's mood was bizarre.

"My niece, Koulin," Huazo explained to Kyoshi. "Those two were the same year at the academy. The bonds forged in school, over the anvil of education, are stronger than any other. I'm sure you understand."

Huazo would have known that, as an Earth Kingdom peasant, the odds of Kyoshi having a level of formal education similar to Rangi or Koulin were nil. Her petty dig hurt less than the way Rangi's face shone for her friend. She couldn't remember ever being greeted in such a manner.

Seeing she'd scored a hit, Huazo decided to leave on a high note. She made a show of covering her small-mouthed yawn. "Apologies, Avatar; I'm so exhausted from my journey. I should make for my lodgings. I'm sure I'll see you and your companions during the festivities. Koulin! Come now."

Rangi and Koulin reluctantly pulled themselves apart. Huazo got back in her palanquin. Kyoshi, with feet planted, watched the laborious, lengthy process of the Saowon contingent reorganizing itself. It turned its head like the slowest serpent in the world, without any spitting this time, and marched back to town.

Sanshur Keohso suddenly appeared by Kyoshi's side, gazing at the retreating column with her, as if the task of seeing off the Saowon had required the two of them equally. "Fork-tongued fiends, they are. I'm glad the Avatar's here to keep them in line."

She glared at him. "It was your side I caught throwing rocks!"

"Huazo and her clan have been biting off chunks of the other islands like lion vultures!" he said, as if that was an excuse for the behavior of his kin. "I'll be a cremated pile of ashes before I let her have Shuhon! Her and that by-blow son of hers!"

"We're not rubes!" another man shouted from the fairground crowd. "We know about the dirty tricks Chaejin the Usurper is pulling in court!"

"We support the legitimate Fire Lord Zoryu, long may his flame burn," Sanshur said. "Are you going to tell us we're wrong for being loyal to the crown?"

"The Fire Lord doesn't need you starting violence for him!"

"So we should let them insult us? Like what she did to your companion?"

Kyoshi had no answer for that. She looked to Rangi and Hei-Ran, but they said nothing. There must have been some kind of Fire Nation rule at work where they couldn't in good conscience tell their own countrymen how to interpret their personal dishonor.

"Don't worry!" Sanshur declared. "We've got your back against the Ma'inka worms! You can count on us!" The fairground workers rattled their tools, shouting praises of the Avatar and the Fire Lord while heaping scorn upon the Saowon.

Hei-Ran stepped closer to Kyoshi. "Let's just leave," she whispered. "Remember we have a mission here. If we get caught up in this nonsense, we'll make it worse."

"Are you sure? Sanshur's men seem really riled up."

"It's not Sanshur's men I'm worried about."

Hei-Ran glanced at her daughter. Rangi stared out to sea, lost somewhere in the churning waves.

Leaving wasn't easy. They had to wander the tents, looking for Atuat and Jinpa. They found them near the gambling tents offering the highest stakes. The monk appeared to have aged a decade, sweat and furrows marking his brow.

"I had a run of bad luck," Atuat explained. "But Jinpa here got us back to breakeven."

The remnants of shock lingered on his face, like he'd witnessed the desecration of a holy relic. "I've . . . never seen anyone play Pai Sho quite like the doctor. You'd almost have to be a genius at the game to do what she did."

At this point Kyoshi was simply glad the two of them hadn't drowned in the sea or gotten stuck in a hole. They headed back to town. As they walked, Hei-Ran gave Kyoshi another meaningful look. Rangi was storming off ahead of the group.

Kyoshi caught up with her but was at a loss for what to say. "It's nice to know there's at least one tolerable Saowon," she ventured. "Koulin must remind you of the good old academy days."

"Kyoshi," Rangi said slowly. "I was *miserable* at the academy."

"What?" She nearly stopped in her tracks. "Weren't you the number one student in your class? Didn't you graduate from officer's school early?"

"Those things aren't mutually exclusive," Rangi said. "I had motivation to get the scores I did. I couldn't get out of that place fast enough."

There must have been signs Kyoshi missed along the way. How else could she have misunderstood such an integral part of Rangi's life so badly? "I'm sorry. I—I didn't know."

"It's not your fault. I've only mentioned bits and pieces of those days, never the full story." Her tone was carefully measured, composed with effort. "You do remember when I told you the other students used to spread rumors and gossip about my mother, right?"

"I do." It had been a secret shared on an iceberg drifting in the ocean, the two of them lying under the same blanket together. Not circumstances easily forgotten.

Rangi jutted her chin in the direction of the town. Kyoshi knew she was pointing at Koulin, wherever Huazo's niece was. "It's a Saowon signature technique. Delivering insults with plausible deniability. There were some vicious little monsters at school, but her, she was the worst."

"You couldn't . . . call her out?" Kyoshi wasn't sure at what age the Fire Nation allowed Agni Kais. And after what she'd personally been through on the *lei tai*, she had mixed feelings about the practice of duels in general. But she assumed the behavior Rangi was describing would have ended in some kind of challenge.

Rangi shook her head. "She was careful not to say anything to my face that warranted it. She left that to cronies who were too weak for me to confront without looking like a bully. I know exactly how Lord Zoryu feels, trying to win a war of insults against an enemy he can't confront."

She bit her lip, trying to convince herself more than anyone. "And what could I have done, really? I was the headmistress's daughter. Any fights I got into would have reflected poorly on her, or made it look like I was abusing my status. Was I supposed to go whining to a teacher that the other kids were saying mean things about my mother?"

Kyoshi couldn't believe it. "I thought the academy was this . . . this wonderful experience that shaped you."

"It did. I learned everything I know there. But I wasn't happy until I left and found a purpose on the outside." She gave Kyoshi a tilted smile full of heartbreak. "Serving the Avatar."

Kelsang used to say there was pain and joy in all things, often when trying to comfort Kyoshi about her earliest years in Yokoya. During her visit to the Fire Nation, Kyoshi had been thrilled each time she discovered another little cache of information about Rangi, like unearthing another bit of treasure. But under the shine was life, grubby and dirty and impossible to burnish.

She would take it anyway. Along with everything else about her girl, no matter how unexpected or painful. It took every ounce of her willpower not to lean over and give the Firebender a forbidden kiss on the top of her head.

Together they walked down the street that bisected the guest districts, cutting across the wedges of restaurants and shops. Rangi pointed out some festival-related traditions they saw along the way. Paper streamers strung over doorways were meant to comb the entering visitors for good luck. Shopkeepers cooked pots of beans to represent the inventories being counted. The dark, sugary drinks sold everywhere symbolized the prodigious amount of ink Avatar Szeto used over his career. Had it not been for the unpleasantness by the beach, they could have pretended they were here to enjoy themselves.

But reality intruded yet again, once they rounded the corner of the inn they were staying at. A huddle of men came into view. Kyoshi could tell from the clouds of dust and swearing, the way their fists rose and fell, what lay at the center of the ring. Their victim.

She lowered her shoulder into two of the men at once, sending them flying away from the group. Rangi took the other two attackers by the backs of their collars and yanked down, slamming them to the ground.

Kyoshi expected the dazed and bleeding youth they'd been beating to be a Saowon, isolated from Huazo's group, but judging from his clothes he was a local like the other four men. "What is going on here?" she bellowed.

"We caught this traitor putting up a stone camellia banner over his stall!" said one of the men wriggling in Rangi's grasp.

"I just wanted some business," mumbled the young vendor as he shakily got to his knees.

"And that was more important to you than the honor of your clan? No nephew of mine is going to toady up to the Saowon!"

The ringleader tried to kick more dust in the direction of his beaten kinsman.

Kyoshi shared a worried look with Rangi. It had taken less than an hour since the arrival of the Saowon for a fight to break out, and it hadn't even been between rival clans. Kyoshi could see the grains of violence crystallizing into a fuller shape. Under their feet, North Chung-Ling was priming to explode.

SPIRITUAL EXERCISES

"IT DOESN'T surprise me they were related," Nyahitha said when Kyoshi told him about the act of battery she'd stopped. "Enemies are enemies, but no one can shame you like your own family."

She and Rangi had immediately hauled the offenders to the town jail. But the local judge's indifferent response to the crime and his strong family resemblance to the uncle of the victim meant it was unlikely they'd be locked up for longer than overnight. She would have to remember the troublemakers' faces if she saw them around town in the morning.

Kyoshi followed Nyahitha on a narrow path that crept along the rim of the caldera. It was just the two of them. Her entire party had shown up to his tent at the appointed time. He'd taken one look at the motley group before declaring that spiritual breakthroughs were not a group activity. He would need the Avatar alone.

Climbing up here had been sweaty work in the humidity of the island. It was easier to talk now, exposed to cooling breezes that ran across the edges of the cliff heights. "It's not a good sign though," Nyahitha said. "Fights don't usually break out until later in the festival, once the alcohol starts flowing. I'm sure you have plenty of drunken aggression in the Earth Kingdom, but here, where you've got to avenge every stupid slight upon your name . . ." He grimaced. "I tell you, I don't love that part about my country."

Kyoshi knew the feeling. The Earth Kingdom's hidebound, corrupt habits had caused her no end of grief. "At least there won't be any Agni Kais," Nyahitha said. "It's a spiritual offense to burn another person during a holiday."

They walked farther until they came to a bluff that overlooked a growing plain, a flattened gentle slope that bore the marks of plow and hoe. Most of the ground had been upturned and emptied.

"There's not enough light to see it clearly now, but over there are the melonyam fields," Nyahitha said, pointing to a still-green patch on the opposite side of the village. "They're an extremely sensitive crop, so they stay in the ground until the very end of the festival. I'd be surprised if they even survive that long though. This town is withering, Avatar. The tourist money helps, but it's not enough."

"Do you think the rumors are true? Could the spirits be angry at Lord Zoryu for some reason?"

"*Man guesses, spirits act,*" Nyahitha said, trotting out an old expression. "You could try asking them yourself once you figure out how." He pointed to a stump on another nearby clearing. "That's where we'd tie up your flying bison, if you had one."

Kyoshi frowned. "I do have a bison. Or at least access to one."

"What?!" Nyahitha's shout echoed in the evening air. "Why didn't you say so? We've been hiking for an hour! We could have flown here in minutes!"

"You didn't tell me where we were going! I thought the walking was part of the spiritual exercise!"

The two of them held back from swearing at each other. Between the Flying Opera Company's obsession with Pengpeng and Nyahitha's grumbling that she hadn't brought Yingyong, Kyoshi was beginning to think the world would be better off if the Avatar simply reincarnated as a sky bison from now on. At least then it would be universally beloved.

"All right, just sit," Nyahitha said. "Anywhere is fine as long as you give me some space in front of you."

Kyoshi took her position. "We're not doing incense, are we?" She'd had bad experiences with incense, to say the least.

"No, we're not doing incense." Nyahitha's approach seemed to forgo as many spiritual trappings as possible. He'd left behind his ridiculous fake Fire Sage outfit and wore a simple cotton robe, notably devoid of any clan symbols.

"You know, I just thought of something," Kyoshi said as he sat down across from her. "If it doesn't work out with Kuruk, you could guide me to Yangchen. She mediated between humans and spirits."

Nyahitha let out a long hiss through his teeth. "I . . . don't think Yangchen will be as much help as you think."

"That's nonsense. Yangchen was the perfect Avatar." Or at least better than Kuruk in every way possible. "She'd be able to help me somehow."

"If you reached her, maybe. Some sages, including me, believe you have to go down the chain of your past lives in reverse order if you want to communicate with them. You can't talk to Yangchen or the older Avatars before you manage to connect with Kuruk."

"Great!" Kyoshi said, throwing up her hands and breaking her meditative posture. "So on top of everything else, Kuruk's a wall keeping me from my full potential!"

"He's not a— I swear, I would have known you were his reincarnation from the start and saved the Earth Kingdom a lot of trouble had they brought you before me! You two are *exactly* alike!"

Kyoshi sputtered, indignant to her very core. How dare—the nerve of him to insinuate such a—

Nyahitha quickly constructed a list on his fingers. "You both idolize Yangchen to a fault, you're both stubborn as rocks when it comes to what you want, and neither of you have any control over your emotions! Mark my words, you're going to botch up bad someday because of your personal feelings, just like he did!"

"I'm glad you could tell all of that from the *two* conversations we had!" Kyoshi had thought the days of mystical tutors unilaterally declaring who she *really* was inside were over, but apparently not. "Now can we get down to business?"

Nyahitha wiped his mouth and calmed himself into a state more becoming of an Avatar's spiritual guide. "There's a number of ways Kuruk might talk to us," he explained. "The most straightforward is if you were to simply have a vision of him. This method tends to be successful in locations with meaning for the past Avatars. This spot right here was where Kuruk would meditate and recover from his own spiritual journeys."

A vision in an important location to the Water Avatar. That could explain his appearance in the Southern Air Temple. And, she thought with some displeasure, the wreckage he'd made of Yangchen's island.

"The downside is that any messages you get from a vision tend to be one-way only," Nyahitha said. "Not as useful if you have to ask him questions. Another way to have more of a conversation is if he took over your body and spoke to me in person. I would have to relay whatever you want to ask him."

Kyoshi frowned. She was distinctly uncomfortable with the idea of being possessed by someone else. Kuruk was one of the last people she wanted controlling her body, even if he was her own past life.

Nyahitha noticed her reluctance. "If you don't like that, the final method, which is the most difficult and least likely to happen after one session of practice, is if you managed to meditate your way into the Spirit World. There, you could talk to him face-to-face. This is the level of communing that most people associate with the Avatar's abilities. It's the most efficient and clear way to draw on the wisdom of previous generations."

He paused.

"But?" Kyoshi asked.

"Kuruk's spirit isn't necessarily going to be there to greet you. And your body is rendered physically helpless while your spirit is on the other side. And sometimes you don't remember anything you learned once you come back to the physical world."

Maybe she was better off inhaling the gas inside the dirty tent. "Communing doesn't sound like the great and useful power it's described to be."

"Nothing is useful until you practice it." Nyahitha brought

his hands together, fingers to fingers, palm to palm. After a deep breath he drew them apart, creating a small, flickering fire in the empty space. It hovered in the air, the size and gentleness of a candle flame.

His voice lost its cantankerous edge. "Focus your attention on this single flame," he said. "It is one flame, and it is many. It changes with every moment."

Kyoshi relaxed into the shape of her guide's words. "No fire is ever the same fire," Nyahitha said. "No Avatar is ever the same person. You and the flame change with every moment, every generation. *You* are one flame, and you are many."

The sounds pouring forth from Nyahitha turned into echoes of themselves, an overtone, a reverberation. They lost their meaning and found their weight. "One and many. You are the flame. One out of many, one and the many."

The clouds picked up speed. The trees whispered in her ears. The stars winked, yawned, and turned in for the night. Nyahitha's voice became her own. She was repeating after him unbidden, and crowds of her selves shouted back in response, a swearing-in ceremony where she was the leader and follower at once.

And then.

THE MESSAGE

THE ICE of Agna Qel'a was so clear and pure Kyoshi instinctively rubbed her arms to warm them. Despite the sudden shift, the yanking of her mind across the world, she knew exactly where she was and what she was looking at. She had the certainty of being here before.

Kuruk sat at a great feast, long tables of ice laid out with raw and roasted meats, choice slivers of fish. To him and the rest of his kinsmen, the glacial hall was warm and bright as could be with the heat from dozens of blubber lamps, and they laughed at the shivering foreign dignitaries in red furs and green coats who tried to raise their cups with their thick mittens for toasts. Over the course of the night he pried at his elders, asking them, How did you know? What were the signs? *He hadn't ever bent the other elements until they told him to try, confident in his success. Weeks ago, he'd been astonished*

*when the glowing crystal they gave him rose into the air under
his command.*

*The sages of the Northern Water Tribe only gave him mis-
chievous grins in response and assured him the unrevealed
procedure had gone flawlessly, an auspicious sign for his era.
Yangchen's successor would be worthy of her legacy and her
peace would continue for a hundred generations. Kuruk gave
up, smiled, and nodded. Though tonight was meant to be a celebration, everyone else's absolute certainty in him kept the joy
from fully reaching his heart.*

Kyoshi was watching a memory of her past life. She stared at
a young Kuruk from every angle at once, recognizing what was
going through his mind with each twitch of his handsome face.

"Kuruk!" she tried shouting, to no effect. Her voice left her
body, but there was no round trip, no echo. These were images,
not people who could hear her and talk back. She was imprisoned, an audience in someone else's performance, forced to
watch a play she had no chance of altering.

*Earthbending came so easy for him. Too easy. The rocks
danced at his command, but his form was improper, his wiz-
ened master from Ba Sing Se grunted. Too loose and wiggly,
not enough stamping around. He wasn't adopting the attitude
of an Earthbender. Kuruk struggled with why the influence of
his waterbending style was considered a detriment to the other
forms of bending. The elements—they were all connected. One
flowed into the next, sharing the same energy. He wished his
older teachers could see that. To be of one mind instead of four,
wasn't that the strength of the Avatar? To constantly switch your
identity back and forth,* Waterbender-Earthbender-Waterbender-
Firebender-Airbender, *the strain would tear you apart.*

Surprisingly, the only person who agreed with him was a younger member of the Earth Kingdom delegation, some prissy kid from the Gan Jin tribe. Despite the difference in their personalities, Kuruk began to hang out with Jianzhu more and more. It was clear the uptight boy needed a friend. And the Avatar needed one too. He had plenty of people who liked him, but that wasn't the same thing as true friendship.

It took a surprisingly long time for the two of them to sit down at a Pai Sho table together. By the time the first game concluded, Kuruk's bond with Jianzhu was absolute.

The two of them put on their masks and suffered through the lecturing of their elders all the way through his mastery of fire and air. Best to simply comply than fight tradition along every single front. He pretended to be a model student in front of his teachers, held his tongue on corrections he could have made to their forms. He even invented a technique that could have earned him arrows, a way to create a cushion of air under a heavy object so it could be slid and moved over a floor with ease. A perfect way to arrange all those statues they had lying around the Air Temples.

The people who knew Kuruk as a child would have been surprised at his good behavior. There was a reason for it though, a reward that lay at the end of the elemental cycle. A sky bison. You could have all sorts of adventures once you had a flying mount at your disposal. The world opened up, unconstrained by distance.

That was how one of the junior monks of the Southern Air Temple caught him and Jianzhu sneaking into the pen, hoping to experiment with a joyride, and pinned them to the wall with a blast of air that rippled their cheeks for minutes on end.

Jianzhu's hair stuck up like cactus thorns as the two of them knelt in front of the abbot of the temple and Kuruk's elders, trembling at what punishments they might receive. Idiots, *they were told.* Every Avatar normally did a bit of independent traveling; they could have simply waited for their chance. Now, on their first trip, they were going to get chaperoned into oblivion.

The monk who had roughed them up so badly was assigned as a companion to the Avatar, despite his protests that he wanted nothing to do with two bison thieves. They were shocked to learn he was the same age as them, his hulking size and enviable beard making him seem older. It was a good punishment. The Avatar had this Kelsang fellow pegged for a no-fun grump.

"No!" Kyoshi thrashed back and forth, unable to break free. "*NO!*"

She had weathered the nausea of having to look at a younger version of Jianzhu smile and enjoy himself. She'd swallowed her hate by reminding herself the man was dead. But seeing Kelsang again was too much.

She couldn't warn him of the monster sliding into his life in the disguise of a friend. She couldn't change his fate. She was watching a wave crash inexorably against the shore, where it would break up and dissipate, irrecoverable.

The last member of their group would be an adult. The three of them would be accompanied by one of the strictest, harshest senior teachers at the Royal Academy. A Sei'naka man. The most powerful clan heads in the Fire Nation thought twice about trifling with a Sei'naka. But as fate would have it, the man got sick. He sent a younger relative in his stead, assuring them the arrangement would be only temporary. Kuruk knew he had to pull every string he could to make it permanent once he saw Hei-Ran.

He was convinced the spirits had given him a vision that day in First Lord's Harbor. The girl who arrived was a walking dream of night-black hair and fierce lips and eyes that cut like knives. He had to ask quickly. He had to make her feelings clear, while his heart pounded in his chest like a battle drum giving him the courage to approach someone so beautiful. He turned on his charm, a weapon that had never failed him in the past.

It took less than a minute for Hei-Ran to coldly proclaim she wasn't interested in a relationship with the Avatar. Jianzhu and Kelsang bonded for the first time over their mutual friend's misery, slapping each other's backs and laughing at how brutally he'd been shot down. But while the two of them had their fun, they'd missed Hei-Ran giving Kuruk a slow blink, a smirk, and a little comment that romance was forbidden . . . while on duty.

Finally, world travel on a bison. As the breeze ruffled their hair, the sun warm on their skin, Kuruk surprised his companions by asking for more bending training. Why? they asked. They were young, not the established experts in their disciplines. And Kuruk was a bending prodigy, already a master of all four elements. What need did he have for further practice?

He explained that the distinction between the best Pai Sho grandmasters and those journeymen who were only mediocre was that the true geniuses simply played more games than their lower-ranked counterparts did. They never stopped learning. Jianzhu, Kelsang, Hei-Ran—they could make the Avatar better. They could make each other better. Constant challenge was the key to growth.

And so they practiced along the stops of their journeys. They practiced with each other, identifying and correcting and destroying each other's habits, until it felt like the four of them could speak without speaking, their spirits merging into a single pool. Kuruk knew his companions had the potential for greatness, unorthodoxy, far beyond what their elders expected or even wanted of them.

Kelsang confirmed it one night when he admitted he'd visited the Spirit World unintentionally. His descriptions of colorful, translucent creatures, talking plants, shifting landscapes, had confused and upset the older monks who thought of the realm outside the physical as an austere place of blankness mirroring the detachment of the visitor.

That was exactly it, Kuruk said. The instant the facts disagreed with their preconceived notions, people lost their minds. That settled it. Kelsang was going to guide the Avatar to the Spirit World.

The monk agreed readily, eager for someone to share in the wonders he'd seen rather than ridicule him for it. They picked a meadow in the Earth Kingdom near Yaoping where it was said Yangchen liked to practice using the Avatar State to power her airbending. Kelsang and Kuruk sat on the grass, facing each other.

Though the exercise had been his idea, Kuruk didn't still himself into meditation right away. He took a moment to watch Kelsang's breathing rustle the coarse hairs of his mustache. He felt Jianzhu and Hei-Ran's eyes on his back, their gazes filled with warmth.

His friends. He loved them so much. Life was good. It was simply good, and the world was a wonderful place.

had the potential for great spiritual discipline," he said as he continued picking his way through the narrow path. "You must have had a good teacher showing you the fundamentals."

His pity was worse than his antagonism. "You're not the first old man I've meditated with, if that's what you mean." She'd learned at the feet of a supposed immortal. It would have reflected poorly on her if she hadn't picked up a trick or two about the inner mind.

Nyahitha shrugged. "Whoever it was has my regards. I could feel the veil between worlds thinning around your shoulders, Avatar. The spirits of the islands came through and spoke to you tonight. It's just a matter if you can decipher their hidden messages."

Dawn breaking further put the rugged handsomeness of the Fire Islands on full display. The sun gilded the fields below them, and from this high up, the disk of North Chung-Ling looked like an artist's gentle stamp on a nature painting. But as the glare in her eyes lessened, restoring the farmed land to its natural colors, a jarring discrepancy arose.

Kyoshi stopped where she was and pointed at the hillside melonyam field. "Did the spirits do that?" she asked. "Because if they did, I think their message is pretty clear."

The melonyam leaves created a dense blanket of vegetation over the soil. But many of the plants had, in a single night, dried and turned sickly yellow in swathes that stood out clearly against their green surroundings. From this distance, the dying crops formed patterns that looked like giant brushstrokes.

And the perfectly legible characters they spelled out were *Hail Fire Lord Chaejin.*

INTERLUDE: SURVIVAL

YUN THREW up his hands as Father Glowworm bore down on him. *This is it*, he thought. *This is where it ends.* The boy who'd turned out to be nothing would fittingly vanish without a trace.

But his body was stronger than his will. Out of sheer memory and practice, the forms carved into his muscles and bones, his gesture of surrender turned into a Sky Piercing Fist, an uppercut.

The earth. The earth that loved him when nothing else would. He should have known that even in his lowest moment, he would never be abandoned by his element. A focused blast of mud and loosened rocks lashed Father Glowworm across the iris. The spirit shrieked and halted its charge.

Yun stared at his own hand in shock, as if this were the very first act of moving earth he'd ever performed. Tears welled in his eyes, blurring his vision.

"Oh look." He wiped his face with his arm and sniffed. "I can bend here."

The duel raged for three days and three nights is how his fable would have gone, if told by another.

In truth, he didn't know how long he battled Father Glowworm. Time seemed to work differently here. At one point he remembered crawling on his hands and knees for the edge of the swamp, willing to put his lips to the bottom of a puddle, needing to drink more than he wanted to defend himself. But tendrils of slime had blocked his path, forcing him to turn and continue to fight. It was no longer about predator and prey, but whose hatred and stubbornness would see them through.

Yun had to strategize which parts of his body he could sacrifice, like he was one of the wound dummies he and Master Amak used to practice on. A twisted elbow was better than a broken rib. Bleeding from the head was fine but he had to protect his arteries. Above all, he could not lose consciousness, whether to exhaustion or a knockout blow.

And he gave as good as he got. He battered the spirit with columns of solid stone, sprayed it with clouds of pebbles, nearly caught it in a giant hand of mud. An observation throughout the fight gave him slivers of hope, peeking through like rays of sunshine. Every time he struck home and truly wounded the spirit, it shrunk in size. A marker of progress.

"So," Yun wheezed during a lull while bent at the waist and heaving for breath. "How do I stack up against Kuruk?" His blood and sweat dripped off the tip of his nose, pattering and mingling on the ground. "I have it on good authority I'm his equal when it comes to earthbending."

His enemy continued to flit through the trees, but at a slower, ragged pace. The spirit had lost control over much of its slime. It had fewer weapons to work with. "You presumptuous little stain. If Avatar Kuruk hadn't weakened me all those years ago, I would have finished you in an instant."

"And yet here I am!" Yun screamed, wasting precious air, agonizing his own torn muscles. "How inconvenient for you!"

Father Glowworm chuckled, knowing Yun could have been addressing someone else. "Yes," the spirit said, considering his words. "You are more trouble than you're worth. There are easier meals to be had."

It gapped itself between two slender trunks, looking like a vertical squint of contemplation. Father Glowworm had started the battle the size of a wagon wheel but was now no bigger than an overgrown calabash. "What do you say to a truce of sorts? I have a proposition for you."

After earthbending and Pai Sho, dealmaking was what Yun excelled at. He pressed a thumb to one nostril and expelled a clot of blood from the other. "I'm listening."

"I can grant you some of my power. You'd be able to create passage between the worlds of human and spirit. In return, you would bring people to me. Not many. I don't want to become well known."

I could get back home. Sacrificing innocents did not sit with Yun, but it was important to hear the other side's entire terms during a negotiation, no matter how outrageous. "What does it take? For you to give me such power?"

"Our forms would need to intertwine, but only briefly. It's a simple act. A physical one."

"You would . . . possess me? Pass through me?"

"Call it whatever you wish. As long as we both let our guards down long enough to merge together."

The spirit turned magnanimous with its explanation, revealing more than it felt was needed. "You might notice some changes to your physical nature as a result, but it's no issue. If anything, you'd become stronger."

Yun knew a double-edged statement when he heard one. But keeping his good looks was not a concern. He fought through the pain in his arm and held his hands up. No sudden earthbending moves. "I accept."

Father Glowworm relaxed its tendrils. A layer of slime blanketed the ground. "Come closer."

Yun approached slowly. Scattered teeth rolled under his feet and trails of mucus clung to his soles. Nestled in the fork of a tree, Father Glowworm pulsed with anticipation. The branches surrounding it looked like part of a face. During their fight it had never left the partial cover of the grove. Yun remembered how the spirit had preferred to remain within the stone tunnel Jianzhu had opened in the mountain, back in Xishaan. An unprotected eye needed a socket.

A welcoming energy radiated from the spirit, promising terrible transformation, the liquid dissolution and rebirth of a larva wrapped in its cocoon. It had opened to him. It had made itself ready for its end of the bargain.

So had Yun.

He threw his hands apart. The entire floor of the grove followed them. The ground layer containing the roots of the trees washed to the left and right, dividing right down the middle in a line that ran under Father Glowworm.

The spirit suddenly had its clothing and protection stripped away by the tidal act of earthbending. It fell to the new level of ground Yun created and howled in surprise.

Yun nearly did the same. The brute force act had taken every ounce of his power. Kyoshi could have done it easily. But the effort of washing away the topsoil had almost killed him.

He had one last move to make. Hurling his arms back together, in a hug almost, he caught Father Glowworm in the jaws of an earthen vise. Crushed in his stony grip, the spirit shrank further.

"Wretched boy!" The spirit wriggled with impotent fury. "I offered you power and you resort to tricks? Not even Kuruk would have disgraced himself in such an— *aaagh!*"

Yun closed his thumb and forefinger. The boulders squeezed closer together. "Shut up about Kuruk."

Under his unrelenting pressure, Father Glowworm had been crushed down to the volume of a sea prune. "Stop! Without merging with me you can't return to your home!"

"I know." Yun reached out and plucked the shrunken eye from the rock. It was wet and sticky like a sea prune too. "It's just going to be on my terms, not yours."

"What are you doing!?" Father Glowworm shrieked in his fingers, no less loud for its diminished size.

"Exactly what you were going to do to me." Without giving it any further consideration, Yun popped the eyeball into his mouth.

The sphere burst between his teeth. The bitter taste of the jelly inside washed over his tongue and a scream rang through his limbs, vibrating his bones like the strings of an *erhu*. The sickly clouds overhead fled for the cover of the horizon. He could feel the trees hiding their faces in shame.

He didn't need to be told by an older, wiser master to understand. Combining with an immortal being in such a sacrilegious way created a permanent hole in the weave. It was a crime against order. An abhorrent violation of spiritual balance.

Yun swallowed his mouthful and let change overcome him. He'd never been a picky eater.

RESIGNATION

KYOSHI AND Nyahitha ran down the mountain as fast as his old bones would let them. Which, in his panic, was surprisingly fast.

"The spirits speak in subtle ways, do they?" she yelled at him. She skidded over a patch of wet rock, nearly turning her ankles. What she would have given for the hidden forces behind the movement of the world to stay hidden in her life.

"This isn't a spiritual message! It's a declaration of war! If either the Saowon *or* the Keohso see this, North Chung-Ling will drown in blood!"

He was right. Chaejin had been working the angle of being favored by entities beyond the physical realm. The sudden, inexplicable appearance of this message overnight would infuriate Zoryu's supporters and embolden his own. If a single misplaced banner could cause a fight to break out, a provocation of this size could be the prelude to a full-blown riot.

It didn't make sense why spirits would care which brother sat on the throne. Did Chaejin's training at the High Temple earn him some kind of goodwill with the islands themselves? Had he struck some kind of supernatural bargain? Despite the visions she'd had, the foe she was trying to rescue Yun from, she couldn't bring herself to believe the spirits would scrawl someone's name into the landscape like a vandal. And it didn't seem like Nyahitha did either.

It occurred to her she had no way of undoing the message. Not unless she was willing and capable of destroying the entire hillside or setting the last remaining crops of a hungry village ablaze. She could see Chaejin's smug grin, taunting her as she ran. *The Avatar can't fight history.*

She and Nyahitha were only hurrying toward the inevitable. By the time they reached the village center, astonished people were already stumbling out of their homes to stare at the giant writing.

Nyahitha came to a stop and doubled over, his hands on his knees. "We're too late," he said over his heaving gasps for breath. Inhaling so much gas could not have been good for his endurance.

"Find my friends and tell them what happened." The Avatar was going to be needed here in the middle of North Chung-Ling. The Saowon and Keohso clansmen were beginning to gather in force.

From one side of the square, Sanshur and a very large group of toughs filed in. These were battle-scarred men Kyoshi hadn't seen before at the fair, or around town. Based on the way they carried themselves, she guessed they were seasoned fighters and guardsmen that must have come from other settlements on

Shuhon Island. After seeing Huazo arrive yesterday, Sanshur had called for backup from his clan.

The Saowon contingent packed the opposite end, basking in what the dawn had brought. The men behind Huazo and Koulin laughed and cheered for the ostensible will of the spirits. It was too early for anyone to have put on armor, so they were dressed in wide-sleeved cotton summer robes printed with bright red and white stone camellias. The disparity between the Saowon's crisp, boldly dyed fabrics and the faded, tattered rags of the Keohso locals made the choice of clothing look more like mockery than fitting in.

"Sanshur!" Huazo called out. For a delicate-looking person, she had a powerful voice when she needed it. "Look at what the spirits have wrought!"

"Spirits nothing!" Sanshur screamed, his face as scarlet as Huazo's outer jacket. "Mark my words; this is Saowon treachery and naught else!" His outrage couldn't hide the fact that he was speaking for the benefit of the villagers who weren't die-hard Keohso loyalists. He was deathly afraid of the stain this message would leave on his clan.

Men who were fearful for their image tended to act rashly, and in this regard Sanshur was no different than the boy in Loongkau who'd attacked Kyoshi with a rusty *dao*. At his signal the Keohso battle line began edging forward.

Huazo wasn't fazed. The smirk she shared with her niece said she wanted this clash just as much as Sanshur. "Why don't we ask the Avatar how to interpret these symbols? She's right over there. Avatar Kyoshi! You can read, can you not? How should we interpret this miracle? Do you think our dear, departed Lord Chaeryu might be speaking to us from the great beyond?"

Kyoshi tried to come up with a relevant answer that would both make her sound like a spiritual authority and change the direction this encounter was heading, but there was nothing she could say as loudly as an entire hillside. She ran into the middle of the shrinking space between the two clans.

"Stand down, all of you!" she shouted. Kuruk's memories had been a stage play, but here she was the actor now, not the audience. And a bad performance could lead to a national disaster. "I want everyone to go back to their rooms immediately!"

"Right, because there's nothing to see here!" a Saowon man hooted.

"Get out of the way, Avatar!" Sanshur yelled. "This isn't a foreigner's business! Insults and perfidy of this size need to be answered, holy day or not!"

The taboo against Agni Kais during the festival was working against her. Another time of the year, the clans could have satisfied their honor through the firebending duel. Without the release the ritual provided, the situation was dissolving into something more dangerous and unknowable.

Huazo stood fast. Her men streamed past her like river water around a stone. Koulin marched at their head, the older Saowon warriors confident in her as the point of their spear.

Kyoshi heard footsteps rushing at her from behind. It was Rangi. Without so much as a nod, her bodyguard stepped neatly in to cover her flank, fitting to the Avatar as closely as a hilt to a blade. She looked haggard and exhausted, like she'd spent all night awake worrying about Kyoshi's spiritual trials. But she was here, thank the stars. Now, together, they stood a chance at keeping the peace.

The two clans closed in, catching them between the jaws of a vise. "Listen to the Avatar!" Rangi shouted at the Keohso. As a member of the Fire Nation and a neutral clan, hopefully she could arbitrate successfully. "Kyoshi is the highest-ranking Firebender present, peer to the crown, and the final word when it comes to the spirits! You are beholden to her as much as you would be to Szeto himself!"

She turned to address the Saowon and her former classmate. "Koulin," Rangi pleaded quietly. "Help us stop this. You don't need to bear your aunt's grudges for her. I'm begging you."

Koulin raised a hand, halting the Saowon advance. She came closer, alone. She paused in front of Kyoshi and Rangi, and gave them a warm, thoughtful smile.

"Oh, Rangi," she said. "My dear friend."

She lowered her voice so only Kyoshi and Rangi could hear. Koulin's pleasant, pretty features twisted into a disdain so deep it cast grooves over her face. *"Of course the daughter of a shorn, honorless animal would resort to begging,"* she whispered, with the deliberate intent of an assassin.

Rangi blinked. She nodded. Then, before Kyoshi could stop her, she struck Koulin across the jaw.

The Saowon had found their excuse in Rangi's attack. The Keohso took it as an example to follow. All around Kyoshi, the rival clan members roared and charged each other.

She was still trying to process what had just happened when a man slammed into her back. She whirled around and flung the offender to the side, bowling over two of his kinsmen. Or his enemies. Already the lines had merged into a pitched brawl with no defined front. Keohso and Saowon fought each other tooth and nail, with everything short of drawn blades and firebending.

Kyoshi spun on the balls of her feet and lunged, sending a blast of wind hurtling at the biggest clump of people she could pick out. It flattened them like wheat in a storm, but with the combatants already locked together, they simply continued their fight on the ground, grappling in the dust. Thrashing bodies piled up at her waist like snowdrifts, impeding her movements.

She forced her way to the pocket of space that had formed around Rangi and Koulin. Huazo had disappeared, leaving her niece to manage things. Rangi raised her hand to Kyoshi, a silent order not to interfere. Koulin wiped the blood off her smirk. The blow had been hard, but she'd rolled with it, expecting and wanting it.

"What do you say?" she asked Rangi. "After-Curfew Rules? No burns or closed fists?"

"I was thinking the same thing," Rangi replied.

The two of them walked right up to each other. Instead of resorting to graceful punches and kicks in the long, far-reaching style Kyoshi was accustomed to seeing from Firebenders, they grabbed for the backs of each other's necks and fell into an exchange of brutal, vicious strikes with their knees and elbows.

The first blast of heat made Kyoshi think they'd broken the festival's prohibitions. But then she remembered skilled Firebenders could do extreme damage from the concussive force of their bending alone. Each time Rangi and Koulin rammed a knee into the other's ribs, or aimed an elbow at their opponent's temple, they let out a shock wave that rattled Kyoshi's teeth.

There was no way they could keep this up. They absorbed each other's blows with their shins and forearms, their skin reddening from toeing the line of open flame. Koulin attempted to smash her forehead into Rangi's eye and just barely missed, cutting a gash along the cheekbone.

Rangi staggered away, her knees wobbling. Koulin followed in pursuit, hungry to exploit her advantage. But she'd fallen into a trap. With the extra space, Rangi turned her back to Koulin and leaped into the air.

It was a move few others but Kyoshi would recognize. Jet-stepping, but not the way Rangi had used it in Chameleon Bay. Flames shot out from only one of her feet, propelling her into a backflip, pinwheeling her around with extra speed and force. Her knee came crashing down on Koulin's head like a sledgehammer.

Koulin was out before she hit the ground. She fell face-first, as limp as a wet rag. The whole fight had passed in seconds.

Rangi, breathing heavily from exertion and pain, but somehow completely calm, crawled on her knees over to Koulin. Without hesitation, she turned the unconscious girl over and raised her fists to strike her helpless opponent again.

"What are you doing!?" Kyoshi screamed. She grabbed at Rangi and pulled her off Koulin.

"I—" Rangi struggled to find an answer. Horror seized her as her mind finally caught up with her body. She stared at the roiling battle she'd sparked over the town square, and then at Koulin, who wasn't moving at all. "I—"

Kyoshi had seen Rangi start a fight once, on a *lei tai* platform, but it had been a calculated maneuver, not a complete breakdown. If the madness of family honor could make someone as disciplined as Rangi lose control, then there was no telling what would happen if this violence burst the bounds of North Chung-Ling and Shuhon Island. "Take her to Sifu Atuat!" Kyoshi ordered.

Still in shock, Rangi laced her arms under Koulin's and slung the girl over her shoulders. She staggered through the melee, threading into the open spaces she could find. Kyoshi had to trust in luck and whatever remained of clan honor that no one would strike them from behind.

She couldn't use earth in the frenzy, not without risking serious injury to her targets. She resorted to pulling Keohso and Saowon apart with her bare hands, hurling opponents as far away from each other as she could. Sometimes she had to crack their skulls together first. Pair by pair, she worked her way through the crowd, creating peace through brute force.

Kyoshi spotted Jinpa coming to her, quelling the violence in his own way. Many of the fighters simply stopped when they saw him, the grace of an Air Nomad enough to calm their tempers. The ones who didn't he wedged apart with his staff, smacking them on the shins and hands like an angry schoolteacher until they let go of their enemies.

"Avatar!" he yelled. Their combined efforts were working, slowly, and she could hear him over the lessening din. "Atuat's set up a field hospital in one of the restaurants." He pointed to one of the buildings closer to the Saowon side. "Our inn didn't have enough space to hold the injured. Rangi's there right now."

The village bystanders were already dragging the more badly beaten warriors in that direction. Kyoshi was going to tell Jinpa he'd done well, that their whole team, despite its many mistakes and humiliations and failures since coming to North Chung-Ling, had done well. But when she looked around and saw the brawl dying down to its embers, there was no reassurance. Only the pounding thought in her head that everyone in the village was here, watching the fight or participating in the fight or recovering from the fight.

A deep, queasy sickness rippled through her core. "Where's Hei-Ran?" she said. "Who's with her?"

"She's still back in our inn . . . by herself." Jinpa realized it too and swore a curse unbecoming of his people.

This whole showdown. A more perfect diversion could not have been designed. After all, why would Yun switch tactics if she kept falling for them?

Kyoshi barreled straight for the inn she hadn't slept in yet, knocking men down, trampling them in her haste. Jinpa fell behind, struck in the neck and knocked to the ground by an errant Saowon elbow. There was no time to wait for him to rise to his feet and shake it off. She had to get to Hei-Ran.

The street she was trying to reach lay several blocks away from the square, and as she gained distance from the noise a ghostly silence fell over her like a cloak. Her own footsteps and ragged breathing were louder than the clash of knuckles on bone she'd been listening to until now. She found the corner where the man from yesterday had nearly caved in his nephew's head and went inside the inn.

Inside, the common room was warm, cheery, and well-lit.

This establishment was deep in the Keohso side of town, so cushions and throw rugs adorned with the winged peony lay over every surface that would hold them. A Pai Sho board made of weathered wood had been set up in the middle of the floor. On one side sat Hei-Ran. The other, Yun.

"Don't move, Kyoshi," Yun said. "She's in grave danger right now." His eyes stayed on the board, examining the game that lay in its middle stages. He'd been forcing Rangi's mother to play.

Instead of his Earth Kingdom clothes, Yun wore pilfered Saowon robes, a stone camelia emblazoned on his shoulder. He'd snuck through the chaos outside by blending in. No bending tricks. Just the skills of an infiltrator, his learning made possible by the woman who sat across from him.

"Kyoshi, remember what I told you." Hei-Ran spoke with the same calm determination she had before cutting her hair and letting go of her honor. Now she was ready to give what little she had left. "Remember what's important. You won't get a better opportunity than this."

Yun placed a tile with finality, making the sharp *click* against the board that signaled the pieces had been carved from high-quality stone. "My victory in eighteen moves, Sifu," he said. "No need to continue. It's over."

Hei-Ran bobbed her head in agreement.

The Pai Sho tiles flew from the board into Yun's hand, following his motions. In an instant, they merged and reformed into a long thin spike that he pointed at the base of Hei-Ran's neck.

Kyoshi screamed and threw her hands up, pushing against the dagger with her earthbending, but Yun maintained his grip on the stone. His bending opposed hers, the same way she and

Jianzhu had warred against each other in the stone teahouse of Qinchao.

Only, right here and right now, Yun was stronger than Jianzhu. Despite Kyoshi's resistance the entire way, he sank the dagger into Hei-Ran's throat.

WEAKNESS

OVER THE sound of the Avatar shrieking, Yun and Hei-Ran stared at each other. He held on to the stone spike, as if he wanted to maintain a physical connection to her death, the same way he had embraced Jianzhu while killing him. He gave her a parting smile.

But Hei-Ran wasn't ready to say farewell just yet. Her bronze eyes flared with clarity and purpose. As blood welled from her wound, she grabbed Yun by the wrist. She choked involuntarily, her back spasming, and pulled him closer. The dagger plunged deeper into her body.

Yun frowned, not expecting this. He tried to pull his hand away but couldn't. Hei-Ran's final muster of strength had turned her into iron. Scarlet trails poured from from her lips, but she never took her eyes off her former student. Hei-Ran raised a hand and with an effort Kyoshi could see was killing her just as much as the blood filling her lungs, she summoned a ball of flame.

The blaze in her grasp made her look like a Fire Lord captured in portrait, unconquered to the end. She thrust her palm into Yun.

He managed to break free and twist to the side right before the fire punched into his torso. His shoulder still got caught in the flames and he hissed in pain, shoving Hei-Ran to the floor, the motion withdrawing the dagger with a sickening wet sound. He ran up the stairs leading from the common room to the upper level of the inn, clutching his burned arm.

Kyoshi couldn't stop him. The mission was forgotten, the plan was nothing. She had to help Rangi's mother. She dashed to Hei-Ran's side and tried to wrap her mind around the grievous wound, to figure out her next action.

Hei-Ran's fading expression was one of fury, reserved for the Avatar alone. "Go . . . after . . . him!" she gurgled at Kyoshi through her own blood.

Yun had opted for a second-story escape. And he was wounded. Kyoshi could have caught up to him with dust-stepping, her secret advantage from the Flying Opera Company that allowed her to speed along rooftops. But to do so would have meant letting Hei-Ran bleed out. It would have meant Rangi losing her mother again.

She bunched up her sleeves and clamped them to the tunnel in Hei-Ran's throat. Blood kept slipping through her fingers, lessening to give her hope, then pouring out harder in waves. She realized it was the pattern of a heartbeat. She had no time to lose.

She picked Hei-Ran's upper body off the floor in preparation for moving her. "*N-no!*" the Headmistress sputtered. "*Kyoshi!*"

There was a final burst of indignation in the headmistress's eyes, outrage at the weakness of the Avatar, before they closed.

Kyoshi had thrown away her chance to fulfill her duty. She couldn't do what needed to be done. There would be consequences for choosing her personal attachments over all else, in the long run.

But right now, she had to hold on to Rangi's mother as tightly as she could. She lifted Hei-Ran and ran out the door in the opposite direction Yun had gone. They needed a miracle. One who was currently on the other side of town.

Kyoshi sat inside the Coral Urchin Noodle Shop with Nyahitha and Jinpa. The restaurant had been closed for the holiday, so it was dark, and the stoves were cold. Long wooden tables took up most of the floor space. They'd paid the owner handsomely to take over his apartments upstairs as well, where Atuat worked on Hei-Ran, Rangi by their side.

Kyoshi looked around the dark, knotted table at Jinpa and Nyahitha, the arrowless Airbender and the mock Fire Sage. Under normal circumstances these two men would have been her spiritual advisors. What a trio they made.

"The fighting seems to have paused," Jinpa said. He'd been searching for something positive to say for a while.

"Only for the moment," Nyahitha said. "There's too many injured on both sides. Even worse, a few of the younger, stupider fighters met outside the town square and broke the taboo on harmful firebending during the holiday. The Saowon and the

Keohso will lick their wounds for a bit, and then the conflict will spill the borders of North Chung-Ling. Each of the clans thinks they have just cause to attack the other now."

"There's nothing we can do?" Jinpa asked.

"This is what the beginnings of wars in the Fire Nation look like," Nyahitha said. "If Agni Kais and Avatar mediations didn't work in the past, I don't know how they'll work now."

Kyoshi rested her forehead against her knuckles and stared at the whirling patterns in the wood grain. The situation between the rival clans had been precarious already, but her decision to come to North Chung-Ling had pushed the country over the edge. She was to blame for whatever happened next.

And she had squandered the chance Hei-Ran had given her to take Yun down. She'd violated her promise to Rangi to keep her mother from harm. She couldn't simply fail along one path like most people; she had to be torn apart by her failures in every direction.

"How much time do you think we have before fighting begins in earnest?" she asked.

"A few days," Nyahitha said. "If you have a plan, it had better be simple and quick."

She had no plan. She had nothing.

Atuat came down the stairs, wiping her hands with a clean towel. Thankfully there was no blood on it. "She's absolutely livid with you," the doctor said to Kyoshi.

"Which one?"

"Both." Atuat motioned with her thumb up the stairs, where mother and daughter waited. "I would not want to be you right now."

There was nowhere left to show any courage but here, her

reckoning. Kyoshi accepted the pitying looks of Jinpa and Nyahitha and went to go see Rangi and Hei-Ran.

She could tell the room was hotter before she entered it. Kyoshi ducked inside the restaurant's sleeping quarters and saw Hei-Ran propped up on a small bed, a thick layer of bandages swaddling her neck. She was pale from blood loss, which only offset the anger shooting from her eyes. On a table beside her was a piece of slate and several lumps of chalk, taken from the order boards from the restaurant downstairs. She must have been using it to communicate with Atuat and Rangi, unable to talk from her injury.

Rangi stood at the foot of the bed, so stock-still Kyoshi wondered how much Hei-Ran had revealed to her about the conversation they'd had by themselves in the palace stables, about the tactic of luring Yun out in the open.

"You used my mother as bait," Rangi hissed.

Apparently, everything. "I didn't agree to the plan," Kyoshi said weakly.

"Right. You just went along. Neutral *jing*, huh? You kept quiet and you didn't tell me she meant to sacrifice herself. Would you have mentioned it over her corpse? Would you have told me then?"

She wasn't describing the truth of Kyoshi's thoughts. But thoughts didn't matter. Only actions and their outcomes. "Rangi, please! I'm sorry!"

"Don't apologize to me," Rangi said. "There's no need. Because from this point on, I am *nothing* to you. Do you hear me, Avatar Kyoshi? *Nothing*." She brushed past Kyoshi and ran down the stairs.

Kyoshi barely saw her leave. She was too stuck on what Rangi had called her. She couldn't remember Rangi addressing her as "Avatar Kyoshi" during the entire time they'd known each other. Not in Yokoya, not in Chameleon Bay, not in Hujiang or Zigan. Hearing those words from her lips was like a blade coming down between them, cold and sharp and final.

Kyoshi's body began to heave. She took great dry gulps, her insides twisting. Ever since Jianzhu had taken Rangi, she'd been so fixated on what outside dangers might separate them. She'd never thought about losing her by saying the wrong thing or being silent at the wrong time.

She couldn't breathe. She didn't want to. This wasn't a future she could face. She was imprisoned again, like she'd been in Kuruk's memories, forced to watch proceedings that she couldn't bear to witness.

There was a precise little flick against Kyoshi's forehead. Something white and powdery fell to the floor. Hei-Ran had thrown a piece of chalk at her.

The headmistress held up her slate and tapped its surface, showing Kyoshi what she'd written. *Stop panicking*, it said. *She's not leaving you.*

"Bu-but she said—" Kyoshi was a blubbering mess, a wreck threatening to spill its contents into the sea.

Hei-Ran rolled her eyes, rubbed the slate clean, and wrote more on it with a fresh piece of chalk. Her strokes were so fast and efficient she could have outpaced some speakers. She was a career teacher, after all.

She says a lot of things. Yes, she's angry with you. It doesn't mean she'll walk away forever.

Rangi *had* just walked away while making it sound like forever. "How do you know?"

Rub. Scrape. *She's my* daughter. *You think you know her so well. I've known her since she was born.*

Hei-Ran turned the board over to use the back. *Eventually she'll come back with some sign she still cares. It usually takes her a week to forgive me. Give it time.*

Kyoshi wiped her face, sniffling like a child. It wasn't easy to recover from such a blow. What if Hei-Ran was wrong?

The headmistress wasn't going to give her time to ponder the issue. *Yun?*

"I searched the town with the help of some of the more reasonable locals. He's gone. He could be anywhere on Shuhon Island. Or he may have escaped by sea."

You missed your opportunity. Hei-Ran was less angry and judgmental this time. She was simply stating the facts.

"I couldn't leave you to die. For Rangi's sake, I couldn't."

Hei-Ran sighed, wheezing through her nose. The exhalation aggravated her wound and she coughed pink spittle. Kyoshi moved toward her, but she put her hand up to say she was fine. She resumed writing, the chalk dust thick on the slate by now.

He's not the only thing driving us to war anymore. The Saowon and the Keohso will use today as a just cause to fight. They'll both say they were defending their honor.

Kyoshi stared at the strokes of chalk. Not out of a lack of understanding, but because the characters spurred a recollection in her. She had to dig for it, feel it brush against her fingers before she could grasp the idea.

To help the process along, she reached out with her earthbending, applying the gentlest of force against Hei-Ran's board.

At the touch of her bending, the mineral chalk swept clean off the slate. With Kyoshi's level of control, that was the best she could manage. Even with her fans she'd never had the fine-tuning to be able to create words in earth.

But she knew someone who could do just that.

"Yun is working on behalf of the Saowon," Kyoshi said. "They've been abetting him in the Fire Nation in return for his service."

Hei-Ran frowned. *What makes you say that?* she wrote on her newly cleaned slate.

"Everything he's done has strengthened the Saowon's position and weakened Zoryu's. He humiliated the Fire Lord at the party. He created the message in the hillside." How could she have not realized this earlier? Yun may have been trained as a killer, but his specialty was cutting deals. Making sure both parties got what they wanted. The Saowon would shelter him as he worked toward his revenge, and he would tilt the Fire Nation's politics in their favor by sowing chaos.

I don't follow you on the crop writing. But if it turned out you were correct then—

Hei-Ran ran out of room on the slate board and tossed it to the side. She shifted in her bed so she could start writing on the wall.

—Chaejin and Huazo have been acting dishonorably this whole time. A link between the Saowon and Yun would turn them from a clan striving for the throne into a conspiracy of traitors. They'd have to submit to justice if they were found out. The other clans respect strength and cunning but they couldn't possibly forgive inviting a foreign attack on the Fire Nation.

Kyoshi looked at Hei-Ran's cropped hair with new admiration for the woman's sacrifice and iron composure under Huazo's insulting touch. If honor was the reason quoted for bloodshed, conflict could be avoided by stripping it away entirely.

"Right now, it's only a hunch," Kyoshi said. "I have to follow up on a few things to confirm it." She turned to leave, but her path was blocked by Rangi storming back into the room.

Rangi glowered viciously at Kyoshi and pushed a steaming hot bowl into her hands. It was filled with plain yellow noodles.

"You haven't eaten since yesterday afternoon!" she screamed. She hurled a pair of chopsticks on the floor and left as abruptly as she'd entered.

Kyoshi stared at the bowl. There hadn't been any fuel in the kitchen, which meant Rangi must have cooked it with her own firebending. She looked up to see Hei-Ran with an expression that almost crossed the line into smugness.

See? Even faster than I thought. You mean everything to her, Kyoshi.

She was running her chalk down to the nub. *My daughter loves you. Which means you are also my daughter. For better or worse, you are a part of our family.*

Hei-Ran smiled. *Now go on, before your food gets cold. You need your strength.*

Kyoshi bent her trembling knees and picked up the chopsticks, not caring they'd been on the floor. The noodles were unflavored, boiled from dry, and so overly alkaline they still smelled of lye.

They were the best thing she'd ever tasted. Tears ran down Kyoshi's face as she ate her meal, Hei-Ran watching to make sure she finished.

ESCALATION

"**BRING US** down," Kyoshi said. It was just her and Jinpa right now.

"Where?" he said. "By the *Hail Fire*—or the—*Lord Chaejin*?"

"Anywhere!"

Yingyong swooped lower onto the diseased melonyam crop and landed by the left "arm" of the character for fire. The writing was detailed enough that once they dismounted, they could walk between the gaps of the strokes. Yingyong immediately set to rooting through the ground with his nose.

"Boy!" Jinpa scolded. "Don't! Those aren't yours!"

Most people would have assumed the bison would go after the sweet tubers of the healthy plants, but the bison spent his time lapping at the soil itself, aiming his giant tongue under the withering, yellowing melonyams.

"Hey!" Jinpa tugged on his fur. "You'll make yourself sick!"

Yingyong's behavior added to Kyoshi's suspicion. She found a patch of earth he hadn't licked yet and crouched down. Above her head was a sickly plant. She made a face, knowing she was about to live up to an insult that foreigners sometimes hurled at Earth Kingdom natives. She picked up a clod of soil and popped it into her mouth.

"Kyoshi, are you eating *dirt*?" Jinpa said.

She wasn't eating it, was merely tasting it. A crude but effective technique poor farmers like the ones in Yokoya sometimes used to diagnose their field conditions. Kyoshi turned around to face him and spat her mouthful of grit to the side.

"It's salty," she said. "This field's been poisoned with salt."

Kyoshi wiped her tongue on her sleeve and spat again. "Yun bent a message into the soil to kill the plants above it. Huazo supplied the materials. She bought out the local salt-making business just recently."

It all added up. Yun and the Saowon were working together. They'd picked their "Avatar," and Zoryu had his.

"What do we do now?" Jinpa asked.

"Take us back," Kyoshi said. "I want to talk to everyone before I do something rash."

I don't think it's enough, Hei-Ran wrote on her slate.

Upon Kyoshi's return to the restaurant, the headmistress had joined the rest of the group downstairs. Rangi protested her moving about for fear of worsening her injuries. The screaming and scribbling match reached such proportions that Hei-Ran was forced to order Rangi to leave and cool off with a harshly written *young lady*. A chair lay shattered in splinters by the door as her daughter's final retort.

It was Kyoshi alone with Jinpa and the older folks. *I think you're right about Yun working with the Saowon*, Hei-Ran clarified. *But it won't hold up with the rest of the clans.*

Nyahitha concurred. "Your evidence relies on an earthbending technique no one else has ever heard of before now."

"Then I only have one option left," Kyoshi said. "I find the leaders of the Saowon and get a confession from them." A statement from the guilty party was as valid in the Fire Nation as it was in the Earth Kingdom.

No one missed the implication. There was a chance Kyoshi was going to have to confront the Saowon with more than just facts. It was good that Rangi wasn't here. She believed the Avatar had a duty to follow the path of righteousness. She had faith.

The rest of the group, less so. Kyoshi looked around the table at her new set of companions, gathered by chance instead of choice. They made a motley collection of representatives from every nation. She focused her attention on Jinpa.

Hei-Ran, Atuat, and Nyahitha had been weathered by life and its insults, but the Air Nomad was still young. His pacifistic beliefs should have prevented him from accompanying Kyoshi where she was headed. She waited for some kind of gentle counterargument for peace and neutrality from the monk. But it never came.

Jinpa ran a finger over the restaurant's table, inspecting it for dust. The gesture aged him, made him look like he was an investor considering buying the whole establishment. "Just tell me where to take you, Avatar," he said.

What a crew they made. A disgraced Firebender, a sage without sanctity, a doctor who let people die, and an Air Nomad involving himself with the dirty politics of the world. With Avatar Kyoshi at the center. None of them were what they were supposed to be. The Flying Opera Company might have gotten along better with this group than she thought.

Kyoshi beckoned everyone to listen close. "Here's what's going to happen," she said.

The nearest viable port was south of the fairground beach, around a bend of the coast. The boardwalk had been optimistically filled with stalls for snack vendors and bauble sellers to ambush arriving tourists before they even got to North Chung-Ling. Reefcrabs scuttled freely over the jagged rocks. The birds that would have eaten them had too much refuse to gorge on.

Kyoshi and Atuat got there at the break of dawn to wait for Huazo on the damp wooden pier. Kyoshi had gotten the idea in her head that an extra Waterbender might be helpful backup so near the ocean, but Huazo arrived without her niece and only two guards. Her contingent had been left behind in town. It must have suited her to keep a force in Shuhon to meet the coming Keohso aggression, while she made a discreet exit.

"Leaving so soon?" Kyoshi said. A single island-hopping ferry boat drifted nearby in the water, ready to launch. "The Festival of Szeto's not over yet."

Huazo was surprised to see her but, as always, managed it well. "This town has given me what I need."

Kyoshi did not have the patience to bandy in euphemisms anymore. "Where is Yun?" she snarled.

"Yun. Is this the boy the Earth Kingdom thought was the Avatar before you? The one who attacked the royal palace and humiliated Zoryu?"

Huazo's polite front had turned from annoying to nauseating. Earlier, Kyoshi had gone over her plans with her group in a calm, rational manner, but coming face-to-face with one of the people keeping her from Yun was a fresh trial. She was too close to her end goal to remain composed. "I know he's been working for you," Kyoshi said. "Tell me where he is."

Huazo craned her neck forward so Kyoshi could see the perfection of her lying face. "I have no idea who this person is. I've never met him."

Kyoshi drew circles in the air with her wrists, flowing, summoning motions of energy. The crash of the surf hissed in her ears. Water was calmness and tranquility, but it was the rage of a storm as well.

She flung her energies at the ship. The ropes mooring it to the dock snapped like threads. A wave as wide as a river carried the boat out to sea, lifting it higher. Once it reached a hundred yards out, the riptide Kyoshi created froze in a snap, leaving the ferry held in the air by talons of ice. Huazo's men jumped back and shouted in astonishment.

"La's fins," Atuat muttered upon seeing the Avatar's full strength for the first time. "You've got enough raw power to freeze a polar orca solid."

Huazo bade her retainers to stand down as Kyoshi came closer and loomed over her. She stared up in defiance. "You have nothing, Avatar. Try to intimidate me all you want; hurt me even. You'd only be strengthening my clan's position in the coming war. There is nothing you can do to me to get what you want."

In her own way, the woman was as fearless as Hei-Ran. "I had a feeling you might say that. You're coming with me to Capital Island. Alone."

The Saowon matriarch broke out into a smile, as if she'd been handed a gift. "That's right," she said to her guards before they leaped on Kyoshi with firebending. "The Avatar's taking me hostage on behalf of Zoryu. I'm about to be falsely imprisoned."

Her men looked unsure. "Send messages to the rest of the clan and our allies," Huazo said. "Tell them what happened here. Don't start anything with the Keohso until I'm freed from the injustice of Zoryu and his hired bandit, the Avatar." She gave Kyoshi a wink that said *This is how you craft the image of events as they happen, girl.*

Huazo took Kyoshi by the elbow and led her ostensible captor off the dock. The two of them could have been a lady and her maid, out for a morning stroll. "Do you play Pai Sho, my dear?" she asked.

Kyoshi tensed so hard Huazo could feel it in her biceps. "I take that as a no," Huazo said. "I thought as much. You see, my dear, one of the first lessons a player learns is never to interrupt your opponent when she's in the middle of making a fatal mistake."

By the time the three of them returned to the Coral Urchin, Jinpa had retrieved Yingyong and was perched on top of the bison's neck, finishing preparations for their flight. The great beast filled most of the alley next to the building. Hei-Ran waited by the door. She'd removed some of the bandages from her neck but was still clearly feeling the effects of her wound.

Upon seeing her, Huazo burst out laughing. "Oh, this keeps getting more hilarious by the second!" Her grin turned cold and wicked. "You know what this means, Hei-Ran. The Avatar's disgraced herself and you've thrown your lot in with her. When my clan finally triumphs, there will be no mercy for the Sei'naka."

Hei-Ran spoke, the injury transforming her normally graceful voice into a terrible rattling whisper. *"We have no need of mercy. Only justice."*

The dreadful sound coupled with the raw determination in her voice silenced Huazo for once. Kyoshi took the matriarch of the Saowon clan by the waist, eliciting a yelp, and lifted her into the grasp of Jinpa, who swung her up into the saddle. Huazo flumped into the corner like a bolt of cloth, her fine robes and layers of petticoats pooling around her.

Kyoshi faced Hei-Ran one last time. "What if she's right?" she muttered. There was no way the Avatar's reputation would emerge from this affair unscathed. "By doing this I'm ruining my own honor."

"Only because you understand the true meaning and value of the word," Hei-Ran rasped. *"Honor cannot be coveted too dearly, young lady. Sometimes it must be laid down for the good of others."*

As if to quell Kyoshi's doubts, Rangi walked around the corner, holding baskets of supplies. The plan had been to keep her away while the Avatar took off with Huazo, but she'd come back too soon, perhaps unable to find what she needed in markets of the declining town. She dropped her burden as soon as she saw their hostage, rolls of gauze and bundles of medicinal herbs scattering at her feet.

"What is going on here?" Rangi shouted as she ran up to Kyoshi. "Have you lost your mind?"

Kyoshi took one of her fans out. As gently as she could, she earthbent Rangi into the ground, halfway up to her shins.

"What in the name of— Kyoshi, is this you?" Rangi clawed at the ground around her legs, trying to uproot herself. "Stop it! Let me out!"

There are places my daughter will never go, Hei-Ran had once said. There were places Kyoshi would never take Rangi. Just, honorable, kind Rangi who believed in what the Avatar stood for. Kyoshi leaned over and kissed Rangi on the top of her head. "Please forgive me," she whispered, before climbing into Yingyong's saddle.

"Kyoshi!" Rangi screamed, trapped where she stood. Jinpa snapped the reins and Yingyong rose into the air. *"Kyoshi!"*

Kyoshi clenched her teeth and wished the bison could climb faster. She needed to be high in the sky where the air was thin and she could no longer hear Rangi crying her name.

THE COMPANION

"I'M HUNGRY," Huazo said.

If Kyoshi could keep only one lesson she'd learned in her seventeen or so years of life, it was that your choice of traveling companions was the most important decision you could ever make. Forget the Avatars roaming the world with their bending teachers. The Avatars roamed the world with the few select people they didn't want to strangle with their bare hands mid-journey.

"For the last time, there's parched grain in the sack you've been using as a pillow," Kyoshi said.

"And nothing else?"

"And nothing else!"

Huazo made a noise with her teeth. She opened the bag and poured some toasted millet into her palm. Then she tossed it into her mouth, crunching the grain more noisily than Kyoshi expected from a refined noblewoman.

"Chaeryu and I used to fight like this when we traveled," she said. "He loved the idea of being close to nature, so he always packed as little as possible on our trips. If he had his way, there would have been no guards at all in our procession. Just the two of us and what we could carry, tromping through the wilderness of the islands."

The thought of Lady Huazo and the deceased Fire Lord camping outdoors, like the Flying Opera Company and their meals of elephant rat, was so incongruous that Kyoshi's curiosity got the better of her. "You and he really used to rough it?"

Huazo shrugged. "You look so skeptical. Any pastime feels like the most glorious adventure when you're young and in love. Fleeing into the mountains was how we escaped the pressures of the court."

"What happened?"

Huazo knew Kyoshi was pushing it and answered anyway. "What happened was, we were young. And merely in love. What are those compared to the pressures of clan and country? Nothing. At some point, whether it was a suggestion planted in his head by his advisors or an idea he came up with on his lonesome, Lord Chaeryu became convinced he could do better than me."

She picked a husk out of her teeth and flicked it to the side. "It could have been about power, politics. Fortunes rise and fall quicker here in the Fire Nation than in the stagnant Earth Kingdom, Avatar. In those days the Saowon were weak. And I wasn't well-received in the capital as the Fire Lord's mistress. There are certain ways members of the royal family are supposed to meet their future partners and falling in love as teenagers doesn't count."

Huazo lay back against the saddle edge and held out her hand. "Water."

Kyoshi was so enthralled by the story that she forgot to snap at Huazo for being such a demanding hostage. She handed over the water skin and Huazo swigged it until it was empty.

"The millet really dries out your mouth," she said. "Anyway, where was I? Oh, yes. The worst moment of my life. Chaeryu's ministers—a lot of them being Sei'naka clan, mind you—arranged the whole thing like an assassination. It was at one of those blasted, wretched, miserable garden parties. Chaeryu had already been thinking about ending our relationship, but he wasn't sure about it. Not until his advisors trotted out Lady Sulan of the Keohso clan before him."

The woman Chaeryu married, Kyoshi thought. *Zoryu's mother.*

"I was watching his face when it happened," Huazo said. "I saw the exact moment Chaeryu laid eyes on her and thoughts of me vanished from his head. The pieces fell into place for the Fire Lord. He had the excuse, the permission to 'make the ultimate sacrifice' and let go of his love for me. I saw how wide his grin grew when he realized he could pursue the lovely young Sulan and be completely blameless in the eyes of our country."

Huazo smiled with one corner of her mouth and frowned with the other. "He could have fought in his heart a little more. If it was his inevitable and unfortunate duty to cut me loose, he could have done it a little more solemnly, instead of wearing that big, stupid dumbstruck face he used to reserve only for me."

She remembered an important part of the story and giggled. "It was an unfortunate time to be pregnant with his first son. You can imagine Chaeryu's embarrassment when I told him."

Kyoshi wondered if she ever phrased it like that in front of Chaejin, and what her son thought if she did. Parents had ways of offhandedly cutting their children. "So you've been taking it out against the Keohso ever since."

"What? No!" Huazo scoffed. "You make me sound so petty. I dedicated myself to growing the fortunes of the Saowon because that's what clan leaders do. And I was one of the best in our history. You think the other nobles don't try to edge their rivals out or dream of having their offspring sitting on the throne? Every single family of sufficient birth has wanted to own this country since Toz. Your precious Sei'naka women would go for it if they had the strength."

Huazo seemed to enjoy how the Avatar incorrectly dwelled on the level of personal grudges, like a child. "I never hated little Sulan," she said. "She was too pure for court. If you want to hear a story about what she was like, listen."

She traced a character on the floor of the saddle with her finger, the elegance in her penmanship clear to see even without ink. She did it upside down too, so Kyoshi could read it right side up, an understated but extremely impressive feat. The character was *zo*, sometimes pronounced *so*, and it meant "ancestor."

"For generations the character for *zo* has been used for names by the Saowon and only the Saowon," Huazo explained. "But it's the same as the one in 'Zoryu.' Chaeryu gave another woman's child *my* family's character for his name."

Kyoshi sucked in her breath sharply. "See?" Huazo said. "Even you, a foreigner, understand. Agni Kais have been fought to the death for lesser insults. But Chaeryu did it because Sulan wanted to, and Sulan wanted to *because she thought it sounded pretty.* He bowed to her nonsensical whims and in doing so angered an entire clan!"

She threw her shoulders higher. "Me, personally? I was less upset about the insult than I was shocked, completely staggered that Sulan didn't understand it would be a bad idea. How could the future Fire Lady be so naïve? How much damage was she going to cause with her foolishness?"

Huazo tapped her chest with her hand, her fingers crooked like the claw of a raven eagle. "We could have had a Fire Lady who actually knew how to use power! I could have brought success and prosperity to the rest of the country like I did for the Saowon!"

And I could have had a great mentor in you, Kyoshi couldn't help but think about this future that had withered on the vine, one where she had no reason to come into conflict with Huazo. *The Avatar and the Fire Lady, working together as allies.*

"Chaejin is your second chance at the throne," she said. "He's nothing more than your way of reclaiming what should have been."

"Chaejin is my son and I love him," Huazo snapped indignantly. "But yes, him taking the crown from Sulan's progeny would rectify a few mistakes of the past."

"At the cost of plunging the nation into war. You can claim not to hate Zoryu and Sulan all you want, but your actions don't follow your words."

The leader of the Saowon smirked. "Maybe you're right. It's so hard to keep personal matters out of our duties, isn't it, Avatar?" The mask slid back over Huazo's face, hiding the candor she'd shared so openly moments before. "I still don't know anything about Yan. Or was it Yao? I can't remember."

Thank you for making this easier, Kyoshi thought as Capital Island came into view. "Take a left," she said to Jinpa. "I'll need to guide you the rest of the way."

They landed on a rocky coastline, the view of First Lord's Harbor blocked by jutting promontories. Here, the waters were too dangerous for boats to dock or even linger. Powerful waves slammed into the near-vertical cliffs, creating a deafening hiss. The only sign of human interference was a small hut nestled into a crag. Kyoshi had to rely on a faint memory of a written description to find it.

"I thought we were going to the palace," Huazo said.

"We will," Kyoshi replied. "Eventually."

There were no stairs or pathways to the house from the cliffs above or the waters below. A visitor would need a bison or have to be an extremely skilled bender in order to reach it. Jinpa brought Yingyong down as far as he could, but there wasn't enough space to land.

Kyoshi earthbent a ramp so Huazo could disembark. "Go inside," she said. "Make yourself comfortable. There should be more preserved food and fresh water, but I doubt you'll need it. We'll be back in less than two hours."

Huazo sniffed in confusion and disgust at the house. It was covered in a thick layer of seabird droppings. "You're not going to guard me?"

"Where could you go?" Kyoshi said.

Being ordered inside this strange, unexplained house that existed in defiance of logistics unsettled Huazo for the first time since Kyoshi had met the woman. But she refused to show weakness. "Well, it's not an Ember Island bungalow, but it'll do." She fought past her hesitation and marched across the bridge.

Kyoshi and Jinpa watched her proceed carefully inside, perhaps checking for traps. Once she disappeared from view, he turned to Kyoshi.

"That was an incredible story she told you," he said. "Are you two friends now?"

"I don't think so."

"Good. It would be difficult if you suddenly became fond of Huazo."

Again, he showed the lack of a typical Airbender's scruples. By all rights she should have had to lock him to the ground alongside Rangi. Instead he was enabling her the same way the Saowon were doing for Yun.

"Jinpa," she said. "How long have you been traveling with me as my secretary and advisor?"

He scratched the top of his head. He hadn't shaved in a while, and his hair was starting to grow back. "Well, I don't remember the date we made it official. But I suppose you could start counting from when you first had to leave the Southern Air Temple to mop up the splinter fleets of the Fifth Nation before they could reform. Then we went to Misty Palms and ran into that problem with the beetle-headed merchants and their mercenaries. By the time you destroyed the Emerald Claws, people knew they should go through me to talk to you."

Kyoshi nodded. She could count each of those adventures through the scars on her body, up to and including the raid on Loongkau. "Brutal business, all of it. And yet, not once have you ever advised me to follow the path of peace."

Jinpa stuffed his tongue under his lower lip. He looked away from her.

"You've seen me take a lot of punishment," Kyoshi said. "But you've also seen me inflict a great deal of it, and you've said nothing. How odd for an Air Nomad. I don't believe that simple deference to the Avatar is what's keeping you quiet as you watch me violate your spiritual values over and over again."

She'd caught him out. She might not have had the specifics, but she'd caught him out just the same.

"It's as you suspect," Jinpa said. "I'm an Air Nomad. But I'm also something else. I belong to . . . another community."

"Your friends you play Pai Sho with."

"Yes. The senior members of the group agreed I should help you establish your Avatarhood in whatever way I can. Even if your actions go against what I've been taught as an Airbender."

He rubbed the back of his head, uncomfortable with revealing so much. "Having two identities means I serve two different ideals. Which is probably why I'm not very good at either. Sometimes those beliefs come into conflict with each other."

Kyoshi was of Earth Kingdom and Air Nomad parentage. She was the bridge between spirits and humans, a public figure and a *daofei*. Her own half-status made it easier to understand others who were torn in different directions. "I know what Air Nomads believe," she said. "What's the other ideal?"

"The philosophies of beauty and truth. It doesn't sound so different from Airbender teachings at first blush. But to uphold such values requires a deep attachment and love for the greater world that enlightened Air Nomads aren't supposed to have. Some of my friends in the other nations would argue that, on occasion, truth and beauty must be defended with ugliness.

They would claim a gardener who nurtures a flower so others can enjoy it bloom for a few moments must spend much time with their hands buried in dirt."

Kyoshi would have chosen a less pleasant word than dirt. "What do you believe then?"

Jinpa smiled sadly. "I believe I have to make peace with my own choices, just like everyone else."

The tint of pain in his expression reminded her too much of Kelsang for her to believe Jinpa was at complete peace with himself. Outsiders enviously and condescendingly assumed Airbenders lived in a state of innocent bliss, but that didn't give the monks and nuns enough credit for their inner strength. From what Kyoshi knew, belonging to the wandering nation meant a constant struggle with your own morals against the world's.

She didn't ask him to name his group. She'd rather a secret society try to help her for once, instead of coming after her with hatchets. "Perhaps after all of this is done, I can be less confrontational, and start compromising more," Kyoshi said. She could stand to make her long-suffering secretary's life a little easier. He deserved it.

Jinpa glanced at the house where Lady Huazo was resting inside. "I think we're both compromised now. To the palace?"

"To the palace."

THE EDGE

"YOU KIDNAPPED *the leader of the Saowon clan?!"*

Zoryu's cry of shock echoed through the war room. Luckily, the only ones to hear it were Kyoshi, Jinpa, and the multitude of carved dragons wrapped around the pillars and walls. She'd asked the Fire Lord to dismiss his retinue, and then asked him again to dismiss the unseen lurking guards who had undoubtedly doubled in number since Yun's attack.

She'd briefed him on everything that happened in North Chung-Ling, but the details had only made Zoryu more upset. "You were supposed to help me prevent a war, not create one from whole cloth!"

"We *are* preventing a war. The Saowon have been working with Yun. Once we make the connection public, you can deal with them as honorless traitors. No amount of manipulating public opinion or court etiquette or claiming it's really the Keohso's fault can excuse them."

Kyoshi reiterated the plan. It wasn't very complicated. "Get me Chaejin and I'll get you a confession."

Zoryu's mouth flapped open and shut. Kyoshi knew what was happening. The time had come for the Fire Lord to make his move, and even in the face of his own destruction he couldn't do it, didn't want to do it. Whether it was the weakness he'd shown when it came to his brother, or a lack of resolve in general, he couldn't sign the picture that Kyoshi had sketched, inked, and colored in for him.

She surged forward and grabbed Zoryu by the shoulders. Manhandling the Fire Lord was probably punishable by death, but right now Kyoshi could only see a scared young person whose weakness was going to get everyone killed. She saw herself. And she hated it.

"You have to be stronger," she said. She could have been talking into a mirror. "*We* have to be stronger. Our opponents in this game are playing for blood and they're willing to break every rule. We have to break a few as well."

"Kyoshi, if this doesn't work, I'll have only hastened my own demise."

Zoryu might have had his political troubles, but he hadn't lost everything yet. He was still a relative newcomer to a life on the brink. If one path of a fork promised you oblivion, it didn't really matter what the other path held in store.

"There's a saying among the destitute of the Ba Sing Se Lower Ring," Kyoshi said. "The ones who are so poor that if they find a copper piece in the street, they take it straight to the gambling dens and the numbers rackets, because a single coin won't make a difference in their survival. '*You either accept the risk of winning, or the guarantee of losing.*'"

She let the words sink in. "Now, can you get me Chaejin? Yes or no?"

Zoryu worked his jaw around nothing again, and she fought the urge to slap him. But, like a newborn turtle duck taking its first waddling steps to the water, he nodded. "I'll have to bring in a few people, and I don't think I can trust them all to keep their mouths shut, so you won't have much time before word leaks out. But I'll make it happen."

"Be quick about it. I'll wait in my quarters for your signal." She turned to leave the war room without waiting to be dismissed.

"Avatar," Zoryu said, calling her attention back.

His eyes burned with more light than she'd seen from him yet. If the royal portrait artists wanted to capture Zoryu's likeness for the ages, they could do worse than choosing this moment. "I may not be the strongest ruler yet," he said. He already sounded clearer and backed with purpose. "But I would do anything for the sake of the Fire Nation. Please understand that."

She gave him a nod, the gesture of two people about to take a plunge into uncharted depths together.

"I really have to thank you, Avatar," Chaejin said, his words slightly muffled by the burlap sack covering his head. He sat across from Kyoshi in the back of Yingyong's saddle. "You've grown my legend in ways I couldn't dream of. Wrongfully accused, forced to bear the injustice of men while being blessed by the spirits? History will turn my reign into a song for the ages."

Zoryu's agents had found Chaejin so willing to comply with his own abduction that they hadn't bothered to gag or restrain him. The nondescript men wearing the clothing of junior ministers told Kyoshi they'd simply asked him to leave the teahouse where they found him and get into their carriage. They passed through the winding streets of the capital like a noble and a few of his household retainers on a joyride to the isolated meadows surrounding the outskirts of the city.

Only once, when they'd opened the door to the carriage and let Chaejin step out, did they throw the bag over the top of his head as she'd requested. And they did it so clumsily that Chaejin had gotten a good long look at Kyoshi and Jinpa waiting with Yingyong. He'd given her a knowing grin before his face disappeared under the hood.

"I do have one complaint though," Chaejin said, sniffing. "What is that abominable smell?"

"Seabird droppings," Kyoshi said.

"Ah. I knew we were near the ocean. It's hard to tell what direction we went in. I've never traveled by air before."

Kyoshi yanked the hood off his head, which he could have done himself but chose not to in his desire to fully embrace the role of suffering captive. Jinpa pulled his bison down, level with the platform the hut stood on.

"Lovely," Chaejin sneered. "Is this the Avatar's private residence in the Fire Nation?"

"In a way," Kyoshi said. "It used to belong to Master Jianzhu of the Earth Kingdom. Now I own it." She leaned closer to his ear. "Your mother's inside."

To Chaejin, it was a sudden tangent and he laughed. "Very funny, Avatar. Do you and I have business here or not?"

Kyoshi violently ripped away the foundations of the hut with earthbending. Planks and splinters flew into the air like they'd been caught in a tornado. Huazo, suddenly revealed, screamed in surprise.

"Mother!?" Chaejin tried to reach for her, but Kyoshi hadn't made a ramp this time. The gap between Yingyong's saddle and the stone platform was too far for him to leap across. They were, however, close enough for everyone to hear each other.

"What is the meaning of this?" Huazo shouted. "I told you I don't know where Yun is!"

"So now you remember his name," Kyoshi said. She slashed one of her hands at the cliffside. Cracks ran around the rock Huazo stood on, puffing out thin lines of dust. The entire platform lurched, threatening to plunge into the sea.

Chaejin threw out his arms in a panic, as if he could control the earth himself. "No! Stop!"

"Kyoshi, what are you doing!?" Jinpa shouted. "I thought you were just going to scare them a little!" The Airbender's shock was real, and not an act put on to convince the Saowon. She hadn't told Jinpa how far she was truly willing to go. She didn't quite know, herself.

"Where is Yun?" Kyoshi didn't care whether Huazo or Chaejin told her. One of them had to know. "You've been working with him this whole time, in the palace and in North Chung-Ling. Admit it! Where is he?"

The stone supporting Huazo dropped another foot. "Kyoshi, that's enough!" Jinpa said. He gathered the reins to fly them away.

"Don't," she ordered Jinpa. "I might lose control over the stone." One wrong move would send Lady Huazo plummeting into the sea.

"We don't know where Yun is!" Chaejin cried. "We've never dealt with him!"

His denial sent Kyoshi into a rage. With her other hand she grabbed him by the throat and angled him over the saddle railing. Now both of the Saowon threatened to fall.

"Let my son go, you monster!" Huazo shrieked on her hands and knees. "Viper! Animal!"

Kyoshi would be those things if necessary. "I'm only going to ask one more time," she said, and in her heart, she knew it was no exaggeration. She had lost her patience, her honor, her friend. She had reached her limits. She was done, finally done, and unless Huazo or Chaejin answered her, they would be too. "Where is Yun?"

KYOSHI.

She shook her head in confusion. She normally didn't hear Kuruk's voice so clearly. His husky growl pierced through the roar of the waves, the whistling of the wind.

KYOSHI. THIS ISN'T WHO YOU ARE.

Chaejin raised his tear-stained face and wailed in helplessness. It was the same cry the little girl in Loongkau had made, watching her parents dragged into the street. Maybe Kyoshi had cried like that once, as she watched a bison fly away from Yokoya, never to return.

Sobbing, Huazo crawled to the edge of the cliff and reached for her son. It was a fruitless gesture, but she'd be that much closer to her child, whom she loved more than her own life.

Kyoshi finally saw the truth, bare and stripped open. They didn't know where Yun was. They hadn't been working with him. In her frenzy, she had nearly killed mother and son in front of each other.

She tossed Chaejin onto the platform beside his mother before she accidentally throttled him. She could hear Jianzhu laughing in her ear. Or maybe it was Kelsang weeping over the loss of his daughter, her betrayal of his example.

She pulled out her fans, eliciting whimpers from Huazo and Chaejin. Another sharp crack of rock rang out. Instead of heralding a landslide, the entire crag they were on rose higher, riding the edge of the rock wall toward the sky.

Without needing to be told, Jinpa climbed Yingyong in the air, keeping pace with Kyoshi's earthbending. The platform stopped at the top of the cliff, leaving the Saowon level with a wind-scrubbed field of coarse grasses.

"Go," she ordered them. *"Go!"*

They crawled away at first, not trusting the steadiness of the ground or her sudden change in disposition. Then Huazo and Chaejin began to believe they might yet survive. They picked themselves up and ran, the pounding of their feet clumsy and unpracticed. The flatness of the cliff tops meant Kyoshi could see them go for as long as she wanted. Watching them take part in the most humbling, equalizing ritual—the flight for one's life—made them look vanquished and small.

Kyoshi turned around, unable to stomach the sight any

longer. She teetered to the edge of the saddle, dropped to her knees, and retched emptiness into the ocean.

"Kyoshi!" Jinpa dropped the reins and clambered into the saddle with her. He grabbed her by the shoulders, wondering if she was still maddened. "Get a hold of yourself!"

She tried to apologize for risking so much on this desperate, ugly, vile gambit and coming away empty-handed. For being so completely and utterly wrong about the connection between Yun and the Saowon. For almost making him complicit in her crime.

But she was only capable of producing halting gasps. Seeing she was incoherent, Jinpa got back in the driver's position and flew them away, making a straight line for the capital. Kyoshi refused to look over the rails below. If she did, she would see Huazo and Chaejin moving in the same direction.

She'd forced them to their lowest state and terrified them down to their bones. If only that were the end, the conclusion of the Avatar's dealings with the Saowon. How convenient it would be if giving someone enough comeuppance silenced them for good.

But eventually they were going to make it back to their kinsmen, and not long after, the royal court itself. Huazo and Chaejin would spread word of what happened. The story of their treatment by Zoryu and the Avatar would be used as the just cause for their war. Kyoshi had not only fanned the flames. She'd thrown oil onto the blaze.

She thought of Yun playing Pai Sho with Hei-Ran and how he'd predicted the end of their game. How Hei-Ran had all but clasped his hand over the board in agreement. If only she could see so far ahead, read a board and know where the final tiles would fall. But instead she was walled in from every side. To her, the future was an impenetrable blankness where she'd faltered, injured, and made things worse with every step.

Not only was she the loser of the game. It had been a mistake for her to ever play.

SHAPES OF LIFE AND DEATH

BY THE time they arrived at the palace, Kyoshi was a shivering wreck. Jinpa collected the shards of her as gently and methodically as she had once picked up messes in the Avatar's mansion.

First, a place to store the mess. He brought her to her room and sat her on her bed. Then he took it upon himself to find Zoryu and let him know the plan hadn't worked.

The lack of an angry Fire Lord beating down her door to demand answers for her failure likely meant that Zoryu had decided to withdraw and collapse much like Kyoshi was doing now. There was a set length of wick left to burn before his country set blade and fire against itself, and it was exactly however long it took for Huazo and Chaejin to walk back from the cliffside to the capital. A day? Two? As soon as they met up with their clan, a new, bloody chapter of Fire Nation history would begin.

Kyoshi wasted a few precious hours of her remaining time before that moment sleeping. A sympathetic future scribe, slicing the records apart to truly understand *why* the Fire Nation broke out into civil war under Kyoshi's tenure, might declare the Avatar had blacked out from strain and exhaustion. In truth, it was the kind of sleep where she was afraid of tomorrow and what the morning would bring. Tears squeezed out of her shut eyes as she fell into the slumber of weakness. She simply couldn't handle being awake anymore.

Dark grayness was her shroud, until Jinpa roused her, shaking her shoulders. "Avatar. The Fire Lord is calling for an assembly. I'm barred from going, but you should be there."

Huazo and Chaejin must have arrived. At least Zoryu was using his final peacetime moments to speak to his people, rather than hide away. He'd done better than her in the end.

Kyoshi shambled down the halls of the palace. It felt like she was decaying with each step, flakes of her peeling away to reveal hollowness underneath. She was a layer of dried paint surrounding nothing.

She heard an excited titter. A young noble couple rushed past them, paying no heed to the Avatar, the woman holding her skirt so it wouldn't drag, her escort trying to plaster over his grin with solemnness. The briefest whisper passed between them: "... *he's done for* ..."

They appeared to be heading in the same direction as Kyoshi. As she rounded the corner, the hall filled with more members of the court, murmuring to each other. She filed in behind them, carried along by the tide, until she reached a large room they hadn't been to before, a theater with a stage running along one wall. It must have been built so the royal family could take in plays without having to rub shoulders with the residents of Caldera City, or worse, Harbor City.

It was standing room only. Kyoshi lingered near the back. Like with any performance, there was an agonizing wait until the first actor emerged. The crowd hushed when Zoryu walked out onstage, looking haggard and resigned. A wispy mustache had formed over his upper lip like mold on bread.

"My friends," he said. "It has been a difficult time for our great nation. Instead of peace and abundance, this year's Festival of Szeto has brought a horrendous attack upon the sanctity of the palace, the bodies of our court, and the Fire Nation's history itself. The ruination of the Fire Avatar gallery is a grievous wound to my heart. It will never heal."

Zoryu was much better at speaking alone, from an elevated position, than he was at mingling in a crowd where he could be overshadowed by his political foes. The slouch in his shoulders was less pronounced, and there was a flinty look in his eye.

"I told myself that if I couldn't avenge this slight upon our honor, I had no right to call myself Fire Lord," he said. "That much still holds true."

His audience ruffled like stalks of wheat in the breeze. This was no mere update.

About a quarter of the nobles packed into this room were Saowon. They smirked in delight at their victory. The men and women Kyoshi could identify as Keohso numbered fewer than half the Saowon. Rage warped their faces to the point she thought their noses would start bleeding. There was no need for flower symbols to tell who belonged to which clan.

The nobles who weren't part of one faction or the other in this rivalry were already darting their eyes around, wondering if they'd sufficiently hedged their bets in favor of the Saowon. Little rings of space began forming around the furious Keohso as people sought more distance from them.

Zoryu held his hand up. "Let it be known that the spirits of the islands have been watching my reign since its inception, judging my fitness to be Fire Lord. With the attack upon the palace, they put me to the final test." He swept his gaze over the room. "And I have passed it. I have found the perpetrator. Bring him out please."

The declaration was so sudden that Kyoshi chuckled. The perpetrator was Yun. Which meant Zoryu found Yun.

Zoryu had found Yun?

Her laughter iced over in her throat, solidifying into barbs and cutting edges. Two palace guards brought out their blind-folded captive, hunched over from the weight of his iron shackles. Kyoshi could only see the top of his tousled brown hair as he was made to kneel next to Zoryu.

It was happening too fast. The stage felt disjointed in time from the audience and Kyoshi, as if she were stuck in the same trance as her session with Nyahitha on the mountain. She raised her arm toward Yun and opened her mouth to shout, but Zoryu, working on a faster rhythm, launched into the next stage of his speech.

"This man has confessed to crimes against the Fire Nation, for which he will be executed," he said. Kyoshi shouldn't have been so shocked to hear him mention capital punishment. But in a prolonged fit of naïvety, she hadn't considered at all that finding Yun would mean delivering him to a death sentence.

Zoryu grabbed Yun by the head and tilted his face toward the light in the room. It was a meaningful gesture intended to give the audience a better look, both at the captive and Zoryu's dominance over him. "Have you anything to say in your defense, you despicable beast?"

"No." Yun's features were smudged heavily with dirt. He wore the same robes he'd appeared in at the party. "I infiltrated the palace. I assaulted the members of the court. I vandalized the royal gallery. I killed Chancellor Dairin."

Yun took a deep breath. "And I did it at all the behest of the Saowon clan!"

A rumble of shock passed through the crowd. He had to shout to be heard over the din. "I was paid by Huazo of the Saowon to humiliate Fire Lord Zoryu! I blasphemed by faking signs from the spirits of the islands! I committed foul deeds here and in North Chung-Ling to instigate a war that might put the usurper Chaejin on the throne!"

It was a confession to everything Kyoshi thought the Saowon had conspired to. The exact results she'd been hoping to achieve.

The tromping of boots could be heard coming down the hall. Nobles began to shout and shove each other in the crowded room. "Treason!" Zoryu shouted, stoking the fires of confusion and panic instead of calming his subjects. "You have heard testimony of treason against the Fire Nation itself! All citizens who remain true to our country, regardless of your clan! Seize the Saowon criminals, here and now!"

The Keohso were the first to act, barely needing a reason. They leaped upon their enemies and dragged them to the ground, a ridiculous-looking scuffle of polished men and silken ladies flailing away like a drunken rage had suddenly possessed them. This was the brawl of North Chung-Ling writ smaller and better dressed, the grudge of a lowly peasant town continuing in the rarified air of the royal palace. Human beings could drape themselves in titles and etiquette, but at their hearts they were all the same animal.

The unaffiliated nobles had a dilemma thrust upon them. Until now the tides of power had clearly been flowing in one direction. The suddenness of Zoryu's declaration asked them to reverse course, to leap from their doomed boats and start swimming upstream.

Kyoshi saw the flashes of calculation run through the rest of the clans, faster than lightning. It was gang math. The Saowon really had overstepped their bounds recently, hadn't they? They were the largest family, but their numbers paled in comparison to the rest of the Fire Nation, unified.

Fire Nation folk were a decisive people. The rest of the clans found no more upside to being allied with the Saowon. They turned on their neighbors with even greater violence than the Keohso, pummeling anyone wearing stone camellias into submission with demonstrative zeal, needing to make up for lost ground. Palace guards, presumably loyal to Zoryu, were flooding into the room. No one wanted to be caught sympathizing with the traitors.

Zoryu and his prisoner were hustled out the back by guards as soon as the violence started. Kyoshi fought her way to the stage, slipping by men with bloody faces, nearly stepping on a woman crawling along the floor. She hoisted herself onto the empty platform and followed down the dark passage.

Immediately she crashed into a sharp turn. The stage exit was less a tunnel and more a catacomb, twisting left and right and forking into multiple paths. She lit her way through the maze of wooden walls with fire cradled in her hand and chose her route by listening to the sound of chains rattling. Alone, she was faster than two men dragging a third.

She entered a wide, straight corridor where an ambush waited. Half a dozen new guards barred her path, already in fighting stances. Yun's captors made haste for another passage at the end of the hall.

Kyoshi sent forth a snaking torrent of wind from one of her palms that blew past the squad of guardsmen and slammed the exit's heavy wooden door shut. Yun was close to the floor and was weighed down by iron shackles, so he was saved from the brunt of it, but one of his captors was thrown into the back wall and knocked out. The other one tried to pull the door open by the bronze ring handle, but she kept up the gale-force pressure and it refused to budge.

The rest of the soldiers attacked. They were the royal elite, undoubtedly selected from the best of the best to serve in the palace.

But Kyoshi was the Avatar. And she still had a free hand.

She advanced down the hall through the storm of fireballs, deflecting them at first to the left and right, and then simply catching them once she gauged just how far her raw bending strength surpassed her opponents. She didn't have to outthink here in this confined space, or possess better technique. She could overwhelm.

"Call for reinforcements!" one of the guards screamed as his mistimed fire jab dissipated ineffectually against Kyoshi's chest.

But there were only two ways out of the corridor, and she controlled them both. She flicked a single wrist to counterattack.

The dirty secret of airbending Kyoshi had learned through experience was that it was absolutely devastating in close quarters. Surrounded by hard objects, the gentle art of monks and nuns turned utterly brutal. She sent wind back and forth with rapid changes of direction. The guards were taken by their midsections, flung into spine-rattling collisions with the walls and ceilings. They collapsed into armored heaps.

Kyoshi walked up to the shackled and blindfolded man who'd managed to inch himself into a sitting position. "Who are you?" she asked. "Who are you, really? Because I know you're not Yun."

He cringed. "What do you mean? I'm Yun, the man who attacked the palace, the false Avatar—"

She snatched away the cloth tied over his eyes to reveal golden irises. He was Fire Nation, though he looked very much like the man he was impersonating. He had the same handsome planes to his face as Yun, the same hair, the same build. The similarity was amazing, as brotherly as Zoryu and Chaejin.

But Kyoshi knew he was a fake from the first word he'd said out loud. He'd been coached to sound like Yun and was good enough to fool the nobles who'd been at the party. But he wasn't good enough to trick someone who'd lived with Yun and heard every emotion his voice could produce, laughter and despair and maybe even love somewhere in between.

Nor was he wounded in the shoulder. Kyoshi hadn't shared that detail with Zoryu. If she had, the Fire Lord would have undoubtedly burned the man to keep up the ruse.

Kyoshi knelt down and gripped the bindings between his ankles, heating them in her hands. She'd pulled off this metal-snapping trick once before, but back in Governor Te's mansion she didn't have to worry about scorching someone else.

"What are you doing?" the man yelled. He tried to worm free of her grasp.

"Stop moving! I'm getting you out of here! I won't let you die for crimes you didn't commit!"

"You can't! Leave me alone! I need this!"

It took a great deal to distract her so badly that she could feel the pain of burning herself through the numbness of her lightning scars. She hissed and dropped the red-hot iron. "You need to die?!"

"*Yes!* My family in Hanno'wu, we have nothing! Less than nothing! My debts—the Fire Lord promised me they'd be paid off upon my death! This is the last thing I can do for my wife and children!"

Shouts echoed and bounced off the walls. "Please," the man begged. "I was promised a quick and merciful execution. My family will starve if I don't do this. Save me and you'll be killing them."

In his scramble for more arguments to hurl at Kyoshi, the man who was probably a farmer or a fisherman down on his luck resorted to the highest level of politics. "The court needs its scapegoat, doesn't it? I understand the situation; I'm not stupid. Letting me die is necessary for the country!"

He spoke the Fire Lord's argument on Zoryu's behalf. It was necessary. Everything was *necessary*. An innocent man was going to die, and the whole world down to the victim himself was whispering in her ear to stand back and let it happen.

Kyoshi's shriek started low in her stomach and filled her

body. It was a sound of pure and total despair. The country would be saved. Her side had won.

The guards rounding the corner were thrown back by her cries of anguish, the ghost tearing itself free from her lungs. Yun's impostor, so ready to die, shuddered away from her howls like they were curses. Kyoshi screamed in the darkness, over and over again, her hatred for the world and herself spiraling into oblivion.

HOUSECLEANING

SHE FOUND Zoryu in the war room. A large table had been set amid the dragons. On top were two maps, one of the Fire Islands, and another of a single landmass resembling a fish's head. Ma'inka. The island looked like the main dish of a banquet, ready to be carved up and served.

The Fire Lord himself was alone in the empty hall, no advisors to give him counsel, leaning over the strategy table with outspread hands as the heavy burden of rulership weighed on his shoulders. Kyoshi wondered why he stayed there, not reacting to her entrance, until she realized there was one other person in the corner of the room. An artist making a sketch, scribbling diligently on a small canvas.

Zoryu wanted to capture the most pivotal moment of his reign for posterity. The pose was too informal for his entry into the royal gallery. This was meant to be a more intimate masterpiece, something to show his grandchildren and their grandchildren. No glory in victory, for one as wise as Zoryu, only the pain and burden of leadership.

"Leave," Kyoshi said to the artist. The young woman tucked her sketch under her arm and started for the door before remembering to wait for her Fire Lord's permission. Zoryu waved her away.

"Before today, she would have walked straight out of this room without a second glance at me," he said to Kyoshi once they were alone. "I'm making progress."

So he was. "Where did you find the double?"

"Trade secrets of the royalty," he said. "Master Jianzhu and Yun themselves advised me on how to restart the program, back before I knew you existed. *They* advocated the usefulness of having a decoy for Yun. Apparently, the practice is good for making speeches and foiling assassins."

Zoryu chuckled to himself at the irony. "People aren't as unique as they believe themselves to be and the Fire Nation is a populous country. You should check with the Earth King; you'd be surprised who he has copies of lying around."

He eyed her up and down. "I don't think anyone could find your like, so worry not. There will only ever be one Avatar Kyoshi."

It might have been one too many. "What will happen to the Saowon?"

"I will round up and arrest the ones here in the capital. The other clans will do the same across their home islands, on behalf of the Fire Lord. And then I'll have them killed."

Without pausing to consider the weight of what he said, he gestured at the map on the table. "As for Ma'inka itself, I believe the Saowon there will retreat to their mountain forts, at which point there'll be a lengthy siege. Sieges are always unpleasant affairs, but they don't have to be bloody. With the rest of the country's noble houses united behind me, I'll be able to starve the Saowon out. Or to death."

An entire clan of the Fire Nation wiped off the face of the earth. As simple as that. He walked out from around the table and rapped it once with his knuckles. "It's better than what would have happened otherwise. By my best guess, three-fifths of the clans would have joined the Saowon and turned on me, had things continued the way they were headed. It would have been open war across the entire Fire Nation."

Instead of resigning to a grinding conflict of attrition, Zoryu had isolated his enemies, branded them as criminals, and trapped them on a single island. He'd played his tiles masterfully. But there was still a critical flaw in his operation.

"If the real Yun shows up again, your ruse will be exposed," she said. "Everything would fall apart."

"Oh, I know. The Fire Nation would tear itself apart in the chaos and confusion. All I've really done is buy you more time to find him."

The first time Zoryu had explained to her the precipice the Fire Nation balanced on, it had been a cry for help. Now, repeated here, it was an ultimatum. "You're not done assisting me, Kyoshi," he said softly. "You don't want my nation to suffer any more than I do. You and I are still in this together."

A ruler holding his own country hostage. She had been so worried about turning into Jianzhu, as if the Earth Sage had been a special breed of monster threatening to be reborn through her and only her. How laughable a notion. The fact of the matter was the world grew Jianzhus by the bushel. They sprouted from the soil and multiplied from the seas. People sought to emulate Jianzhu with every fiber of their being.

Kyoshi had forgotten her *daofei* oaths. Becoming the lackey of a crown was a violation punishable by many knives. For bending to Zoryu's will, she would be ripped apart by thunderbolts.

The best she could do in her defeat was to save as many lives as possible. "I want clemency for the Saowon, if I'm to help you."

"Why should I give it? Even if they weren't collaborating with Yun, they were undermining my authority. Do you think if they succeeded in taking the throne, Chaejin would have sent me gently into exile?"

Kyoshi thought of a phrase her friend Wong had told her, back in her Flying Opera Company days. *A fight is over only when the winner says it's over.* She had to make sure Zoryu didn't commit an atrocity in celebration of his victory.

"Punish them in accordance for their tricks, but not for an act of treason they didn't commit. There will be no wholesale massacre."

"I'll look weak."

"Good thing you're a savvy politician capable of crafting his image into whatever suits his needs."

He narrowed his eyes at her. "As long as you're asking for the impossible, do you have any more demands?"

"I do. Yun's decoy. I want him sent home alive, and rewarded for his troubles."

Zoryu swelled with resistance. This was a bigger issue for him than the fate of his rivals. "No. I have to hold an execution. I need a body or else the honor of the entire Fire Nation goes unsatisfied. I've heard the stories about you, Kyoshi, and I know the things you've seen. What do you care if a single peasant lives or dies?"

She crossed the distance between them and thrust a closed fan under his chin, stopping short of his throat.

"I care more for his life than I do for yours right now," she said, examining the growing whites of Zoryu's eyes. "Let me make myself perfectly clear. You live on top of what I control. Your islands are surrounded by my waves. You fill your very lungs at my discretion. So if I hear any news about 'Yun' being executed, you will truly learn what it's like when the spirits forsake you in the face of the elements."

Zoryu cowered before her sudden onslaught. They always did. For a brief moment the Fire Lord knew what it was like to be truly helpless.

But unlike so many *daofei* and Triads before him, he found the strength of his title at his back. He was the ruler of the Fire Nation, and Kyoshi was the Avatar. She had her own image, as poor as it was, to think about. Slowly but surely, Zoryu grinned at her bluff.

He did her the favor of not saying out loud how badly she'd overplayed her situation. Instead he took on an air of pity. "Let me give you a bit of advice for when you next see Yun," he said. "I've thought a great deal about this, ever since he first showed up, and I think I know why you've been having so much trouble against him. You don't understand his feelings."

She pressed the fan deeper into the underside of Zoryu's jaw, but he didn't flinch. "Yun hates us," Zoryu said. "Everything he's done so far is because he hates us. You, me, the lieutenant."

"That's not true," Kyoshi snarled. "We were his friends. He's been acting out of vengeance. He *said* so."

Zoryu shook his head. "I don't think he realizes it himself. Consider his deeds, Kyoshi, not his words. Who has he been causing the most pain?

"For starters, me. By my reckoning, he's angry with me for daring to rule my country without his help. He's also furious with the lieutenant for having her mother's unconditional love. What Jianzhu gave him wasn't anything of the sort. And then there's you, Kyoshi."

And then there was her.

"Yun has never been able to let go of the fact that he's not the Avatar," Zoryu said. "To this day he agonizes over what should have been. He grieves for his lost destiny and that grief has turned into blame." He nudged the fan aside, expecting her to lose control of her emotions any second. "Jianzhu and the others might have lied about his Avatarhood, Kyoshi, but only one person truly stole it from him. You."

Seeing he'd rendered her incapable of response, he side-stepped out of her grasp and went back to his map table. "He's punishing us, Kyoshi, for moving on from him and having the things he doesn't. And unless you accept the truth, sooner or later he is going to punish you in a way I can't even imagine."

Kyoshi swallowed the buildup in her throat. She had no way of disproving any of Zoryu's insights other than her own stubborn faith that she knew Yun better. "I suppose you can tell all this because you played him in Pai Sho," she said hoarsely.

"No. I can tell because I'm not blinded by the past, like the two of you are. Maybe he truly is possessed by a spirit. It doesn't change what needs to be done."

He waved at the door. "Now, please, leave me. You have work to do, and I have the future of my country to plan."

SECOND CHANCES

KYOSHI NEEDED to arrange some travel for herself. She couldn't bear having to explain another half-baked plan to Jinpa, nor did she want him present when she carried it out. So, she went to a palace minister with her request for a ship and kept the whole arrangement from her secretary.

The next morning, upon learning a vessel waited for her at the harbor, she left the palace by herself. Guards opened the many doors and gates without her needing to ask, or even break stride. It made her feel like a farm animal being guided out of its pen.

She got into a carriage, which took her through Caldera City, down the volcano's slope, and through Harbor City. News of the Saowon's heinous acts had spread overnight through the capital and the streets were mostly empty, the Festival of Szeto abandoned mid-swing in the face of such treachery. Parade floats remained in side alleys, covered in tarps. Lanterns bobbed in the breeze, unlit. Kyoshi nearly marveled at the speed of court rumors before realizing Zoryu had probably spread the information throughout the island himself.

Like most of the major clans, the Saowon would have had a normal, everyday presence in the capital. Businesses and family homes. That was no longer the case. Primed to look for them, Kyoshi saw signs everywhere of a swift, efficient purge. A lone shop in a commerce street might be closed and dark while its neighbors were still open. A luxurious apartment, most certainly belonging to a noble, had no clan banner on its flagpole. Wisps of black smoke rose in the distance, clustered too near each other to be a coincidence.

She had to fight to keep the sourness in her stomach down. *Better than open war* was not a standard to live by. And yet people seemed content with it.

She reached the docks and found her ship. It was a well-made sloop with a deep keel, a speedy ocean traveler with no need to hug coasts and rivers like squat Earth Kingdom transports. But she winced when she saw the name on the side.

Sulan's Smile. The late Lord Chaeryu might have commissioned it for his wife's personal use before the two of them passed. It looked barely used.

Kyoshi decided Huazo had the right measure of it. Zoryu's mother had no blame in recent events, or at least the same amount of blame as everyone else in this whole affair. Kyoshi boarded the boat and did her best to ignore the neighboring cargo hauler having its stone camellia decorations scraped off by a team of Fire Navy sailors, red paint falling in flakes to the water's surface like clotted blood.

The crew of *Sulan's Smile* left her alone as they sailed in the direction she'd ordered. As she stood on the deck she could feel the water dragging on the hull like fingers, gripping the vessel, slowing it down more than the thin air ever did to Yingyong or Pengpeng. Compared to flying, every method of travel was a slog. She supposed she could have tried to speed them along with waterbending, but she'd heard it was possible to damage and capsize a vessel that way if the Waterbender didn't know what they were doing.

They came to the dark patch below the waves she was looking for. Kyoshi ordered the ship to drop anchor. Captain Joonho, a man with whiskers like spruce needles, stood at the head of his crew of hardy, weather-beaten sailors, waiting for her next command.

"Stay here until I return," Kyoshi told him. "Do not try to come after me, no matter what happens."

"I don't understand, Avatar," Joonho said. "Return from where? There's nothing here."

Kyoshi hoisted herself onto the railing of the ship. "There used to be." She plunged into the water.

She could hear shouting from above the surface. Some of the men might have been inclined to dive in and rescue her, but her orders had been clear.

They would have had difficulty catching her anyway. Kyoshi had worn her full complement of armor so she could sink faster. She kicked downward, swimming for the ruins of Yangchen's island. As before, it took her an embarrassingly long time for her to remember she was a Waterbender. With a flap of her arms, she surged faster than an elephant koi.

Her sight became blackness. The only reminder she was swimming through water was the burning of her lungs as she ran out of air. She fought through the knives in her chest to keep going, but her bravery bought her only a few more kicks.

Her mouth opened and she swallowed to fullness. A cloud of bubbles escaped her throat before the seawater rushed into her body, violating every space she had left. She was drowning.

She'd come here with a crew of strangers because none of her companions would have let her take this risk. Kyoshi fought for as long as she could, wanting to bring her consciousness to the very edge. With her last reserves of thought, she sent out her message.

Kuruk. Get out here now before I die, or I will cross over to the other side and come after you there.

"Kid. You can open your eyes."

Kyoshi blinked awake. It was warm and bright. The scent of grass tickled her nose.

She was sitting in a green field that rolled gently into the distance. On one side of the horizon was a row of trees that looked placed by hand, applied to the top of the hills like Kyoshi's eyebrow liner when she wore her makeup. Opposite the forest was a tall peak jutting high into the air after a few false starts. Lines of clouds converged to a point behind it, as if the mountain were a sun emitting beams of light.

Her predecessor in the Avatar cycle was dressed more casually than the one time he'd fully appeared before her. Kuruk was without his furs and wore only a light blue Water Tribe summer tunic. His arms and neck were still adorned with the sharp teeth and claws of beasts, strung through by leather thongs.

He made a crooked little half smile that tugged one side of his face higher. "I've been trying to get a hold of you for the longest time. But I needed your help to do it. An Avatar talking to their past lives requires true willingness from both ends."

His message to her in the Southern Air Temple. *Need your help.* He hadn't been asking for a favor from beyond the grave. He needed her help in order to communicate properly. Of all the stupid, unclear ways for him to put it. "What did you want to talk about?"

"The same thing as you. Your boy. Him and Father Glowworm. I can guide you to what you seek. It's why you're here now, isn't it?"

So she hadn't been wrong in going to North Chung-Ling to get Kuruk's help. Congratulations to her. Vindication felt about as good as drowning.

She should have just kept her mouth shut and taken whatever assistance Kuruk was offering. But there was an unsettling calmness to their conversation. It was happening in complete silence.

Something was off. "This is the Spirit World, isn't it?" she asked. "Where are the spirits?" The two of them were the only beings sitting in the vast field. Kyoshi had little to base her expectations on, but unless the plants and rocks themselves were alive, this place was as devoid of life as the dried patches of the Si Wong Desert.

Kuruk winced. "Most spirits tend to give me a wide berth."

"Why?"

He didn't want to say. But he was talking to himself. Lying was pointless. "Because I used to hunt them."

Kyoshi rubbed her face, feeling the cracks and lines with her fingers. Lao Ge had mentioned it once. *Kuruk, the greatest hunter that ever walked the Four Nations.* The trophies that had decorated his body the first time he manifested before her in his full regalia. If slaying beasts in the physical world no longer posed a challenge, then it wasn't so far-fetched that a reckless, thrill-seeking adventurer like Kuruk would turn his eye toward spirits. Being the Avatar would have given him the means.

"You," she said. It was hard to speak through the grin ripping her mouth apart and difficult to see through the tears streaming down her face. "You are something else." Letting her feelings run loose was like putting boiled herbs to a burn. It was necessary and painful and it had been postponed long enough.

Kuruk swallowed, unable to meet her gaze. "It's not what you think. Yangchen—"

"Don't you dare!" Kyoshi giggled. Her tears flew down her own throat as she gasped. "Don't you dare bring her into this. You're not worthy of her legacy. Your name belongs in the gutter with mine."

Here she was, in the middle of the most sacred act an Avatar could perform. Except she was Kyoshi, and Kuruk was Kuruk. Had there ever been a worse duo in history, disaster followed by catastrophe?

The hilarity of her situation snuffed itself out like a candle with a glass placed over it. A dead, airless feeling followed. "This isn't fair," she said. "None of this is fair."

The earth around her began to ripple. She heard a flitting, flipping sound like the pages of a thick book being swiped. Starting from the horizon, a crack in the grass began to zigzag and spiderweb toward them. Pieces of the terrain itself started falling into the rift, making it clear that she and Kuruk stood not on solid ground but a fragile, thin surface.

This wasn't bending. It was a reflection of the wounds she'd suffered. Here in the Spirit World, her pain had substance.

"I hate you!" she screamed at Kuruk. The tear in the ground revealed a shade of color underneath that Kyoshi could not explain in the language of the Four Nations. It was the tint of the abyss, the background swirl of chaos. If she fell into it, there would be no coming back. "You had everything handed to you! Yangchen gave her legacy to you, and you squandered it! You left me a world full of nothing but suffering and misery!"

The collapse picked up speed, racing toward her and her past life, threatening to drop them both into a twisted new existence. The landslide consumed the trees, the grass, the sky, abrading reality, shrinking her mind. Nothingness, in an onrushing wave.

Kuruk gazed at the annihilation coming for them both. And in response, he gave her a look of complete surrender. "You have every right," he said gently.

At the very last second, the crumbling halted at the edge of their feet.

Did she?

No, she thought. She didn't.

She didn't have the right to lose herself in her rage and let it take her to oblivion. No matter what she'd been through. She wouldn't allow herself to become a human scar, a compendium of personal loss. She had the obligation to be more than the sum of her grievances with the world.

Gradually, shard by shard, the surfaces and planes of the Spirit World floated back into place, raised from the chasm they had fallen into, affixing themselves to each other like a plate being mended with gilded lacquer. Whether it was her doing, or the work of forces beyond her control, she wasn't sure.

Either way, it was slow going. Rebuilding always took longer than destruction, cleaning a mess more time than making it. Kuruk watched the landscape repair itself, neutrality still lingering in his expression despite the fact he'd nearly taken a plunge into the terrifying beyond with Kyoshi.

"You came here for answers," he said to her, holding out his hand. "I have to show you something."

"Don't touch me." She smacked his hand away.

In the moment they made contact, it occurred to Kyoshi she wasn't wearing her gauntlets in the Spirit World. Her hands were bare, and the red scars of lightning were nowhere to be seen, as if her memories of herself hadn't incorporated the damage to her skin. No one had explained to her what would happen if her form touched Kuruk's in the Spirit World.

There was a flash of light in her head. And when it subsided, Kyoshi found herself imprisoned once again, in the unbreakable cage of memory.

LOST FRIENDS

KURUK OPENED his eyes. He was no longer in Yangchen's meadow near Yaoping, facing Kelsang under the starry sky. He realized the source of his Air Nomad friend's conflict with his elders when it came to what the Spirit World looked like. The realm beyond the physical was different things to different people at different times.

The Avatar was alone, his friend nowhere to be found in the hissing gray swampland. They'd lost each other somewhere in the journey. The water around Kuruk slithered with—not life, but something akin to it and all the more unsettling for the closeness. A scream and the beating of a drum were all he could hear, incessant, hysterical, and only when he braved the foul water and flailed his way to a solid shore did he find the source.

A spirit. Not one of Kelsang's playful creatures but a monstrosity the size of a house, gripping the ground with arms like spider limbs and bashing its featureless head against the earth over and over again, causing itself horrible pain but never ceasing its assault, nor its shriek that came from no discernible mouth. Before he could swallow her horror and try to speak to it, a long tail wrapped around his neck and hoisted him into the air.

Their forms were crushed together. Revulsion seeped through his skin, a feeling of being tied to a corpse. The creature hurled him to the ground and he bounced like stuffed rags, blacking out from a pain to his ethereal form that did its best to mimic the physical. Before he lost consciousness, he caught a glimpse of what the spirit was attacking so ferociously with its skull. It was a pond of ice. The reflection on the silvery sheen was a hillside view of Yaoping Town.

Kuruk woke up with a gasp. Kelsang was still sitting across from him, his eyes closed, murmuring pleasantries like he was attending a tea ceremony. Kuruk got up, ignored the looks of surprise on Hei-Ran's and Jianzhu's faces, and stole his friend's glider.

He rode his own furious squall of airbending to Yaoping. There was no time to explain to the others what he knew in his heart. That monstrous spirit had found a crack between the Spirit World and the world of humans. If it broke through, it was going to slaughter everyone it came across.

There was only one place where someone could see the town from above like Kuruk had, and that was the entrance to the salt mines in the neighboring mountain. He landed the glider and stood before the hole in the world, the gaping maw of darkness. He summoned his courage and ran inside. Better to cross through the rift and go on the attack in the Spirit World. He would have his bending that way. Kelsang had said so.

He found the enraged spirit and began to fight it. He didn't know how long the battle raged. He only knew with grim certainty that the right Avatar had been chosen for this task. This foe was a beast, and he was a hunter. A hunter struck fast and true, and was merciful to their prey. A hunter approached their duty with solemn respect.

It took bringing all four elements to bear against the maddened spirit to bring it down, but bring it down he did. He was victorious. The town was saved. All would be well.

The next morning, his friends found the Avatar crawling blindly through the streets of Yaoping, foaming at the mouth.

It was days before he could speak. Destroying the spirit had cost him a piece of his own, somehow. He was bleeding inside, losing something more vital than blood, vitality leaching away in a manner no healer could fix. He was cold. Him, a child of the north who laughed at blizzards and swam laps around icebergs, was cold. Nothing pumped through his veins.

He tried to tell Kelsang, Jianzhu, and Hei-Ran what happened and could not. The words stuck in his throat. He made up a story about a mischievous spirit tricking him into losing his faculties for a moment. Like what happened to wandering children in ominous folktales.

His friends left him to rest in the bed of an inn. They looked for a doctor. The doctor came by, said there was nothing wrong with his body, and told him to rest. He wanted to die.

One day, when everyone else was out, a friendly maid came by and gave him some distilled wine in defiance of the doctor's orders. It burned his throat going down, the first sensation in days that cut through the chill. He drank more, and more, feeling the liquid press against the wound inside him like a red-hot iron to a severed limb.

When the maid smiled and gently laid a hand upon his chest, the Avatar clasped it like he was drowning.

He couldn't remember the woman's face. But he remembered those of his friends when they happened upon the tangle of limbs poking out from under the covers and the broken bottles littering the floor. Kelsang didn't judge. Jianzhu didn't care, being of the opinion that if the Avatar had a certain desire, the Avatar should slake it. Kuruk would only understand the difference in their reactions later in his life.

And Hei-Ran, though she would never admit it, lost a great deal of respect for him in that moment. The door to the Firebender's heart, while not locked forever, had been firmly shut. There was always going to be a portion of her closed off to those who couldn't master themselves.

But they bounced back. Their adventures went on. The Avatar's friends were remarkable. He loved them so much. He loved their intelligence, their aspirations, their sheer nobility. They were simply good people. There was so much good this group could do for the world.

That was why, when the second spirit attack came, he went to face it alone again. His friends would insist on helping if they knew. But he would never, ever make them suffer what he had, not in a thousand lifetimes. They would be tainted by association with the deed he had to do.

A bad dream during a visit to the Fire Nation showed him a rift in a cenote supplying sacred water to a corner of Ma'inka Island. He ran to the cavern in the middle of the night and dove into the water, defiling it. Instead of dashing his head against the stone bottom, he swam and swam straight down until he found the mass of writhing beaks, snapping and licking their way to the surface. He stabbed with ice and he stabbed with stone, his eyes closed, the screams of terror his own. His former hunting partners of his youth would have scorned him for not performing a clean kill. He could not look upon the dying thing.

Once the deed was done, Kuruk dragged himself over the lip of the cenote, weeping water onto the ledge. The cold emptiness inside him had returned in force. He crawled like a baby until he reached the feet of a man who stared down at him in puzzlement and distaste.

The man was a Fire National from a clan or tribe he didn't recognize. His name was Nyahitha, he said, and after receiving a premonition, the elders of the Bhanti had sent him here to give aid to the Avatar. It was clear he had trouble believing this bedraggled mess was Great Yangchen's successor.

Nyahitha hauled Kuruk to a campsite in the jungle and performed some kind of diagnostic ritual, guiding heat along his energy pathways similar to the way a Northern healer would use the water within a patient's body. He confirmed what Kuruk had already guessed, that coming into contact with these dark creatures and destroying them was causing damage to his own spirit. Nyahitha repaired what he could but admitted a permanent toll would be taken each time another of these battles was fought. Already, Kuruk was going to be out of the running for "Longest Era" in the Avatar history books.

Such terrible bedside manner for a doctor, Kuruk joked. Couldn't he have broken the news a little more gently? Then he threw up blood all over the Fire Sage's robes.

Nyahitha's dire warnings cemented Kuruk's decision not to tell his companions about the spirit incursions. They would follow him into any danger and give their lives to protect his. Staining the vibrant spirits of Hei-Ran and Kelsang and Jianzhu with this sickness would be a tragedy too horrible to consider. He was not going to see that happen, not even if it meant his own oblivion.

He began to take breaks from his missions with them to do research with Nyahitha. They visited the hidden library of the Bhanti, a contender for the greatest repository of spiritual knowledge in the physical realm. Together, under the peaked roofs of the stone pagodas, they pored over scrolls and tomes older than the Four Nations themselves.

They deduced that the spirits were trying to force their way through newly created cracks in the boundary between the Spirit World and the lands of humans. They did not know why or how these cracks were forming all of a sudden. Normally, places where spirits could cross over were ancient and sacred and rare. Special circumstances like the twilights of hallowed dates were required. That didn't seem to be the case anymore.

They also searched for a better technique to subdue their foes but found none. Perhaps it had yet to be invented. Kuruk shuddered as he closed the last promising book in the Bhanti library without finding salvation.

As more attacks came, he realized he could stalk the dark creatures across the Spirit World itself, sometimes following the wake of great disturbances and storms across the ever-changing landscape, and sometimes relying on his own preternatural tracking skills, his ability to cut sign from sheer ice and bare rock and the smallest out-of-place blade of grass. On such excursions he always had to pass through a rift from the physical world to the spiritual, taking on his quarry with his physical body. Without his bending he stood no chance, and it made more sense to fight on the Spirit World side of the border, to minimize collateral damage to humans.

And so he hunted. He walked the realm beyond the physical, searching for spirits with murderous intent trying to force their way into a human population. Each time he found one, Kuruk tried his best to placate the being's anger, at the cost of his blood and sweat and bones. Nothing worked. To save lives, he had to fight. He had to kill.

He and Nyahitha told no one what they did. They were like people graduating from petty theft to organized crime, in too deep to ever extricate themselves. By the time they reached a certain number of hunts, layfolk would have shunned them for the spirits they'd destroyed, let alone the Bhanti or the Air Nomads.

The world went on. It had competent people looking after it. Kuruk, never one for meetings, where the quickest minds were forced to adopt the pace of the slowest, began to sleep through them, exhausted by the lingering pain and the wine he drank to dull it. Jianzhu would inevitably work things out with the diplomats and ministers and ambassadors by the time he woke up.

His nights were spent carousing at parties, in taverns, at contests of bending prowess, trying to feel as human as possible with as many different humans as possible. He secretly hoped Nyahitha would find a sacred text declaring the official treatment for his symptoms was to be close to life, joy, and the touch of warm bodies, but no. The hedonism of his self-prescribed "healing process" was his own weakness showing through, nothing else. Nyahitha partook in the treatment as well, surprising Kyoshi with his indulgences. The formerly austere sage pursued excess with the immoderation of a man denied.

Kuruk barely noticed his friends splitting apart. The treasures of his life scattered over the Four Nations to pursue their own paths. They'd all come to the same conclusion. They were accomplishing nothing of worth in the Avatar's company. It felt like one day he was playing his daily game of Pai Sho with Jianzhu, and the next, he was reading Jianzhu's letter of admonishment for not attending Hei-Ran's wedding.

Hei-Ran. Kuruk had been out of his mind with grief when he showed up at Kelsang's with that poem. A spirit had tried to break through the day before, and his pent-up fury at himself for lying to Hei-Ran by omission about so many different things for all these years exploded. He had annihilated the creature with the full power of the Avatar State, an unworthy act no matter the circumstances. The poem was a feeble attempt to turn back time to a point where he wasn't such a miserable failure who abused Yangchen's gifts, an age where he was still within reach of deserving Hei-Ran's love.

He channeled his sorrow into more research with Nyahitha, longer expeditions into the Spirit World. He finally discovered how the tunnels to the physical realm were being created, his knowledge of beasts coming to the forefront once again. Animals often took over structures created by other animals, like how jaguar beetles would live in the vast complex mounds of angler termites after the original residents moved on to form other colonies.

The cracks in reality were being created by a single spirit.

Kuruk switched his focus to pinpointing the origins of the tunnels instead of the spirits trying to use them, circling closer and closer to the source, until he encountered Father Glowworm. The World-Borer. It Within the Hole.

Finally he'd found a spirit that would talk to the Avatar. He learned Father Glowworm had the power to rasp away at the barrier between the physical and spiritual worlds, leaking wisps of its essence through the cracks it made to bask in the warmth and chaos of the mortal realm at his pleasure.

Did it take the occasional human, here and there? Yes, but what hunter didn't snatch up choice prey when the opportunity presented itself? Father Glowworm was a wise and crafty predator. It could create tunnels to any location in the physical world, but kept the exits in deep, dark places where humans wouldn't notice, and never lingered around the same settlements for very long. If lesser spirits wanted to make a go for the lands of humans using his abandoned passages, that was none of its concern.

Kuruk's mistake was trading names with it. Spirits with self-appointed names were incredibly powerful and dangerous, Nyahitha had told him, and there was a power in introductions. Knowing Father Glowworm's name finalized the curse that had been slowly building upon the Avatar over the years. It dried the ink on the contract.

Father Glowworm knew it too. The two of them were in it together for the long haul, the spirit declared. Perhaps they would have fun.

Kuruk, deadened with exhaustion, showed the human-eating spirit his definition of fun.

Their fight nearly created a gaping hole in the boundary

between realms. Father Glowworm was stronger than the other spirits, and Kuruk was too stubborn to die. Their energies bit into each other like blades clashing edge-to-edge, leaving permanent notches.

With a strike that nearly broke the foundations of the bedrock around them, Kuruk wounded Father Glowworm grievously, the spirit diminishing in size and power several times over. But it managed to escape, wriggling away into an endless labyrinth of darkness.

It was an outcome the Avatar found acceptable. The disappointing secret of Pai Sho most novices never learned was that at the very highest levels, half the matches between masters ended in unsatisfying, inconclusive draws. He'd done lasting damage to his enemy, enough to ensure the spirit would keep out of the human world for at least a generation or two.

And it had marked him in return. Neither of them would ever fully heal from the encounter. They would know each other in their bones forever, like old friends . . .

Kyoshi stepped away from her predecessor's memories gently, like they were pieces of crystal too delicate to handle. Unlike the communing session in North Chung-Ling, where she'd watched his youth unfold by herself, Kuruk had been standing beside her as they silently witnessed the horrors of his later life. There hadn't been a right time to speak to him.

Still, she was grateful for his presence this time around. She couldn't have handled watching those memories on her own.

Father Glowworm had scared her witless, back when she had met the spirit in the flesh.

She looked at Kuruk, examining his strained but stoic face. By the time of his death, he would have been more injury than unbroken skin underneath his clothes. His appearance in the Spirit World must have been altered by his own perceptions and preferences. He remembered a version of himself from before the worst days of his life took over.

The meadow around them had been mended and no longer looked like a broken plate. "Why were there so many angry spirits during your era?" she asked. She understood now that Kuruk had only taken on the creatures that couldn't be appeased by anything but death.

"That's a question for another day," he said. "In order to give you the aid you sought, I had to share memories of my Avatarhood and Father Glowworm. Now that you remember this portion of your past life, you'll be able to find your boy in the physical world. Trust me."

She found herself believing him. "What about the rest of your memories?" The words slipped out before Kyoshi realized she was prying.

Kuruk's jaw tightened. "There's little to see after I lost my friends."

Where was Kuruk? Kyoshi had once asked Kelsang, curious about what happened after their group had split. Traveling the world had been the answer. Breaking hearts and taking names. Being Kuruk. It sounded like the Water Avatar had been living it up by himself, having one great adventure across the Four Nations.

But the grief in his face right now told her differently. After the companions of his youth left his side, Kuruk had been alone. Surrounded by a world that celebrated him perhaps, but completely and utterly alone.

The man in front of her was a physically large person, but looking at him, she could only see the limits of the space Kuruk filled. It reminded her of the way Jianzhu's corpse seemed to shrink after the life left his body. Death and time made everyone small, reduced them to trivialities. She had no doubt her successor would look at her with skepticism, wondering why everyone claimed this Kyoshi person was considered a giant.

"I'm glad I finally reached you, Avatar Kuruk," she said, meaning it wholly.

His shoulders hitched. And then they eased. She didn't consider he might have needed this connection as much as her, assuming a past life could need anything.

"There's one more thing I have to tell you." Kuruk suddenly appeared reluctant, a change of mind taking hold of him. "But I don't know if it's ultimately worth it. I don't want to cause you more pain."

Kyoshi read his grimace and realized another flaw in Kuruk's character. Outside of his bending opponents perhaps, he could not stand seeing other people get hurt. "You might as well."

Kuruk sighed. "Come with me."

They walked side by side. The unreality of distance and solid ground flowed to their advantage. A few strides took them out of the meadow and into the horizon, as if they were spinning the world underneath them with their feet.

She forgot to observe their journey and take in the splendors of the Spirit World. By the time she remembered to look for Kelsang's glorious painted landscapes and curious talking creatures, they arrived at their destination.

They'd gone from nightmare to nightmare. Kuruk and Kyoshi stood at the tip of a drained, dead swamp. Trees that needed their roots submerged in liquid had withered into kindling. The silt floor of the basin had dried into dusty mudcrack.

She had an idea where the water had gone. A great gash in the earth had opened, splitting the width of the swamp's edge. The crack started small and tore away from her feet like the beginnings of a great canyon cut into the desert. The depths were filled with the same wild, clashing, mindless color that Kyoshi had threatened to immerse herself and Kuruk into.

The creator of this tear had stood where they stood now, the origin point clearly marked like a burst of outrage. "Did Yun do this?"

"Yes. The Spirit World reacts to our emotions. The wounds we bring into this place take on physical characteristics. Unlike the rupture you created, this one isn't healing. Your boy is keeping it open and festering by clinging to his anger."

Kyoshi nodded. "I know. Yun's not in his right mind because of Father Glowworm's influence."

"No. You've held on to that excuse long enough." Kuruk was gentle but unyielding. "What I needed to tell you is that spirits can possess a human being's body, and they might even merge with a person to give them new shapes and forms. But they don't take over people's thoughts. Yun is in complete control of his actions. He has been the whole time."

"Oh," Kyoshi said. She wavered where she stood. "Oh." If Kuruk was right about Yun, then Zoryu was too.

"I'm sorry, kid," Kuruk said. "I wish it wasn't so."

The sky, a clear blue sheen, began to swirl around her axis. Clouds appeared for the sole purpose of marking her spiral. Kuruk glanced up with a disappointed expression. *Shame. Looks like rain. We'll have to cut the outing short.*

Kyoshi tried to speak and salt water came out of her mouth. It spilled down her chin and dampened her robes. She wanted to give parting words to Kuruk but her throat was thick with the sea.

Someone rolled her to her side, and the rest of the water came rushing out of her body. She felt the wooden deck of *Sulan's Smile* pressing against her cheek. Captain Joonho and the crew ringed her, frowning with worry. It would be bad luck if an Avatar died aboard their ship, even a foolish Earthborn one.

As Kyoshi lay there, she could feel the gift Kuruk had given her. The battle between the previous Avatar and Father Glowworm had left identifying scars on both parties, marks carved so deep as to be permanent.

She and Yun were the inheritors of that legacy. She could tell where he was. It was a faint presence, flickering at this distance, but it had a direction. She knew if she reached for him, extended the flow of her spirit, she could follow him to his location. He'd likely tracked her through the Fire Nation using the same method. They were each other's beacons, two torches in the darkness.

And he'd used that connection over and over again, to make her suffer.

Kyoshi sniffed and immediately regretted it. She wiped the burning salt sensation from her nose. "I thought I told you not to come after me," she said to Captain Joonho. Several sailors were dripping wet like she was. The strongest swimmers must have fished her out.

Joonho nodded solemnly. "You did. But that was obviously a stupid order and we were never going to obey it."

If only the world were filled with common-sensed people like the captain and his crew. She let her head thunk back to the deck and closed her eyes. "How dare you defy your Avatar," she muttered.

INTERLUDE: THE MAN FROM THE SPIRIT WORLD

AFTER CONSUMING Father Glowworm, Yun went through the checks Sifu Amak had taught him to perform after coming into contact with potentially deadly toxins. There was no burning or numbness in his stomach or on his skin. No tingling on his lips. His vision was as clear as it had ever been. He held out his hand and spread his fingers; they were steady.

No effect. Perhaps he'd drunk enough vileness in his life to render him immune. If there were signs that appeared when a spirit passed into a human, they were masked by his own flesh. He couldn't discern whether Father Glowworm was destroyed, dissipated, or alive somewhere inside him. He didn't care.

He was more puzzled by what had spurred him to behave so. Maybe it was sheer contempt for his enemy. Jianzhu had often told him to try and avoid feeling contempt in his political duties. It made you act irrationally, blinded you to your own gain.

Jianzhu.

Yun gazed around him, his hands on his hips. He decided, quite logically, and of his own accord, that he should start digging. Straight down.

He dropped to his knees and buried his fingers in the damp soil, parting the dirt. He shoved clods of earth—spirit earth?—out of his way, yanking at the remaining roots that laced themselves across his path. He tore at the fibrous weave, sap bleeding into the lines of his palms. Forcing his way through the layer of living vegetation, he encountered darker clay. He went deeper.

He dug as the animals did, not like badgermoles with their bending but in the manner of clawed, malign, lower beasts that never saw the light of day, creatures that laid grubs and grew fat and pulsing and luminescent in the darkness. He flung clods and castings behind him and over his head, though which way was up no longer mattered. He bored deeper and deeper, darker and darker, until the only sound in the pitch black was his own breath, his exhalations hot and trapped against his skin.

Yun woke faceup. He had to pry his eyelids apart with his fingers, glued together as they were with dried tears and sediment. He was lucky. Had he passed out under the sky with them open, the burning sun would have blinded him permanently.

The other part of his body he feared for were his nails. They should have been chipped, shattered, worn down to flakes. He'd scratched away at so much soil and stone with hands that weren't meant for it. But they were fine. Dirty, yes. Kyoshi would certainly give him a scolding later. She hated it when he absentmindedly picked the grime from under his nails throughout the day.

"There's such a thing as soap!" he shouted in imitation of his friend's distress.

His voice bounced off the striated walls of a gully. The runoff that had carved it was long gone. Nothing grew here.

I . . . may be dying of thirst, he thought to himself.

Yun staggered out the path the rain would have taken, had there been any. The earth was so barren and devoid of animal signs that he thought he was still in the Spirit World, doomed to wander a wasteland, until the land sloped away to reveal a town below him.

He picked his way down the rocky hillside, hunching and limping until he remembered he wasn't injured, just tired. And possibly delusional. There was no way any of what he'd gone through could be real, was there? The Spirit World was as much of a state of mind as it was a place, according to some scholars.

The settlement bore marks of cheap, rapid construction, the type of boomtown constructed to exploit opportunities and people in equal measure. He could tell with a couple of footsteps that most of the brickwork wouldn't last more than a few years. Yun kept his mouth shut despite being on the receiving end of a few hard stares from the villagers on the outskirts. Blundering in and shouting, *Hey, what place is this? Where am I?* was an invitation for trouble.

But try as he might, he lost all caution and composure once he saw the well at the center of the square. He ran toward it, stumbling over his own feet, frantic like a pet for its returning master.

A very large man sitting on the porch of one of the nearest

buildings saw him and slowly got up. He walked over, placing himself firmly in Yun's path. A heavy club dangled from his belt. Yun slowed to a halt.

"This is Governor Tuo's well," the guard said. "If you got tags, you can drink." He flicked the carved wooden chits that hung from a string around his neck.

He had the twang of Xishaanese in his fourth-tone syllables. Which meant Yun wasn't far from where he'd first exited the human world, dragged into that cave by Father Glowworm. This town must have been built as part of a new mining operation, its citizens the workforce brought in from afar.

He wondered how many of the villagers knew they could glimpse their futures farther along the mountain range. They only had to look at the abandoned ruins where Jianzhu had brought him and Kyoshi. Once the veins of ore dried up, so would the money. The workers would be discarded just like the husks of their homes. No more use to anyone.

Yun ground his heel into the dust. Through his earthbending he could feel the shape of the well. The weathering told him it had been dug in the distant past, probably a century before any human being realized there was wealth to be extracted from the mountains.

"Did Governor Tuo put that water in the earth? Did he drill that well himself?" Yun's tongue rasped over his lips. It was difficult for the walls of his throat to part from each other. The worst part was he *knew* Tuo, and the parsimonious governor was exactly the type of man who would refuse someone a drink like this.

The guard's hand moved to his club.

"Look," Yun said. "Let me have some water and I'll make sure you're rewarded beyond . . ." The sentence died in a gasp. He was too weak to offer the man a fortune beyond his wildest imagination. It occurred to him that he no longer had any fortune to give. There was a trove of wealth in the mansion in Yokoya and he owned exactly none of it.

"Go try one of the shops," the guard said. He drew his weapon and pointed to the corner of the square. "They can give you their water if they want. But this here is the governor's well."

All right. All right. The first shop in that direction was a teahouse, as far as he could tell. It was just another step added before his destination. No need to despair yet.

Yun teetered over to the building where a chimney sent puffs of friendly white smoke into the air, indicating a stove was burning away, boiling water for tea. The entrance was on the other side. He navigated the alley using the walls for support, skimming his hand against the texture of the brick, and only made it halfway through before slumping to the ground.

Now this *is a familiar feeling*, he thought, his back pressing against the outside of a building he wanted to be inside. Just like the good old days in Makapu, listening in on the classroom. His teeth chattered. He hadn't realized how cold he was.

His head tilted lower. His thoughts drifted to Kyoshi again. He could feel her warmth against his flank as if she were next to him. She wasn't though. She was in Taihua, the wrong mountain range, on the complete opposite end of the Earth Kingdom.

Yun blinked awake from the sleep that threatened to claim him and never let go. How did he know Kyoshi was in Taihua?

He tried reaching for her again. Their distance across the physical realm didn't matter. He was certain of it now. Her spirit was a beacon, a shimmering signal in the darkness. Steady. Reassuring. Unique. It was everything he wanted.

He yanked himself back to his own place in the world, ashamed. *Of course her spirit stands out among all others. She's the Avatar.*

He was too dried out to cry and too weary to cry out. Here, among humans, the earth did not automatically shake itself asunder in obeisance to his emotions. There was nowhere for the pain to go, no reflection of his suffering. Another wave of grief swelled inside him, and he could only cling to his own sides, powerless, trying not to drown.

"Oh come on!" a man shouted loud enough to rattle the waxed paper covering a window above Yun's head. "You're docking me half a week for one missed day?"

"You should be grateful you're not fired," someone else replied calmly, probably the owner of the teahouse. "You miss your shift, you don't get paid. How hard is it to show up for work when you're supposed to?"

"It's because you insist on using that stupid calendar!" said the first one. "The six thousand twenty-whatever-eth day of the Era of Yun? What are you, some Upper Ring ninny who sleeps with a portrait of the Avatars under his pillow? It's not going to make this dump any fancier!"

Yun froze at hearing his own name. They were referring to the Avatar calendar. Six thousand and twenty-odd days into his era meant Yun had been trapped in the Spirit World for about a week.

"I'm surprised you're not a greater devotee," the owner said to his delinquent worker. "Didn't the Avatar save your sorry hide from the big bad pirate queen?"

"Wait, what?" a woman said. Boots clunked to the floor like she'd taken them off a chair to sit up in interest. "I never heard about this. *You* were one of Tagaka's hostages?"

"Gow here is originally from Lansou Village on the other side of these mountains," the owner said. "He got nabbed like a gold piece left in the street. Whisked away like a poached pig chicken."

"Oh, cram it," said the other man. "You tell the story more often than I do." He sounded like he viewed the whole experience as embarrassing instead of harrowing, like tripping into a pile of manure.

Yun squeezed his eyes shut. He'd been thrown one last bit of luck. He summoned the energy to stand up, unsure if he could do it again after this.

There was no door, only an empty frame with a curtain tied to the side. As he entered, Yun knocked on the wooden strut to draw the attention of the people inside. "Sorry to trouble you," he said.

He'd seen finer establishments, to say the least. The interior was furnished with rope spools for tables. The benches were overturned supply crates. The owner, a burly man with heavy-lidded eyes and hairy arms, was in the middle of wiping used cups, evidently the only cleaning they ever saw.

His gaze dipped to Yun's chest, where no tags were to be found. "What do you want?"

"I could use some water. Please."

He heard a laugh come from the woman sitting at a table. She had wavy hair tied back low on her head and a round, flat face. Her boots were caked with dried slurry, but only up to the ankle. She must have been a shift boss from the mines. A regular worker would have been covered in the filth from head to toe, nor would they be in a teahouse in the middle of the day. Yun did his best not to stare at the steaming pot in front of her, or the long, damp leaves poking out from under the lid of her ceramic *gaiwan*.

"Do you have money?" the owner said.

"I do not." His pockets were empty. And after clawing his way back to the mortal world, Yun's once-fine robes were no longer capable of convincing anyone he was rich.

"Then get out." The owner said it with so little malice that it sounded like a pleasant *Good afternoon*.

Yun expected this response, but he had one last desperate counterplay. "I couldn't help overhearing your conversation about the Avatar. You, someone who obviously respects the master of all four elements." He bowed slightly at the owner before turning to Gow. "And you, sir, whom the Avatar rescued from danger."

Gow was thinner in body and face than his boss, and in the habit of shifting his weight from side to side where he stood. "Yeah?" he said defensively, his pinched features turning even narrower in suspicion. "What of it?"

"I know it sounds hard to believe," Yun said. "But I'm the . . ."

He hitched. An era passed in silence, the almost-lie stuck to his lips.

"I'm Yun," he said, recovering. "I am the man your calendar refers to. I led the rescue efforts in the southern seas." He gave it a moment to sink in. "Now, I ask you again, can I *please* have some water?"

Perhaps he would have been taken seriously had he not hesitated over his identity. Perhaps it wouldn't have made a difference. The owner's sleepy-looking eyes sparked with amusement, not reverence.

"I don't know," he said. He tilted his head at Yun. "Gow, is this your savior?"

Gow squinted. "The sailors who picked us up off that iceberg were Fire Navy. I didn't see an Avatar do anything to rescue me."

"Yes, but I—you see, it's—" Yun's hand went to his head. A quick way to explain the complexities and logistics of transporting over a thousand kidnapped Earth Kingdom villagers eluded him.

The owner took advantage of his loss for words by going to the stove and placing a fresh cast-iron pot on it. From the heavy way it clanked, it was full. "I'll tell you what," he said. "You can have all the water you want, provided you stay right over there." He rapped the pot with his knuckles. "Here. Have a drink on me."

Yun's jaw fell. "You . . . What?"

"You're Earth Kingdom. So, if you're who you say you are, then it shouldn't be a problem for you to waterbend some refreshment over to that gaping mouth of yours."

"Seems fair," said the mine boss, grinning wickedly. She took a deliberately long and noisy sip from her own cup.

Though Gow had been angry with his employer moments earlier, he too found Yun's stunned silence a great joke. "Come on, master of the elements!" he guffawed. "Aren't you thirsty?"

There was a ringing in Yun's ears. It was as if he'd lingered too close to a firecracker, spent too much time watching the lit string burn down to its ends, and now he was living in the after-math of the explosion.

"You're asking me to prove I'm the Avatar," he whispered hoarsely. "For a drink of water."

There was no more. There was no more left in Yun. There was no more he had to give. He raised a trembling finger. "I risked my life for you," he said, pointing at Gow. "I risked my life to save yours. You wouldn't be standing here right now if it wasn't for me."

Gow's eyes went wide. He tried to protest, but something blocked the words from leaving his throat. The owner and the mine boss looked like they were going to mock him for being singled out, but Yun fixed them with stares. "And you two. You couldn't just . . . you couldn't just *help* me."

"Hey now," the woman said, suddenly finding a cliff on the other side of the door they'd opened. She scraped backward in her chair, jarring her table. Her cup tipped over, sloshing its contents to the floor. "You can—you can have mine. You can have what's left." She grasped clumsily at the pot she'd been drinking from but only managed to get the lid, not the handle. "Take it. Take it!"

It was too late for that. "I dedicated my life to people like you," Yun said. He couldn't tell if he was laughing, crying, croaking out bestial sounds of fury. The human speech was mixed in somewhere. "I wanted you to thrive. I wanted you to prosper. I tried so hard."

There was a crash behind him. He saw the owner of the teahouse fleeing out the back of the shop. Yun swept his hand over the air and a string of filthy ceramic cups flicked out like a whip, flattening themselves into a knife's edge. They slashed across the back of the big man's legs, sending him to the floor with a gruesome thud.

Knocked out. Yun would have to wake him up at some point. He turned back to Gow and the mine boss, who trembled in place, stuck with fear. He watched their foundations sway, trying to figure out whether or not he enjoyed it.

He decided it didn't matter. Yun reached over Gow's shoulder, giving the man a conspiratorial smile, and closed the door curtain from the inside.

Yun drank the stagnant, sulfurous water from the thick-walled bucket. It sloshed down the front of his chest, puddling on the ground in front of the town well. It was the best drink he'd ever had.

He poured some out on the face of the well guard lying at his feet. Unlike some people, he shared his bounties. "How's the governor's water taste?" he asked. The liquid splashed against the corpse's glassy, unblinking eyes and pooled in its open mouth.

Around him the town was silent. Everyone who could run, had. He would have to learn to control his energies at some point if he didn't want people fleeing him on sight.

Yun drew another bucket and poured it over his head, repeating the process until his runoff no longer contained streaks of bloody crimson. He threw the wooden vessel to the side and listened to its hollow clank.

See Kyoshi? he thought. *I can bathe without hot water, no problem.*

His friend's presence beckoned to him from across the world. Though he wasn't certain on the details, he was convinced there was a permanent connection between the spirit that took him and the Avatar. Kyoshi was Kuruk. And he was . . . he was who he was.

"Well," he said out loud to no one. "It looks like I've been fired."

Perhaps it was for the best. He would need the free time, because he had a list of things to do. Lots of personal business to take care of. And at the top of the list was paying his respects to Jianzhu.

Filled with new purpose, Yun took off down the road, whistling as he went.

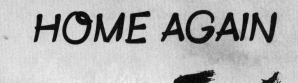

HOME AGAIN

YOKOYA HAD never been wealthy. But now, without Jianzhu's presence, its prospects seemed even grimmer than Kyoshi remembered as a child. The ghosts of the sages who had fallen here would take a long time to relinquish their hold on the moldering docks, the hardened, rocky fields, the sparse, weather-beaten houses.

A month had passed since Zoryu's "victory." Kyoshi walked slowly through town, wading through her own past. The queasiness in her stomach told her she'd been wrong back when she'd declared her ties severed with Yokoya after Kelsang's death. She was and would always be from this village. Only home could make you feel this bad.

She passed one of the logs pounded into the earth in an attempt to please the spirits and shook her head. Perhaps the ones who inhabited this peninsula were gentle and satisfied by stakes in the ground. It wasn't out of the question. The spirits, as she was learning, were subject to all the variations and complexities of human beings. There were the terrible ones, the irrational ones, the cruel ones, the harmless ones, the ones who would talk to you and the ones who would force you to guess their whims like a servant groveling before a silent, smirking master.

Motion caught her eye, children scampering from cover to cover. They poked their heads out from behind doorways and corners of houses, whispering to each other. She wasn't wearing her makeup. They were just rude the way children were, peering at the stranger.

The adults gave her perfunctory nods as they continued their sweeping, the never-ending sweeping. Pushing dirt around from one place to the other was a burden and obligation shared by the lowly of every nation. She had no doubt that if she visited one of the poles at length, she would see the commonfolk doing the same with the snow, herding the drifts from one end of a village to another.

It was a small mercy that she didn't see Aoma or anyone else from that crew. Then she remembered the reason. It was the middle of the workday. The villagers her age would be toiling in the fields, stooped among the furrows, or out at sea hauling in the day's catch. She, the exalted Avatar, had stepped off a pleasure craft belonging to the royal family of the Fire Nation. There was no sense or structure to it, the way the world scattered lives into the wind like chaff to land so far apart.

She left the village and made her way deeper into the fallow sections of land. The path made a sharp turn around the hillside, and she braced herself for what she was about to see.

The Avatar's estate, in all of its shabbiness.

Facing the results of her own neglect was difficult. It made her wonder if she could ever call herself a tidy person again. The once-vibrant colors of the walls badly needed a fresh coat of paint. The south-facing gatehouse was empty, and some of the iron studs of its heavy doors were beginning to rust. The lawn was overgrown and patchy with weeds.

It was a testament to how much effort was needed to maintain a large manor in good order, to fight the ravages of time and decay. It took so much energy to remain frozen in an eternal state, never changing. Once you gave up, turned your attention away for the slightest second, collapse progressed further than you expected.

Kyoshi shoved the gates open, the metal groan announcing her presence. The garden had thrived and died in equal measure, certain shrubs coming to dominate the others. Balance had been lost, or perhaps it had been restored to a form displeasing to humans. Thin tendrils of vines curled over the outdoor sculptures and had taken root in the sands of the meditation maze. Hardy weeds had taken the place of precious, ephemeral flowers.

There was a message for her, written in pebbles over the ground.

I'm inside.

Even with the house in its current condition, there should have been someone to greet her. The halls looked completely abandoned. Kyoshi's footsteps echoed and creaked over the wooden floors as she checked each section of the mansion in turn. She found what she was looking for in the dining room.

Yun sat at the head of the long table with a small place setting in front of him. He was calmly eating a plate of dumplings. Auntie Mui stood at attention behind him, tears in her eyes.

It was the garden party all over again. Kyoshi's first thought was to separate hostage and captor, to free Mui from whatever bonds Yun had her in and get her to safety. But before she could, Mui let out a sob and bounded over to her.

She collided with Kyoshi and wrapped her short arms around the small of her back, the highest she could reach. "My girl, my girl!" she said, weeping with joy. "At last, my girl and my boy are both finally home!"

Kyoshi stared hard at Yun over the top of Auntie Mui's head. He met her gaze and sipped his tea.

"This house will be a home again," Mui sobbed, her tears forming a damp spot on Kyoshi's robes. "We'll clean up the rooms. We'll have the guests coming back. The two of you, you were the heart of this place. And now you're together again. Everything will go back to the way it was."

"Yes, Auntie," Kyoshi said, never dropping her eyes from Yun's. She gave the older woman a gentle squeeze and patted her on the back. "Everything will be all right from now on. I promise."

Yun smirked. *Lying to our elders now, are we? How low.*

"Auntie," he said. "We should have a big dinner tonight to welcome Kyoshi home."

"Yes!" Mui's eyes shone with happiness. "Of course! I'll need to do some shopping in town. What would you like to eat, my dear?"

"Stalknose mushrooms," Kyoshi said firmly. Mui would search Yokoya end-to-end before realizing she couldn't find them. The futile quest would buy Kyoshi more time.

Mui nodded, undaunted. She hurried out of the dining room, paused by the doorway to give her children one last beaming look, and then disappeared down the hall.

Yun gave it enough time for Auntie Mui to leave the mansion before speaking. "She'll be gone for a while," he said. "And she gave the remaining staff the day off. The house should be empty." He popped the last dumpling into his mouth and laid down his chopsticks, chewing in contemplation. "If there's anything I've missed about this place, it's Auntie's cooking.

"So what have you been doing for the past few weeks?" Yun said once he was done. "Mastering the Avatar State? Or some other secret fighting technique you wanted to use against me?"

"I was learning healing. My teacher says I'm the fastest study she's ever seen."

"Are you here to look at my arm then?" He rolled the shoulder Hei-Ran had injured. It was probably the reason he'd laid low until now, and it had recovered enough not to bother him. "Are you going to try and make me all better?"

Now, it seemed, they were both ready. "No, Yun," Kyoshi said. "I'm here to put you away."

Yun leaned onto the table, chin in one hand, interested in this new development.

"You can't be allowed to show your face in public again," Kyoshi said. "Zoryu's managed to contain the damage you've done in the Fire Nation, but if you resurfaced now, the country would fall apart."

"So? I don't care about that anymore. And the beautiful thing is I don't have to. I used to have to negotiate, accommodate, bend over backward to make people happy, but those days are over. You know what I spent the last few weeks doing while I recovered from my injury? I thought about all the liars and backstabbers I've met across the Four Nations who kissed my feet when I was the Avatar."

A blissful thought crossed his mind and he smiled. "And I realized that I could kill them all," he said. "Not an exaggeration. With enough time I truly think I could actually kill them all. I know their names. I know how they're connected. Most important, I know why they would deserve it."

Kyoshi had hoped she could talk some sense into Yun. She'd hoped his rage had been sated upon leaving the Fire Nation and that he might come along with her quietly. But it was clear now. Yun's rampage was never going to end with Jianzhu and Hei-Ran and Lu. In his eyes, the whole world had wronged him. He wasn't trying to balance the scales with his killings. He was trying to smash the device into bits.

"Yun," Kyoshi said. "You're not going anywhere."

"Oh? What are you going to do? Send me to the prisons at Laogai? Lock me up below the house in a cage, like Jianzhu did to Xu Ping An?"

So he'd known about that. "I don't want to fight you, Kyoshi," Yun said. "But you're not leaving me much of a choice here."

Knowing the truth, that Yun wasn't being controlled by a spirit, that this was the real him, was as painful as Kuruk had warned. Talking to Yun was like pulling out barbs. Little pieces of her flesh were tearing away with every word, irrecoverable. But it had to be done.

Kyoshi drew her fans. "I didn't say you had a choice."

His brows shot up, as if he were only now seeing her for the first time. His friend had been suddenly possessed by a spirit. Yun rose from his chair and slapped his thighs. "All right, Kyoshi. Let's see how this plays out."

He flicked his elbow, like a greengrocer bouncing an apple, and a square stone column burst through the floor of the dining room, snapping planks and overturning the heavy table to the side. It reached the ceiling before stopping.

Kyoshi didn't move or flinch. The attack wasn't directed at her. He was just setting up the game board, bringing in earth the two of them could use.

The stone had thrust into the house exactly between her and Yun, equal in distance. He leaned to the side, his grin serving as a salute and a signal. *There. Fair for both of us. Have at it.*

As if a frenzy had fallen upon them both, they began punching bullets from the monolith, chipping off fist-sized rocks and sending them speeding at each other. They were aiming blind. Yun's projectiles smashed through the plaster of the walls behind her. She ducked and circled, never letting up her own barrage. Yun matched her in violent parody of the gentle spiraling footwork of airbending, keeping to the opposite side of the pillar. The vicious hail of stones whined by her ears.

Kyoshi ended the challenge early by shoving the entire pitted and cored stone column at Yun. It sawed through the dining hall as easily as a finger opening an envelope, ripping its way outside the mansion itself, leaving a gash of sky and field behind.

She cleared the dust with a blast of air. Yun was no longer in the room with her.

There were three exits he could have taken. She chose the one that led to the central part of the house with its many rooms and corridors. It would make for a more interesting battleground and therefore it would be the one Yun favored.

Kyoshi stepped through the lanes of her own memories. The

mansion's paths solidified, changing from phantoms to solid terrain. She knew which floorboards creaked. She remembered which turns were sharp.

A spike of earth burst from a nearby painting on the wall, aimed at her head. She blunted it with brute force, holding out her fans, grinding the stone to dust a foot away from her face with sheer willpower.

"Such strength!" she heard Yun hoot.

She followed his voice. She passed the woodpile where she'd once stolen a maul and used it to bash open her inheritance. The door to the kitchen, where she inadvertently revealed the first sign she was the Avatar. Kelsang's meditation alcove. It was a drubbing from her past. These were the lumps she had to take.

Kyoshi rounded a corner and a wall of bricks laced itself together, barring her way. "Hey, now," Yun called from the other direction. "You know how I never liked you going into my room."

"And I never did," Kyoshi said without turning around. "Not even after I took over the house."

"Thank you." He was nearing her from behind. "It's the small kindnesses that mean the most."

She flung a thrust kick at him, a torrent of air shooting from her foot, enough wind to scrub the hall from the floor to the ceiling. Only after she heard a crash against the back wall did she let up and look. The force of her airbending had sent paper screens and hallway tables all the way to the other end, smashing them to bits. No Yun though.

"I was wondering when you'd bring the other elements to bear," he said from somewhere close by. He knew the house as well as she did, every nook and hiding place. It had been his domain before it had been hers.

Kyoshi moved toward the back of the house, where the expanse of the training ground lay. She entered the empty courtyard. It smelled like rotting straw, the stuffing of the target dummies moldering from disuse. Many of the clay earthbending disks had shattered on their own, exposed to seasons of cold and heat that bleached them from brown to white.

She walked to the center, exposed and vulnerable to attack from all sides. "Yun," she said. "Can I tell you something?"

"Of course." He echoed off the surrounding walls, impossible to pinpoint.

"It's time to let go." Kyoshi lowered her hands. "Whether you kill me here today or not, you have to let go of what happened."

Yun emerged from one of the alcoves. A shadow fell across his face, blanking out his expression. A wave of malice as tangible as the elements came pouring forth from him, the sickening wrongness she'd felt when he first came back to the world of the living. "Let go?" he snarled. "*Let go?*"

She'd been trying to pick the words that would help him, and instead she'd struck a nerve. "You have the gall to say that, after helping me kill Jianzhu?" Yun shouted. "You got exactly what you wanted, Kyoshi!"

She closed her eyes and let the violence of his emotions wash over her. It was a test of her root. When she opened them again, she was still standing firm.

"And it didn't bring me peace. It was wrong that you were lied to, Yun. It was wrong for Jianzhu to do what he did. But he's gone. Whatever pain and anger you have left—you have to live with it. You can't put it on anyone else."

If the boy she knew was still inside somewhere, he would listen to what she had to say next. "You don't deserve to hurt more people because of what you suffered, Yun. You don't deserve to hurt me."

Yun paused. For a moment, Kyoshi thought she'd pierced through the blinders and chains trapping her friend. There was a chance she'd defied the odds and broken through to him.

But a confidence born from a terrible place straightened his spine. "Oh, Kyoshi. You've got it all wrong."

The motion he made with his ink-stained hand resembled the waterbending of Tagaka the pirate queen. A wave of liquid as high as Kyoshi's shoulders struck her hard from behind, knocking the wind out of her.

In her surprise she thought somehow Yun had learned to waterbend. He'd finally figured a way around the immutable laws of the world. Were there two Avatars now? Or he'd stolen a portion of her bending, the element she'd overlooked the most for lack of experience? It was only when the splash around her solidified, trapping her limbs like a tree caught in an ice storm, did she understand.

He'd liquified the stone floor of the courtyard and sent it crashing over her. He'd melted the rock without heat. Yun's earthbending skill was such that he could treat his native element like water.

Kyoshi was encased from the back, gripped as tightly as a turtle duck by its own shell. She couldn't move her arms and legs or turn her head. Yun approached, avoiding the centerline of her mouth and any potential dragon's breath.

"I can't believe you think I would ever hurt you." He gently tugged the closed fan out of her right hand. "You, the one innocent party in this whole affair! I would never hurt you, Kyoshi. For Yangchen's sake, I used to be your whole life!"

He dropped the weapon, and it pinged against the ground. "I know what's happening here. Your duties have gotten to you, haven't they? I remember what it was like, carrying the weight of the Four Nations on my shoulders. Jianzhu used to liken them to unruly students in a classroom, requiring the guidance of a strong hand."

He paused and chuckled. "I used to believe it meant showing the way, leading by example. Now I know better. The world is a child refusing to listen, screaming in tantrum. It needs to be slapped a few times until it learns to be quiet."

Yun relieved her of her other fan and tossed it over his shoulder. From the little shake of his head, he wasn't only disarming her. He was removing the parts of her that confused him, trying to reduce her back to the state he was familiar with, the serving girl. The Kyoshi in his memories didn't carry around implements of war.

He would have her immortalized. But certain injuries couldn't be undone. Yun frowned deeply when he saw the scar around her throat, an indelible sign of change.

"See this? This is what I'm talking about. Look at what you've suffered for the sake of duty." He pinched the collar of her armored robe, rattling the links of mail inside. "They forced you to hide in this shell. They turned you from a gentle girl into a walking terror. Avatarhood is a curse. Look how it's made you treat me, your oldest, truest friend."

"Listen to me, Yun." Kyoshi found herself bolstered by an unfamiliar, terrible, powerful feeling.

Pride. Pride in herself. Pride in her duty, no matter how great and terrible and ill-fitted to her it was. Despite the opposition of man and spirits, this was the Era of Kyoshi. There would be no other.

"I wear these clothes because I choose to," she said, loud enough to ring across the courtyard. "Those marks are who I am." She locked their gazes. "And I have friends much truer than you."

A water whip lashed down from above. Yun only managed to leap back at the last second. The liquid cracked like leather where his feet had been.

Up on the roof, across the shingles, a slender woman in a fur skirt rode a tide of water. She sent another lash at Yun, forcing him farther away from Kyoshi.

"Wong!" Kirima shouted. "Get her out of there!"

On the other side of the training ground, a huge man flew into the air, stepping on pillars of earth so delicate they seemed like threads. Despite his massive bulk, his flitting movements were as elegant and well-balanced as a sparrowkeet's.

"Hold still!" he shouted at Kyoshi.

Like she could do anything else. Wong was one of the few Earthbenders Kyoshi knew who had fine enough control to free her without hurting her. She felt the stone crumble away from her back and arms. She burst from her prison, a statue freeing itself from the marble blank.

She barely missed wrapping her arms around Yun in a grapple. He skated away, moving the earth under him instead of his legs. He angled a slab above his head to block the torrent Kirima rained down upon him, waiting a moment before sending his makeshift lean-to flying back at the Waterbender. She yelped and teetered to the side, narrowly avoiding the missile that gouged a trench into the roof.

"Cute," Yun snapped at Kyoshi. He pointed his index and middle fingers downward and waggled them higher in imitation of someone walking, or in this case, dust-stepping. "Cute technique. I never heard them coming with their feet off the ground. Tell me, is Rangi here too?"

The air above his head shimmered. Yun glanced up and quickly rolled out of the way before the Avatar's bodyguard slammed her flaming fist into his skull. Rangi's fiery impact broke the portion of the floor he'd been standing on. The Firebender withdrew her hand from a smoking hole in the ground and stood up to face him.

"Yes," Rangi said. "I am."

Above them, Jinpa circled on Yingyong, the platform she had leaped down from. After they left the Fire Nation, Kyoshi had sent him to collect her friends, giving him the hideout locations and code words he'd need to gain Kirima's and Wong's trust. She'd made him memorize parts of the *daofei* oaths so he could quote their pledge to defend their sworn sister.

And lastly, because she knew her friends well, she'd given him a lot of money from Jianzhu's vaults to bribe them. *So* much money.

Lao Ge hadn't shown, but the old man could hardly be counted on in the best of times. No matter. The Flying Opera Company was reunited, standing at Kyoshi's back. She had never felt stronger.

"Are these them?" Yun asked her. "Are these the *daofei* you've supposedly been running with? This is the scum you're calling your companions nowadays?"

"Eh," Kirima said. She whirled her mass of water into a rotating ring around her waist. "We don't socialize enough for that." Wong shot Kyoshi a hurt, accusing look for not being in touch more. He was always the most sensitive of their bunch.

Kirima sent a fresh torrent at Yun. He raised a neat shield of earth to block it again, but it was caromed off to the side by Wong's own stone. The blast of water knocked Yun's feet out from under him.

Kyoshi tried to sink his limbs into the ground, like he'd done to the nobles of the Fire Nation court, but Yun simply pulled free of the solid rock, dusting it off him like flour from his hands. "The earth is *my* element," he said, ignoring the giant plane of tiles twice his height that Wong was folding over him from behind. "I just let other people borrow it sometimes."

The sheet of flooring crashed down on Yun. It would have flattened a normal person, even a skilled Earthbender, but for Yun, all it took was a flick of his shoulders for the slabs of rock to splash off his back. The stone shattered around him in a neat circle, organizing its own debris for his convenience, spreading away from him like the petals of a flower.

He looked up at Wong. "Sorry," he said to his astonished fellow Earthbender. "I guess the Avatar's friends will have to try something else."

"Sure," Rangi said. She stepped forward and inhaled so deeply it could be heard over the courtyard. She exhaled and then breathed in again slowly, not caring how big of an opening she was leaving on herself. She was almost constraining her power instead of releasing it.

Upon her third pulsing, charging breath, she lunged, releasing a flame so intense it nearly turned from yellow to white. It was pure avenging wrath given solidity.

Nothing would withstand such a blast. Yun slid to the side, riding a swell of earth under his feet. Rangi followed his trail, snapping the columns of the training ground with the continued force of her firebending. She was trying to scorch out of existence the man who'd nearly killed her mother.

She ran the fire after Yun as he escaped along one side of the training ground. Her rage carved holes into the walls of the building, consuming its value as fuel in moments, leaving charred, blackened ruins behind.

The flame didn't run out until it reached the corner of the yard. Yun hopped off the stone he'd been riding and backed away a few steps from where the smoking trail of fury ended, his eyes wide with surprise. There was a momentary break in the fight. The ferocity of the attack had shocked everyone but Rangi herself.

"Wow," Yun said. "You're really playing for keeps."

Rangi responded by inhaling through her nose again.

Yun's head tilted and his eyes went dark. "I guess I should too," he said. He sank into a deep stance. Kyoshi realized, with sudden fear, that it was the first time she had ever seen him perform a fundamental of bending, like a beginner.

He swung his fists, snapping with his waist, and the earth began to violently twist back and forth. Kyoshi and Rangi were thrown off their feet, the solid ground pulled out from underneath them. The sturdy foundations of the mansion wobbled like jelly.

Yun's stance was low and wide, but his arms were as loose as rope darts as he painted his destruction. It was Jianzhu's personal style of earthbending, warped to liquify and annihilate the stone instead of constructing from it. Around them the walls folded in on themselves, sucking downward in a groan of tearing wood as if the house had been built on quicksand instead of bedrock.

Kirima and Wong finally lost their vaunted balance and tumbled off the roof into the courtyard. They tried to right themselves midair by dust-stepping and mist-stepping, but the technique still needed a firm base to work. The vibrating ground shook apart the tiny columns of their elements, and they crashed to the earth, hard.

Kyoshi had ordered Jinpa to stay floating above the fight, both to save him from having to participate in violence and also to rescue anyone who might be in trouble. Now the Airbender decided, correctly so, that they were all in trouble. He came flying down on Yingyong to pluck whomever he could to safety.

Yun raised a hedge of stone spears. A nightmarish memory of Kelsang gliding over the iceberg spread across Kyoshi's vision. "*No!*" she screamed.

Jinpa saw what was going to happen and rolled Yingyong around so that the bison's back faced Yun, covered by the large saddle for at least a measure of protection. But the maneuver left the rider horribly exposed.

The first sharp point took a chunk of fur out of Yingyong's tail. The second and third buried themselves in the floor of the wooden platform. But the fourth spear landed home. It ran Jinpa through the shoulder, pinning him to the saddle horn.

Yingyong let out an anguished roar on behalf of his master and pulled out of the dive. In a moment of terrible slowness, he drifted over the battleground, letting Kyoshi see her friend from the Southern Temple.

Jinpa stared at the stone embedded in his body. The shock in the monk's eyes faded to accepting calmness. He leaned back against his bison's withers as if he were taking a nap.

Yingyong had had enough. With a powerful stroke of his tail, the great beast fled into the sky, trying to take his Air Nomad companion away from the danger.

"It was a mistake to bring others into this," Yun said, shouting to be heard over the grinding of the soil and the house finishing its collapse into rubble. Wong and Kirima had recovered and managed to get a sense of timing over the spasms of the ground. They sprinted and skimmed over the earthquake to get around to his blind side, their feet blurs of motion. Yun didn't turn his head. "You've just left yourself so . . . vulnerable," he said to Kyoshi.

He hammered his fists down. Cracks parted underneath the oldest members of the Flying Opera Company, neatly placed pitfalls that swallowed them up to their knees. There was a pair of sickening crunches as their own momentum broke their legs. They let out brief screams before clamping their mouths shut, unwilling to give Yun the satisfaction of hearing their pain.

With only a few gestures of earthbending, Yun had plucked away the foreign elements from Kyoshi, leaving behind only what she'd started with in Yokoya. Her and Rangi. He condensed the shaking of the world down to just the patch of ground under their feet, yanking the surface out from under them each time they tried to stand, intentionally undercutting them into the most clownish, humiliating postures. It was no coincidence that the only way for them to stay stable was to remain on all fours, bowed before him.

He pointed at the corner of the decimated training ground. Broken earthbending disks flew across the courtyard and smashed into Kyoshi and Rangi. The training tools were designed to break apart into dust upon impact, but they were also meant to leave lasting bruises, under the belief that the best and fastest teacher was pain.

Yun struck them about the shoulders with the flying lumps of clay, in the stomach and back. Kyoshi knew he didn't want to knock them out. He wanted to chastise them. This was a punishment befitting of those who overstepped their bounds.

To put the finishing touches on his statement, he made sure Kyoshi and Rangi each took the final training disk to their jaws. The impact flung them head over heels, laying them out on their backs, leaving them both gasping at the sky overhead, choking on the suspended dust.

"Kyoshi," Rangi coughed. "Do you remember what I tried to teach you so many times since Governor Te's? And you could never do it? I think you have to do it now."

"I can do it. But not for long."

Yun allowed them to stagger back to their feet, presumably so he could knock them down once more. Kyoshi and Rangi looked at each other, the white powder caked on their features, the mention of the Flying Opera Company's moonlight raid hanging in the air. And in an instant, they were possessed by the exact same idea.

Of course they'd been losing. They hadn't put on their faces.

Rangi pressed her palm to her bleeding lips and swiped a

crimson bar down her chin. It was the most distinctive mark of a benevolent river spirit worshipped in Jang Hui, the same design Rangi had chosen the first and only time she'd ever worn the Flying Opera Company's colors.

Kyoshi gathered the blood streaming from her nose with her fingers. She closed her eyes and dragged crude red streaks across them, tapering back over her ears. It was a far cry from her normal makeup, the fine oil-based stuff from Ba Sing Se, but it would do.

Together, the two of them wore white and red again. Like *daofei*.

"I remember Qinchao," Yun said. "You showed a face like that to Jianzhu, once."

"And now I'm showing it to you," Kyoshi said. Before he could reply, she ignited the air under her feet.

Flame shot out from her soles, lifting her off the treacherous ground, propelling her body forward. She thrust her hands behind her for extra speed, bending concentrated fire from them, torching her own skirt. She was jet-stepping, using the form of elevation that the one Fire Nation member of the Flying Opera Company had innovated.

In his surprise Yun tried to send out another pulsing earthquake to knock her off-balance, but jet-stepping didn't involve touching the earth at all. He couldn't take the ground from under her feet anymore.

Kyoshi rammed him hard in the stomach with her shoulder. He went rolling over the courtyard, shifting the ground underneath him to halt his skid. As he came to a stop, he pulled up another wall of earth to protect him from the blasts of flame

Rangi rained down from above as she hovered high in the air, standing on nothing but the counterforce of her own bending.

This was their one shot, and they both knew it wouldn't last long. Jet-stepping without pause was impossible even for a Firebender as gifted as Rangi. Kyoshi put her hands together and shot a massive yellow fireball at Yun, hoping its size and overwhelming power would count for something.

She still missed. Yun smirked as he dodged out of the way of the rolling sphere. But Rangi acted faster and better than them both. From her higher vantage point she spun her arms in a circle, mimicking a Waterbender, redirecting the flame Kyoshi had put out into the world. Kyoshi saw her fireball change course behind Yun like the orbit of a comet and come around for a second pass.

Caught off-guard again, the barrier Yun raised at the last second wasn't as thick as he needed it to be. It exploded under the weight of the flame. There was a burst of blinding light. Smoke and dust flew everywhere.

The raw power of the Avatar's fire, guided by the refined skill of the Avatar's firebending *sifu*. In tandem, maybe they'd done it.

But when the column of smoke cleared, Yun wasn't there. There was nothing where he stood except for a patch of loose, crumbly earth. "Kyoshi!" Rangi shouted from above. "He can tunnel—"

Yun rose up behind her, carried by a rising mound of soil like a waterspout, and drove his hand into the small of Rangi's back.

Rangi's lips parted. Her flames sputtered out. Yun let the girl who once defended him with body and mind, spirit and honor, fall to the ground.

Kyoshi managed to reach her in time before she dashed against the earth. She caught Rangi in her arms. Her back was wet with blood. Yun had stabbed her with a spike of earth like the one he'd used on her mother, angling the puncture wound underneath her armor.

Kyoshi shut her eyes. She knew if she opened them, light would shine forth, the elements would flow through her, and her bending would rage, unstoppably, until she was left victorious, the last person standing. A thousand voices told her so. It had been decided long before she was born that power was adequate compensation for losing what she most held dear.

But what was the point anymore? What did the generations have to offer her but sorrow and pain? All she knew as she rocked back and forth, cradling the girl she loved in a lullaby of grief, was that if Rangi was taken from her, she would no longer be Kyoshi. She would no longer be human. She would be forever on the other side of the rift, among the swirling colors of the void she'd glimpsed in the Spirit World, watching humans from afar, a terrible and alien presence.

"Kyoshi."

Rangi's voice was the only sound that could make her see right now. Her Firebender reached for her face.

"Stay here with me," Rangi whispered, a faint smile on her lips. She shuddered, and her hand fell before she could touch the Avatar one last time.

Kyoshi looked up at Yun. The bloody earthen dagger in his

hand crumbled to dust. "It shouldn't have been this way," he said. "But this is how it *will* be, over and over again, if you keep trying to stop me."

She'd wondered why Kuruk had nearly let her destroy her surroundings in the Spirit World, and why he'd taken her to the site of the damage Yun had caused. Yun had failed his portion of the test. He would rather break the world than his own self-regard.

Kyoshi knew what he wanted to hear, despite what he'd said before about her being innocent. There was only one thing that would placate him. "I'm sorry," Kyoshi whispered softly under her breath. "I'm sorry I stole your Avatarhood."

"Hmm?" Yun came nearer. "You'll have to speak up."

"It was yours, and I took it from you." She didn't raise her voice, kept it so he could barely hear her. "I'm sorry I robbed you of everything, Yun. I'm sorry I stole your future."

He kneeled down beside her so he could drink in her confession. He needed to hear it from her. But she just needed him close. Within arm's reach. "I regret everything," Kyoshi said, trembling. "I regret what I did to you so much."

"Good." Yun nodded solemnly. "That's good to hear. What else are you sorry for, Kyoshi? Maybe you should apologize for what you said to me earlier. Telling me I should just forget what happened. That was a terrible thing for you to say."

"I'm sorry for saying you had to live with your pain." Kyoshi put her palm to his chest in a gesture of comfort. "Because you won't."

The cold she sent through his body formed a tunnel of ice between his ribs. It happened so fast, and with so much force, the moisture in the air behind him turned to frost. His back sprouted vaporous wings of crystal that disappeared just as quickly.

With his heart and lungs frozen solid, Yun fell to the side.

Kyoshi took the hand with which she'd killed one of the two people she'd loved and placed it against the wound of the other. Water. She needed more water. Her tears of light weren't enough.

"Please," she said into the past.

There. In the distance. She could feel a response. She could hear the voices helping her, guiding her where to look. Kuruk no longer blocked her path. The Water Avatar opened the door and showed her the way.

The broken ground in front of her rumbled and cracked. A tiny trickle of water leaked out, from the well that supplied the mansion. It was the same water she'd hauled up by the bucket during her servant days.

She nearly laughed at perhaps the most underwhelming use of the Avatar State in history. She'd once pulled earth from the seabed through the depths of the ocean. But this was better, in her mind. Healing was better than destruction. The water coated her hand and began to glow.

She had to reduce her power as much as she could, in order not to damage Rangi further. But there was no more fear in Kyoshi's heart. She would be her own miracle this time.

Kyoshi watched Rangi's eyes flutter open. The Firebender looked around the plain wooden room, the broad wooden chest with its myriad little drawers, the charts of energy paths on the walls. She struggled to her elbows atop her bed. "How did I get into the infirmary?" she wheezed.

It was one of the few sections of the mansion still standing. "I brought you here after stabilizing you," Kyoshi said. "I've been working on you since."

"Yeah," Kirima snapped. "Leaving *us* to suffer the whole time." She waved at her leg and then Wong's, immobilized in the splints. They sat in chairs against the opposite wall. "You didn't even give us anything for the pain!"

"Jinpa needed the medicine more!" Kyoshi yelled. The monk lay in the other bed, swaddled in bandages. He'd been dosed with herbal concoctions to dull the agony of his shoulder and gone slightly loopy as a result. He was busy drawing patterns in the air with his good arm and quietly singing tavern songs that a monk shouldn't have known. Perhaps Kyoshi had given him too much.

"This guy's not a member of our group!" Wong protested. "Did you swear oaths of brotherhood to him too? Because you're not allowed to do that! You can only do the actual swearing part to one group!"

"Shut up and stop whining!" Kyoshi missed the two of them so much it hurt. "The world's greatest doctor is on her way here right now. She can treat you better than I can."

She turned back to Rangi. "You're not properly healed. You're just not bleeding anymore. In all likelihood you're going catch a fever from the dirty wound or a punctured gut, and I don't have the experience to do anything about it. You might even have permanent damage." Atuat's hurried, emergency-focused training hadn't granted Kyoshi as much healing ability as it did knowledge about what abilities she lacked.

Rangi saw her distress. "Kyoshi, I don't care."

"I do!" Kyoshi's confidence had vanished as she'd struggled with Rangi's injury. It had come down to luck and less than an inch. Maybe Rangi had twisted slightly at the last second, or her armor had deflected the blow. The thin stone blade missed her lung. If it hadn't, there would have been no helping her.

Kyoshi was ready to call herself the most fortunate Avatar in existence. "You're going to get worse before you're better, but Sifu Atuat should be here by then. Your mother too."

Rangi grew still. "Does that mean Yun is . . . Is it over?"

The others, noticing her shift, went silent. Kyoshi had been asked that very question long ago, after the final time she'd seen both Jianzhu and Yun under the same roof. One her greatest fear, the other her greatest regret. Both of them now gone.

The hollowness left behind let her know the answer for certain this time. "It's over," she said.

Rangi cupped her hands over her face. She sniffed, sharp little noises ringing in her palms. Kyoshi pressed her forehead to Rangi's.

And together they cried for their friend.

THE MEETING

KYOSHI KNEELED before the stone.

Using her fans, she'd tried to engrave it with the information normally written about the deceased for posterity, but each time she tried, it was too much for her to bear.

The year of his birth—the same as hers, the year Kuruk died. Family name—like her, Yun didn't have one. The ease with which he'd assimilated into high society had many visitors convinced he came from a noble family of prominent standing, but the truth was he was a commoner, the same as Kyoshi. The date of his death—

Sometimes people used the Avatar calendar to precisely mark when their loved ones had passed. Doing so in this case would have meant Kyoshi writing her own name on Yun's gravestone. She had to leave the space blank.

So it came to be that his marker was unusually sparse. *Yun. From Makapu.* The rest of the stone was empty, as if it could still be filled with an unwritten destiny. She'd buried him on a hill, where he could see the village by the waves below and watch the clouds drift overhead in the skies above.

Everyone had left except for Rangi, who lingered by Kyoshi's side. It was the three of them together, like it had been in the very beginning.

"Was I right?" she asked Rangi and any spirits listening nearby. The muscles in her chest were tired and aching from grief. "Was I right about anything at all? What will they say about me? Avatar Kyoshi, who killed her friend because she couldn't save him?"

"I don't know," Rangi said. "I can't tell you anything for certain about the future. Only that I'll be there with you." She leaned over, supporting herself on the crutch she'd taken from the infirmary, and kissed Kyoshi on the top of her hair. Then she limped down the hill, leaving Kyoshi alone with her memories.

Kyoshi waited and waited until finally she thought of the right farewell to give.

"I wish it could have been you, Yun. If it couldn't have been me." Neither part of it was a lie.

A gust of wind swept her hair. She heard a chirping sound, perhaps a bird disturbed in its nest. She looked behind her.

From a nearby bush, a snout poked out. Its owner emerged into the clearing. A four-legged animal resembling a falconfox, only without the beak and feathers, furry all over.

The beast stared at Kyoshi with glowing green eyes. It padded over to her, sniffing along the way, until it was close enough to nuzzle at her.

She didn't know what to do except offer her hand. The fox . . . fox licked her palm, the roughness of its tongue tickling her skin. She risked scratching it behind its ears. Creatures like this didn't live in Yokoya.

The strange animal leaned into her touch, enjoying the contact, until it suddenly and arbitrarily decided it'd had enough. It chirruped at her again, throwing wide jaws set with small, pointy teeth, and then dashed back into the bush.

A few seconds later it came back. Somehow it looked annoyed with her. The fox padded around in a circle. "You . . . want me to follow you?" she said.

It scratched impatiently at the grass until she got up.

Kyoshi followed the fox through the woods, over the edges of the hills, down and up ravines. There was no trail and she nearly fell several times, off slippery stones and bridges of rotting logs. She didn't know where they were going, and though she had spent nearly a decade in the village, she couldn't boast knowledge of every inch of the mountain. Wandering was dangerous and expended energy. The younger version of her liked to stay put.

Speaking of which, getting lost as an adult wasn't a good idea either. "We've gone too far," she said to the fox. Then she realized she was talking to an animal. She'd gone too far indeed, in the head.

The fox jumped between two thick trees. Kyoshi sighed and wedged herself through the space. She stumbled into a clearing.

In the middle was a spring, a little pool with clear, fresh water bubbling up from the earth. It was hemmed in with mossy stones, and the lip jutted out over the slope of the mountain. It was beautiful.

Kyoshi understood once she saw the water. Kuruk had sent the fox to guide her to a spiritual site so they could commune. Her connection to the Water Avatar, as it had been made obvious, was strongest near his native element.

She saw a flat table of a stone, perfect for sitting on to meditate. The fox watched her climb onto it and take a cross-legged position. She arranged her hands with her thumbs touching to make a circle, preferring it over the knuckle-to-knuckle contact master Airbenders used to align their tattoos.

As Nyahitha had observed, it didn't take her long to detach from her body and the physical world once she closed her eyes. Perhaps because the realm of humans hadn't cared for her much, it was easy to separate from it. Or she'd simply gotten more skilled with practice. It was difficult for her to admit, but at the cost of sufficient effort, sometimes heroic, inhuman effort, things could get better over time.

She smiled once she felt a presence across from her. "I don't want to relive memories of you swimming in this pool," she said to Kuruk.

"Sure?" a woman's voice replied in confusion.

Kyoshi's eyes snapped open. It wasn't Kuruk sitting in front of her.

"No," Kyoshi whispered. Her heart pounded between her ears. Bile surged over her tongue. "No no no *no NO!*"

She wasn't ready. She wasn't ready to see her mother's ghost. What kind of cruel trick of death was being played on her? How had Jesa of the Eastern Air Temple come back to haunt her?

Kyoshi scrambled back over the rough stone. She flailed her arms to ward off the tall, beautiful Air Nomad woman, the one who'd abandoned her in Yokoya, never to return. "You're not here! You're supposed to be dead!"

The spirit parted her lips and raised her dark brown eyebrows. The act scrunched the blue arrow tattoo lying over her shaved forehead. "I . . . know? Kyoshi, who do you think I am?"

Kyoshi caught her ragged breath. She squeezed her hands under her arms to still their shaking. She forced herself to think rationally about it, instead of panicking over the same slight laugh wrinkles about the eyes that Jesa had, and the deep gray eyes the statues at the Air Temples couldn't capture. People could resemble each other. No one's face was as unique as they thought it was.

"Yangchen," Kyoshi said. "It's you."

The Air Avatar gave her a mildly embarrassed smile. Even that she shared with Jesa. It was too much, and Kyoshi burst into tears. "You look just like her," Kyoshi sobbed. "You look just like my mother."

Yangchen was surprised. But being the woman of legendary compassion, she knew exactly what to do. She opened her arms and Kyoshi fell into her embrace. The feeling of Air Nomad robes against her face reminded Kyoshi of Kelsang, and her bawling reached a higher pitch.

"Oh, my child," Yangchen murmured, despite what they'd just established to the contrary. She hugged Kyoshi to her chest and stroked her hair. "I'm sorry. I'm so sorry I wasn't there for you before. But I'm here now. Everything is going to be all right."

If there was a good Avatar for Kyoshi to thoroughly embarrass herself in front of, it was Yangchen. Szeto or one of the others known for their rigid discipline probably would not have let her finish crying in their arms. They wouldn't have let her be weak for once. Yangchen not only soothed Kyoshi with a gentle touch, but she let her take as much time as she wanted to compose herself.

"I have so many questions," Kyoshi said, once she could sit up straight again. "You're the first person I've been able to talk to about being a proper Avatar."

Yangchen tilted her head. "Was Kuruk not able to guide you? You couldn't have reached me without connecting to him."

"Kuruk spent his days battling dark spirits, not—" Kyoshi was going to finish with *not making any sort of impact*, but that was doing the Water Avatar a disservice. Her world could have looked very different had Kuruk not made the choices he did.

Yangchen read her thoughts, a feat made easier by the fact they were the same person. "Let me ask *you* a question, Kyoshi. Have you ever wondered why there were so many angry spirits during Kuruk's time?"

"I asked him, but he wouldn't tell me. Did he provoke them? Turn them dark somehow?"

"No, Kyoshi." The Air Avatar had no hesitation in answering, only an underlying sadness. "I did."

Yangchen used Kyoshi's surprise to begin her explanation. "I tried my best to nurture human growth in the Four Nations," she said. "When people inevitably butted against the spirits, I sided with humans more often than not. The Heartwalker of Yaoping Mountain, the phoenix-eels living in the underground caverns of Ma'inka, General Old Iron. Many spirits came to me with complaints of human transgression against their territories.

"I told them they should leave the physical world alone and trust their lands and waters would be respected by the humans living nearby. And I trusted those humans to respect the balance of their surroundings. Some people upheld their ends of the bargain. Many more did not."

The sigh she let out was imbued with a heavy guilt. "Kyoshi, every Avatar makes mistakes, and I was fairly consistent in mine. When humans violated the promises I made on their behalf too many times, the spirits turned dark and wrathful. Those were the ones Kuruk was forced to hunt down."

"But none of that was your fault!"

Yangchen skewed her face to disagree. Kyoshi couldn't believe the embodiment of serenity could wear so skeptical an expression.

"I gave each nation everything it wanted but only realized my error too late. People shouldn't have everything they want. No one is entitled to their every desire. To live in balance, we must willingly decide *not* to take all that we can from the world, and from others."

She glanced at the pool beside them. "My choices ultimately led to Kuruk's suffering. The poor boy thought it was his duty to maintain my legacy and reputation. So, he did it alone, without sharing his burden. I might have done things differently had I known how much pain I'd be causing my successor."

Kyoshi didn't know how to respond. "I can sense you're a little disappointed," Yangchen said.

Not disappointed. Just confused. She had wanted desperately to meet Yangchen, the woman who supposedly knew exactly what to do in any given situation. Kyoshi had hoped to gain some insight into what her future as the Avatar held, and how she should meet the challenges to come.

Reaching Yangchen was supposed to be the end of her journey, not the beginning of fresh uncertainty. Kyoshi had come to accept the mantle of Avatarhood proudly. But how was she to fulfill her duty the right way without knowing what to strive for?

"Let this be my first piece of advice to you, Kyoshi," Yangchen said. "There's a thousand generations of past lives in the Avatar cycle. You could spend a thousand years talking to us, and you still wouldn't know how best to guide the world. This is what you must forgo, Kyoshi, the easy answers. You must give up your desire for someone to tell you your choices were correct in the end."

Kyoshi bit her lip. "I don't fully understand, but . . ."

Yangchen read her thoughts again and smiled. ". . . you'll keep trying anyway. That's the spirit, Kyoshi."

Their surroundings began to thicken, the physical world becoming dominant once more. Her past life had decided they were done for now. They could always talk again in the future. The Air Avatar might have sought to impart upon Kyoshi the importance of self-reliance, but simply knowing she wasn't alone was an immeasurable comfort.

"One more thing," Yangchen said.

"Huh?"

"You broke one of the sacred Air Temple relics. A clay turtle." Yangchen flashed Kyoshi a frown befitting the powerful lady of steel who'd famously enforced a great peace upon the world. "See that you replace it. There's only one more lifetime after yours before it's needed again."

Before Kyoshi could apologize, Yangchen vanished.

Kyoshi blinked. The Air Avatar's exit was as undramatic and straightforward as the woman herself. Yangchen came and went like the wind.

Kyoshi wondered if the encounter had changed her somehow. She couldn't detect a difference within herself, but maybe one would become clearer with time. She remembered what Nyahitha said to her over a flickering light, how a fire was never the same fire. Kyoshi wasn't the same Avatar as Kuruk or Yangchen. She wasn't even the same Avatar she'd been a day ago.

In the future, perhaps, she'd become finalized like carved stone. It would be easier to deal with the world then. She could only hope.

As she stood, her legs filled with the ache of blood rushing back through her veins. It was a good sign she was still human. She saw the fox basking on a warm stone nearby. It opened a single green eye, and then stretched to get up with her.

"You're a spirit, aren't you?" she said to the creature. She'd expected it to be long gone, having fulfilled its mission of leading her to Yangchen. But it was still here, waiting. "Well, if you're going to stick around, do you think you can guide me back to my friends?"

The fox yawned in response. It picked a route out of the clearing and down the dangerous slope, moving slowly enough for her to follow.

She still had to be careful not to lose her balance and fall. Kyoshi kept her eyes focused on her difficult path, sometimes stumbling but making sure to catch herself, taking one step at a time.

EPILOGUE

AFTER A long day in the tower study, surrounded by relics of his ancestors and the journals of Toz the Strong, Fire Lord Zoryu dismissed Chancellor Caoli, the late Chancellor Dairin's former student and successor. The two of them had been spending a lot of time together, crafting how this period of history would be viewed by future generations. Caoli had imaginatively suggested calling it "The Camellia-Peony War." Despite war being precisely what Zoryu had managed to avoid, he liked the sound. It was pretty and poetic.

The skies were gray outside his window, rare for this time of year. Zoryu sat in his chair, a high-backed piece carved by a Sei'naka craftsman, and watched evening fall to darkness.

The word he'd received from the Avatar indicated she'd tidied up the mess that had spilled out of the Earth Kingdom. He didn't take the girl for a strong liar. Yun was out of his hair.

His ruse would hold. The fake Yun still lingered in the prisons, though not in bad conditions. Huazo, Chaejin, and the other Saowon in the capital were under house arrest. Their relatives in Ma'inka couldn't act militarily without risking their lives, and so remained bottled up on their home island. An observer might mark this as the moment the Fire Nation was truly saved.

Zoryu knew better. Only fools thought they were ever saved. His struggles were just beginning.

Huazo and Chaejin's ploy for the throne was the symptom of a deeper sickness within his country. As long as the clans held power and were sway to the greed and hatred of their ruling families, the Fire Nation would constantly erupt in these fevers of civil conflict. It had in the past. Without change, the future would be no different.

He dreamed of the day when the citizens of the Fire Nation stopped using the silly insignias of their home islands as reasons to start fights. He longed for the ability to take the surplus of one island to feed the hungry of another. He wanted his country to stop burning itself in the name of honor.

To make his dream come true, he would have to break the clans. All of them, including the Keohso. There could be no true strength in the Fire Nation unless the fealty of its citizens was reserved for the Fire Lord alone.

It would be a generational project. Remolding the country would take decades, centuries. Zoryu would not live to see his great work completed. But he'd planted the seed by ruining the Saowon, one of the most powerful families of the age. He'd proven it could be done. His children, and his children's children, would have to continue his efforts to weaken the clans, destroy them, render them irrelevant.

And then one day, one day, a Fire Lord of his bloodline would look upon his strong, united country, and sit the throne in peace.

But right now, Zoryu had to figure out tomorrow.

He considered the Avatar's ultimatum. Sparing the Saowon appeared to be simple. It was anything but. There was nothing he could do with them. The clan was dishonored, aimless, in disarray. Yesterday he'd flirted with the idea of incorporating them into the standing Fire Army, but he doubted they would readily accept subservience. And worse, the burden of supporting them would fall on the Fire Lord's coffers.

The simplest and best solution was the one he'd decided on first. You didn't have to pay a salary to a corpse. He would cull the Saowon, like the nation's farmers had done to their plagued pig chickens.

He would merely have to go back on his word to the Avatar. Defying Kyoshi was the option without cost. The islands would be refreshed in the blood of his brother's clan.

Zoryu heard thunder outside his window. The night skies opened and began to pour.

He had to stare at the falling sheets of water for a good minute to believe they were real. Rain, so late in the season? It almost never happened.

The tension left his body in an uncontrollable giggle. For rain to come after the Festival of Szeto was the ultimate sign of good fortune. It would accumulate in the mountaintops, refill the cenotes, and ensure a productive start to the next growing season. It would stir the seas and attract migrating silverskim fish closer to the islands, into waiting nets. By this time next year, the Fire Nation would enjoy a bounty beyond imagination.

Not even Lord Chaeryu of the green fields could boast of such a blessing during his reign. This was a sign from the spirits. The islands approved of Zoryu's plans. For once, in his entire life, he felt lucky.

He hadn't been this happy in a while. That was why it took more than one lightning flash for him to notice the man crouching in his window.

Zoryu shrieked and fell out of his chair. The man stepped inside the room, dripping water on the floor. By the light of the candles in the study, Zoryu could see the intruder was old. Very old. But he moved with a slinking, deadly grace, as if his tattered robes covered the muscles and scales of a dragon.

"Hi!" the man said brightly. He took no heed of the rain he was drenched in. "You must be Zoryu."

He smiled, and then frowned. "You *are* Zoryu, right? I've heard there's been a lot of funny business going around recently involving people who look like each other. You wouldn't lie to me about being the Fire Lord, would you?"

Something about the old man made Zoryu certain he could have had the greatest double in the world, a living talking mirror, and this person would still be able to tell them apart. "I'm Zoryu," he said. His voice sounded tiny, like he'd shrunk back into the boy Chaejin used to boss around in their youth. "Who are you?"

"You can call me Lao Ge. Or Tieguai. I don't care. Listen here, young Zoryu. Normally I—*glahck*—the people I visit." He drew his finger across his throat as he made the sound. "But today I'm delivering a message on behalf of a friend. Consider yourself lucky."

"What's the message?" Zoryu asked shakily. He had a good idea already who it was from.

"That powerful people like yourself are still beholden," the old man said. "That you can still be reached. My friend had a hunch you might be inclined to go back on your promise and shed a little blood. Hide a few atrocities. This is your reminder to be the benevolent Fire Lord she knows you were always meant be."

Lao Ge pointed at himself. "Now, me? I approve of your sort of ruthlessness. But my friend has a softer heart. Not a whole lot softer, mind you, but she prefers it when people *live*." He shrugged as if it were the most ridiculous idea he'd ever heard.

"So she sends an assassin to threaten me?" Zoryu rose from his seat, indignant. "I am the Fire Lord! I am the reigning head of state! Is this how the Avatar conducts diplomacy now?"

The old man put a single finger on Zoryu's chest and shoved. Zoryu flew back into his chair hard, nearly tipping it over. Shooting pain rippled from the single point of contact. He had to check he wasn't bleeding.

"You don't understand," the old man said. "She told me to tell you she realizes her entire mistake was trying to dabble in politics with you."

His voice dropped into a deadly register. "My friend is not a diplomat. She is the failure of diplomacy. She is the breakdown of negotiations. There is no escalation of hostilities beyond her."

He stood back, a grandfatherly smile on his face once more. Deciding the message had been sufficiently delivered, he hopped onto the window ledge to leave. Zoryu didn't know how. The drop from this height was at least a hundred feet.

The man looked over his shoulder for a parting word. "Some people in my country like to believe Avatar Yangchen watches over them. But you, Fire Lord. I can assure you that Avatar Kyoshi watches over *you*."

Zoryu balled his fists. The feeling of powerlessness infuriated him, made him slip into childish retorts. "She can't watch me forever!" he yelled.

The old man tilted his head back and laughed to rival the thunder.

ACKNOWLEDGMENTS

I'd like to give my thanks to Michael Dante DiMartino and everyone who helped create Avatar. I'd also like to thank Anne Heltzel, Andrew Smith, Joan Hilty, Stephen Barr, and my friends and family for supporting me. And Karen, I guess.